PRAISE FOR SA

"A very engaging saga . . . . For Western readers the novel not only offers an example of contemporary Iranian fiction; it also provides a rare glimpse of the inner workings of an Iranian family. Such a prospect is even more intriguing because the novel is written from a woman's point of view, by an Iranian woman writer whose life covers one of the most turbulent periods in Iran's history."

—Washington Post Book World

"Savushun is important for many reasons . . . . Its protagonist embodies traits, self-questioning and quandaries found in many educated Iranian women, meaning that Savushun can serve as an important window into a room in Iranian culture not often visited or accurately described."

—Choice

"It is a meandering novel about fallible human beings, who are confused about what is happening and confused too about their role in a country which in 1940 (and in the 1960s) had lost its sense of direction. At first, incident follows incident as in an unedited diary. Threads of a plot are picked up and dropped, but slowly those threads are drawn together in a phantasmagoric modern-dress version of the betrayal and martyrdom of Siyavush."

—Times Literary Supplement

"Daneshvar lovingly details the old Persian customs and way of life. And the conflict between an understandable yearning for peace and tranquility in the face of change and tragedy is movingly evoked. It is a sympathetic but never sentimental account of one woman's right of passage. A timely and welcome debut."

—The Kirkus Review

"Simin Daneshvar is a writer of the first order. She does not belong only to Iran, but to the world."

—Wallace Stegner

"It is one of the most outstanding works of fiction in Persian literature."

—Dr. Hamid Enayat, St. Anthony's College, Oxford University

Also by Simin Daneshvar

DANESHVAR'S PLAYHOUSE
TRANSLATED BY MARYAM MAFI
$22 ✦ ISBN 0-934211-19-1

SUTRA AND OTHER STORIES
TRANSLATED BY HASAN JAVADI AND AMIN NESHATI
$24.95 ✦ ISBN 0-934211-42-6

Also Available from Mage Publishers

THE LION AND THE THRONE:
STORIES FROM THE SHAHNAMEH OF FERDOWSI, VOL. I
TRANSLATED BY DICK DAVIS
$75.00 ✦ ISBN 0-934211-50-7

FATHERS AND SONS:
STORIES FROM THE SHAHNAMEH OF FERDOWSI, VOL. II
TRANSLATED BY DICK DAVIS
$75.00 ✦ ISBN 0-934211-53-1

IN THE DRAGON'S CLAWS: THE STORY OF ROSTAM AND ESFANDIYAR
FROM THE PERSIAN BOOK OF KINGS
TRANSLATED BY JEROME W. CLINTON
$17.95 ✦ ISBN 0-934211-56-6

EPIC & SEDITION: THE CASE OF FERDOWSI'S SHAHNAMEH
BY DICK DAVIS
$29.95 ✦ ISBN 0-934211-55-8

NEW FOOD OF LIFE: ANCIENT PERSIAN AND MODERN IRANIAN
COOKING AND CEREMONIES
BY NAJMIEH BATMANGLIJ
$44.95 ✦ ISBN 0-934211-34-5

A TASTE OF PERSIA: AN INTRODUCTION TO PERSIAN COOKING
BY NAJMIEH BATMANGLIJ
$17.95 ✦ ISBN 0-934211-54-X

SIMIN DANESHVAR
SAVUSHUN
A NOVEL ABOUT MODERN IRAN

TRANSLATED FROM THE PERSIAN BY
M.R. GHANOONPARVAR

INTRODUCTION BY
BRIAN SPOONER

MAGE PUBLISHERS
WASHINGTON, D.C.
2001

COPYRIGHT © 1990–2001 MAGE PUBLISHERS
DESIGNED BY MOHAMMAD & NAJMIEH BATMANGLIJ

LIBRARY OF CONGRESS CATALOGING-IN-PUBLICATION DATA

Danishvar, Simin
[Savushun, English]
Savushun / a novel by Simin Daneshvar;
translated by M. Ghanoonparvar;
introduction by Brian Spooner.–1st ed. p. cm.
Translation of Savushun   I. Title.
PK6561.D263S213 1990
891'.5533–dc20
90-5608 CIP

ISBN 0-934211-31-0

MAGE BOOKS ARE AVAILABLE THROUGH BOOKSTORES
OR DIRECTLY FROM THE PUBLISHER.
VISIT MAGE ON THE WEB AT http://www.mage.com
OR CALL 1-800-962-0922 OR 202-342-1642
TO ORDER BOOKS OR TO RECEIVE OUR CURRENT CATALOG.

CONTENTS

Culture-specific Persian terms, which are italicized
in the text, as well as relevant information, are
provided in the Glossary, arranged
alphabetically at the end
of the volume.

INTRODUCTION

FIRST PUBLISHED in 1969, Simin Daneshvar's *Savushun* has gone through sixteen printings and sold half a million copies—a record for a work of literature in modern Iran. The reason is not obscure. Daneshvar's style is sensitive and imaginative. Her story follows basic cultural themes and metaphors. It goes straight to the hearts of a generation of Iranian readers, striking special chords of emotion and memory of the recent past.

Savushun enriches a generation's understanding of itself. It encapsulates the experience of Iranians who have lived through the midcentury decades which led up to the 1979 revolution. They feel immediate identity with the major characters, each of whom struggles in their own day-to-day lives with the social and historical forces that gave prerevolutionary Iran its characteristic hopelessness and emerging desperation—so inadequately understood by outsiders.

The work of translation is long overdue, but may in fact be more successful with Western readers now than earlier. In the 1970s we were too confident in our outsider's view of Iran to appreciate its full significance. The revolution shattered that view and brought home to us the extent of our outsiderness. Iran today seems incomprehensible to outsiders. This novel helps us to reconstitute our earlier view, to rebuild our dialogue, and to trace the historical and cultural continuity through the 1979 revolution into the present.

The translation of such a novel into English presents special problems. If it means so much to Iranians, will the Western reader understand it? Should we expect that any novel could convey a single package of meaning to two culturally distinct readerships—especially when it deals with historical events and interests that have recently separated them? Though the work of translation was unusually challenging, I think its success is facilitated, perhaps even ensured, by the humanity of Daneshvar's central characters. This humanity shows irrepressibly through several passages that are not otherwise directly translatable from one cultural discourse to the other. Although the lives in the novel are so obviously different from Western lives, as non-Iranians we also can relate to them immediately and unconsciously—to the underlying human nature we share with them, and which the author so sensitively develops in the course of her story.

Most of the action takes place in a middle class, land-owning household in the town of Shiraz in southern Iran. The events as they unfold are seen through the eyes of the young wife and mother, Zari, whose first concerns, whether unconsciously or consciously, are her children, her husband and the security of her family and household. Much of what she does not experience herself is narrated to her by visitors participating in family situations. The centrality of the life of the family and of Zari within it is a major factor in the book's appeal. Using the household as a stage, the author weaves a narrative of steadily increasing complexity, involving a variety of situations and personalities that work through the gamut of Iranian collective concerns. The household includes Zari's maturing son, her twin daughters, her widowed sister-in-law, and devoted servants. Her principled husband spends extended periods away in their village. Frequent visitors to the household include her ambitious brother-in-law and headstrong tribal leaders who are in rebellion against the government. Other significant characters include the governor and his family, officers and policemen, and the British (including Scottish officers and an Irish correspondent). But the essential field of action is Zari's evolving sense of herself and her vacillation between her fears for herself and her family and her respect for her husband's ideals. She works these out in her personal experience of childbirth and charitable work in a mental hospital and through participation in weddings and contact with disease. The narrative is developed within basic Iranian paradigms of womanhood and married life. Each character plays out the role that is inherent in their personalities. Even divorced from its essential historical context this makes for an unusually good novel. But understood in its context it is a unique piece of literature that easily transcends the boundaries of the historical community in which it was written.

Nevertheless, the more we know about the historical web in which these characters live—which is an integral part of the consciousness of the Iranian reader, but alien or unknown to us—the better we shall be able to appreciate the novel. The major strands of this web are the interests, privilege and influence of foreign powers, corruption, incompetence and arrogance of persons in authority, whether in national and local government, the army or the police, the paternalistic landowner-peasant relationship, tribalism, the fear of famine, and the intellectual appeal of Soviet-inspired communism as a way to escape from hopelessness. Other important strands include the implications of the author's choice of location in and around Shiraz during the Second World War, opium addiction and the interplay of Islamic and pre-Islamic ideas and rituals.

The story's main concern are the years between 1941 and 1945. Iran had been occupied by the British and the Soviets, joined later (in 1945) by the Americans, because it sat astride the supply lines from India and the Middle East to the Soviet Union. The Allies considered the occupation necessary because they could not afford to allow the possibility of German activity in the area. Many influential Iranians were ready to collaborate with the Germans in order to counteract the suffocating dominance of British and Russian interests that had become a fact of life.

The Russian expansion through the Caucasus over the past hundred years had become a threat to Iranian interests towards the end of the eighteenth century under Catherine the Great. Later, in 1828, the Treaty of Turkmanchai set the tone for the next 150 years by forcing Iran to cede most of her Caucasian territory and to grant extra-territorial rights to Russians on Persian soil. Meanwhile, the British were anticipating the extension of Russian interests towards India and from the beginning of the nineteenth century actively sought to dominate Persian foreign policy and to influence the Persian economy. Since then competition between Russia and

Britain (since 1947, between the Soviet Union and America) has dominated Iranian political life. All the modern borders of Iran were drawn by Russian and British teams during the nineteenth century, with only minor revisions since. In 1907 Britain and Russia concluded an agreement whereby they avoided direct competition with each other by dividing Iran into zones of influence for the purpose of commercial development. This caused outrage in Iran, although it made little difference to the existing state of affairs.

In 1941 Britain occupied the south while the Soviets occupied the north. Reza Shah Pahlavi, who since 1925 had achieved a measure of success in extricating the country from its economic and political dependence, was forced to abdicate in favor of his son (who reigned until 1979). From 1941 to 1945 Iran was reduced to the most abject state of dependence of its modern history—while still nominally retaining its own independent government under the young Shah. The occupying powers subordinated everything to the economic and political objectives of supplying the eastern front and winning the war, with disastrous results for Iran's small economy. The worst of the results was widespread famine, especially in 1942–1943, triggered by a poor harvest the previous year. Existing extremes of poverty were exacerbated, disease rates increased, and typhus became a chronic problem. Corruption, incompetence and arrogance characterized almost anyone in authority, in national and local government, the army and the police. The influence of the occupying powers had a Christian-religious extension in the south, and a communist-ideological extension in the north, both of which were socially disruptive. In particular, the Soviet presence encouraged the formation and development of the Party of the Mass *(Tudeh)*, a political party which found appeal among middle class urban intellectuals. All of these factors are significant in the novel.

Apart from these results of external influence, the author makes excellent use of purely internal factors. The southern town of Shiraz, which provides the setting for the story, is more than any other town central to Iranian historical identity. It evokes images of shrines and Sufis, of the tombs of the great poets, of Persepolis and the great monuments of pre-Islamic Iran, and, in the hinterland, of the nomadic tribes. It is not easy to convey in a few sentences the significance of tribalism in the Iranian consciousness. Iranian writing has exaggerated the fear and dislike of the city dweller for the "uncivilized." This is somewhat overcompensated for by the work of anthropologists, who have provided monographs on particular aspects of the tribal experience, but none summarizing the significance of this other way of living for the society as a whole. Historically the tribes have represented the spontaneous organization of populations that were not controlled by any central or urban government. When the government was weak tribes often terrorized the countryside. In the early part of this century tribal leaders played a significant role at the national level. However, since they are essentially the antithesis of strong government, Reza Shah made a special point of bringing them under control. He did this by depriving them of their economic resources, and by forcing them to settle. On his abdication the leaders escaped and within weeks the tribesmen were back on the migration trail. The Qashqa'i confederacy, which was the most powerful in the Shiraz area, was pro-German and kept a German military adviser for a while until they found that he could not deliver the arms they wanted. There was sporadic fighting throughout the period of the Allied occupation. All this is there in the novel.

Against this background—corruption, disease, famine, insecurity, and foreign dominance—provincial life continues. Everyone works out their own day-to-day lives. The demoralization is evident in the exploitation of any position of power, by the governor and his family, by petty officials, in the arrogance and incompetence of army officers and of the paramilitary gendarmerie. Socialist ideas provide hope for the young. Opium offers an option for the old. But Zari's husband, Yusof, who is the hero of the work, displays a calm, responsible, human decency. He is accused of idealism, but is never fanatical. He is a landowner but treats his peasants fairly and with no more paternalism than is inherent in the system. He is frustrated by the indecency and injustice around him, but he stands firm against the time-serving maneuvers of his brother and others, who see no point in making things worse for themselves for the sake of abstract principles and with no prospect of any return.

Savushun, the title of the novel, is a folk tradition, surviving in southern Iran from an undatable pre-Islamic past, that conjures hope, in spite of everything. It is evoked in some detail in the final pages—a metaphor for the flame of idealism against a backdrop of hopelessness and helplessness, a basic metaphor that is found in many traditions, religious and secular. In Iran over the centuries it has become entangled with the Shi'a Muslim passion of Hoseyn, the Prophet's grandson, and the tragedy of Karbala. It suggests the transformation of hopelessness into salvation. This is the essence of Iran, with no compromises, in a novel of universal appeal.

BRIAN SPOONER
FEBRUARY 28, 1990
UNIVERSITY OF PENNSYLVANIA

CHARACTERS

Abolqasem Khan: also referred to as Khan Kaka, brother of Yusof and Khanom Fatemeh.

Bibi Hamdam: mother of Malek Rostam and Malek Sohrab.

Dr. Abdollah Khan: old, kindly, popular family physician.

Ezzatoddowleh: prominent aristocratic woman; mother of Hamid, childhood friend of Khanom Fatemeh.

Fasihozzaman: title of Bibi, mother of Yusof, Abolqasem Khan and Khanom Fatemeh.

Ferdows: young maid in Ezzatoddowleh's household.

Fotuhi: high school teacher active in socialist groups.

Gholam: servant in Yusof and Zari's household.

Gilantaj: youngest daughter of the governor of Fars Province.

Haji Mohammad Reza: a dyer by profession; neighbor and family friend to Yusof and Zari.

Hamid: son of Ezzatoddowleh.

Hasan Aqa: a dry grocer; brother of Hoseyn Aqa.

Hormoz: son of Abolqasem Khan.

Hoseyn Aqa: an herbalist by profession; neighbor and family friend to Yusof and Zari.

Kal Abbas: husband of Ferdows and doorman at the home of Ezzatoddowleh.

Khadijeh: maid in Yusof and Zari's household.

Khan Kaka: see Abolqasem Khan.

Khanom Fatemeh: also referred to as "the aunt" and Qotsossaltaneh; sister of Yusof and Abolqasem Khan.

Khanom Hakim: female British doctor in charge of the missionary hospital.

Khosrow: son of Yusof and Zari.

Kolu: son of Yusof's shepherd.

MacMahon: Irish correspondent; friend of Yusof.

Majid Khan: friend to Yusof.

Malek Rostam: a tribal leader; brother of Malek Sohrab; friend to Yusof.

Malek Sohrab: a tribal leader; younger brother of Malek Rostam.

Marjan: twin sister of Mina, daughter of Yusof and Zari.

Mehri: also referred to as Mehrangiz, friend to Zari.

Mina: twin sister of Marjan, daughter of Yusof and Zari.

Miss Fotuhi: sister of Fotuhi; patient in the insane asylum.

Miss Masihadam: young midwife and physician.

Naneh Ferdows: mother of Ferdows.

Qotsossaltaneh: see Khanom Fatemeh.

Seyyed Mohammad: works for Yusof as a foreman.

Yusof: husband of Zari.

Zari: or Zahra; the protagonist of the story; married to Yusof.

Zinger: British sergeant, formerly a sewing machine salesman.

In memory of my friend Jalal,
who was the glory of my life, and whose death I have mourned
as a Savushun mourner.

Simin

The King of the Turks listens to the words of pretenders
Shame on him for the cruelty of spilling the blood of Siyavash

Hafez

1

IT WAS the wedding day of the Governor's daughter. The bakers had put their heads together and baked a loaf of flat *sangak* bread the likes of which had never been seen before. In groups guests came to the wedding room to see the bread. Khanom Zahra and Yusof Khan, too, saw the bread up close. When Yusof's eyes caught sight of the bread, he said, "Stupid cows! How they kiss their butcher's hand! What a waste! And at a time like this . . ." Those nearby who overheard Yusof first edged away, then left the room altogether. Zari stopped herself short, took Yusof by the hand and, with pleading eyes, said, "For God's sake, can't you let me breathe in peace, at least tonight?" Yusof smiled at his wife, as he always did, spreading his pursed purled lips to show his once sparkling white teeth, now stained by years of smoking the hookah. Yusof walked away, but Zari stood there, staring at the bread. She leaned over and lifted the corner of the hand-printed tablecloth, which hid two wooden doors stuck together. Around the borders of the cloth, in floral and paisley patterns, were trays of wild rue and figures of the legendary lovers, Leyli and Majnun. In the very center sat the reddish loaf of bread, decorated with a poppy seed inscription: "To our benevolent Governor—from the Bakers Guild." Along the sides of the bread, "Congratulations" was written over and over in saffron and nigella seeds. What an oven they must have needed! Zari thought. What a mound of dough!

How much flour they must have used! And, besides, as Yusof said, "At a time like this!" At a time when this single loaf could make a whole family's evening meal. At a time when to get bread from a baker you need to be a hero like Rostam. Lately the rumor had spread through the city that the Governor had threatened to throw a baker into his oven, to set an example for the other bakers. Anyone who bought bread from that baker came down with severe stomach cramps, writhed in pain like a wounded snake, and vomited as if stricken by the plague. They said that his wheat had so much darnel in it that his bread was as black as ink. But then, as Yusof said, "Were the bakers to blame?" The city's food supplies, from onions to wheat, had been bought up by the occupying army, and now . . . How can I ever convince those who heard Yusof to pretend they didn't . . . ?

She was still lost in her thoughts when a voice broke in, "Hello." She raised her eyes from the bread to see Khanom Hakim, the British doctor, standing next to Sergeant Zinger. They all shook hands. Both the foreigners spoke Persian, although a broken Persian. Khanom Hakim asked, "How the twins have been?" and explained to Sergeant Zinger, "All three children by my hands have been delivered." The Sergeant retorted, "I could never have doubted that." Then she asked Zari, "The child still has been on a pacifier?" Khanom Hakim said so many "have beens" and "had beens" that she even wore herself out. Afterwards she said some things in English Zari did not follow, even though she had studied at the British school and her late father had been considered the best English teacher in the city. Her mind was elsewhere.

Zari had heard it but couldn't believe it, until she saw it with her own eyes. The present Sergeant Zinger was none other than the former "Mr. Zinger," the Singer sewing machine salesman. He had come to Shiraz at least seventeen years ago, and still did not speak good Persian. With every sewing machine he sold, this giant corpulent man gave ten free sewing lessons. Maneuvering his weight behind the sewing machine, he would teach young girls the fine points of embroidery, eyelets, and double pleats. Curiously enough he never once chuckled at the figure he cut. But the girls learned well, Zari too. When the war began, Zari heard that Mr.

Zinger had overnight donned the braids and stars of an officer's uniform. Now she saw that his sergeant's uniform suited him well.

She thought, What self-control he must have had to live with these lies for seventeen years. A fake profession, fake clothes, all lies, from head to toe. And how skillful an impostor he was at his job. With what cunning he made Zari's mother buy a sewing machine. Other than her husband's pension, Zari's mother had no other income. Mr. Zinger had told her that a girl with a Singer sewing machine in her dowry needed nothing else. He said anyone who had a Singer sewing machine could even make a living with it. He claimed that the rich and the noble in the city had all bought Singer sewing machines as part of their daughters' dowries and then showed Zari's mother a book in which he had recorded the names of his most noteworthy clients.

Three Scottish officers with pleated kilts and women's stockings joined them. Then, Yusof's friend MacMahon, whom Zari had seen many times, came in. MacMahon was an Irish war correspondent who carried a camera around. He asked Zari to explain the wedding layout, and Zari launched into a description of everything: the silver flower vase and the candelabrum and mirror; the shawl and ring wrapped in cashmere, the bread and cheese, the green herbs and wild rue . . . and the two large sugar cones placed at each end of the tablecloth, which were especially made at the Marvdasht sugar factory for the Governor's daughter's wedding. One sugar cone was dressed in a bridal gown, the other in a groom's outfit and a top hat. In the corner of the room was a baby carriage, covered inside with pink satin and filled with candy and coins. Zari lifted a cashmere cloth from the horse's saddle and said, "The bride sits on the saddle so she will always be riding her husband." Everybody laughed and MacMahon clicked pictures.

Zari noticed the Governor's younger daughter, Gilantaj, motion to her. She excused herself and walked over to the girl. She had honey-colored eyes and straight brown hair that touched her shoulders. She wore short stockings and a skirt that reached above her knees. She must be the same age as my Khosrow, no more than ten or eleven, thought Zari.

"My mom asked if you could please lend us your earrings,"
Gilantaj said. "My sister will wear them just for tonight and
tomorrow they will be returned to your house . . . It is Khanom
Ezzatoddowleh's fault; she brought a green silk braid for the
bride to wear around her neck. She says green brings good luck.
But my sister has nothing green to go with it." Gilantaj recited her
lines like a school girl. Zari was stunned. How were her emerald
earrings spotted and singled out? Who ever thought of mixing and
matching apparel for the bride in the middle of all this commotion? Probably something Ezzatoddowleh cooked up. With those
crossed eyes of hers, she spies on everyone in the whole city and
keeps track of what they own.

Her voice trembling, she replied, "These were a gift on my wedding night, a memento from my mother-in-law." She remembered
the night in her bridal chamber. Yusof put the earrings on her ears
with his own hands. Amidst the hullabaloo and the commotion,
before the eyes of all the women, while sweating, Yusof had
trouble finding the holes in her earlobes. The crude women had
jumped at the opportunity to repeat the proverb about ears
being pierced in the father's home and what happens in the husband's home.

Impatiently, Gilantaj said, "They're playing the wedding song.
Hurry up. Tomorrow morning." Zari removed her earrings. "Be
very careful with them. The pendants might fall." If hell froze over
she would see her earrings again. She knew all right, but how could
she refuse to hand them over?

The bride now entered the room for the wedding ceremony.
Ezzatoddowleh was holding her arm. It was amazing how every time
a new governor came to the city Ezzatoddowleh wormed her way
into the family as a friend and adviser. Five little girls in frilly dresses looking like little angels, each carrying a bouquet of flowers, and
five little boys in suits and ties followed the bride. The room was
packed. Ladies applauded. The foreign officers were still in the room.
They too applauded. After all, the show was put on for them. For
Zari, this pageant was like a procession in a passion play. The wedding song was being played. The bride sat on the saddle in front
of the mirror, and Ezzatoddowleh rubbed the two sugar cones togeth-

er over her head. With a needle and red thread, a woman pretended
to sew up the lips of the groom's relatives. The foreign officers chuckled. A black maid like a genie appeared in the room, carrying a charcoal brazier in which wild rue seeds were burning. But the room
was so crowded that no genie would have fit in. All the villains of
the passion play are here, thought Zari. Marhab, Shemr, Yazid, The
Frank, Zeynab the Unwanted, Hend the Liver Eater, Ayesheh, and
this last one, Fezzeh. Suddenly it dawned on her: I'm beginning
to sound like Yusof.

The room was warm and permeated with the smell of wild rue,
tuberoses, carnations, and gladiola, which could been seen in large
silver vases here and there between the ladies' skirts. The flowers
were brought from the Khalili Garden. Zari did not hear the bride
say, "Yes," giving her consent. Gilantaj touched Zari's arm and whispered, "My mom said thank you. They look good . . ." The rest
of what she said was lost amid the cheers and the loud and dis-
cordant military march which followed the wedding song. It
sounded like battle drums were being played. Ferdows, the wife
of Ezzatoddowleh's doorman, elbowed her way up to her mistress.
She handed Ezzatoddowleh her purse. The mistress opened it, pulled
out a bag of candy and silver coins and showered them over the
bride's head. And, so that the foreign officers would not have to
bend over, she handed them each a coin. She also gave one to
Khanom Hakim. Up until then, Zari had not noticed Hamid Khan,
but became aware of his presence when he began to talk.
Addressing the foreign officers, he said, "My mother's hands will
bring good fortune and luck—" Then, turning to Zari, he asked,
"Khanom Zahra, please translate for them." Her former suitor! You
wish! Zari thought. I had enough of you when the history teacher
dragged all the ninth-grade school girls to your house under the
pretext of showing them a historical monument, and you checked
us up and down with your lewd eyes and showed us your bathhouse and exercise room, constantly repeating that your grandfather, the grand police chief, built the mirror hall, and Lotfali Khan
had the mirrors painted . . . And then how rudely your mother
came to the Shapuri public bath on our bath day, intruding in our
private cubicle, to look at my naked body with those crossed eyes

of hers, checking me over. Luckily, though, Yusof had already asked
for my hand. Otherwise, my mother and brother may have been
fooled by your pretentious lifestyle.

Following the wedding ceremony, the celebrations began in the
courtyard garden and on the front veranda. They had decorated
the cypresses, ornamental palms, and sour orange trees with lights,
each tree a different color. Large trees with large light bulbs and
small trees with small ones. Just like stars. Water flowed down the
two sides of the stairs leading into a pond. A rose-shaped light glowed
in the middle of every step and water passed over its red reflection
and poured into the pool. The large garden patio was carpeted for
dancing. Zari figured that the wiring for the lights in the waterscape was hidden under the carpets.

Large, ornate china bowls full of fruit, candelabra with three
branches, and baskets of flowers were arranged alternately all
around the pool. The candles on the candelabra were lit, and as
soon as one was blown out by the breeze, a servant would immediately relight it with a short-handled torch.

The Governor himself, tall and broad-shouldered with a white
beard and moustache, stood by the side of the pool welcoming the
guests. The last to arrive was a cross-eyed British colonel, who entered
hand in hand with Zari's former headmistress. They were accompanied by two Indian soldiers bearing a basket of carnations
shaped like a ship. When they reached the Governor, they put the
basket down by his feet next to the pool. The Governor, who was
busy kissing the British lady's hand, did not notice the flowers. He
shook hands with the colonel a second time and then stretched his
hand to the Indian soldiers, who clicked their heels, saluted,
turned about, and left. The military band was playing a march.

Then the other musicians arrived. Ne'mat played the *zither*, a
pot-bellied man played the *tar*, and a boy who had plucked his eyebrows sang, "My flower, my flower, my silver-braided beloved,"
and danced. Afterwards he sang, "My darling, you are a willow leaf,
a willow leaf." Then they played the drums and a few men and
women in borrowed Qashqa'i costumes did a poor imitation of
a handkerchief dance. Zari had seen all sorts of fake things but had
never in her life seen counterfeit Qashqa'is.

Now the musicians, who had come all the way from Tehran just for this wedding, had their turn. To Zari's ears, their tunes sounded all muddled. The mere sight of the large platters of cookies and pastries and bowls overflowing with mixed nuts made her stomach turn. It dawned on her that the first platter had probably been sent by the pastry guild and the second by the nut-sellers guild. The five-tiered wedding cake, flown in by an airplane, was a gift from the Head Command of the Foreign Troops. The cake was placed on a table on the veranda. A bride and groom were standing hand in hand on its top layer. Behind them was a British flag. Everything was made of pastry.

The whole scene seemed like a movie, especially with all the foreign officers in uniforms adorned with braids and medals, Scottish soldiers with pleated kilts, and several Indian officers with turbans. And if Zari hadn't lost her earrings, she may have even enjoyed the spectacle.

First the bride and groom danced. The long train of her gown dragged over the carpet like the tail of a shooting star, the stones, glass beads, and pearls sparkling in the lamplight. But she was wearing neither the green silk braid nor the bridal chiffon. Only the earrings were in place. The bride danced once with the British colonel and then with Sergeant Zinger, in whose arms she looked like a vulnerable little creature. It seemed that he even stepped on her feet a few times. Then the foreign officers approached the other ladies. The women, in their colorful dresses, were dancing in the arms of strangers, the officers, while their husbands sat on the sofas and watched. The men looked like they were on pins and needles. Perhaps they were happy. Or maybe they were mad as hell. You never know what is going on inside somebody else's mind. At the end of every dance, the officers brought the ladies back to their places, as if they couldn't go back on their own. Some officers clicked their heels and kissed the women's hands, which prompted their husbands to jump up and quickly sit down again—somewhat like a spring that had been wound up. MacMahon was the only one who didn't dance. He just took pictures.

Sergeant Zinger walked over to Zari, clicked his heels loudly, bowed, and said, "Shall we dance?" Zari excused herself. Zinger

shrugged his shoulders and went to Khanom Hakim. Zari looked
at her husband, Yusof, who was sitting a few chairs away. Yusof's
eyes, darker than the clear sky of these spring days, were fixed on
hers. He winked at her and made her feel warm inside. Yusof always
seemed to have a teardrop hidden in his eyes, like two moist emeralds, like the emeralds in her earrings.

The Colonel and Zinger, sometimes together and sometimes
alone, took some of their men to the end of the garden, returning in a few minutes straight to the bar, where they drank to each
other's health. Zari saw Zinger whisper something in her husband's
ear. Yusof got up and accompanied Zinger past the decorated cypress
and sour orange trees to the end of the garden. They returned quickly and did not go to the bar. Sergeant Zinger signaled to the
Colonel, whose eyes became even more crossed as he scowled. Yusof
sat down next to Zari. His face was flushed and his blond moustache trembled. He said, "Get up, let's leave quietly." Zari brushed
her hair over her left ear, which was visible to her husband and
said, "As you wish."

She was getting up when MacMahon appeared, goblet in
hand, and sat next to her. He took Yusof's hand. He had had so
much gin that he could barely keep his eyes open. He asked in
English, "Did you lock horns with the tailor general again?" He
sighed and continued, "It is more difficult for you, not that it will
be easier for us. Did you like the poem that I read to you early this
evening? Did you? Now, I'm considering writing a poem about your
city." He pointed to the slice of lime in his goblet and said,
"The lime, with its delicate green skin and odor that combines all
the scents in the meadow, and the cypress, so free-spirited and
restrained, are among the major plants in this city, and humans
must naturally resemble the plants of the region in which they are
born. Delicate and restrained. They have sent me to ask you why
you are not delicate and moderate. I am making good progress,
Yusof, even though I am dead drunk! How well you accom-
plished your mission, oh Irishman, ever-drunk poet!" And looking at Zari, he said, "To your health." He took a sip and placed
the goblet on the table.

"Get up," he continued. "Let's go over there and sit on that bench next to that ship of flowers which has anchored at the grassy shore. Zari, you come too. The presence of a beautiful woman is always exciting. This warship with its cargo of flowers is a gift from the General Command of our troops.

"Now that's better. Where is my glass? Zari, fill our glasses.

"We are kin, aren't we, Iran and Ireland? Both are the land of Arians. You are the ancestors and we the descendents! Oh, our old, old ancestors. Give us solace. Give us solace! Oh, Catholic Irishman, the patriarch, the ever drunk! I know that in the end, one day, on a lousy rainy day, you will fall into a ditch and die, or in a poorhouse look for an old woman to call "mother!" Well, your mother and the neighbor girl who brought your mother a glass of warm milk . . . your mother was knitting woolen argyle socks for her son at the front . . . like the ones I have on. Your father was a night watchman in charge of the bomb alert siren; he knew that airplanes drop bombs in our neighborhood, and he knew that our house was about to be hit by a bomb and knew that mother was knitting woolen argyle socks for her son at the front. When they pulled her out of the rubble, she was still holding her knitting needles, and now father has sent a letter. He has written that he is sorry that . . . he is sorry that . . .

"Now, oh patriarchal Catholic family, by confessing and other such absurdities you got up and migrated to London, for what? Had you stayed home and fixed up your poor, miserable Ireland, liberated it, you would not have lost so many to migration. In exile, I remember, you told tales about Ireland, you boasted of its abundant poets and sighed for your poor country. I remember you said there was no corruption among the youth of your country, and your audience would retort, 'Is it not so in England?' Who were you trying to fool? You had forgotten the drunkards of Ireland. You had forgotten that every week a ship would arrive and, in exchange for its cargo, load up the girls and boys of your country to take to America. And they pretended not to notice that they were sending their criminals to the colonies. Just like our tailor general. The tailor general is upset with you. He can't stand the sight of you. He feels the same way about me. Yesterday, I told the Consul to forget about Yusof. The tailor general wouldn't hear of it." He drank again and continued:

"Some people are like rare flowers; others are envious of their splendor. They imagine this rare flower will absorb all the earth's energy, devour the brightness of the sunshine and the moisture in the air, and usurp their place, leaving them no sunshine and no oxygen. They are jealous of it and wish it did not exist. Be like us or don't be at all. You have a few rare flowers here and there, you have oleander, which is good for repelling mosquitoes, and fine herbs, which are good for sheep. Well, it's always the taller and more fertile branch that becomes a tree, and now this taller tree has its eyes peeled, ear to the ground, and can see well. It is being told, 'Don't look, don't listen, don't talk.' And the ever-drunk Irish poet, the war correspondent, is sent to him to soften him up, and this correspondent has his father's letter in his coat pocket, right here, and his father has written, 'I am sorry that . . . I am sorry that.' Well, if you give in, it will all be over."

He took another sip. His eyes now only slits, he said despondently: "Oh Ireland, oh land of Arian descendents, I have composed a poem about a tree that must grow in your soil. This tree is called the Tree of Independence. This tree must be irrigated with blood, not water. Water will dry it up. Yes, Yusof, you were right. If independence is good for me, it is good for you too. And the story you told me was very useful to me. You told me about the tree in your legends, whose leaves when dried and applied to one's eyes like *kohl*, can make one invisible and capable of doing anything. I wish there were one of these trees in Ireland and one in your city."

He paused to light a cigarette and continued, "I've said all this nonsense to soften you up. When my father's letter came—'I am sorry that, I am sorry that'—I sat down and wrote a story for your twins . . . for Mina. Well, Mina and Marjan are the twins. Where is my story? I put it next to my father's letter. I want to build an airplane that drops toys for children . . . or pretty stories. Once upon a time, there was a little girl whose name was Mina. This girl was the only girl who cried for the stars when they were not in the sky. In all my life, I had never seen a child who cried for the stars. Only Mina. When she was younger, her mother would pick her up, show her the sky and say, 'Moony, moony, come, come;

go into Mina's chest,' or something like that. That's how Mina fell in love with the sky. Now, every night when it is cloudy, Mina cries for the stars. I hope their maid will sweep up the sky; she is a slob. She only displaces the dust, scattering it in the sky. On the nights that the maid has done the sweeping, at least some of the stars are visible. But what a treat when mother sweeps; she sweeps the sky clean, collects the stars and the moon, puts them in a gunnysack, sews up the top, and locks the gunnysack in the cupboard. Now, Mina has found a way. She teams up with her sister and steals mother's keys, and goes to sleep hugging the keys. Without the keys, they can't sleep at all. I have never seen another girl who thinks as much about the stars, and I have never seen another city in whose cupboards you can hide stars."

MacMahon took another sip, and said, "This is the end of Mina's story. Say, 'Well done,' Yusof. What a story I've made from a few fabricated and real things you reported from your twins. You said the people in your city are born poets. You can see that the people of Ireland are the same." And he became silent.

Zari did not notice that her brother-in-law, Abolqasem Khan, had suddenly appeared before them. MacMahon got up, took his goblet and left. And Khan Kaka sat down. He blinked and asked, "Are you drinking whiskey?" "No, it's gin," Zari answered. "Would you like me to pour you some?"

Khan Kaka said quietly, "Brother. You're being stubborn for no reason. After all, they are our guests. They won't be here forever. Even if we don't give it to them willingly, they'll take it by force. They're not deterred by the locks and seals on your warehouses. And besides, they don't want it for free. They'll pay cash for it. I've sold everything in my warehouses in one shot. I've even collected a down payment on the wheat that is just sprouting. After all, they are in charge."

"There is nothing surprising and new about the foreigners coming here uninvited, Khan Kaka," Yusof replied. "What I despise is the feeling of inferiority which has been instilled in all of you. In the blink of an eye, they make you all their dealers, errand boys, and interpreters. At least let one person stand up to them so they think to themselves, 'Well, at last, we've found a real man.' "

Dinner was announced, and the guests started toward the building. Zari, her husband, and her brother-in-law only pretended to join the others. Khan Kaka turned to Zari, blinked and said, "Sister-in-law, say something. See? How easily and openly he insults his elder brother." And Zari responded, "What can I say?"

Khan Kaka turned to Yusof and said, "My dear friend, dearest, you are young and do not understand. You are risking your own life and creating trouble for all of us by being so stubborn. After all, they have to feed that big army. You know yourself that an army that big can't be kept hungry."

"But my peasants and the people of my city can be kept hungry," Yusof said bitterly.

Khan Kaka said, "Look, my friend, last year and the year before that you got away with it and didn't give anything, which we somehow made up for. But this year, that just won't do. Now, they need food and gasoline more than they need cannons and rifles."

Gilantaj approached them and said, "My mom says please come to dinner."

They began to walk toward the table. Abolqasem Khan whispered to Zari, "I hope he doesn't get some crazy notion not to come to the celebration tomorrow afternoon. They have invited Khosrow, too. I will personally come and pick you up."

Zari said, "Tomorrow is Thursday, and you know that I have to keep my charity vow."

Abolqasem Khan blinked and said, "Sister-in-law, I beg you."

When they got home, Zari sat on the bed. She took off her shoes. Yusof was straightening his pants on the bed to put them on the clothes hanger. After he put on his pajamas, he went to the next room, which opened to their bedroom. Zari could see him from where she was sitting. He was standing by the twins' bed, watching them. Then he moved out of sight, but she knew that he was straightening the pillows. He would take Zari's keys, which they had hidden between their pillows. She knew that he would kiss them and that he would say, "My cutie dolls." When she heard the door, she knew that Yusof had gone to Khosrow's room. She knew that he would pull up his cover, kiss his forehead and say, "My son, if I don't succeed, you will. You are dearer to me than my life. If I don't see you one day, I'll feel like a chicken with its head cut off," or words to that effect.

Yusof came back to their bedroom. Zari had not moved from where she was sitting on the bed. Yusof asked, "Aren't you going to sleep?" and gave her the keys, laughed, and said, "Those two little devils are really something, the cutie dolls." And sitting next to her, he said, "You probably want me to help you with the buttons on the back of your dress. I'm sorry, I forgot." Without turning her back to him, Zari said, "What a pretty story MacMahon has written for them."

"Did you understand it all?" asked Yusof.

"Yes, I've gotten used to his Irish accent," she replied.

"Do you know what Mina told me today? When I tossed her up in the air and caught her in my arms, she asked, 'Daddy, has Mama given you two stars? I can see them in your eyes.' "

Zari laughed. "The child is right. Two stars shine in the depths of your eyes. Your eyes . . . God protect them, are like emeralds." She couldn't finish the rest of the sentence.

Yusof began undoing the buttons on her dress, and said, "Good heavens, what are all these buttons for?" He continued, "Early this evening, I said things to MacMahon that will be the end of me if Zinger hears them." He undid all the buttons and her dress dropped to her waist. He began to undo her brassiere and said, "I told MacMahon, 'Yes, friend, the people of this city are born poets, but you have stifled their poetry.' I said, 'You have emasculated their heroes. You haven't even left them with the possibility of struggle so that they can write an epic and sing a battle cry.' I said, 'You have made a land devoid of heroes.' I said, 'You have turned the city into a graveyard; the most thriving part of the city is the Mordestan District.' " He undid the brassiere, put his hands on her breasts and said, "I feel sorry for your breasts, how tightly you bind them." Zari felt a shiver shoot through her breasts. Her nipples became ever more firm. Yusof kissed her shoulder. His lips were hot. Zari said, "Didn't he ask where Mordestan District was?"

Yusof said, "Yes, he did. I said, 'It is the district whose inhabitants are for the most part unfortunate women who make a living by selling their bodies; and you send the Indian soldiers to them. As for yourselves, you have it made.' I said, 'You have stifled poetry, and in its place, the *droshky* drivers, whores, and dealers have learned a few words of English.' All MacMahon had to say was, 'Don't tell me these things. I, for one, have a heavy heart because of this war.' "

Yusof stroked his wife's hair and reached to kiss her behind her ear. Zari turned, putting her arms around her husband's neck as tears began to flow down her cheeks. Yusof asked with surprise, "Are you crying because of what I've done? I can't be like everybody else. I can't watch my peasants go hungry. A country can't be completely without men."

Zari said, crying, "Let them do whatever they want, except bring the war to my nest. What business is it of mine that the city is like the Mordestan District? This home is my city, my country, but they even drag the war to my home."

Yusof held her face in his hands, kissing her tears. "Get up, wash your face," he said. "Now is no time for this kind of talk. Your face is all puffed up like one of the faces they mold onto mud bricks. I swear to God you are a thousand times prettier than those puppet faces you put on. Get up, dear, I want you."

She turned off the light so Yusof couldn't see the scars on her belly. Yusof said these scars looked like a map. He would kiss the stitch marks and say, "You have suffered all this for me." Khanom Hakim had stitched up her belly like a wrinkled tablecloth.

When she came to the bed, Yusof's warm, hairy legs touched her own cold legs. His large hand caressed her breasts, and as it reached lower, she forgot everything—the earrings, Sergeant Zinger, Khanom Hakim, the bride, the marchers and the drums . . . the cross-eyed and the bald in the wedding ceremony . . . she forgot them all. But in her imagination, she could hear the quiet flow of water from a waterscape over bright red flowers, and she could see a ship full of flowers which was not a war ship.

2

I T WAS dawn on Thursday morning when Zari got up and
tiptoed out of the bedroom. After she freshened up her face
and brushed her hair, she went to the parlor where her sister-in-law, Khanom Fatemeh, was serving breakfast. She was
sitting behind the boiling samovar. The twins, Mina and
Marjan, were already chirping and bouncing like sparrows
around the breakfast table. It was to ensure their safe delivery and that of their brother, Khosrow, that Zari had made
a vow of charity, promising to take fresh bread and dates every
Thursday to prisoners and mental patients. Because Zari
was slender and her hips were small, her deliveries had been
difficult. At the beginning of each pregnancy, she would
decide to give birth at home and would make arrangements
with the best midwife in the city, but, in the end, she would
wind up, on the one hand, with Khanom Hakim at the missionary hospital and, on the other, with vows of charity and
oblations. As for Khanom Hakim, she was quick with the
knife. She would cut and sew. For Khosrow's delivery, the agonizing pain had led Zari to make a vow to take homemade
bread and dates to the mental patients, and five years later,
when with great fear and apprehension she became pregnant
again, she made a vow beforehand to do the same for the prisoners.

The children's aunt poured her a cup of tea, put it in front of her and asked, "Well, what happened at the wedding?"

Zari said, "I wish you were there. Once again there was a quarrel between the two 'governments.' "

The aunt said, "I know my brother, Khan Kaka. And I know Yusof, too. Abolqasem Khan is not sincere. And ever since he began thinking about becoming a member of parliament, he is even less sincere."

"He made me promise to go to the Europeans' celebration this afternoon, come what may," Zari said. "What am I going to do about my vow?"

"Don't worry. I'll ask Haji Mohammad Reza, the dyer, to go to the mental hospital with Gholam. And I'll go to the prison with Hoseyn Aqa, the herbalist. Sakineh has the oven ready. And the dough has risen. I checked on her after my prayers. I think she's baking the bread. You go ahead, sister. I don't want a quarrel to start between the brothers."

Khosrow came to the parlor. Mina clapped her hands and said, "It's my brother. He gives me horsey rides, right, brother?" There weren't many words she could pronounce properly. She pronounced the "s" as "sh," the "k" as "g" and "t" and "r" as "l." Her twin, Marjan, who was fifteen minutes younger, imitated her and was like an apprentice to her sister. Marjan hugged Khosrow's leg. "You play with him first and then I will. All right?"

Khosrow hurriedly patted the twins on the head and said, "I've got to go to school now." He sat at the table. Mina pulled at the table cloth. The samovar rocked and almost fell over. The aunt grabbed it. "God protect them, they can drive a person crazy." She gave them each a lump of sugar. Khosrow reached for the sugar bowl, "May I, mother? This afternoon Sahar is going to be shod." He took five lumps from the sugar bowl and put them in his pocket. He took the cup of tea from his aunt and reached for two more lumps of sugar and put them in his pocket. The aunt asked, "Are you drinking your tea without sugar?" He said, "Yes. I'll be late for school." Khanom Fatemeh gave him another lump of sugar. "At least drink your tea with this." She laughed and continued, "Khan Kaka has taken a gunnysack of sugar and twenty packages of tea, which were his peasants' shares, to Seyyed Moti'oddin. I have heard that he even attended the Seyyed's prayer service, this from a man who never in all his life knew which direction he should face to pray."

Khosrow said, "Auntie, I've seen Seyyed Moti'oddin. I saw him the day Gholam and I went to the Vakil Bazaar to buy a bridle and saddle for Sahar. He was riding a white donkey and had one arm stuck out of his *aba,* holding it in the air like this." Imitating the Seyyed, Khosrow held his arm up and away from himself, rocked back and forth on the chair as if he were sitting on a donkey, and continued. "As the people passed by, they kissed his hand and went on their way. Gholam and I kissed his hand too. He lowered his hand for me because otherwise I couldn't reach it."

There was a knock at the garden gate. Zari's heart sank. Maybe her earrings were being delivered from the Governor's house, but that early in the morning? The sun had just come up. She went to the veranda. Gholam, in his shirt and pajama bottoms, was coming from the stable at the other end of the garden. He wore his felt hat, as always. Gholam was bald. He opened the gate. Abolqasem Khan came in, straight as an arrow. I hope my earrings are sent back before Yusof wakes up, Zari thought. How gullible I am! How? By whom? What earrings?

She returned to the parlor and sat down to wait. When Khan Kaka entered, his sister said, "Speak of the devil. I was just talking about you."

Abolqasem Khan blinked, "You were probably saying that with all my running around, I'm sure to become a member of parliament. I will become one. I have met with the Colonel and the Consul. The Governor has promised, too. Only Seyyed threw a cog in the wheel. One day he praises me from the pulpit, but the next day he denies everything he has said."

"Maybe your gift of sugar and tea didn't impress him very much!" said Khanom Fatemeh.

Khan Kaka nodded toward Khosrow and reproached Khanom Fatemeh with, "Sister, have you lost your senses? What sugar, what tea?" The aunt said calmly, "I am the eldest of you all and I have the right to give you advice. The path you have chosen to follow is not the right one. And, as for Khosrow, he is no stranger."

Khan Kaka blinked and said angrily, "Then the path that your favorite brother, Yusof, is following is the right one? With one hand he takes coupons for sugar, fabrics, and lump sugar from the government and, with the other, distributes them among the villagers. Simpleton, what do you gain in such a transaction? Whenever he goes to a village he takes medicine for the villagers. I swear to God if you bring all the medicine in the world into these villages, it won't do any good."

Khosrow stood up and said goodbye. Khan Kaka asked, "Where is he anyway?"

Zari was making a fresh pot of tea. "He's awake," she said. "He'll be right with you."

Khan Kaka said, "Always sleeping! In the village, too, he is either sleeping or reading a book under the mosquito netting. I work like a dog, getting burned and wrinkled under the sun, while His Honor protects himself in wrapping paper. My dear, a peasant must fear his landlord. You have to stand over the peasant's head just like an elephant trainer. A peasant must be flogged and bastinadoed. There's an old saying that a peasant must always be kept hungry. Yusof has no idea about the winter crop or the summer crop. He just keeps looking at the sky. If it doesn't rain, he gets depressed, not about himself, but about the villagers and the sheep. And when you give him advice and try to reason with him, he quotes you in Arabic, "The harvest belongs to the one who cultivates the land, even if the land is usurped."

The aunt said, "With such good deeds, even if he gains nothing in this world, he'll have the rewards of the next. Besides, Khan Kaka, what business is it of yours what he does? He's not giving away your wealth, you know."

Sahar's neighing could be heard from the garden. Zari knew that Khosrow would drop by the stable before leaving for school. He would bring Sahar to the garden and let him loose. When he heard Sahar, Khan Kaka stood up, went to the parlor window that overlooked the garden, and said, "He's become a real beauty. The animal shines like gold! How he rolls on the cool grass! Look, he stood up—those eyes so well set, that wide forehead. He's thrusting his ears forward. His yellow mane—he's holding up his tail. And he's holding his head high. He's imitating his mother."

Sahar neighed again, indicating his pleasure. Abolqasem Khan came back to the table and sat down. Khanom Fatemeh sighed and said, "Thank God you finally said something positive about this household and quit criticizing it."

Khan Kaka laughed, "Everything he does is on a whim. Who keeps a horse in this day and age except my brother? Who else has three horses in the stable?" And he mimicked Yusof, "I like to ride a horse to the village. I ride the bay mare myself; my foreman rides the roan; and the sorrel colt belongs to Khosrow."

Yusof came in. He wore a thin *aba* over his shoulders. He said good morning and, with a surprised gaze, first looked at his brother, then at his sister, and finally fixed his questioning eyes on Zari. Zari shook her head. He asked, "Did Khosrow leave?"

"Yes."

"Where are Mina and Marjan?"

The aunt answered, "They're watching Sakineh bake bread and are probably jabbering away like chatterboxes."

Yusof sat down and asked Khan Kaka, "Has anything happened, God forbid?"

Abolqasem Khan did not answer. Instead, he took a small book out of his pocket, placed it on the table, closed his eyes, and said, "Swear on this Koran that you will come this afternoon and won't let your tongue get the better of you. Now, if you don't want to sell them the surplus provisions from your villages, don't. But you don't need to tell them that you won't. Give them some vague promise, like, 'Come back at harvest time.' You'll have to go to the winter pastures in a few days, anyway. Tell them that as soon as you have your harvest, you'll hand it over to them. Who knows what tomorrow may bring? They might be defeated and get the hell out of here. Rumor has it that Hitler is working on a bomb that will destroy the whole world . . . Now, swear . . ."

Yusof sighed and said, "I didn't say I wouldn't come this afternoon, so there's no need to swear. But as for deceiving them, I have to be honest. I won't lie and cheat, even if it costs me my head."

"Just for my sake," Khan Kaka said. "I haven't said this before, but I'm saying it now. My father, Haj Aqa, God rest his soul, spent a great deal on your education. But he didn't spend anything on me. And when he was dividing up his wealth, he gave both of us equal shares. Did I say anything? And Khanom Fatemeh's share fell into your hands. At least now that things are finally working out for me, help me get somewhere in this world. 'Strangers I don't complain about, alas, it's friends who are the cause of my woes.' "

Khanom Fatemeh broke in: "Khan Kaka, I only know that neither your father nor your grandfather ever gave in to anyone, neither to the filthy Europeans nor to our own nouveau riche. Our late father, Haj Aqa, did not remove his turban to the end of his life and was confined to his house a lifetime. In that parliament—I forget what it was called—to hell with its name—he did not vote for the one he was supposed to. If Yusof was his favorite son, it was precisely because he had a temperament like his own."

Khan Kaka shouted angrily, "Now you, too, are putting me down. If Haj Aqa had had any sense, we would have been millionaires by now. He spent all the money on that Indian slut of a dancer, Sudabeh. My mother died of grief in exile because of him. If he had had any sense, he wouldn't have married you off to a worthless idiot like Mirza Miyur's son, who got himself killed on purpose, and you wouldn't have had to be a maidservant in the home of . . ."

Zari interrupted her brother-in-law, "Khan Kaka, Khanom Fatemeh is older than any of us here and deserves the most respect. Without her, I wouldn't be able to manage this big house and garden by myself. Besides, we don't even consider her a guest."

"Yes, I know," Khan Kaka said. "She eats her own pottage and stirs someone else's porridge." He got up and suddenly, in an unusually soft and mild tone, added, "This is not the way to do it. So early on this holy day, instead of giving to charity and praying for the dead, I am making them tremble in their graves. Well, let bygones be bygones. I hope you will forgive me."

Zari accompanied the two brothers to the garden to see Khan

Kaka off. Sahar was grazing. When he smelled the stranger, he raised his head, his red nostrils flaring. Khan Kaka stood before him. The colt backed up and neighed. His mother neighed back from the stable. When Yusof stepped forward, Sahar sniffed the sleeve of his *aba,* raised his head, and took a deep breath, inhaling the familiar scent. Yusof patted his mane and neck. As Yusof and Zari returned from seeing Abolqasem Khan off, Sahar galloped from one end of the garden to the other. "Zari, look! He's chasing the butterflies." Sahar must have gotten warm, because he dropped on the grass that was still in the shade and rolled around in it several times. Then he stood up and suddenly lunged toward a yellow and brown butterfly.

When they reached the veranda, Yusof stopped, looked at the garden and said, "Your city is beautiful. It's a pity that summer is coming and I won't have time either for you or your city."

Zari asked, "My city?"

"Didn't you say last night that your city is this house?"

Zari laughed. "Oh, yes. This is my city, and I love every inch of it—its hill in the back, its veranda that runs all around the house, the streams on both sides of the patio, those two elm trees at the edge of the garden, its sour-orange grove which you planted with your own hands, that 'seven-graft' tree to which you yourself added one graft every year, the distillery next door with its mounds of flowers and herbs every season, flowers and herbs whose very names make you happy . . . its pussy willows, citrons, fumitories, palm pods, sweetbriars and most of all its orange blossoms and the scent that comes to our garden; the sparrows, starlings, and crows that consider our home their own. But the sparrows make me angry. They build their nests on the ledge of the sash window or on the treetops. Their eggs fall onto the ground and break all the time. They are so careless."

Yusof smiled. "Your voice is soft as velvet, like a lullaby. Tell me more."

"Tell you what? About the people in my city? About you? About the children, their aunt and our neighbors?"

Yusof added, laughing, "About Haji Mohammad Reza, the dyer."

"About Haji Mohammad Reza, the dyer, with the colorful

fabrics that he drapes under the sun along poles in the street and
his arms that are purple up to his elbows, about Gholam, about
Hoseyn Aqa, the herbalist, and Hasan Aqa, the dry grocer on the
corner, about Khadijeh—that's enough. You won't let me go get
to my work."

They could hear the sound of donkey bells. Yusof said, "They've
brought orange blossoms for the neighbor's city. What a scent there
is in the air!"

Zari couldn't tear herself away. She stood there until the donkeys entered the neighbor's garden and scattered their scented loads
on the patio in the middle of the garden. Only yesterday morning she had taken the twins to see the mound of orange blossoms.
Mina had clapped her hands and said, "Oh God, so many stars!"
And Marjan had laid her head on the flowers, saying, "I want to
night-night here." And all this time Zari was watching the old distiller and his three sons with fascination. The old man was kneeling down before the orange blossoms, filling up the baskets. His
sons put the baskets on their heads to carry them to the distillery tub. Zari didn't know why the old man called Marjan Narcissus
and Mina Tangerine . . . When he had finished with the baskets,
he made Narcissus and Tangerine, as he called them, a carousel
out of an apple and four sticks of wood, and he put the carousel
in the stream so that the flowing water made it turn. The children
were delighted, as if they owned the largest carousel in the world.
Zari wondered why the old man didn't marry his sons off. Clearly
it was time for them to take wives. But why would people who
work with so many flowers need wives?

3

WHEN THEY cleared away the lunch, Zari brought a hookah to her husband. Khosrow had been restless at lunch, and he was getting more restless as time passed. He seemed to have tears in his eyes that he was trying to keep from flowing. Zari put the twins to bed for their nap and returned to the parlor to take the hookah away. Khosrow was pacing back and forth, his father watching. "Why did we make all these preparations?" he asked. Khosrow answered despondently, "So he won't be afraid."

"It wasn't just because of fear."

Khosrow sat down next to his father and said, "Whenever the blacksmith came, I would lift his leg myself. At first, he was terrified and would buck, especially when the blacksmith drove the nails in his hooves. Of course, in the early days, he tapped them in gently. But yesterday, he pounded them very hard."

"Well, we did this so the colt wouldn't be frightened or pull his leg back when he's being shod and make the nail go into his flesh. Now, today, I will lift his leg myself, just as if I were your horse's midwife." And turning to Zari, who was now sitting down, he said, "You have put the hookah in front of you as if you meant to smoke it." Zari took a puff off the hookah, which made her cough, and she gave up the idea.

"Father, will you let me come and watch?" Khosrow asked.

"Of course. Weren't you there when he was born?"

"Yes. I remember it so well. Sahar stood up immediately. The mare cut his cord with her teeth and began to lick and sniff him. You put your *aba* on Sahar so he wouldn't catch a cold and rubbed his body until Gholam brought the blanket." Then he laughed and said, "He's become quite mischievous. He bites his mother, then he regrets it and licks her." He then asked: "Father, why do I love Sahar so much? I always want to talk about him. When I'm sitting in class, I can't wait for the bell to ring so I can come home and play with Sahar."

The father said, "There's nothing wrong with loving, son. Loving lights up one's heart. But hostility and hatred darken the heart. If your heart gets used to love, when you grow up, you will be ready to love the good and beautiful things in this world. The human heart is like a garden full of buds. If you water the garden with love, the buds will open. If you hate, the buds will wither. You have to learn that the objects of hatred and hostility are not goodness and beauty, but ugliness, dishonesty, and injustice. This kind of hatred is a sign of passion for honesty and justice."

"Dad, you're talking above a fifth-grade level again," Khosrow said.

"Didn't you understand what I said?"

"Yes, I did . . . You said there is nothing wrong with loving Sahar. Then you said I must water the buds."

Zari laughed. "As the saying goes: 'While you was telling me all them things, I counted a hundret and thirty ants go into a hole.'" Turning to Khosrow, she added, "I think you should get up and go to your uncle's house, go see Hormoz, and come back after Sahar is shod."

Yusof said, "No, Zari, Khosrow must learn how many nails you have to suffer through in order to have shoes on your feet. He must learn that in this world, pain and suffering . . ."

"Father, will it hurt him a lot?" Khosrow asked.

"No. The important thing is perseverance. We have made him get used to not being mischievous and to tolerating pain, whereas other horses . . ."

Khosrow interrupted his father again. "Father, the herd of horses that you told me about in a story didn't have bridles and shoes."

"Of course they didn't."

Zari asked, "What story was that?"

Yusof said, "I don't remember myself."

Khosrow stood up and said, "Don't you remember? You told me the story the night Sahar was born. Since that night, Gholam and I have talked a lot about the horses in the herd. Gholam said, 'Your daddy made it all up so you wouldn't cry.' "

Zari swallowed her laughter. "What was the story?" she asked.

"Father, I'll tell it . . . Once my father was the guest of a tribe. One moonlit night when the air is clear and the sky full of stars, my father and a few others go hunting. Suddenly they see a herd of wild horses in a very large field. Now, the horses are just standing there. The stallions are in a very large circle with their backs to the center and their faces to the field. The mare, who is giving birth, is in the middle, surrounded by the stallions—the stallions are embarrassed to look because when a mare gives birth, the colt comes out of some very, very bad part of her body. My father and the others don't go nearer, otherwise the horses might attack them. No, wait, the horses are standing like that so the mare won't worry, otherwise she will be afraid that some wild animals might attack her foal. Oh, I forgot to tell you. An experienced mare was standing as the midwife by the mare who was in labor . . ."

Yusof asked, "Did I say the baby comes out of some very, very bad . . ."

"No, Daddy, Gholam said this."

And Gholam entered wearing the felt hat that he always wore. Khosrow asked, "Has the blacksmith come?"

Gholam, addressing Yusof, answered, "His wife is here and says he has got a fever."

In the afternoon, Gholam came with two porters . . . Two large trays full of bread and dates covered with a printed cloth were waiting for the porters at the edge of the pool in front of the house. The aunt, wearing her *chador*, was seated next to one of the trays. Haji Mohammad Reza, the dyer, was pacing by the garden gate. But Hoseyn Aqa, the herbalist, had come inside and was standing by the orange grove looking at the orange blooms. Zari would alternate, going to the prison one week and to the mental hospital the next, and there was always a volunteer who would go to the place Zari herself could not visit that week. When there were no volunteers, the neighbors, Hoseyn Aqa and Haji Mohammad Reza, never let her down.

Zari, Khadijeh, their maid, and the aunt had been stuffing pieces of bread with dates. Now Zari stood at her vanity putting on make-up. She could see the garden from the bedroom window and could hear voices. She heard the aunt ask one of the porters, "Well, how much do you charge?"

The first porter answered, "Where am I supposed to go?"

The aunt said, "The Karimkhani Citadel, the jail."

"God grant you a long life," the porter said. "I don't want money. Give me homemade bread instead."

"Where am I supposed to go?" the second porter asked.

The aunt said, "You go to the mental hospital."

The second porter said, "I'll take bread, too."

Zari smoothed out the powder on her face and came to the veranda.

The aunt explained, "Sister, they want to be paid in bread."

"All right," said Zari, telling Gholam, "Give them each ten loaves."

"I have to go farther, but that's all right," the first porter said. "He has a sick child. It is the fault of the foreign troops. They contaminated the Vakil water reservoir."

The aunt said, "Goodness gracious!"

"As if their being here wasn't enough, they brought their diseases, too," Hoseyn Aqa said.

The first porter said, "Out of charity, you look after the prisoners and the mental patients on Thursdays, but no one looks after us."

"God bless them," said the second porter. "Let Him take care of us too."

Gholam brought the bread. Both porters had unwound the loincloths they had coiled to use as pads on their heads, had them ready in their hands, and carefully wrapped the bread in them. They tied the cloths around their waists. Their bellies looked swollen. "What are you going to put on your heads for padding?" asked Zari.

"If we don't," the first porter said. "they'll snatch the bread, especially since it's homemade. Homemade bread is as sweet as rose petals. The smell makes your mouth water. Good thing you've covered the trays with cloth."

"You are going by *droshky*," Zari said. "No one will have a chance to grab the bread."

"You'd think the lady's not from this city," the first porter said.

"Gholam," said Zari, "go ask Khadijeh for Khosrow's and his father's loincloths and give them to these men to coil up. They can't just put the trays on their bare heads."

A car stopped by the garden gate and honked. She saw Abolqasem Khan come in with his son Hormoz. Oh, my God, I haven't finished all I have to do yet, she thought, and ran inside. She hurriedly took off her house dress, put on her woolen sweater and skirt and looked for her shoes. She heard Khan Kaka, call, "Hey, folks, are you going to be long?" Then, the aunt's voice was heard: "Don't rush, this is the first day she's not delivering the charity food herself. Just for your sake—"

And again it was Khan Kaka's voice: "We've got a long way to go. We have to be there at five sharp."

"Isn't it next to Seyyed Abolvafa?" asked the aunt.

"No, sister, it's a *parasang* farther."

"Will you do a good deed and help these poor fellows? While they are getting ready, take us in your car."

"Are you afraid you'll be late for your opium, sister?"

Zari was combing her hair. She thought, Sister and brother are about to have an argument.

She heard Hormoz mediate, "Auntie dear, would you like me to go? I like to talk to prisoners. I've gone three times with Hoseyn Aqa, haven't I, Hoseyn Aqa?"

Khan Kaka's angry voice was heard. He reproached Hormoz, "Here you go talking nonsense again."

Khan Kaka came to the veranda and, smiling, addressed Zari and asked, "Sister, how many hours have you spent in front of the mirror? Where is my brother? Where is Khosrow?"

Zari did not answer Khan Kaka. She was listening to the aunt, who said, "Let's get going, Hoseyn Aqa. Help put the tray on his head."

And she heard one of the porters say, "With God's help," as he lifted the tray, and then, "By the grace of God."

Sergeant Zinger himself came to welcome them and together they passed by the fruit orchards. Zari was hot, but knew that it would get cold at night. She was walking together with Khan Kaka, ahead of everyone else. Yusof and Zinger followed them, and Khosrow and Hormoz were walking behind. They passed a farm that had lettuce standing in rows, like soldiers in a regiment, under a layer of dust, and then they walked by farms that were bright in the sun and exposed all they had, ripe and unripe—cucumbers, eggplants, tomatoes and watermelons. Khan Kaka said, "It's time to water them."

To the left of the farms, soldiers and officers were sitting or standing under the tents, and cars and trucks were parked next to the tents in rows or at random. Zari heard Yusof say, "Such wine shall never suffice our intoxication," and then Sergeant Zinger ask, "What do you mean?" Khan Kaka stopped and turned toward them. Zari was also obliged to stop. Abolqasem Khan turned to Sergeant Zinger, blinked, and said, "If I may, Your Excellency, what my brother means is that a glass of whisky is nice, but one cannot get drunk on a single glass alone." Khan Kaka pushed Yusof ahead and he himself walked alongside Zinger.

The guests were ushered into the headquarters, which was in a large tent. Khan Kaka had hurried so much that they had arrived early. They greeted Khanom Hakim and a Scottish officer and exchanged pleasantries with them. A map of Iran was spread out on a table in the corner of the tent. Khanom Hakim was pacing in the tent and looked like she was memorizing something from a piece of paper. Zari glanced at the map. They had put so many colored markers on the map that even if you knew what the markers meant, you would still be confused. Yusof went to the map, followed by a distraught Khan Kaka. Yusof said, "They have really chopped it up." Khan Kaka put his hand on his brother's arm. An Indian soldier came in with a tray full of glasses, iced fruit drinks, and colorful alcoholic beverages. Zinger guided him to the table with the map. He said to Yusof, "Now, drink." The three each picked up a glass. Zinger lifted his glass and said, "To Iran, much greatest than France. And Tehran, greatest than . . . than . . . Vichy," he finished in his broken Persian. Yusof lifted his eyes from the map, looked at him, and said, "But, unfortunately, we did not fight!" Khan Kaka blinked and said, "But, as for the Vichy mineral water for indigestion . . ."

Zinger interrupted him and asked Yusof, "Why unfortunate you said?"

"Because we suffer the consequences without having tasted heroism or honorable defeat," Yusof replied.

Zinger said harshly, "If you able fight. This good word I found. It was dunnage. We ripped, it had no blood. Instead of blood, it was filled with straw."

Yusof laughed involuntarily, placed his hand on Zinger's shoulder, and said, "My dear Zinger, you knew yourself it had no blood, and that was precisely what made it hideous and banal. We didn't even know we should not fight, so that if we were defeated we would have a proud defeat."

Zinger held his hand in front of Yusof's face, signaling him to stop, and said, "Whoa . . . Say it slow so I can come with you."

Khan Kaka blinked and said, "What's done is done, like spilled milk, my son."

"You poetry recite and make lose my mind," Zinger said angrily.

Other officers, British, Scottish, and one Indian, joined them in the tent. Hormoz whispered in Zari's ear, "If Mr. Fotuhi were here, he would point to my uncle and say, 'This is what a man should be.' He drives us crazy with his constant talk about the bravery of Jalaloddin Menkoberni. If he could only see my uncle."

Zari was preoccupied with watching Zinger. She saw him take Abolqasem Khan's arm and heard, "Advise your brother. God gives you a bounty. Give it to us. This bounty belong to all, belong to mankind. All this too much for you. Was not necessary . . ."

Yusof laughed and said, "Just like B.P."

Zinger seemed taken aback. His face and neck turned a darker shade of red. He put his glass on the map and said, "You did not know. You not necessary. We brought out. Brought to those who need." And suddenly becoming friendly, he took his glass and said, "To your health."

The Governor, with the cross-eyed Colonel ahead and the new bride and groom and Gilantaj following them, entered the tent. The officers stood at attention and the Governor nodded. Little by little, the commander of the troops, managers of the city newspapers, and directors of departments, all with their wives, came in and crowded the tent. The odors of feet, alcohol, sweat, and women's perfumes mingled. Now, three Indian soldiers were serving them. Zari signaled to Khosrow and Hormoz and the three of them together went toward Gilantaj. Zari had decided to disregard formalities and remind her of the earrings. She introduced Khosrow and Hormoz to Gilantaj. The girl put out her hand and laughed. Both her cheeks formed dimples. The new bride, wearing a wide-rimmed straw hat and green sunglasses, walked toward them. She said, "Dear Zari, I am most grateful for your gift. I will always keep them as a memento."

Zari looked at her in astonishment. Since when had she and the Governor's daughter become, unbeknownst to her, such bosom buddies? In the three years since they had come to Shiraz, all in all, she had seen her three times—well, maybe four times, and counting her wedding, five times. She opened her mouth to say, "What gift? They borrowed it. If you don't believe me, ask your sister standing right here!" But not a sound came out of her mouth. In her heart, she cursed herself for being such a coward and thought, Spineless women like me get what they deserve.

The new bride glanced at Hormoz and Khosrow and said, "Zari, dear, I didn't know you had such grown-up boys, you being so young and beautiful. Tell everybody they're your brothers, not your sons."

Khosrow interjected, "Hormoz Four-Eyes is my cousin."

Hormoz blushed and took off his glasses. But Zari knew that he couldn't see a thing without them. She wanted to punch her son in the stomach for being so impolite. Hormoz Four-Eyes! Historical Hormoz! Calling his older cousin such names, and in front of class people like the Governor's daughters! This time, the new bride beat her to it: "Hormoz Khan, are you Mirza Abolqasem Khan's son? I know him very well. He has been so kind to us! What a nice man. He makes us laugh so much. Don't be embarrassed; put your glasses back on. I wear glasses too. Even my sunglasses are prescription. Last night, I had a hard time without my glasses."

The sound of drums and trumpets rose and the Colonel and the Governor came out of the tent followed by the guests. Zari felt as if she were being led to the gallows. They reached a large open area where chairs were arranged in the shape of a horseshoe and were filled with thousands of soldiers, most of them Indian. The officer who was walking behind the Colonel gave an order and suddenly everyone stood up, making quite a clatter. Several wooden platforms were joined together and covered with carpets to make a stage. Around it, five flags were flapping; among them Zari recognized the British flag.

Khanom Hakim walked on stage and went up to the microphone. The boards squeaked under her feet. She welcomed the audience in Persian, reading from a piece of paper in her hand. Her voice was trembling until she collected herself. Her teeth looked yellower that usual in the afternoon sun. From what she said, Zari gathered that a show had been arranged for their fighting boys who had come on leave to the city of flowers and nightingales. They needed to be entertained in order to fight the monster of fascism with a strong spirit and send that Satan to hell. They were all grateful for the hospitality extended to them by the Iranians, who had made their war against this Satan, that is, Hitler, easier. She also said that Hitler was a microbe, a cancer, and the cancerous growth had to be removed.

After all, Khanom Hakim was not only a midwife, she was also a surgeon, and very handy with a knife. Moreover, as she said, she "also brought good tidings and guidance." Every night, she would line up the expectant mothers and those who had been knifed in the streets, along with their kith and kin, to show them films. Silent films, of course. She held a long stick and pointed to the people on the screen, explaining in her awkward Persian: "This has been Jesus Christ . . . This has been Mary Magdalen . . . This has been Judas Iscariot . . ." Then she would preach in the same Persian, especially about Satan and the fires of hell. Zari had seen all sorts, but this one was something else: Really, why would a midwife, surgeon, and missionary show up in a place like this? There is probably some wheeling and dealing between the Satan she preached about and the one that the fighting boys wanted to send to hell! As for the fighting boys, most of them are Indians. As Khan Kaka would have said, "They eat their own pottage and stir other people's porridge. But the people of our city have nicknamed the latter Satan the Imam of the Age. I have heard it many times with my own ears."

MacMahon came on stage and brightened up the scene. He wore a red cape and black boots. He looked like a movie star whose name Zari could not remember no matter how hard she tried. What a pity he was fat. He spoke in English, but Zari did not understand many of his jokes. After he said two or three sentences, the laughter of the officers and most of the soldiers rose to the sky. Even the Governor and the Commander laughed. One of the news-paper managers laughed the loudest. Probably some laughed out of hospitality to the foreign guests. Some wanted to taunt the Fascist Monster. Zari, well known in town for her knowledge of English, didn't understand a word of it anyway. MacMahon recited a poem, complete with gestures. The poem was about a soldier abroad who traps a foreign girl and gets as much out of her as he can . . . shoes, hat, money on top of that . . . but when the girl says "I'm pregnant, marry me," he confesses that he has a wife and kids. MacMahon rocked an imaginary cradle. He put his arms around an imaginary woman and even said in Persian "I have a wife and kids." The audience laughed. It was not a belly laugh.

Then he recited his own poem. The one about the Tree of Independence. "A strange tree which draws its strength from the soil and blood. This tree has a gardener who looks like a prophet. Of all the trees, the gardener only loves this one. When it is time to water it, he shouts: Blood. All the people gather around the tree and cut open one of their veins. This tree has a cool and vast shade. All the people sit under it, and forget their sorrows. People dry up and grind its fruits and leaves to apply to their eyes. As a result, pride, hope and self-confidence nestle in their hearts, replacing cow-ardice, suspicion and lies, and they all become men of courage and honor."

Then the show began. A bearded Indian with a turban came out dressed in white from head to toe and sat cross-legged on the stage. He adjusted the microphone and began to play a reed. From the pit in front of him, which Zari had not noticed before, a dark woman peeked out a few times and stuck out her tongue. She had put a red dot between her eyebrows. The woman came up and stood next to the man. She wore a yellow sari with gold embroidered trim. Her voice was so high she kept making squealing noises. The woman was old. When she shook her hands, her bracelets jingled. Her voice was drowned out by the ruckus and whistling of the Indian soldiers. Her neck seemed double-jointed. Her head was as flexible as a snake's. Her eyebrows wiggled up and down. How much *kohl* she had wasted on her eyes! The woman kept dancing back and forth in front of the pit. The rhythm got faster and faster. A rubber tube with a snake head was stuck up from the pit, stiff and erect. The woman reached out and pulled the tube. Then she coiled the rubber tube up like a long snake in a corner of the stage.

Next a skinny man with bushy eyebrows, a salt-and-pepper moustache, a top hat, tails and an umbrella in hand came on stage. The reed player continued playing. The woman reached into the pit and took out some items one by one: wood, pieces of board, the red cape that MacMahon had worn, a dunce cap, a box, a hammer and an air pump. Now the woman became the assistant to the man with the bushy eyebrows. The man made a scarecrow out of the wood and took the rubber tube from the woman and covered the trunk, arms and legs of the scarecrow with it. He put the cape on the scarecrow's shoulders, which had a snake head, and put the dunce cap on its head. He glued a moustache over its lip. The moustache covered the entire width of the snake's face. He also took a swastika from the woman and pinned it to the cape. Then he went to the air pump and attached it to the scarecrow and began to pump it up to the beat of the music. The scarecrow kept getting bigger and bigger. Its head, its body, its hands and its legs kept swelling. It became astonishingly huge—taking over most of the stage—and the Indian with the turban had to move aside. Someone behind Zari's whispered, "It's Hitler." Suddenly, drums pounded. First a fat man with a small pipe in the corner of his mouth, and then Uncle Sam and various Scottish officers, with and without kilts, others with hammer and sickle insignias, all poured onto the stage. Each was carrying a bow and arrow. The men on stage fingered the scarecrow. One of the officers kept holding them back and saying, *"Nyet, nyet."* Then he finally consented and yelled, *"Kharashu! Kharashu!"*

The drums pounded harder; the officers with bows and arrows went to work, and each shot an arrow into the scarecrow's body. The punctured scarecrow began to deflate. It gave out one last hiss and plopped onto the ground. The crowd cheered and applauded. Then there were other shows.

4

ON SATURDAY afternoon, Sahar was shod by a blacksmith who wasn't their usual. Khosrow was at school and did not witness the event. When he came back, he looked reproachfully at his father, who was saying, "We had no choice. It would have been too late." Then the conversation turned to hunting and his father promised to take him and Sahar along. Until Thursday afternoon, when the riders rode through the garden gate, all Khosrow could think or talk about was hunting and whether or not Sahar would be able to come. And now it had been some twenty-four hours since Zari had seen her son. She had worried constantly and imagined the worst. The aunt had consoled her, saying, "They are galloping on their horses enjoying themselves, and you imagine they have been injured or thrown off the mountain."

Zari instructed Gholam to sprinkle water on the front patio and place the wicker chairs next to the pool. They would surely show up before sunset on Friday. Mina and Marjan were hanging around the pool, and as soon as their mother turned her back, together they stuck their hands into the water.

There was a knock at the garden gate. Zari went to welcome the riders. Gholam was opening the gate wide. A *droshky* drove in and Zari was taken aback. But they had gone on horseback! When the *droshky* reached Zari, it stopped. Two women got out. They had on *chadors* and were covering their faces tightly. What huge women! They were wearing thick Abadeh-made *maleki* shoes, and how big their feet were. How tall and broad-shouldered they looked under their *chadors*. Zari said hello. The women nodded. One of them paid the *droshky* driver with a rough-looking, thickly veined hand. She was wearing a man's watch. Zari tried to remember where she might have seen them before, but couldn't. Perhaps they were old friends of Khanom Fatemeh, who was now smoking opium on the veranda. Were they the manly, macho women of the type who were afraid of no man in the world? Or were they female thugs?

Her attention turned to Mina and Marjan, who had stuck their arms up to their elbows in the water. She shouted, "Get away from the pool." When they got to the chairs, she asked the women to have a seat. But they paid no attention and kept walking toward the house. It was obvious that the shorter one was laughing, because her shoulders were shaking under the *chador*. Still puffing on her opium pipe, the aunt looked at the women and said, "I don't recall having met you before." The women passed through the veranda, opened the parlor door, and went in. Surely they were not two of the mental patients to whom she had given bread and dates yesterday with her own hands. But no sane person would walk into somebody's home, wander around like a sleepwalker, not say a word, and to top it all off, treat it like her ancestral home. Zari followed the women into the parlor. She said, "Why don't you have a seat? To tell you the truth, I still cannot recall who you are." One of them asked in a husky voice, "Where is Yusof Khan?" Zari answered, "He's gone hunting with Khosrow."

It was a man's voice. And it was familiar. This was probably a practical joke. The women sat on the sofa in the parlor and both dropped their *chadors*. Wide eyebrows, black eyes, long eyelashes, hooked noses with dark, drawn faces. They couldn't have been more alike than two halves of an apple. Only one was younger and the other older, and the older one had a moustache, to boot. What a sight. Amazed, she shouted, "Malek Rostam Khan! What kind of get-up is this? You scared me half to death."

Malek Rostam put his finger to his moustache and said, "Shhhh! Quiet. We'll wait here for Yusof."

Zari went to the veranda. She saw the twins sitting by their aunt, watching her smoke. She returned to the parlor and handed two fans to Malek Rostam and his brother Malek Sohrab, and said laughingly, "You sure had me fooled! After all these years, you drop in like this."

Malek Rostam asked anxiously, "When are they coming back from hunting? Might they not come back today?"

"I'm expecting him any moment now," Zari answered. "Why do you ask?"

Malek Rostam said, "I heard he's going to the winter pastures tomorrow. Why hasn't he come back yet?"

Zari brought glasses of iced drinks for the guests and then fruit and mixed nuts. She opened the parlor doors. But they did not let her turn on the lights. She sat in front of them and asked, "Well, what has brought you here?"

Malek Rostam stroked his moustache and said, "Sohrab was sent by my uncle. I just came along because I missed you."

"And wearing *chadors* was probably Sohrab Khan's idea," Zari said. "Sohrab Khan, you haven't given up your childish antics yet. Do you remember what hell you used to raise?"

Malek Sohrab laughed. "How could I forget? But we used the *chadors* as a disguise. If we get caught, they'll make mince meat out of us."

Zari turned to Malek Rostam and said, "Remember the good old days! We were so carefree!"

And she recalled one of those days in the first year of her marriage. It was the year the tribal chief had been arrested and taken to Tehran, and the tribe was pulling itself together. When Yusof and Zari arrived, a large group came to welcome them. They even cheered, but, as Yusof said, it was only half-hearted. The welcoming party seemed disheveled, dejected, and depressed. Before the couple had reached the Khan's large, five-pole tent, most of them had scattered. Malek Sohrab was sitting on the chief's seat. When he saw them he said, "Welcome to our portable capital." Zari had never in her life seen a prettier tent. What rugs! What cushions! What beautiful leather coffers! All around the tent were painted images of Rostam, Ashkabus, Esfandiyar, and Sohrab, and other

figures Zari did not recognize. It was funny. Malek Sohrab was both
a child and not a child. He got up, pointed to the picture of Sohrab
and said, "This is me!" Zari said, "God forbid," because that picture depicted Sohrab with his side ripped open by a dagger.
Then he pointed to the picture of Rostam and said, "And this one
is Malek Rostam, the oldest son of the tribal chief's family."
Zari watched Malek Rostam whisper to Yusof. Malek Rostam had
a sad smile on his face. Then Malek Sohrab pointed to the picture of a severed head in a basin full of blood. Tulips had grown
around it, and a black horse was sniffing them. Malek Sohrab said,
"This is my brother that Bibi has not yet given birth to!" "You can't
fool me," Zari said. "I bet this one is John the Baptist."

Malek Sohrab laughed. "Okay," he said. "I'm ready to bet."

"What do you bet?"

"A Brno rifle."

He then called Yusof and showed him the picture. "Your wife
says this is John the Baptist."

Yusof smiled and said. "Forgive her. My wife has come to her
husband's home straight out of school. Her mind is still full of the
Bible stories she had to read every morning in school."

"Wait, I know," Zari said. "It's the severed head of Imam
Hoseyn . . . and that horse . . ."

"Don't embarrass me more than you have, dear," Yusof said.
"This is Siyavash."

Malek Sohrab went and sat in the chief's seat again and said,
"Total number of troops, six thousand. Slaughter one hundred and
fifty sheep a day." He paused. "And you, Khanom Zahra. I hear
you have brought your bridal carpet as a gift to the chief. We can't
accept it. The warp and weft of this carpet are made with toil and
affection." And he asked Zari, "Did you see the layout of the tents?
Did you see how the armed guards are standing prepared with their
rifles? Do you hear the sound of trumpets and drums? This military march is being played in honor of your arrival."

He hadn't yet finished his sentence when their mother, Bibi
Hamdam, came in. After greetings and customary pleasantries, she
said, "Get up, child. Are you talking nonsense again? They have
caught two chickens. Run and cut their heads off before the sun

goes down." Malek Sohrab got angry. He stood up, made a face at Bibi and left. When he came back, he threw the dead chickens on his mother's lap.

Malek Rostam interrupted Zari's reminiscing as he asked, "Khanom Zahra, you seem distracted. Maybe we are imposing on you?"

Zari laughed. "What are you saying? I was remembering the first night that I came to the tribal chief's tent. It was in the first year of our marriage."

She turned to Malek Sohrab. "Do you remember what you did to Bibi that night in front of me, the new bride?"

"I remember it well," Malek Sohrab said.

"Well, you were a child," Zari said.

"I was not a child," he replied. "I was unruly and rebellious."

"I remember Bibi Hamdam had to change her pants," Zari said. "I counted. She was wearing eight pairs of pants. Bibi caught a cold . . . and you, Malek Sohrab, kept saying a tribal woman should not get sick."

"I remember well," Malek Sohrab said. "That night I won a Brno rifle from you, which you never paid up."

At this time, Khadijeh came in and asked Zari for the keys to put the children to sleep. She looked at the men in *chadors* in amazement and asked, "You are sitting in the dark! Shall I turn on the lights?"

"No."

Malek Rostam said, "I remember, it was the year that I got malaria and came to you for refuge. I stayed bedridden in your house for three months. Those days no one dared to even say hello to us. You nursed me like a sister. I won't forget it. The washerwoman had not come and you washed my clothes with those small, delicate hands of yours. Yusof himself put bedpans under me." Turning to Sohrab, he added, "Sohrab, I should leave. I shouldn't have come here." Sohrab answered him in Turkish. The two brothers switched to Turkish for a while. Zari did not understand anything, and she got worried again.

The sound of hooves could be heard on the gravel in the garden and Zari ran to greet the riders. The lights in the garden were lit. They had shot two deer. A fawn was on the back of the roan horse which their foreman, Seyyed Mohammad, with his thick salt-and-pepper moustache, was riding. The riders dismounted. Khanom Fatemeh also joined them and said, "Tired, I bet."

Khosrow enthusiastically explained, "Mother, Sahar has been very bad. He chased this fawn and caught it on the neck with his teeth. Needless to say, he fell down himself and hurt his knee. Now I'll have to treat it with burnt hazelnut oil. Do you have any hazelnuts, mother?" Zari said, "There are some on the table in the parlor, in the bowl of mixed nuts." Then she thought about it and said, "But don't go in now. We have guests you don't know."

Yusof had gone to the twins' bed; they were sleeping on the other side of the pool under mosquito netting.

The husband and wife went into the parlor. Yusof switched on the lights. He told Malek Rostam, "I was expecting you, but not today. You've come too late and at the wrong time. Today, I'm not even happy that you've come. Why you? Why should you consent to this kind of thing, despite all the discussions we've had?"

Yusof sat on the sofa and Zari sat in front of him on the floor and pulled off his boots. Malek Rostam dropped his head and chewed on his moustache. Sohrab rolled up his *chador* and tossed it into a corner and sat erect. Yusof continued, "You dug the rusty old rifles out of the crevices in the mountains and every nook and cranny, polished them, and once again took up your pillaging and fratricide. What could we possibly say to each other?"

"Khanom Zahra is no stranger," said Sohrab. "We had to take our revenge. How long must we suffer? It was that general amnesty which they later ignored, and how. They started out fine, but took a wrong turn. They took bribes, looked for excuses, sowed hatred, and carried out executions. As for their so-called settlement plan, they wasted all the money they had on rubbish. They built a few mud houses in places where there was no water and said, 'Go live in them.' Instead of books, teachers, doctors, medicine, and sympathy, they gave us bayonets, tanks, guns, and animosity. Now it is natural for us to go back to our own business and take revenge."

Khadijeh brought in a hookah and put it in front of Yusof. Zari said quietly, "Take the boots and have Gholam clean them. And bring some tea." Yusof took a puff off the hookah and said, "There you have it, Sohrab my friend, you've gone back to your business. In other words, the tribe has become a business for you. You use it to make deals."

Malek Rostam supported his brother. "Believe me, it was a case of mindless planning. As you know, I am among those who agree with the settlement idea. But it seems that's not what's really wanted. There are forces at work that will block it, or wish to see us collapse from within and disappear, or maybe want to keep us in our present condition."

Holding the hookah mouthpiece in the corner of his mouth, Yusof said, "You yourselves prefer the present situation too. If you had helped, maybe the settlement plan would have gotten somewhere. But, my friend, you are used to milking your peasants. You don't even see them as human beings. For you, they are no different from your sheep. You sell both for cash."

Malek Rostam faced Yusof angrily. "Don't speak to me like that, Yusof. You are my dear friend and classmate. We have broken bread together many times. But . . ."

"I know no other way to talk but the way I do. You know me. I speak my mind, even with my dearest friends."

Malek Rostam said calmly, "I know better than anyone else that tribal life, despite its excitement and glory, is not a proper life. You know that I myself prefer to be a Qashqa'i of the soil, a farmer, rather than a Qashqa'i of the wind, a nomadic herdsman. I know it's not right for thousands of men, women, and children to wander aimlessly with their livestock, looking for grass and water, from this end of the Gulf to that mountain peak. I know that we shouldn't make the lives of so many people dependent on cows, sheep, and fodder. But is it all in my hands alone? Am I the tribal chief? What can a lone man do?"

Yusof put the hookah aside: "If there is a will, a lone man can join forces with others. There are many who know and can tell right from wrong. But they are not united. Band together with these other lone men. Even if you don't, the next generation will. They pass through cities. They see prosperous villages, schools, mosques, bath houses, and hospitals. They realize what they are missing and will in the end do something about it."

Malek Rostam said, "You know, all this talk won't do any good now—"

Khosrow clicked his heels at the door, said hello, walked to the mixed nut bowl, picked it up and left.

Yusof turned to Malek Rostam and asked, "What's the story about the Malekabad Pass? I've heard rumors, but I wanted to hear it from you."

Malek Rostam said, "I swear by the hair on your head it wasn't anything important. The Ezhdahakosh clan disarmed a group of riders, cut a few people's heads off and captured about ten rifles, some bullets and some twenty horses. That's all. They have done it on their own accord, too. The Farsimadan clan informed my uncle. My uncle himself does not condone petty theft."

Malek Sohrab broke his silence. "Brother," he said. "Tell Yusof Khan the story about the captain's pups."

Rostam didn't say anything, so Sohrab continued: "The captain in charge of the settlement plan had a dog who had a litter. Some kids from the Ezhdahakosh clan threw stones at the dog, a purebred that looked like a wolf. Then, out of fear, they stole the dog and did away with it. The Farsimadans told on them. Well, the captain forced three women from the Ezhdahakosh clan to nurse the pups."

Zari felt her stomach turn, but Yusof smiled and said, "Dear Sohrab, this story is ten or twelve years old. You yourself have told me the same story three different times."

Malek Sohrab said boldly, "Was it fair to let me tell it a fourth time?"

Yusof said, "At first I didn't remember, but it all came back to me when you told it. What do you think? I'm only human. Like everybody else, I can make a mistake." And, turning to Rostam, he asked, "Well, now what do you want from me? So far we've just talked nonsense. Let's get to the heart of the matter."

"Believe me," answered Malek Rostam. "I don't agree with all of my uncle's actions. I even opposed his sending me to you as a go-between. I don't want our friendship spoiled. But at this sensitive moment I can't refuse to back him."

It seemed that in the beginning he was saying only Sohrab had been sent by the uncle and he himself had missed us, Zari thought.

Yusof said, "You haven't told me what it is you or your uncle want from me."

Malek Rostam again dropped his head and became pensive. Malek Sohrab said, "Help."

"What kind of help?"

"Sell us all your food supplies. We are willing to buy even what you have not yet harvested, at any price you say."

"Who put this idea into your head? Zinger? So far, there has only been talk of buying the surplus grain; now they want everything?"

The brothers exchanged glances and remained silent. Yusof shouted, "You want food to give to the foreign troops in exchange for weapons you will then use to shoot your brothers and compatriots? Like that saying we have, 'We stretched it one way, it didn't work, now we'll stretch it another way!' Don't you have any brains? These mysterious hands that do not want you to make a go of it were thinking of a day like this. So, what happened to all that bravery, honor, and dignity?" His blond moustache trembled.

Malek Sohrab almost pleaded. "Do you know that the tribe has been stopped at Kamfiruz? Do you know that they have not been given permission for summer migration? We are surrounded by our own government's cannons and guns. The green grass on the mountain slopes is drying up untouched and our sheep are weak for lack of fodder and are panting for lack of water."

Yusof grew angrier. "Look, my dear Sohrab. Don't try to pull the wool over my eyes, little boy that you are! I don't expect it from you! I know that you have sold most of your sheep to the foreign troops. Your sheep are now frozen and are being kept refrigerated in the Ahvaz-Bandarshah railroad cars."

Rostam kept staring at the floral design in the carpet. His brother answered, "If we hadn't sold them, they would have died on our hands. Believe me, our sheep couldn't walk on their own. They had to be taken in trucks."

"What did you do with the money?" Yusof asked. "Did you buy weapons? Golden ewers? Golden vats? Did you sew up a crown inside your double-flapped Qashqa'i hats? Are you flattered by your uncle being addressed as His Royal Highness?"

Malek Sohrab could take no more. Standing up, he said, "Yusof Khan, our friendship has its place, but there is a limit to everything. What gives you the right to call me a little boy, to say that we have no brains? You're not all that smart yourself, otherwise you, not your brother, would run for parliament."

Yusof said angrily, "Whose representative would I be? Zinger's? The kind of candidate on whose behalf you would mediate makes me shudder."

Malek Sohrab became even angrier. "A fine human being you are! You say whatever comes to your mind. Do you ever think that you might be wrong? Who has made me a mediator? Why do you keep patting yourself on the back? Who do you think you are? And then, what mistakes? What does a golden ewer have to do with us? You even blame us for Davud Khan's deeds? Why? What gives you the right?"

Yusof shook his head. "You are all cut from the same cloth."

Malek Rostam, addressing Sohrab, said, "Sit down, brother. You agreed not to insult my friend." Then the two brothers spoke in Turkish. Rostam's voice was harsher and Sohrab's softer, until finally Sohrab sat down and muttered, "I apologize." Yusof pulled the hookah closer. Zari said, "The charcoal is burned out. Let me replenish it."

Yusof sighed and said, "I have fire in my own head," and puffed on the hookah.

Sohrab smiled. "I didn't mean to offend you; I apologize again."

Yusof laughed. "Dear Sohrab, you showed you have guts. I liked that. Only you don't know the whole story." He put the hookah aside and continued, "You know, I neither agreed with you when you flirted with the Germans nor do I now that you have made a deal with their enemies. It was you who made Hitler into the Imam of the Age. But those kind of tricks won't work here. It was your flirtations that gave these people an excuse to come here."

"Well, brother, after all, it is war," Malek Sohrab said softly. "A war is not a dinner party. The troops have to be here to protect the oil and the Gulf waterways. They would have come anyway. Besides, they come here on leave and for treatment. The main camp is in Khorramshahr. They have no other choice."

Yusof said in a fatherly tone, "You even defend them, my dear boy? This is their war. What is it to us? Hitler is from their own continent. They fattened him up themselves. Let them pay for it. Pay for everything. Pay for the pain they caused those who, as Zinger puts it, have the bounty but don't know how to make use of it. But they never say who is responsible for this not knowing how."

Malek Sohrab glanced at his watch and said, "It's late and I have a headache. Do you have an aspirin? Make sure it's Bayer."

Zari took the hookah and left, returning with the Bayer aspirin and a glass of water. Yusof was saying, "I assure you, in order to dissuade their ally from the proposal I mentioned, with your help, they will orchestrate a maneuver and will have a group of people killed by your hands. These people never say 'no' to their ally. They will present him with a fait accompli so that he will give up his plan on his own. Remember what I am telling you! They will stain your hands, while they sit on the sidelines watching the show. A real fratricide will begin."

"We've got to be going," said Malek Sohrab. "We'd better get back to the main point. You still haven't said whether you will sell us the provisions," looking as if to encourage Yusof.

Malek Rostam laughed and said, "He didn't? How do you want him to say it? With that lengthy sermon he delivered—"

Malek Sohrab persisted, "Believe me, we don't want to sell all of it. Our people are hungry. They are dropping like flies because of disease and starvation."

Yusof conceded, "I'll accept Rostam's promise. If he promises to buy enough to feed only your people and my food is used for no one but your people, I have no objection. Tomorrow, I'll go to Kavar. I know that you have been held back there, too. Bring camels and load up the supplies, but only to feed the tribe. Bahman Dam is a *parasang* farther. You'll have a watering place. And I'll give you a grazing pasture free of charge."

Rostam said despairingly, "I can't double-cross you."

Yusof said, "I know that you can't." He hesitated for a moment and said, sympathetically, "Rostam, come on. Turn back from the path you've decided to follow. Let us at least create a home and hearth and faith for one clan, one family. Teach them trades. How many times have I told you this? My uncultivated lands are waiting to be used for houses, schools, bathhouses, hospitals, mosques, and grazing pastures."

Malek Sohrab interrupted. "What you propose does not agree with us. We have lived freely, nature always within our grasp. We have ridden horses on its mountains and valleys, we have rested in its fields, and camped beneath its sky. We cannot be imprisoned in houses."

Yusof added bitterly, "Of course, except for us khans. We khans have always had the best gardens in the cities, which are now the headquarters for the foreign troops, the best houses . . ."

Malek Sohrab, knowing what Yusof was about to say, interrupted once more. "Believe me, Yusof, our people love the kind of life they live. If they become settled, they'll get depressed."

"Because they have only known this way of life. But, dear Sohrab, when a person cultivates a plot of land, labors on it and harvests it, he depends on the land. Nature is also within reach in the village. When he is settled—"

But Sohrab completed Yusof's sentence with, "He becomes stupid, dumb, narrow-minded, and cowardly," and immediately changed the subject. "May I ask you a question? What are you going to do with all your crops, the grains and dates that you have? It is now the season for the summer crops. What will you do after you harvest the crops? Will you hoard it?"

"I'll give the peasants their share in full and take the rest to the city. That's to make up for all the unfair landowners who have sold both the peasants' share and the people's food to the foreign troops. There are five of us, all major landowners, and two of us are members of the city council. We have all sworn an oath to take charge of the city's food supplies. We have also gained the mayor's support. I know that you are man enough not to expose us. But I want you to know that we are not hoarders. The hoarders are those who send their own people's food to North Africa and . . ."

Malek Rostam smiled sadly. "Probably Majid is with you too. I hope to God you'll be able to do something."

Malek Sohrab asked, "What will you do about the Governor?"

Yusof answered, "The Governor is, after all, a human being too. He will consent to stop a famine and the unrest in this corner of the country."

"I'm not optimistic," said Malek Sohrab. "It's a risky business. As long as it's only talk, they'll leave you alone. But when it comes to action, they'll stop you somehow." He got up and put on his *chador.*

Yusof said, "We'll do our best" and then added, "Stay for dinner."

Malek Sohrab said, "No, we'd better go. They'll be worried about us; they might think we've been caught. Could you have a *droshky* called for us?"

Malek Rostam got up. He put on his *chador* inside out. Zari laughed and said, "You have it inside out. The seams are showing."

Yusof addressed Rostam and said, "You stay. I'll take you at dawn myself."

Rostam said, "All right."

They went to the garden together, sat on the wicker chairs, and waited for Malek Sohrab's *droshky.* The veranda lights were on. Zari walked to the edge of the veranda. She saw Khosrow squatting by his aunt's brazier of hot charcoal, roasting hazelnuts in a skillet. Khanom Fatemeh was grinding hazelnuts on a flat stone. Sahar was on the veranda, too, his reins tied to a door handle. Zari heard Yusof say, "Why haven't you removed the bridle from the animal? Why have you brought him to the veranda? The horse is tired, son. Take him to the stable. Leave the treatment for tomorrow morning."

Khosrow got up and said, "Father, the hazelnut oil is almost ready. I'll rub it on his knee and take him to the stable. I brought him to the veranda because he was playing around, chasing the fawn. The fawn would have been awakened in the dark, frightened, and would have run into the branches and bushes. So I brought Sahar here to keep him near me."

The aunt picked the hot hazelnuts out of the skillet with her hands and burned herself. She put the nuts down, blew on her hands and said, "Brother, tell Gholam to kill the fawn tomorrow. First of all, there wasn't enough game meat for everyone. They will gripe about it. Secondly, keeping deer brings bad luck. In fact, I wish the men in this family would stop hunting. Just last year, Khan Kaka shot a pregnant deer. When they tore it open,

I saw the nine-month baby lying in the belly of that poor thing. I hit myself on the head and said, it's too late now. Khan Kaka's family . . ."

Zari quietly said to the aunt, "Put on your *chador.* Those are men sitting in the garden."

The aunt raised her hands to her face and said, "God protect me! Come not Lucifer! It's the end of the world," and she hurriedly pulled her *chador* over her head.

When the *droshky* arrived, Malek Rostam also got up and said, "Let me go, too. I must get to my uncle. I think you're right. My uncle has walked into this trap blindly."

Yusof only asked, "Blindly?"

5

TEN DAYS had passed since Yusof had left for the winter pastures, and the weather in the garden wasn't much better than where he was. Summer always hurried in like this, chasing away spring. It was afternoon and Gholam was sprinkling water on the patio in front of the house. Zari, carrying gardening clippers, was looking for flowers to pick. But there were none worth picking in the garden. Mina and Marjan, chirping like birds, followed their mother from one bush to another. By the stream around the patio there were some cockscombs so wilted and dusty that not even an old hen would have looked at them twice. By another stream, the faces and heads of the snapdragons were all covered with dust. Some more humble plants were straining to close their eyes and sleep as the sun set. The only hope was for the tuberoses, which Gholam claimed would, "blossom when there is a full moon." The orange-blossom petals had dried up completely and, under the trees, looked like dried and shriveled brown stars. How one missed winter, when the narcissuses opened at the edge of the streams, and gave their reflections to the passing water as a memento. The water flowed on, losing the reflections, pouring into the pool without a witness. One could only hear its current. And when spring came, the white and purple violets gracefully greeted the passing water without promise or memento.

Mina asked her mother, "When will father come to toss me up in the air? You won't do it, so I won't talk to you anymore." And Marjan pursed her lips into a bud—the most beautiful bud in the world—and finished her sister's sentence thus: "I won't, I won't, I won't talk to you, never ever anymore!" and, "Now toss us up in the air once."

Zari picked Mina up and tried to toss her in the air, but couldn't. She said, "God bless you, you've gotten heavy. I can't do it." She patted the child on her chubby thigh and put her down. Mina said, "Father's hands are big and he can. Your hands are small and you can't. Let your hands get big."

Khanom Fatemeh walked into the garden through the gate. She had been to the public bath. She was holding a wet sack on the palm of one hand. Mina and Marjan, excited, ran to her and said together, "Auntie, auntie, what did you bring us?"

"Fresh walnuts."

"All right, give them to us."

"I hope you had a nice bath," Zari said, reaching for the sack over the heads of the children. She took the walnuts to wash them. When she returned, Khadijeh had put the aunt's satchel on a wicker chair and was folding her *chador.* Mina was chasing Marjan. Khanom Fatemeh, with a red scarf over her hair, took her towels out of the satchel and spread them on the clothesline. Zari put the plate of walnuts on the table, and the children rushed up. She said, "If I had known, I would have asked God for something more substantial." The aunt said, "The city has gone to the dogs. Wherever you turn, some dark Indian chases you and says, 'Lady need! Lady need!'" She rinsed her hand in the pool, held it away from herself, sat on a chair and continued. "The kids chased that scrawny scarecrow of a man, clapping and singing, 'Chelep chelep kiyaneh? Piti, pati pitaneh. Sleep mama, sleep mama.' The Indian swung his chain in the air, wrapped it around his finger, turned back, stomped his feet on the ground, and hissed at them. They all ran away."

Khadijeh came in and left. She returned again and arranged the hot charcoal brazier and the aunt's opium paraphernalia on the floor of the veranda. She also made her tea. Zari and the twins joined the aunt on the veranda and sat down. Mina asked,

"Auntie, did the Indian cut off the children's heads?" And Marjan opened her eyes wide and said, "Sure did. He put them at the edge of the flower garden and cut their heads off, didn't he?"

The aunt said, "My boy is late. His last difficult exam was today. Maybe he didn't do so well. I say, sister, we should send Gholam after him."

Abolqasem Khan approached the veranda through the garden. He was talking to himself and gesturing with his hands. Zari's heart sank upon seeing him. Lately, whenever she saw him it was like seeing her executioner. Every time he blinked his eyes, it seemed as if he intended to disrupt her entire life. As he neared the veranda, Zari got up and said, "Please come up here."

"No. I'm fine right here."

Khanom Fatemeh puffed on her opium pipe and said, "Good news, I hope." She placed the pipe at the side of the brazier, poured a cup of tea, and handed it to her brother. Zari watched Abolqasem Khan put a lump of sugar in his mouth and pour some of the tea into the saucer. "Has anything happened?" she asked. Abolqasem Khan put the saucer down at the edge of the veranda. "Any news from my brother?"

"Nothing yet."

Khan Kaka said, "I don't know how to tell you this."

Zari felt dizzy. She sat down and asked, "My God, has anything happened to Yusof?" The aunt shouted, "Out with it. Hurry up and get this suspense over with."

Khan Kaka blinked and said, "This morning I had a telephone call from the Governor's house. They said Gilantaj Khanom has heard a lot of good things about Khosrow Khan's colt—she likes it, and they would like to buy it. Send them the horse; they will gladly pay any price for it. God knows, since this morning I've felt like my guts have turned inside out. I'm so distracted I can't even think straight."

Zari's eyes filled with tears. Through her tears, she looked at the aunt, with her flushed face, wet eyes, braided hair, long red scarf, and trembling hands as she packed a lump of opium into the bowl of the pipe. The opium fell out of her hand into the fire and the opium smoke rose. She said, "May God destroy their hearth and home. I'm so upset I could pick up this burning brazier and drop it on my own head. Didn't you tell them this horse is the boy's whole life? Had the cat got your tongue?"

Mina came up to the aunt. She opened her small fist. She had a walnut in the palm of her hand. She tried to put it in her aunt's mouth. She said, "Eat it, Auntie. I was saving it for my brother."

Zari called Khadijeh. "Come take the children to Haji Mohammad Reza; show them the snake that was caught yesterday!" Marjan asked, "He pulled off the snake's fangs, right?" Zari answered, "Yes, dear. Don't be afraid." Mina took Marjan's hand and said, "You can play with it for a minute and then I'll play for a minute, right?" Khan Kaka asked, "Do they play with snakes?"

"No, Khan Kaka," Zari answered. "Haji Mohammad Reza wouldn't let them handle the snake . . ."

Khan Kaka laughed. "Everything in this household is out of whack. I thought perhaps . . ." And he decided not to continue. Instead, he blinked and asked softly, "Did you find a snake in the house?"

Zari did not want to even think about her son losing Sahar. The more they talked about the snake the better, "Yes. Yesterday while we were sitting on the veranda a female snake fell from the cornice over the sash window onto the patio. Gholam was sprinkling water. He hit it on the head with the watering can and stunned it. The snake raised its head momentarily before falling back again. Then Gholam killed it with a shovel. He told me the male snake would surely come after its mate. So he called Haji Mohammad Reza, who wrapped some felt around his hand, climbed on the roof, found the nest and caught the male snake."

Khanom Fatemeh said, "I got so mad I dropped all my precious opium in the fire."

Khan Kaka returned to the main subject. "Don't think that I want to hurt my nephew. I swear by my own son's life, I am very fond of Khosrow. I told the Governor's secretary on the phone, 'This child is very attached to this horse; he never lets it out of his sight. I'll be happy to go to the village and bring back one of my best horses for the Governor's daughter—her name escapes me,

Gilantaj, Mazandarantaj, I don't know whatever the hell Taj it is
. . .' He said, 'To tell you the truth, Gilantaj Khanom had
typhoid. Now that she has recovered, she insists upon having your
nephew's horse.' "

Fatemeh Khanom put some opium in the pipe, took a puff, and
said, "Why didn't you tell them his father has gone to the winter pastures? Wait until he comes back next week to ask his permission. Don't you know that my sister-in-law won't move a
step without Yusof's permission?"

"As God is my witness, I told them. The Governor's secretary
said, 'Will your sister-in-law refuse you something as insignificant
as a horse? It will be paid for; nobody is taking it for free, sir.' "

The aunt put the opium pipe aside and poured two cups of tea,
placed one in front of Zari and took the other herself. "You
yourself are the cause of all this trouble," she told Khan Kaka. "You
are willing to go to any lengths to become a member of parliament.
How on earth would that snip of a girl know that Khosrow has
a horse? You got yourself into a fine mess and don't know how to
get out of it."

Khan Kaka vowed, "I swear to God, to the immaculate imams,
on seven Korans, I never spoke of the horse. Do you know what
Ezzatoddowleh is like? She is there from dawn to dusk, plotting
against everybody in the city. She's become a wheeler-dealer. I wanted to ignore it, but the Governor himself called just before I came
and asked, 'What happened to the horse?' I answered, 'Your
Excellency, my brother is in the winter pastures.' He said, 'Come
on, friend. My daughter has just recovered from an illness. Send
the horse for a few days. As soon as she gets tired of it, we will send
it back.' "

Zari thought, Maybe he is telling the truth. She looked at
Khanom Fatemeh, who was gathering the ashes around the fire with
a pair of tongs. Her eyes were filled with tears. She said, "This city
has gone to the dogs. I will leave everything and go away. I'll go to
Karbala and live next to the holy shrine, just like my late mother."

"With what passport?" Khan Kaka shouted angrily. "With
what exit permit? It's not for nothing that they say women are
half-witted. And on top of that, while there's a war going on? Do

you think it's that easy to go?" And, turning to Zari, he continued, "They'll send for Sahar tomorrow morning."

Zari said, "You seem to have left us no choice. It's my own fault for being a coward. But this time, I am going to stand up to them." And suddenly she felt her spirits were raised. She continued, "I'll go to the Governor myself. I'll tell him, there's a limit to everything. Is it only your daughter who can take a fancy to a horse? Can't she stand the sight of anybody else in this city who has something nice? What's mine is mine, and what's yours is mine too?"

Khan Kaka looked at her in amazement, "You're turning over a new leaf, sister-in-law. You're starting to talk like Yusof."

"If a thousand people talk like Yusof, everybody will figure out what is what. The men must stand up, and if they have gone to the winter pastures, their wives have to take their place. When a lot of people show courage and prove their mettle, eventually times will change."

Khan Kaka held his head in his hands and groaned. "I swear to God you have all lost your minds. That one says she'll leave everything and go. This one says she must stand up to the Governor. See what a mess you've gotten me in! And all for a trifle of a thing like a horse."

Khosrow came out of the stable with Sahar. When had he come home without Zari seeing him? He let Sahar loose in the garden and came toward the veranda. His eyes shifted from his uncle to his mother to his aunt. All three were pouting. "What's happened?" he asked. Khan Kaka laughed, blinked and said, "I am going hunting. I'm going to take you with me. Don't listen to what women say, they are all cowards."

"How did you do on your exam?" the aunt asked.

"Fine, Auntie. I think I'll get a couple of hundreds." Turning to his uncle, he said, "Should I bring Sahar?"

"No, my boy. It is a long way. Sergeant Zinger will be there, too. I want to show them that you and Hormoz have become real men. You ride all sorts of horses; you are good shots—"

Zari interrupted. "Khan Kaka, he cannot go. It is his examination time."

Khosrow answered in astonishment, "But, mother. My exams were finished today. Please let me go." Again he addressed his uncle, "But if only I could bring Sahar along . . ."

"Sister," said Khan Kaka. "Let him come and see the world, become a man, fearless; I won't let a hair on his head be harmed."

Khanom Fatemeh had dropped her head and looked thoughtful. She interrupted her brother, "Khan Kaka, the man that you want to make out of him and the one that his father wants are as different as night and day. Leave the child be. Stop all this lying and making things up . . ."

Khosrow pleaded, "Auntie, Mother, let me go. I'm grown up now."

Khan Kaka said joyfully, "Go, boy, get ready for the trip. I'll let you shoot my own Brno, if it's not too heavy for you."

"I have my own gun," Khosrow said and left.

"Do you think you can fight the Governor?" Khan Kaka said sympathetically. "With the kinds of things Yusof has been saying and doing lately, he is risking his life. At least let me make up for his unruly behavior. I tell you, I have heard he has provoked Malek Rostam who, in turn, has drawn a gun on his uncle and has now taken refuge with Yusof. I have heard that he has distributed food supplies among thirty tribal families. On top of all that, Malek Rostam, who is more stupid than Yusof, and that dimwit Majid have joined hands and are building houses for these thirty families and putting ideas in their heads.

"They are building them each a rickety hut out of thistle with piped water on the roof. Water drips constantly on the walls so the gentleman of the house can sit in it and titter. Well, you wise guys, what use are food supplies to tribesmen? What use do they have for thistle huts? For as long as the world has turned, they have been satisfied with acorns, wild almonds and pistachios. What do they need a house for? Black tents are more than enough. They are rebelling against the government. Just a few days ago, they disarmed a gendarmerie regiment on the Takab Pass. Yusof has taken an oath together with a few other daydreamers like himself to take charge of the city's food supplies. So what is wrong with bribing the Governor to change his opinion of Yusof? As I said, you can't quarrel with the Governor."

Zari said despondently, "You can't with the Governor and you can't with Sergeant Zinger, either. They are sworn brothers. The whole city has become like the Mordestan District."

Khan Kaka interrupted her. "God Almighty! Again repeating Yusof's words. Sister-in-law, don't argue. Don't I have authority over my brother's worthless colt? I swear on the soul of my father, Haj Aqa, I will not let Khosrow grieve. I'll take him hunting; I'll keep him in the village for a few days. I'll give him any one of my colts he likes. Early tomorrow morning, when they send for the horse, give it to them and get a receipt. When we come back, tell Khosrow the horse died. This is the only solution. In the village, I will hint to Khosrow that his horse is sick, that in this world one should never become attached to anything whose loss would cause grief . . ."

The aunt raised her head and said, "Why don't you practice what you preach?"

Khadijeh came and collected the opium pipe and paraphernalia. Zari asked, "Where are the children?" Khadijeh said, "They're standing with Gholam watching some tribal men and women playing music and dancing. They're in such tattered rags that if you poured a ton of millet on their heads, it would all be caught in the holes; not one seed would reach the ground. Poor things!"

Khan Kaka snickered. "Oh God! Why does everyone in this household feel sorry for nomads, peasants, and porters?"

"Khadijeh, fix me up a nice hookah and bring it here," Zari said.

Khosrow returned to the veranda. "Mother, give me the key to the cupboard. I want to take my gun," and added, "Have you seen my hunting pants? I've looked everywhere, but I can't find them."

"Never mind the pants, friend. We have lots of hunting pants there," said Khan Kaka.

Zari felt her throat burning. She took the keys out of her housedress and dropped them on the carpet. When Khosrow left, she burst into tears. What a bind I am in, she thought. The deals are already signed and sealed. I have to go along. But there is still time. Tomorrow morning when the Governor's messenger comes, we'll tell him Sahar died, and that's that.

"Sister-in-law, as God is my witness, I can't bear to see you in tears," Khan Kaka said. He stopped talking when Khosrow, dressed in traveling clothes, his gun over his shoulder, came to the veranda carrying a saddle bag and said, "I'm ready."

Zari dropped her head and held back her tears. Khosrow kissed his aunt, then put his arms around his mother's neck, lowered his face to his mother's damp cheeks and said, "I'm not going to the end of the world. Mother, tell Uncle to let me take Sahar." Khan Kaka blinked and said, "Come, boy, let's go. Gholam will take care of Sahar." And he said goodbye and started off. Khosrow whispered in his mother's ear, "I can't not go. Then Uncle would think I'm afraid of guns."

Sahar stood quiet and motionless under the sour-orange trees. He did not move, even when Khosrow came to him. Khosrow took Sahar's face in both hands, straightened his mane, and said, "Mother, don't forget to give him sugar cubes. Gholam knows; he will prepare his barley and groom him, too." Sahar bent his head and kicked the dirt under the trees, and when Khosrow went up to the veranda, he stuck his ears forward and neighed. His mother responded, neighing from the stable.

Zari could see the horse through her tears. What noble eyes! What long eyelashes! she thought. Why don't you look me straight in the eye? Why do you lower your eyes? Why don't you say, 'You cowardly woman, I know tomorrow you will betray me?' Poor mute thing!

"I'll drop everything and leave this place," Khanom Fatemeh said. "What do I want a dashport for? I'll go illegally. I'll change my money to gold *dinars* and sew them in the lining of my jacket. I'll take a suitcase and get myself to Ahvaz. The rest is easy. I'll walk my way through the palm groves. I'll find the Arabs; I'll give each a gold *dinar;* they'll put me on a boat and take me across the river. Then I'll be free. I'll be neither oppressor nor oppressed. It won't be my country, and I won't be so heartbroken." She pounded her chest with her fist and said, "Oh, Imam Hoseyn, summon this lonely slave to yourself!"

Khadijeh brought in the hookah and asked, "Did you want the hookah, ma'am?" Zari took a puff. She coughed. She took another puff. She was getting sick to her stomach, but continued puffing and exhaling the smoke through her nose. Khanom Fatemeh said sadly, "Because things are so tough, it's easy to turn you on to the hookah and then to opium. Sister, if you can help it, don't smoke. Addiction is a bad thing." She took off her scarf, turned her head toward the sky, and in a reproachful tone said, "Oh God, I am not being ungrateful. But in this world of Yours, I have known nothing but sorrow. My good husband suffered until he could not take it any longer and drove his horse towards the concrete pillars that we call the Consul's Daughters, outside the British Consulate, and hit himself against them. My only son died young. He got boils in his throat and died before my very eyes. In this city that's gone to the dogs, they could not fill a prescription for him. Maybe You made me suffer so much to see if I have the patience of Job. I don't. I don't. I don't. At least let me have this one wish. Cast me into exile! Cast me into exile!"

Zari wiped her tears with the back of her hand. "Sister, don't make me so sad. You want to leave everything and go where? At least this is your own home. Your son and husband are buried here. When you miss them, you can visit their graves. Who will you turn to there?"

"To Imam Hoseyn."

"It's hot there. The climate won't be agreeable. Here, there is our large garden. My children are like your own. We live together like two sisters. Besides, how are they going to send you money?"

"I'm just a single woman. I can survive on bread alone if I have to. Am I more special than my mother?"

Khadijeh came to the veranda. "The children are being difficult," she said. "They won't eat their dinner no matter how I try to coax them. They wore me out."

Zari got up and said, "I'll come myself." Then she went to the parlor. Marjan was sitting on the table rubbing her eyes, and Mina was standing next to her. Looking like a frightened child, she was anxiously staring at the parlor door. When she saw her mother, she laughed and stretched out both arms to throw herself in her mother's arms. Zari sat next to them, filled the spoon, and brought it up to Mina's mouth, but Mina pushed it back. She tried to give it to

Marjan, but she also refused, shouting, "I don't want rice pudding."

"Why?" Zari asked.

"I don't like it."

"All right. Then eat plain bread."

Marjan said, "The kid who threw the stone asked for bread. He said, Go get me fruit from the tree." And she rubbed her eyes. Zari asked, "What kid?"

Marjan said, "The same kid who didn't have shoes. The same one whose mama danced. His daddy sat down and said, 'Ouch.' His foot had an ouchie."

"See, that poor kid didn't have bread to eat. Now you don't eat rice pudding and honey."

"Gholam hit him," Marjan said.

They wore Zari out before they ate a bite. When she was taking them to bed, she saw the aunt, who had not budged from her place. She was still sitting by the burning brazier.

The children were restless and wouldn't go to sleep. Obviously the agitation that Khan Kaka had brought that afternoon had also affected the children. Zari said, "If you close your eyes, I'll tell you a story." "I'm afraid," Mina said.

She didn't know why she remembered MacMahon and the story he had written for Mina and Marjan. The night of the wedding of the Governor's daughter, when they went to dinner, even though he was drunk, MacMahon had managed to get a plate and silverware for Zari. How crowded it was and how everybody was rushing greedily forward. No one would leave the dinner table to make room for the latecomers. They weren't stricken by famine, but they acted as if they were. Neither did they have barefoot children begging for bread, and to get it, throwing stones at the feet of children who don't like rice pudding and honey.

To at least show her gratitude, Zari told MacMahon, "I enjoyed your story." MacMahon laughed, even though his eyes were barely open. He said, "I'll polish it up and send it to a publisher of children's books."

Then the Governor came and invited MacMahon to a table, still untouched and especially set for foreigners, and mentioned a whole roasted pig. But MacMahon was not tempted and said that he preferred to stay with his friend's wife. Zari thanked him again and said, "I hope you succeed in making that airplane full of toys."

MacMahon sighed and said, "Who will build an airplane that will drop consolations for despondent men? I am sorry that . . . I am sorry that . . ." Yusof walked toward them with a plate full of sweet rice. "For the three of us," he said.

MacMahon, addressing Zari, continued, "When I think about it, I see that throughout our lives we are all like children happy with our toys. And what a calamitous day when our delights are taken away from us or we're prevented from having them. Our children, our mothers, our philosophies . . . our religions . . ."

Yusof laughed. "Now, have a bite. I've never seen a drunk who could philosophize so soberly."

"Believe me, it won't go down my throat," MacMahon said. "If you strike a match, I'll catch on fire."

Marjan interrupted Zari's daydream. The child sat up on the bed. "I'm afraid of the snake!"

Zari collected herself and said, "Go to sleep, dear! There is no snake. The snake is in Haji Mohammad Reza's yellow box. He's pulled its fangs and it's locked in the box."

She began telling a story. "Once upon a time, there was a man who had built a big, big airplane. This airplane was loaded with toys, storybooks, fruit, treats, and sweets for children."

"Mother, was there a snake on the airplane, too?" Mina asked.

"No, dear, there was no snake. The airplane was loaded with things that children like. This airplane flew over the cities and dropped whatever the children wanted."

"But they would break," Marjan said.

"No, the airplane would fly low over the roofs and the children would hold their skirts under the airplane, and the pilot would drop whatever they wanted in their laps."

"Would he give them to my brother?" asked Marjan. "He doesn't have a skirt."

"Yes, he would give them to the boys who had no skirts. Sometimes he would land the airplane on the roof and—"

Marjan asked, "Would he give them to the kid who threw stones, too?"

"Of course."

"Good," Marjan said.

"Let me tell you. He would land the airplane on the roofs and take the good children for a ride in the sky. They would pass by the stars and the moon. They were so close to the moon and the stars that if they reached out they could gather up the stars and collect them in their laps."

Marjan interrupted again. "Tell him to bring his airplane on our roof and give Sahar to my brother, all right?"

"All right," Zari said. "Now, go to sleep."

Now you've grown up, she thought. When a child develops a memory and can remember the past, she is no longer a child, even if this past is only a few hours old.

When the children fell asleep, she went to the veranda. The aunt was still sitting there with her hand under her chin, staring at the brazier, which no longer had any fire. "Are you still thinking about the trip?" Zari asked.

The aunt lifted her head and Zari was taken aback by her tearful eyes. She blinked and her tears flowed. She answered, "Yes, sister. My heart is heavy. Since nothing worked out for me in this world, at least I should prepare myself for the next. If a person lives next to the tomb of an imam, Nakir and Monkar won't come to him on the first night in the grave, and there will be no questions and answers. At the time of death, first his holiness the Commander of the Faithful and then Imam Hoseyn will come to the person's bedside. And if she is a woman, her holiness Fatemeh will come. The deceased will go before God hand in hand with these immaculate ones."

Zari said, "Amazing. With the message that he brought, Khan Kaka made us all distraught! Even the children. Yesterday, they saw Haji Mohammad Reza's snake without being afraid, but tonight they were afraid and couldn't go to sleep."

"You are right. It's been a long time since I've thought of my loved ones who passed away so young. Tonight, they all appeared before my eyes."

Zari said, "I married into your family so many years ago and have never heard you mention your son or husband. Tonight—"

"I've always kept my pain to myself," said the aunt. "I've never told anyone what I've suffered."

Zari sat down, holding the aunt's hand in her own. "But you've always said yourself that if one talks about it, one's sorrow will be lifted. You said, His Holiness Ali bent his head into a well and passed his sorrow to the water he could not see. You said you were sure that the wells dried up from hearing Ali's sorrows."

The aunt shook her head and chanted, "Were I to grieve for you, I would sink my head into a well, like Ali."

"Am I not as good as a well?" Zari asked.

"But you are young. I don't want to burden your youth."

"I have also had my share of sorrow."

"I know," the aunt said, and began to speak of the sorrows that until that night Zari had never heard her utter.

6

T HAT NIGHT," she began. "I was sitting next to this very brazier here, and just like this lonely night, I was stirring up the fire and pressing the ashes with the tongs. I was looking at the brass figurines around the brazier, holding hands as they are now. I counted them that night. There were thirty-two figurines—figurines without eyes and eyebrows. They haven't changed; they are still the same thirty-two.

"Sudabeh the Indian sat up with me until morning and shed as many tears as I did . . . When the child died . . . in that garden . . . all alone . . . I knew that he was dead, but I picked him up and ran up to Sardozzak. The child was six years old. Had it been now, who would worry about veils and having to cover up in front of men? Who would have to think about opium and get convulsions from opium withdrawal? I went to our own home. My father, Haj Aqa, was sitting with Sudabeh by this brazier in the room with the sash windows. I wished my breath could turn everyone into ashes. Sudabeh took the child from me. I saw that she got upset, but she tried not to show it. What a woman she was! She really broke Bibi's heart, but what a woman she was. She left and then came back. I asked, 'What did you do with my child?' She said, 'Who knows, maybe Mohammad Hoseyn's pious breath will blow life back into the child.' I said, 'You are talking blasphemy, woman. Only God can give life. As the Koran says: *I breathed into*

him of My spirit.' I had studied Arabic and Persian with my
father and geography and geometry with Mohammad Hoseyn,
Sudabeh's brother. When my father returned from Tehran, he was
forced to retire and stay home. He didn't go to lead prayers anymore. He had to stop teaching at the Khan Seminary. He only
taught at home. He would sit in the room with the sash windows,
and men would come, kiss his hand, and ask his opinion on the-
ological questions. I would listen from the adjoining room.
When my father returned from Najaf, everyone in the city went
on foot, all the way to Bajgah, to welcome him. The first day that
he led the congregational prayers, all the clerics in the city, even
the prayer leaders, attended his service. When he appeared on the
pulpit, the Vakil Mosque was so packed you couldn't breathe.

"Oh God! I was myself quite a woman. More than ten times I hid
the secret letters that Haj Aqa wrote with onion juice in my blouse,
took them to Shah Cheragh Shrine, and delivered them to the people that I was supposed to. I remember it as if it were today, a meeting place between two stone lions in front of the holy shrine.

"Mohammad Hoseyn and his sister Sudabeh had just come from
India. Sudabeh didn't become my father's wife, even to the end.
She would say things were easier the way they were. Of course,
she was the one who made my mother Bibi homeless and broke
her heart. But what a woman she was! She was a dancer! I'll never
forget the day that my father gave a party in the Rashk-e Behesht
Gardens. He had invited Sudabeh. She was short. She had a
black mole above her lip. She had an olive complexion. She was-
n't all that pretty. She had big, thickly made-up eyes and long hair.
When she wasn't smiling, she looked like an owl. But when she
smiled, she looked as sweet as a bouquet of flowers. Everyone, men
and women alike, stood around the patio and clapped. She
looked like she was naked and covered only with jewels. But she
wasn't. She had a jewel-studded necklace under which she had covered her body with a kind of flesh-colored stocking. Up to that
day, I had not seen Sudabeh dance. It certainly was nothing
ordinary. All the parts of her body moved—not just shoulders, belly,
eyes, and eyebrows. She even moved her chin, nose, ears, and the
pupils of her eyes. She pretended to be dancing on the corpse of

a man. For the second dance, she wore a blue silk dress with a yellow border and had two pigeons nestled on her breasts, real live pigeons. The pigeons' feathers were dyed mauve. She was holding a piece of blue silk the same as her dress and danced slowly, as if she were afraid that the pigeons would wake up. When she finished her dance, she made the pigeons fly off into the air. After the third dance, she was hot. She sat by the waterscape in a pink satin dress and stuck her bare feet in the water. Haj Aqa—the city's most highly regarded religious scholar—was sitting across from Sudabeh and fanning her."

"It wasn't for nothing that my father invited Mohammad Hoseyn to give me lessons. I studied geography and geometry with him. I drew maps. I was so busy with my work I didn't know what was going on around me. The first day that an airplane came to the city, as early as dawn everyone took along small rugs and went to Bagh-e Takht to watch. I was sitting on the roof in the sun, drawing a map of India. The airplane passed over my head. I didn't even lift my head to look. Oh God, a person like that shouldn't become an opium addict!

"Mohammad Hoseyn was a sun worshiper. Every morning and evening he went to the roof and gazed at the sun. The sun had ruined his eyes. He had stared so much into the sun that his pupils looked white. He did magic, too. He fried eggs in a felt hat floating on the pool. He made gold coins out of little pieces of paper. He swallowed my Haj Aqa's pocket watch and took it out of Khan Kaka's pocket. He was also a palm reader. He read my palm, too. He said that I would have twelve sons and all of them would become ministers. And I said, 'Then my sons will form a cabinet.' My father said that Mohammad Hoseyn had spiritual powers. But in the city people said that he was into black magic and witchcraft. Whatever it was, God rest his soul, he did a lot for me.

"Mohammad Hoseyn had shrouded and buried the child that very night. From that day on, for a week, he made me sit every day across from him, stared into my eyes and said, 'I'll hypnotize you and you will see your child in your sleep. You'll see what a good place he is in and how happy he is.' But I wouldn't go under. He said my resistance was high. He blackened my thumbnail with ink and said, 'Now, stare at your nail. The child will appear now. Don't you see him? Here he comes. When he comes, ask him what he wants. Does he want watermelon?' But I couldn't see anything, no matter how much I stared.

"That night, Sudabeh the Indian and I sat up until morning. She didn't become my father's wife. She never did. But what a woman she was. One of those women who could draw people to herself as if by magical rays. Those she attracted would never be able to free themselves from her spell. It has nothing to do with beauty or ugliness. It has to do with what a person is made of. Everyone was astonished by Haj Aqa, my father. They probably even cursed him behind his back. A cunning man whose identity we never discovered had ordered a bundle of hand-printed cloth from Esfahan, depicting Sheykh San'an. They were inscribed with 'Sheykh San'an goes to Europe.' Sheykh San'an was depicted as an old man with his finger in the corner of his mouth who wore an *aba* and turban just like my father. His followers were shown going after him, and a lewd woman as sitting higher up. Those days, no matter whose house you went to, they had one of those curtains. When people want to be wicked, they sure know how to do it. Haj Aqa said himself, 'They took the mosque and my lessons away from me. In other affairs, too, God forbid, I cannot interfere. I tried it and saw the consequences. After all, a person must do something greater than what he does in his daily life. He must try to change something. Now that there is nothing else for me to do, I love.' He would recite the verse: 'Love has been the cause of much and will be the cause of much again. Love changes the dervish's woolen garment for a Christian girdle and does so again and again.' He said, 'The inscriptions in the Kaaba are the novice alphabet of love.' The clerics had spread a rumor that he had become a Babi and that he went to the sword cutler's bazaar every day on a pilgrimage. But since he was a generous host and could at least solve their problems over the telephone, they did not excommunicate him openly. Besides, the cleric's turban no longer carried any weight and most of them had been exchanged for hats.

"Haj Aqa said, 'My turn has not come yet.' He said, 'This is not the time for me,' and stepped aside. But he never went along with them. He was like that from the beginning and remained so to the end. During the quarrels between the police chief and Mas'ud Khan the Gold Teeth, most of the people put British flags over their portals so that no one would dare loot their houses. But not only did Haj Aqa refuse to put a flag up, along with the head rabbi, he took the wounded from the Jewish district to the doctor or brought a doctor to them. How he talked, counseled, and reasoned with the armed men to dissuade them from plundering the Jewish district. But they were the paid mercenaries of the police chief.

"Through a window they had shot a Jewish woman who was nursing her baby. With her breast still in the baby's mouth, she passes out. When Haj Aqa arrives, he takes the baby under his *aba*. Child in arms, dressed in his turban and *aba*, he goes to Dr. Scott, the European doctor in the missionary hospital. And, who is this Dr. Scott? The special physician to the police chief and his family, who refuses to make house calls for those who have been injured by the cronies of the police chief. That day, my father single-handedly shuts down the hospital and sends Dr. Scott and several Armenian nurses to the woman and the other wounded in the district. The woman recovered. Do you know who she is? The same Tavus Khanom who, after all these years, still brings Yusof wine and got rid of your moth-infested cashmere for you.

"I remember Felfeli, Musa's drummer, was among the wounded. They brought him to our house and laid him in the vestibule on the stone platform where the doorman stands. Blood was gushing out of his wounded thigh like water from a fountain. And the vestibule was covered with blood. As bad luck would have it Haj Aqa wasn't home and Bibi got sick to her stomach seeing all that blood. I threw a *chador* over my head and ran all the way to the office of Dr. Abdollah Khan and his brothers. Their office was in the Gowd-e Araban. Actually, they hadn't put up a British flag over the door of their house either. The father, Haj Hakimbashi, was still alive. There were four brothers. Three were doctors and the fourth, a pharmacist. They had a drugstore, too. God rest their souls, all of them, only Dr. Abdollah Khan is still living. Their office was so full of wounded and dead people that you could hardly move. I begged and cried. So Dr. Abdollah Khan came back with me. It was said that his hands were blessed and helped him cure the ill, even though he was quite young. But as fate would have it, when we got there Felfeli was finished. He was covered with a bedding cloth. His relatives had descended into our house and were all wailing. And Bibi had fainted. And where do you think our house was? Right across from the Center of Intrigues, that is, across from Ezzatoddowleh's father's house. Ezzatoddowleh had just married and she and her husband were living with her parents. That whole mess could be blamed on Ezzatoddowleh's husband, the police chief's son-in-law. Of course, Ezzatoddowleh and I had taken an oath to be sisters, but at that time no one worried about her real sister, let alone a sister by oath. It was only out of respect for Haj Aqa that our house wasn't attacked. Besides, there was fear that he might issue a religious decree for a holy war. You see, all of these things happened long before my father went to Tehran.

"I'm sure that if my father had wanted to he could have hypnotized anyone. He would stare right at the space between your eyes and who could have resisted it? Still, a man like that became enslaved by Sudabeh, the Indian girl, and broke Bibi's heart. Oh, God, don't put us through such a test!"

"Bibi heard about it and saw it, but wouldn't say a word. It is all done and over with now. She wouldn't even talk about it with me, her own daughter. Everybody in the city talked about Haj Aqa and Sudabeh, the Indian girl, except his wife, who was the one person who mattered.

"But while my mother lived in this house, Haj Aqa did not bring Sudabeh and Mohammad Hoseyn to live here. He married me off. Khan Kaka got married, and Bibi chose the life of a wanderer. My husband was a cloth merchant. He did business with Egypt and India. When you hear Khan Kaka saying sarcastically, 'the son of Mirza Miyur,' all the time breaking my heart like a china bowl, this is because the father and son imported *miyur*. Nowadays, no one imports *miyur*. When you wore *miyur*, you felt refreshed, because it was so cool and soft. It was good for undershirts and baby clothes. My husband committed suicide. He drove his horse into the concrete pillars in front of the British Consulate.

At sunset. Because of our son. And also because they made it so hard on him. My father said that he was ahead of his time and stepped aside. But that poor man was young. God forbid—bite my tongue—just like Yusof. Yusof is ahead of his time, too. But that poor soul, too, like Yusof, said that we must try to change the times. He was only beating his head against a stone wall—as he literally did in the end. To tell you the truth, these are times for rogues like Khan Kaka. It will be a long time before people like Yusof have their turn. I'll never forget when my family was destroyed and Yusof wrote me, 'Sister, try to stand on your own two feet. If you fall, you should know that no one in this world will bend over to take you by the hand and lift you up. Try to pick yourself up.'

"Thank God, Bibi was not there to see my misfortunes. One night Bibi invited Khan Kaka, me, and our families for dinner. That night, I saw her looking at us as if she wanted to keep a mental picture of our faces. It had been some two years since Yusof had gone to Europe. When you see Khan Kaka sitting here and saying over and over again that my father did not spend money on his education, he is lying. Haj Aqa wanted to send both of them together. Khan Kaka didn't want to go. He said, 'Figure out how much you want to spend on my education and give me land instead.' And that's what Haj Aqa did. Bibi bid us farewell. She said that she was going on a pilgrimage to Her Holiness Ma'sumeh in Qom and then to the shrine of Imam Reza in Mashhad, and that her trip would take a month or two. We didn't know then that she was leaving for Karbala—and illegally, for that matter. All she took along was the money that my father had given her, some jewelry, a suitcase of clothes, and an ewer. And she gave me her emerald earrings to give to Yusof so that if anything happened to her on the trip, he could put them on his wife's ears with his own hands on his wedding night. A month later, her letter came from Karbala saying that she had become a resident pilgrim near the shrine of the imam and that we shouldn't worry about her. I haven't told this to a single soul, sister—keep it to yourself—my mother had ended up working as a housemaid in Karbala, as Khanom Fakhroshshari'eh's maid. For as long as she was in Karbala, she nei-

ther asked for money nor did my father . . . No, wait, three or four
times on my insistence and Khan Kaka's, Haj Aqa sent some money
through someone or other. But whether or not Bibi received it,
I have no idea. She never sent letters. In the same first letter she
had insisted that we not write her letters. All she wanted to
think or talk about was His Holiness Imam Hoseyn.

"I was talking about that night. I was sitting next to this brazier you see right here and was patting the ashes and then spreading them out. The fire had just about burned out. I was spend-
ing a night of lamentation. Sudabeh, too, sat up with me until
morning. What a woman she was! What a pity that she broke Bibi's
heart so.

"That night I said to Sudabeh, 'I still don't understand, with
all the suitors you have, what do you see in my father that you
would even drive my mother out of her own house?' She said that
she couldn't help it, that she knew she had ruined the reputation
of a Shi'ite cleric, a highly respected religious jurist. She knew that
she had made an innocent woman homeless. But she had no control over it. She said that in a previous life, someone had been close
to someone else but they were separated. The first one keeps coming back to this world to find the second, who suffers separation
and who waits. How could they let each other go once they had
found and recognized each other? First, there were two plants which
had been entwined around each other and one of them had
withered. In the next life, there were two migratory birds who lost
each other when they were flying south or north. In the life
after that, there were two intimate deer, one of them killed by a
hunter and the other one grieving the loss. Then there was a father
and daughter, then a sister and brother and . . . and when they
finally find each other, how could they let each other go? This is
what she said. But she wouldn't become my father's wife. And she
never did. She stayed in my father's house until she grew old.

"When my husband died young, following Yusof's sugges-
tion, I decided to run the land that my father had given to me as
a wedding gift. I wore pants, sat on a horse, and rode all over the
opium fields. And how old do you think I was? Twenty-eight. I'd
even bastinadoed the villagers. God forgive me my sins. It had been

some three years since Bibi left. How old do you think that unfortunate woman was when she died? Forty-four. Fakhroshshari'eh sent a telegram to Haj Aqa saying that Bibi was ill. Haj Aqa met with all sorts of people and, to be fair, did his best to get exit permits for us. Once he did, he sent a telegram to Yusof, to go straight to his mother from where he was. And, unbeknownst to Khan Kaka, he sent him twenty pounds. But in the telegram nothing was said about Bibi being on her death bed. That's why Yusof got there too late. When he arrived, we had Bibi buried in the catacombs of the shrine. Khan Kaka went to a great deal of trouble and spent a lot of money out of his own pocket to get permission to have her buried there. We were sure that as soon as we turned our backs her corpse would be taken out to the public cemetery. But even one night in such a sacred shrine was something, and she had gotten her wish.

"God, what a mess it was! My mother was in the throes of death in a two-by-one room on a torn straw mat with a shredded quilt. It was so hot that she kept saying, 'I'm burning up!' There was neither a basement nor cold water. Fakhroshshari'eh would call her, 'Fasih, get me a hookah. Your soup is too salty today, I guess because you miss Haji.' How dreadful! No, Khanom, no title. My mother's name was Fasihozzaman, which means the eloquence of the age. What eloquence! She never uttered a word about what had befallen her. We even heard the story of her being a housemaid from Fakhroshshari'eh. She talked about Bibi as though she came from a long line of devoted servants. I haven't told a soul about it. We haven't even told Yusof. What's the use? He was a twenty-year-old boy, he couldn't have taken it. Do you think he could take it even now that he is in his forties? We never did find out how Bibi got to Karbala, but we heard that when she got there, she fell into the clutches of Sheykh Abbas Qomi. Sheykh Abbas wore a long gown to look like an Arab and scared the pilgrims with threats that he would report them and do this, that, or the other. Out of fear, Bibi had dropped the suitcase, taken her ewer, and run away. But, as luck would have it, her birth certificate was in her suitcase. She paid the mortuary officials the hundred *tomans* that Haj Aqa had given her to get a birth certificate off a dead person."

Khadijeh came to the veranda and asked, "Aren't you going to eat dinner tonight?"

Zari said, "We'll call you when we're ready."

The aunt said, "That's enough, I've talked too much and given you a headache. Let her bring dinner so we can eat a bite, go to sleep, and see what tomorrow brings."

7

ARLY THE next morning, Zari instructed Gholam that if someone should be sent by the Governor and ask for something, he should say that his mistress is not home and he can't do anything without permission. If the messenger insists that he has come for the horse, Gholam should play dumb and say that he's got the wrong place. We had a horse, but it died. And if he made a fuss, to give him the roan horse.

It was the day to irrigate the garden. Zari came to watch the grass and the tree trunks soak up the water and quench their thirst. She reveled in their renascence and wanted to breathe in the smell of the damp soil.

The gardener and Gholam, shovels on their shoulders, trousers rolled up, and in bare feet, went from one end of the garden to the other either blocking the water's flow or releasing it. Mina and Marjan were getting in their way and slowing them down. Finally, their mother told them to build a mud house under one of the elm trees near the stable. She said they could plant flowers in it and have a wedding celebration for their dolls. She convinced them that if they didn't stay in the shade, Lady Sun would get angry and stick hot prods into their soft and tender flesh.

Mina began designing the house. "Here will be the pool, here's a cupboard and here's a cold oven."

"Then, where is the stable?" asked Marjan.

With much fear and trembling they caught a baby frog and put it in the stable. The baby frog leaped away. But there were plenty of them in the garden.

Gholam redirected the water toward the elm trees and the children's house filled with water. The water also ran under their little feet. They squatted down. Zari said, "Now get up," and all the while she kept her ears cocked to the door so that she could run and hide if anyone knocked. Mina shouted, "Bad Baldy," and Gholam said, "It's a flood, dear."

There was no sign of any messenger that day or the next. Zari was less worried, thinking that they had changed their minds. The aunt said, "Thank God. We worried so much over nothing. They probably just said something in passing, and to win their favor, Khan Kaka made some promise and did his, 'For sure sir, yes, sir.' "

On the third day, early in the morning, Zari had just come out of the mosquito tent when there was a knock at the gate. Gholam went to answer and Zari peeked to see who it was. She saw a gendarme and Gholam kissing each other on the cheeks. The gendarme gave him an envelope.

Gholam brought the envelope to Zari. Zari said, "You seem to know him."

"We are from the same village. He's from Bardeh. He always wanted to be a gendarme and now he is one."

Zari went to the veranda and waited until the aunt finished her prayers before opening the envelope. It was a letter addressed to her in a very good handwriting. She read the letter aloud:

"My Dear Madam. If I were not sure of the kindness of the people of this city to strangers and of the generosity of your honorable family, I would never make such a request of you. My daughter, Gilantaj, was afflicted with typhoid for some time, such that the physicians had given up all hope of her recovery. Now, divine kindness has been bestowed upon us and my child has recovered. My daughter is fond of horseback riding, but no matter how hard we searched throughout this city we could not find a tame horse which my daughter could ride. Believe me, the general sent two of the best horses from the army stable. But they were big, unruly horses, not suitable for a child who has just recently left her sick bed. My honorable friend, Mr. Abolqasem Khan, promised to send your son's colt for my daughter. I have heard that he has gone on a trip. Now, I will plead with you most humbly to loan us your honorable son's colt for a few days through the carrier of this letter. As soon as Gilantaj wearies of horses and horseback riding, it shall be returned. Sincerely . . ."

The letter had been written by someone else, because the Governor's signature was in a different handwriting than that of the letter. Zari turned to the aunt and said, "Now what should we do?"

The aunt said, "We have been caught off guard. You can't win either way. If you give them the horse, I know that Yusof and Khosrow will raise hell. And if you don't, you remember what a scene Khan Kaka made that day. We'll be at odds with him forever. If he doesn't become a member of parliament, he will say it was because of our pettiness."

"It's a foregone conclusion now," Zari said. "I can't send the roan. What should I do?"

"I don't know what we can do but sit here and wonder," the aunt said after sighing.

They brought the gendarme in. They sat him down on a chair next to the pool. Khadijeh brought him breakfast and put it on another chair. The gendarme took off his hat and put it on his knee. Zari watched him empty the sugar lumps out of the sugar bowl into his pocket and gulp down his tea straight. And what huge bites he took! Gholam was sitting across from him at the edge of the pool.

Zari came by the veranda and asked, "Are you the gendarme who guards the gate of the Governor's garden?"

The gendarme answered with his mouth full, "Uh huh," and hastily swallowed his food.

"Do you have a wife and kids, too?" Zari asked.

The gendarme smiled from ear to ear. "We got my cousin to be my wife just before New Year."

"When will you bring the horse back?"

The gendarme said, "The lieutenant gave me this mission. He said that I was a good boy. But he didn't say when to bring the horse back," and smiled again from ear to ear.

Gholam interrupted. "It isn't mating season now, brother."

The officer took an envelope out of the pocket of his uniform, got up, and gave it to Zari. "The secretary gave me this. He said it is eighty *tomans.*"

Zari opened the envelope and counted the money. It was actually eighty *tomans.* She whispered to the aunt, "They imagine they have even paid for it."

"For now," the aunt said. "let him take Sahar until we think of something later."

Zari said, "Gholam, go get Sahar out of the stable."

Gholam said, "Ma'am, I swear to God, these people do everything backwards. Mating season is past. And besides, Sahar is still—"

"They don't want it for mating," Zari sighed. "The Governor's daughter has taken a fancy to Sahar."

Gholam took off his felt hat. His bald head had turned red and was soaking with sweat. He said, "Khosrow Khan left Sahar in my care. Should I give him up to some stranger? Never, never!"

Khanom Fatemeh said, "Gholam, you see that they have sent a gendarme."

Gholam said, "What makes this poor fellow a gendarme? This poor fellow is a simple, honest man." And he turned to the gendarme and continued. "Brother, go tell your master the horse is dead and get a reward from this lady here."

"Aren't you and I from the same village? Where is your loyalty?" the gendarme said. "His excellency the lieutenant instructed me to bring the horse no matter what. He gave me a mission. He said I was a good boy. He said, 'Don't you bring the sorrel horse, or you can resign and go straight back to the village to your mama.' That's what he said himself."

Gholam put his hat back on. "Anybody who wants Sahar, can go take him out of the stable, if he dares. I'll hit him so hard on the back with the shovel that he'll go straight to his mama."

Zari said commandingly, "I give the orders around here. I am the mistress of the house. Go get Sahar out of the stable."

Mina and Marjan had awakened and came to the veranda. Khadijeh was following them to wash their faces.

Gholam said to Zari, "Ma'am, listen to me and don't do this. Think about tomorrow when your son returns and he will be heartbroken. Think about the day after, when the master comes. Don't be afraid of these people. Tell them you won't give it to them, that's all. What can they do to you?"

The gendarme said, "Aren't you from my village?"

He started walking. Gholam asked, "Where are you going?"

"I'm going to the stable."

Gholam said, "I don't care if we are from the same village. If you dare take one step toward the stable—"

"I don't have my gun with me. I'll go fetch it now."

Gholam grabbed the gendarme by the collar and shouted, "Now, you want to show off your gun to me? Weren't you the same vagabond orphan who went stealing chickens at night? Did your lieutenant tell you to threaten me with the gun?"

The gendarme broke away from Gholam. "I swear to God, no. But he said, 'Resign and go straight back to the village.' How can I go back?"

"Gholam, don't insist," the aunt said. "Khan Kaka has promised. For now, let him take Sahar. I've come up with a good idea. I'll bet the horse will be back here before Khosrow returns."

Gholam went and got Sahar out of the stable and put his reins into the gendarme's hand. When the gendarme tried to mount the horse, Sahar shook himself vigorously, kicked, and reared up on his hind legs. He raised his head and neighed as if from the depths of his belly. The roan horse and the mare neighed in unison from the stable. The gendarme stepped back and dropped the reins. Sahar turned toward Gholam and sniffed his rolled-up sleeves. The gendarme kept fumbling and was soaking with sweat. He straightened Sahar's mane, stroked his neck, took a lump of sugar out of his pocket, and held it in front of the horse's mouth.

Finally, he took the horse's reins. Zari gave him the money and said, "You can have that for yourself!" The gendarme's eyes sparkled. He put the money in his uniform pocket and dragged Sahar away. The children watched, horrified, and no matter how much Khadijeh begged them to come and have breakfast, they wouldn't.

Zari felt as if the garden had lost all its luster. Khanom Fatemeh cursed and, turning to Zari, said, "What did you tip him for, sister?"

Gholam stood still, watching Zari, whose eyes were filled with tears.

Khadijeh said, "Ma'am, may your riders be safe. The mare is young, it will give birth to another Sahar."

The aunt said, "I bet I'll get him back within three days. You did a good thing to return the money ahead of time."

Zari said, "If hell freezes over, we'll see Sahar again." She asked Gholam to make a grave near the stable, to dig up the weeds, and make a smooth surface. She told him to arrange some rocks in a rectangular shape on the ground and put a few pots of petunias over the make-believe grave.

The aunt said, "For now, wait and see."

Zari told Gholam, "If you tell Khosrow, I'll have the master fire you."

They went to the parlor, and Khanom Fatemeh telephoned Ezzatoddowleh and invited her for lunch the day after next.

And when the day after next arrived, even though Zari had never liked Ezzatoddowleh, she did everything she could to be hospitable to her. She took her white scarf, gloves, and dark glasses, and wrapped them in a bundle. She gave her guest a brand new house *chador* with quince blossom prints to wear. Ezzatoddowleh had brought along her favorite maid, Ferdows, but Zari sent Ferdows to Khosrow's room to rest. And although from early that morning she had closed up the parlor windows and drawn the wicker shades, she still brought a straw fan and placed it before Ezzatoddowleh. In order to make her feel welcome, she said, "You have beautiful hair!" Ezzatoddowleh answered, "God bless yours." It was still a long time before noon, but Ezzatoddowleh neither touched her beverage nor ate any fruit. She ordered tea to be made for her, which she only tasted and did not like. She said, "Coupon-rationed tea tastes like boiled tea." And then at lunch, it wasn't clear what she ate. She barely tasted a spoonful of rice, *khoresh,* and kabob before pushing the food aside. She asked for *verjuice,* which she mixed with grated cucumbers, bread and onion. She said it was good for the pain in her leg. Unfortunately, the *verjuice,* too, was last year's.

In the afternoon, Zari spread out a mat and brought an eiderdown pillow and a thin sheet. Ezzatoddowleh lay down with the fan in her hand and ordered Ferdows to come and rub her feet. Khanom Fatemeh also lay down next to her on another mat. Zari left the sisters by oath together and went to her bedroom. She quietly opened the bedroom door to the parlor in order to hear their voices. If Ezzatoddowleh would take the initiative, she could get Sahar back. She might even retrieve her emerald earrings, and then all Zari's patient suffering would not have gone unrewarded.

Zari could hear Ezzatoddowleh very well. She was saying, "Bless your heart, Ferdows, rub harder. That's it. Have you done your prayers? Get up, girl, go do your prayers."

It was obvious that Ferdows had left, because the aunt was now getting around to the point. It was a pity that Zari could not hear every word she said. In contrast, Ezzatoddowleh spoke loudly. She was also lying closer to the bedroom door.

8

"NOW I understand," Ezzatoddowleh said. "When you called, I asked myself, 'Why is it that my sister has thought of me? We only see each other on holidays and at funerals. Now, I understand that you have a problem that I can help resolve.'

" . . . Horse? No, as God is my witness, I never knew your nephew had a colt named Sahar. I had heard that your brother keeps horses at home. I thought, If you have it why not flaunt it? But, as for me having tempted the Governor's daughter to ask for your nephew's horse, never ever.

" . . . It's true, I can't stand the sight of your brother. If Zari had not married into your family, I would have destroyed her whole family. Yes, it's been thirteen or fourteen years. But how could I forget? A distinguished lady like myself getting up and going as a suitor to those beggars' house. The room they entertained in was no bigger than the palm of your hand, the size of our prayer room. There was so much smoke from the hookah you couldn't see in front of you. Her mother looked like a skeleton. I would be ashamed to see Naneh Ferdows looking like that—white hair, yellow complexion, front teeth missing, and wearing a wrinkled, old dress. Her armpits stank so bad I had to hold my nose. Well, woman, you could make a short visit to Manavaz to get a set of teeth. Comb your hair. Rub a little rouge on your wrinkled cheeks. After all, a suitor has come, and a distinguished lady like myself. You should consider yourself lucky that, of all those girls, my innocent child likes your daughter. I told Hamid a hundred times, 'Isn't it beneath your dignity to marry the daughter of Mirza Ali Akbar the Infidel, the scribe at the Sho'a'iyyeh school?' Why are you offended? Wasn't I telling the truth? My son said, 'I'm looking for something I don't have myself.' I said, 'What does this girl have except for a pair of pretty eyes and eyebrows?' He said, 'She is also chaste, modest, and educated.' I said, 'Dear—may your mother give her life for you—chastity, modesty, and education won't buy bread.' In any case, it was their own fault they didn't seize what Lady Luck offered them. I sent Kal Abbas, the doorman, to their filthy house. He came back and told me, 'They had consulted the Koran by divination and it was unfavorable.' The family of Mirza Ali Akbar the Infidel and divination? And Hamid kept insisting that this was the woman he liked and wanted. And it was beneath my dignity to go back to their dump of a house. But I did go. Twice. Three times. On the last day, the mother came out with it and said that you had taken the customary shawl and ring to ask for her daughter's hand and that they had already promised her to you. I wanted to come and dissuade you by telling you that her mother had cancer and reminding you that once a beggar, always a beggar. But you had long turned your back on sisterhood and solidarity. How quickly you get offended! Am I not right?

"No, as God is my witness, I didn't put it in the girl's head to take your nephew's horse. And still . . . I promise I'll do my best. I'll go and say the boy is dying of grief; it isn't fair; send the horse to its owner. Did you say that you sent the money back, or not? It would be better to persuade her to ride the horse. The horse will take off and bring her straight to his old stable. She will then forget all about horseback riding. No. Not that I would talk about injustice and cruelty and say that everybody spits and curses at the Governor, no, I can't do that. Unlike you, I don't hurt my friends.

"All right. Just for your sake, I'll do this. But you know me, I hold grudges. Right! But I also understand friendship and sisterhood. I'll tell you the truth, about the business of the emerald earrings. As soon as I came to the wedding and saw your sister-in-law, who looked like living in her husband's house had agreed with her, I decided to make her suffer by taking away those precious earrings of hers. You didn't know? How could that be? You mean she hasn't said anything? That's exactly what I meant. How could you expect the daughter of Mirza Ali Akbar the Infidel to turn out better than this? There is no reason for you to get offended. I am not lying. Yes, it was my doing. I sent Ferdows on the double to the thread and lace sellers bazaar to buy green silk, which I threw over the bride's shoulders. Then I said, 'Go borrow the emerald earrings of Yusof Khan's wife,' knowing that they wouldn't give them back. Now, why are you feeling so upset? Let the one who has lost her earrings feel bad. For my sake, don't be upset, sister. I also knew that they were mementos . . . All right, I'll try to get the earrings back, too. You don't need to tell me how. I know how."

"Come on, let's once again be the kind of sisters we were before. Do you remember when we were both kids and we had a celebration? We brought a cleric to recite the sisterhood vows and they sprinkled candy over our heads? But you have changed. Since your son died and your husband passed away so young, it's as if you were taken away somewhere and replaced by someone else. Do you remember as soon as we could figure out what was what, we both fell in love with Marhamat Khan, the doctor? He had come from Tehran and was said to have studied in Europe. I remember the day that we both made ourselves up so no one would recognize us and went to the doctor's office. There, we counted eleven other daughters of the rich and aristocratic families in the city who had put on makeup with the same idea. Pretending to be sick, they had come to parade themselves in front of the doctor. Do you remember Etrat, who became Etratosaltaneh later on, wore a starched scarf on her head? Ah, youth . . . the good old days. You had pulled some of your hair out so you could tell the doctor that you were going bald. I came up with the idea that I had a cancerous cyst in my right breast which appeared on and off. He rubbed a wad of cotton soaked in iodine where you had pulled out your hair and told me that I was hallucinating. In the end, he didn't marry either one of us and got himself a wife from Abadeh.

"Then each of us followed our own fate. I married first, but we both had bad luck. Maybe you were luckier than I was in the beginning. But your luck didn't last either. I felt it was even beneath me to open my heart up to you, my sister. It is said that every unlucky woman is lucky at least for the first forty days in her husband's house. But for me, it didn't even last forty days. All the dowry I had, my father's house and belongings, all fell into the hands of that ingrate. And a distinguished lady like me, the granddaughter of the police chief . . . a police chief whose ancestors were, generation after generation, the crownless and throneless kings of Fars. You know, on the third day after the wedding, we had a fight and he said, 'Don't give me the police chief's granddaughter act. Your ancestors were all traitors. As for your great-grandfather, he didn't let his own benefactor enter the city, and as a reward for this treason he became a close adviser to Agha Mohammad Khan.' He said, 'Don't boast of your grandfather's house to me. Its every pebble, stone, and brick was laid over the corpse of a noble, hard-working person. Its mud and straw plaster was mixed with the blood of the brightest and wisest men of the era.' . . . Are you, too, saying that he was right? Right, my foot!

"That very afternoon, when my brother came, he got all humble and polite. You should have seen him with his 'Yes sir, yes sir!'

"It was the first month of our marriage when he fell in love with Nimtaj, the wife of Mas'ud Khan the Gold Teeth. Major Mas'ud was appointed by the government as the chief of the police department. But you should remember that well. You were not yet married. My uncle and my brothers did not want the city to fall into the clutches of Mas'ud Khan, the police chief. From his very first day on the job, they began disrupting things and finally started that riot. I saw my ingrate of a husband suddenly change. He turned into the instigator of the quarrel and my house became a meeting place for my uncle's armed men. I said, 'Didn't you say that my brother, father, and ancestors were all traitors? How come you are now beating your chest to defend them?' I had been informed that he had fallen in love with Nimtaj. May God not rest your soul, man!

"Major Mas'ud, who realized that he could not stand up to his opponents, fled early one morning on foot. He tried to get to the shrine of Seyyed Abolvafa and take sanctuary there. My ingrate of a husband chased him on horseback, caught up with him near Seyyed Abolvafa, and shot him in the back. That poor young man kept writhing on the grass and asking for water. Everyone went to watch him die, but no one would dare put a drop of water in that poor young man's mouth for fear of the armed men. But your father, Haj Aqa, took the initiative. He told the armed men, 'You have gone mad and your master has gone mad, too. You will pay for the killing of this young man right here in this world. You will always have the scene of his agonizing death before your eyes.' And then he took that poor young man in the *droshky*. I heard that he died right in that *droshky* in your father's arms. Let me also say that my ingrate of a husband was afraid of your father. My uncle was afraid of him, too. Several times they wanted to loot your house, but my husband wouldn't let them. 'You'll get yourselves in hot water," he said. 'He will issue a decree for religious war; Sowlat will also come to his aid and then who can fight a whole tribe?'

"But I liked Nimtaj. That same night, she went to the home of Sheykh Razi and took sanctuary there, until he arranged for her trip and sent her to her parents. When my ingrate of a husband came to see her, the bird had flown the coop.

"May God not forgive you, man! He wasn't worthy of a distinguished lady like myself. When we had a fight, he would say, 'You're cross-eyed, and they forced me to marry you.' He said, 'I don't love you, but I don't want my son to be insulted by people saying that his mother is a divorcee.' And I, unfortunate fool that I was, was head over heels in love with him. And he knew just what to do to keep me from rebelling completely. A thousand times I found blonde and black hairs and sequins from women's dresses on the collar of his jacket. He had lost all shame and would bring prostitutes to the house—first in the outer courtyard and later in the inner courtyard. In the end, he had fallen for a hundred-*toman* whore. He said, 'A hundred-*toman* whore is too important to take to the outer courtyard.' They'd sit on the wooden platform we put over the pool and I'd send them trays full of liquor. I'd soak tobacco in *arak* and fix him a hookah. He was such a hypocrite that he would say his prayers first and then sit down to drink. He would recite in Arabic, 'Draw not near unto prayer when ye are drunken.' I watched them from behind the sash windows until dawn. In the morning, he would kiss my hands and feet and say, 'What can I do? That's the way I am. I just get excited looking at a woman's *chador*, no matter who the woman is.' I'd cry out loud, tears streaming down my face, and say, 'Forget about paying me my rightful share of marital property, just set me free. Go away and leave me alone. The house and everything in it is mine anyway. I don't need any mere shells of men around here.' I'd threaten him by saying that I swear on my only son's life I'll go to Haj Aqa's house, my sister's house, and take sanctuary, that Haj Aqa is not the kind of man whose words can be ignored. 'God damn him,' he would answer, 'Whose house? Haj Aqa himself is one of the great lovers of our time. He keeps a woman at home without having married her.' He said, 'I won't even listen to God, let alone Haj Aqa.' He was right; he had turned away from God. In the end, he wouldn't even say his prayers.

"When he was on horseback and people greeted him, he wouldn't answer. He would signal to his attendant to answer their greetings. This is the first time I'm saying all this to you. When your son and husband died, you forgot your sister.

"What was the story of Ferdows and her mother, you ask? You've heard some things, now you want to hear it from me? Sister, I have nothing to hide from you.

"One night after the evening and night prayers, I was coming out of the New Mosque. I saw a little girl sitting by the mosque door with a bundle beside her. She was crying so hard that it would break a heart of stone. I asked, 'Dear girl, why are you crying?' She said, 'My mistress has kicked me out, and I don't know how to get to Bajgah.' You see, she had brought me here from Bajgah.' I took her to our own house, thinking it would be a good deed. Next morning, I sent for a midwife. I thought maybe someone had gotten her in a bad way and then it might be blamed on my innocent son Hamid.

"To make a long story short, sister, within a week's time, either the father or the son got the little girl in trouble. I thought that they would at least leave a little village girl alone. I never found

out which one of them was responsible. I branded the girl, but she
wouldn't tell. She only cried so hard that it broke my heart. I did-
n't want to ask Hamid, because I wanted to keep our distance as
mother and son.

"Ferdows remained in our house until she grew into womanhood. As soon as she started her periods, she began to bloom. Her
cheeks became rosy, the dimple on her chin deepened, and her eyes
had such a twinkle in them. I was afraid and was looking for a solution, but before I had a chance, her belly swelled up. It wasn't clear
if it was the father's doing or the son's.

"In any case, I had to dump her on Kal Abbas, the same Kal
Abbas whose mother used to go to the Jewish district once a month
and buy him a little girl for three *tomans*. Then she would put a
fake satin dress on her and as soon as the dress was worn out, she
would take the girl back to her family. But do you think Ferdows
was going to consent so easily? I locked her up for three days during the cold winter solstice. All she had to feed on were her own
tears. I told her, 'You shameless girl, what do you want from me?
Am I being unfair not to send you back to Bajgah with this swollen
belly of yours?' She'd say, 'I'll go to the police station, make a com-
plaint, and disgrace you.' That little village twerp, what things she
knew! I said, 'I'll give you anything you want, just get yourself out
of my sight.' She had set her hopes on the bastard she was carrying
in her belly. She'd say, 'The child is yours; his inheritance will be
millions of *tomans*.' Finally, I beat her as hard as I could. I was in
luck when she began bleeding and Khanom Hakim took that bastard out of her belly. When the baby was gone, she lost her
spunk. Finally, she consented to my bringing her mother from
Bajgah to be with her. That's how I brought Naneh Ferdows to
my home. We settled on six *qarans* a day for her wages. Naneh
Ferdows is a shrewd woman. She's useful, but ungrateful."

9

KHOSROW, COVERED with dust and dripping with sweat, returned from his trip. He was carrying his rifle on his shoulder and a few dead partridges in his hand. He entered the *howzkhaneh,* the basement room which had a little gold-fish pool inside. Zari was cleaning it for the summer days. He held out the partridges to his mother, who was straightening the corner of a carpet and said, "Look, I shot them myself."

Still looking down, Zari said, "I saw them."

"Aren't you happy I came back?"

"Of course I am."

"I'll give one of them to Sahar. He won't eat it; he'll just play with it." Then he said, "No one is happy that I came back. Gholam was sitting in Haji Mohammad Reza's store, and when he saw me, he turned his head away. I came to you first, but you didn't even kiss me. That's all right."

Zari bit her lip. "Take the partridges to the kitchen. Give them to the cook to have them plucked. It's so hot. Tell her to cook them with rice for tonight—rice and raisins, which you like, dear."

When Khosrow left, Zari cursed herself, her ancestors, her fears, her school, her cowardice, and Ezzatoddowleh. As she was saying goodbye, Ezzatoddowleh had promised the aunt that Sahar would be back in his old stable within three days. So where is he? Zari wondered. She sat by the little goldfish pool and turned on the fountains. At first the water was muddy and came out in little spurts, but then it became clear and shot up. The girls came in. Both sat together by the pool and held their hands under the fountain. Zari made them promise, for the umpteenth time, not to let Khosrow know who had taken Sahar and to tell him that Sahar had died.

Khosrow came in. He didn't even notice Mina and Marjan. "Mother, where is Sahar?" he asked urgently.

Zari did not answer and quickly washed the children's faces with water from the fountain.

"My uncle said that Sahar has caught glanders and that glanders is dangerous. Was he right? Sergeant Zinger also said that glanders has been going around. Mother, he even mimicked my father. I almost hit him. He said, 'As your father says, this is another souvenir of the foreign troops!'"

Trying to change the subject, Zari asked, "Was Zinger with you all the time?"

"No, he was with us only the first few days. There was a woman with him who knew Persian well. But she was just like a man. She had a bit of a moustache and was wearing boots. She was a good rider. Now, tell me, where did you send Sahar?"

"Well, why did they leave?" Zari asked.

"Who?"

"Zinger and that old woman!"

"How should I know? What is this, a catechism? Now you're probably going to ask what we ate for dinner, what we ate for lunch ... Won't you please tell me where Sahar is?"

"You left us and went away for such a long time. After all, you were our man of the house. And now that you've come back, you won't tell your mother where you went and who you saw? Did you have a good time?"

Khosrow answered impatiently. "Well, we went hunting. On the third day, when we got back at sunset, another European with dark glasses came and took Zinger and the woman away. Uncle sent three armed men and our guide along with them. They went through the mountains. Hormoz Four-Eyes said, 'You can be sure they're going to the tribe.' Now, tell me, where is Sahar?"

Zari bit her lip. "God help us!" she said.

Mina got up from the pool and said, "Brother, Sahar got an ouchie and died."

"Died?" Khosrow shouted. "But why?" And through his tears he asked, "Mother, is she telling the truth?" He continued, "I guessed it myself. I saw the flower pots on his grave."

Zari sighed and said. "What could I do, dear son? It was his fate. Your uncle took you away to the village especially so you wouldn't see him die. At least he died peacefully. For your sake, we buried him in the garden."

Khosrow squatted by the little pool. "I knew in my heart of hearts that something would happen. From the way Uncle talked. He kept telling me to be strong and patient. He said when one loses a loved one, one should do thus and so. And then he spoke again of glanders. Strange! Last night, I dreamed that I was chasing game on horseback. My uncle and Zinger were there too. Zinger had spread a map over his saddle and was looking for the game through his long binoculars. You see, that's what he did on the first day, and Uncle kept saying, 'See, the Europeans do everything according to maps and calculations, even their hunting.'"

"Especially when they want to hunt people," Zari interrupted sorrowfully. "Well, you were saying ..."

Khosrow recalled the rest of his dream: "But I was riding Sahar, not my uncle's horse. We were coming down the mountain. Suddenly Sahar reared in the air. His legs and mane were in the air. I was suspended in mid-air, still riding him. Beneath me, the earth seemed the size of a walnut. When we were coming back this morning, I told Uncle my dream. He said, 'Something must have happened to Sahar. But don't you be sad! To hell with it. You can take any one of my colts you want.' I said, 'Uncle, it's impossible. When we left, Sahar was fine and healthy. How can it be? For me, no colt in the world can take Sahar's place.'"

He began to sob, "Now I remember. When we were leaving, Sahar was stomping the ground and digging it with his hoof. The poor animal knew he wouldn't see me again, but, stupid fool that I am, I didn't. Mother, why do I feel like this? It's as if someone is grabbing my heart and squeezing it."

Zari put her arms around her son's neck, kissed him, and
said, "Splash some water on your face, you'll feel better, my darling." She herself felt all torn up inside. "Invite your classmates
this afternoon for Sahar's memorial service. I'll prepare tea and beverages for them."

"Will you make *halva* too?" Khosrow asked.

"If you wish, of course," Zari said. Then she thought a moment
and said, "Sure, I'll make *halva* too. When the scent of the *halva*
rises, Sahar's soul will know that we are thinking about him."

"Brother, will you let us come too?" asked Mina.

Khosrow kissed his sisters and said, "No, dear, it is a service for
men only."

The men-only memorial service was actually held in the garden that very afternoon. At least twenty children of all sizes
came. Gholam had swept the top of the make-believe grave and
spread a carpet over it. Zari could see the children from the
veranda, all kneeling in silence. One little boy was even wearing
a black shirt and gazing at something. When she looked closely,
she could see him holding his thumbnail in front of his eyes, probably to stop himself from laughing. In the end, he exploded into
laughter, and all the children except for Khosrow, and Hormoz,
who was sitting next to him, burst out laughing too. The ceremonies
were disrupted. Zari could not take it any longer. She went into
the parlor. It was swarming with flies. She picked up a fly swat-
ter and started killing flies left, right, and center. She could hear
the children playing in the garden. She looked through the parlor window. They had gone after the unripe fruit on the trees. But
Khosrow and Hormoz were still sitting on the carpet and Gholam
was going toward them, holding a tray of coffee. Khadijeh
brought the dishes of *halva* and put them on the carpet. Hormoz
seemed to raise his mouth to Khosrow's ear. Imitating adults in
mourning, Khosrow hit his forehead with his hand and then put
his hand over his eyes.

When the children left, Khosrow and Hormoz came to the parlor. Khosrow's eyes were red and Hormoz's glasses fogged up.

"Dear, don't worry," Zari said. "As Khadijeh says, 'the mare is
young, she will give birth to another Sahar for you.'" She thought,

If, as his aunt says, he sees that little snip riding Sahar, then that will be the end of us all! Amazing how we raise them with lies and deception!

"I'm not crying just for your sake, but my heart is aching," Khosrow said.

Hormoz took off his glasses. He took his handkerchief out of his pocket and cleaned them. His eyes looked sleepy. "I've been saying to Khosrow, 'Brother, this is the beginning of our lives. We have lots of hardships like this ahead of us. We shouldn't give up that easily. Besides, see how many people are dying every day of typhus or starvation. What is a colt compared to all these people?'"

Zari looked at Hormoz. She didn't know whether they were his own words or if someone had taught him to say that. In any case, he was four years older than Khosrow. The death of people compared to the fake death of a colt! she thought.

She remembered that afternoon in the missionary hospital when her mother was passing the final hours of her life. Zari had no idea, even though Khanom Hakim had said, "The cancer now has been spread to all her body and no longer the surgeon's knife has been able to do anything." Zari's mother looked at her out of the corner of her eyes and said, "Stay with me tonight!" But how could she? Khosrow was three years old and would let no one but Zari feed him. And if Zari did not lie down next to him, he wouldn't go to sleep. Besides, they also had guests. Yusof had invited a bunch of people. She told her mother, "I have to go. We have guests. I'll come back tomorrow morning."

"Tomorrow morning?" her mother asked and did not insist any longer. Instead she said, "If you can, send me some soil from the holy shrine. If your sister-in-law isn't busy, have her come and bring me some."

It was late at night before Zari came home. The aunt said her prayers, smoked her opium, wore the long-sleeve dress which conformed to the unveiling ordinance, and put on her gloves and facial veil. And how could the aunt go all that way alone, late at night? Besides, a person who still has her faculties wouldn't die that quickly. Khan Kaka arrived before all the other guests, and when he heard about it, he said, "I'll be happy to go with Khanom Fatemeh." But in those days, Khan Kaka didn't have a car and they couldn't get a *droshky* either. But they went. It was after eleven o'clock by the time they got back. Zari was serving dinner. Khosrow was still awake. He was going from one guest's arms to another, being sweet and adorable. Zari did not even get a chance to ask Khan Kaka, "How was she?" The aunt went to sleep as soon as she got back. And Khan Kaka had so much *arak* to drink after dinner that he got drunk. He was crying his eyes out and calling for his own mother, saying, "Dear Bibi! Dear Bibi!" He threw several glasses at the walls and doors and broke them. Then he gagged so much that the guests got upset. Finally they took Khan Kaka to a corner of the garden where he could throw up out of everyone's sight. When the guests left, they told Zari that her mother had died. She died before the soil of the shrine had gotten there. Only a nurse, who couldn't speak her language, was by her side.

Just then Mina and Marjan came in, each holding a doll. Mina said, "My uncle gave it to me." Then Khan Kaka came in, followed by Gholam, who was carrying two gunnysacks full of something.

Abolqasem Khan blinked. "The first lime crop." At Zari's signal, Gholam took the gunnysacks to the storeroom.

Abolqasem Khan hugged Khosrow and asked, "Shall I have the colt you liked brought to you from the village?"

"No, Uncle," the boy replied. "I don't want a horse at all." Mina walked up to him with her doll, put her hand on her brother's knee and said, "Did you see my doll? Would you like to have it?"

10

THE MIDWIFE, who was from the province and had studied in Tehran, had just opened an office and was swamped with patients. Only through persistence had Zari been able to get an appointment with her for seven o'clock Thursday evening. In the afternoon, she finished her work very quickly at the insane asylum. The number of patients was a little over half what it had been the week before. The director, a short man with a complexion the color of opium, received her every Thursday. He would only allow her to go about her charity work after he had been paid sufficiently. He wanted money, not only for himself but for the other nurses as well. He told her that most of the patients had caught typhus and that the few hospitals in the city had no more room left. Besides, even if they had room, none of them would have hospitalized these patients. Zari looked at him and thought that he didn't look all that well himself. Not that he ever looked particularly well. Who could, after putting up with the mental patients so much? His eyes kept darting about.

Gholam put the tray of bread and dates down on the floor of the large room in the men's ward. Unlike the past, no one paid much attention. Zari looked at the men in the room, their heads shaven and wearing gowns that had once been white. All were silent. It was as if they were listening to voices that only they could hear and answering them in a murmur. They would take the bread and dates from Gholam absentmindedly. Zari felt depressed. She had a feeling that today her vow of charity had not been fulfilled. She would probably not make anyone happy. Dejectedly she began to distribute cigarettes and matches. A patient who considered himself the supreme ruler of the universe had always asked for the pressed, filtered Homa brand of cigarettes. But this time he took an Oshnu cigarette and lethargically placed it between his lips, without lighting it. The windows did not have blinds and the sun shone inside. The flies buzzed around and checked out every nook and cranny in the room. They flew around the bread and dates which were still in the patients' hands.

"Ali," called the head nurse. Ali was Zari's favorite, a tall, young man who looked German and had escaped from the insane asylum three times. Twice his relatives had found him, each time around the high school where he had studied. The last time Gholam had found him on a hill near Yusof's garden. Gholam said, "He followed me like a lamb and I took him on foot to the asylum. Hunger had worn him down." He had told Gholam, "They deceived me; they whispered in my ear: 'The airplane is ready, please get on it and go to Europe to see your uncle.' I came but I couldn't find the airplane, no matter how I tried. Maybe the airplane left me behind. You see, I have a lot of enemies." He had also said, "I drank water from the gutter and I stole a piece of bread or a bone from the dogs. Yesterday, I swiped a piece of raw meat from a dog and ran away. I washed the meat in the gutter and ate it. I got sick to my stomach and now I have diarrhea. I pass blood too. I looked for our house a long time, but I couldn't find it. My father must have arranged to have the house lost so I couldn't find it." From that point on, they kept Ali in the basement of the asylum in stocks and chains. Zari would visit him there and take him bread and dates. When he saw Zari, he would smile. He had asked Zari to bring him an *Essential English III* text and Zari had done so. From then on, he had not spoken a word in Persian. He spoke a language that no one understood.

Ali came. He had gotten so thin that Zari felt a pang in her heart when she saw him, even though Ali did not recognize her. His gaze i

ndicated that he did not know who she was. He did not use his mad
e-up foreign language either. In Persian, he said commandingly,
"A pincer's movement equals typhus plus famine plus cheating on
examination. Oh, mad men of the world, unite!"

Seyyed from the Gowd-e Araban district was sitting in a corner, silently. Normally when he saw Zari, he would put his hand
under his belly, scratch, and say, "Fire, fire, I am on fire," and then
he would say, "I am Ilanoddowleh. I am Veylanoddowleh." He
would take the gifts from Zari and in exchange give her love prayers,
charms, witchcraft, and talismans on imaginary slips of paper, saying to her, "Account settled. But wash your dress in the mortuary water, spread it on the grave of a murdered person, and give
it to him to put on in the morning. Leopard whiskers, and
brains of black donkeys . . ."

Then there was the patient who wrapped any piece of material
or rag he could find around an imaginary wound on his leg and
would stretch the bandaged leg and fan it—but the fan had
slipped from his hand.

When Zari, Gholam, and the director were walking by the flowerless garden of the hospital, they saw a young woman sleeping on
an old quilt under a pine tree. As soon as the woman heard footsteps,
she opened her eyes wide. Zari recognized her, even though her complexion had turned the color of the soil in the garden. She was the
same woman who sometimes claimed to be the Wife of God and
sometimes said that she was God Himself. When the four-o'clocks
in the garden bloomed in the days when someone had the patience
to water them, she would pick off their red petals and rub them on
her cheeks waiting for God. They said that, looking at the sky, she
chanted in a language resembling Arabic and believed that God was
waiting for her on the roof, but she wouldn't go because she was a
woman and should, therefore, not take the first step.

The Wife of God was now lying down under the pine tree, her
skin twitching and lips blistered. Perhaps she was going to join God
in a few moments by her own free will. Zari thought, I wish she
would mediate for everyone before God. A sound came from the
woman's lips: "Water." The light blinded her and her eyes closed.
Gholam ran off.

"Why is she lying down here?" Zari asked the director.

"She's caught typhus."

"Well, all of them will catch it."

"They'd be better off," the director said. "They'd all be free. Their relatives pray for relief from their suffering. What's the use of keeping them?"

Gholam came rushing with a glazed bowl full of water. He bent over and put the bowl to the woman's lips saying, "Drink, sister." The woman couldn't. Zari took her handkerchief out of her handbag, wet it and wiped the woman's lips and face with it. Then she folded the handkerchief, soaked it in the bowl and lay it across the forehead and eyes of the Wife of God.

Then they started on their way. The director walked along with them explaining, "Three of our nurses caught typhus and are now sitting comfortably under the Tuba Tree in the next world. The Wife of God will also start on her way tonight." And since Zari cast a reproachful glance at him, he continued, "It's amazing. When the fever rises, their insanity leaves them. If we could save them from this disease, perhaps God would make them recover altogether. But what's the use? Should they become sane, they would just be beginning their misfortune. Their families are used to life without them and no longer have the patience nor the room for them."

In the women's ward, she saw the crippled woman she feared because the woman considered her responsible for her affliction. In her heart of hearts, Zari felt guilty about her condition. The woman always started by saying, "Whore. Motherfucker. You've come back again? What do you want from me?" When the woman's legs had still been fine, she had asked Zari for a pair of old sandals, *givehs* or *maleki* shoes from Abadeh. She said, "I'm a respectable woman, I can't walk barefoot to the latrine." She said, "May God strike Khanom Esmat dead. If she had spent my dower money and the one-eighth of my inheritance on me and not on that cuckold of a roughneck who sleeps in her arms, now I wouldn't have to ask a person like you who is no better than a Mordestan whore."

But the following week had been Zari's turn to go to the prison, the week after that she had forgotten the request, and by the time she had bought the new shoes and taken them to the woman, it was already too late; the woman had become paralyzed. Even though it was obvious that her paralysis had nothing to do with her having or not having shoes, from then on, whenever she saw Zari, she would shower her with insults the likes of which Zari had never heard in her life. But the nurses said that at night she would hug her new *givehs* and go to sleep.

Zari's eyes searched for the teacher with one false eye. She, too, was not very happy with Zari and would not allow her near her. Zari always left her share of bread and dates on a ledge. The teacher sometimes was kind enough to address Zari with phrases like, "Look at this slut, what a perfume she's put on herself! Pew, pew. Now you're happy, you little slut, you can come and kiss my butt. Do you remember, you were working as our seamstress? I knew that you would finally show your true colors. With that driver who had a wife in every town . . ." And she would touch Zari under her chin and say, "You slut!" Then, suddenly, she would get angry and shout, "You've sewn rat poison into the dates. You've taken out the date pits and replaced them with ratsbane. This is some *ranginak!*"

It was said that after veils were banned, the Governor, the military commander, and the director of education had gone to visit an elementary school where she taught first grade. As soon as the director of education saw her, he began to shout and reprimand her. Apparently, she used to put a pencil between the tiny fingers of the first-grade students and squeeze them together only to laugh at how they squirmed. The reprimands of the director concerned corporal punishment. In any case, she fainted, being frightened by all those dignitaries, and fell to the ground. Later, when they grabbed her by the legs, took her to the office, and brought her to, she kept looking at everyone bewilderedly. She had taken her glass eye out, put it in the palm of her hand and scared everybody by showing it to them. One day, she did the same thing to Zari. Until that day, Zari had not known that she had a glass eye, even though she had noticed that her right eye seemed fixed in its socket. The lady teacher was agitated that day. As soon as Zari came in, she went to her and said, "Take it," and opened her hand into Zari's. She looked and saw that she was holding an eye in the palm of her hand, a large glass eye.

Now, upon asking, she learned that the same woman had
been the first victim of typhus. The director said, "We didn't know
she had caught typhus. Of course, she had a high fever. She prepared herself for the grave. That is, she tied anything within her
reach around herself and said that she was wearing a shroud and
began reciting the Koran from memory. She recited very well.
Instead of cursing Satan, she cursed the Cardboard Man. I suppose the Cardboard Man was the director of education the year
before last or earlier, the one who wanted to fire her. Then she said
her last prayer, threw herself into the pool, and died that night."

Zari then went to Miss Fotuhi, whose bed was next to the window and who always watched the garden, hoping for her relatives
to come and take her to the 124,000-square-meter garden. She knew
the Fotuhi family. They were well off. Earlier, when she had
gotten ill, they had kept Miss Fotuhi at home. But when they could
no longer control her and lost all hope of her recovery, they sent
her to the asylum. Before the war, she had a private room, and her
mother, while she was alive, would visit her regularly. On occasion she even took her home for a week or two until she could no
longer take it and would bring her back by force, plant her in the
asylum office, and disappear. Miss Fotuhi's brother was a
well-known teacher in the city and the idol of adolescent boys. The
best he could manage was to attend to his sister now and then.
They had really abandoned her there and left. But she wouldn't
give up hope. She was waiting for them to come and take her to
the 124,000-square-meter garden. She had an olive complexion, wide joined eyebrows, protruding teeth, and salt and pepper
hair. She never accepted food from Zari. There were others who
were greedy and sometimes stretched out their arms two or three
times. But Miss Fotuhi would not stoop so low. When the fruit
in the garden was ripe, Zari would take large baskets loaded
with apricots, tart apples, cherries, peaches, and pears to the asylum, but Miss Fotuhi wouldn't even look at them. Several times,
Zari made a special basket for her and put it on the window sill.
She heard from the nurses, though, that as soon as she stepped out
of the room, the other patients would snatch and plunder it, and
this was just another headache for Miss Fotuhi. When the patients

got the tart apples, they asked for salt. They would break the apples in half with their fists, sprinkle salt on them, and let them get succulent and tempting. It would have made anybody else's mouth water, but Miss Fotuhi would just stare into the garden waiting for her relatives to come and take her to the 124,000-square-meter garden. Other patients wouldn't even give up apricot and peach pits. They would break them open with their teeth, or hit them with a rock on the floor of the room, and eat the kernels inside. As the director said, on their one-*toman*-per-day ration, how could these patients fill up their stomachs and get any strength? Most had gone mad from poor nutrition.

Once the distribution was over, Zari would sit by Miss Fotuhi's bed and listen to her complaints. Miss Fotuhi disliked all the patients and would not speak to any of them. The patients had nicknamed her "Princess." The *Iran* newspaper, which was published in the large format and was mailed to Yusof from Tehran twice a week, lined notebooks, and pencils were the things that Miss Fotuhi wanted. She would say, "I will permit you to help the world of science and literature." Miss Fotuhi loved the serial stories in *Iran*. She said that she was writing her autobiography in the notebooks. Once one notebook was filled, she would ceremoniously entrust it to Zari and say, "Rent me a safety deposit box in the National Bank. Get the money for it from my brother and store my work there for safekeeping. There might be a fire here and all my work would be destroyed." The first time Zari had believed it and had read Miss Fotuhi's notebook. It consisted of some incoherent ideas written in a jumbled handwriting. Where legible, it described a 124,000-square-meter garden with man-made waterfalls and lakes and with water lilies blooming on the water and acacia and ash trees, and a well-built man with a large forehead and white behind the ears who was waiting in ambush behind an ash tree, and herself, wearing a white wavy silk dress, roaming gracefully like a partridge with her protruding firm breasts, and the well-built man who would come out from behind the tree with his arms open and catch her off guard and embrace and squeeze her. He would hold her so tight that her breasts felt as if they were about to be squashed. And at the end of the notebook, she had written,

"Completed, the sorrowful story of Fotuhi's daughter in Nay
Prison." Under this sentence was written, "Some lines from the
daughter of Fotuhi:
    'To cow's milk they accustomed me,
    But the calf died—it was not to be.
    I was a young babe when my mother expired,
    And for my care a wet nurse was hired.
    My luck failed again, and so I cried,
    When I learned my wet nurse too had died.' "
    Zari knew that these lines were not written by the daughter of
Fotuhi, because the aunt, too, often hummed the same verses. Of
course, the daughter of Fotuhi, when she still had her faculties,
was pretty good with her pen and wrote articles in the local
newspapers about women's rights and against the injustices of men.
She also managed a magazine in which she incited young women
to action.
    Miss Fotuhi was not at all one to have been ignored. She was
the first woman in the city to wear a blue, bell-shaped *chador* and
abandon the black shroud, as she called it. The unveiling law had
still not been officially announced when she even let go of the blue
bell-shaped *chador.* In her better days, she would complain to Zari.
"Alas, no one appreciated me. Men were not ready to accept a
woman like me. First they thought I was honey and they wanted to dip their fingers in it, and when I told them to get their paws
off, they either ridiculed me or ignored me." And suddenly she
would shout, "They drove me crazy! They drove me crazy! I
told them, I will not give it to you, I will not give you what you
want from me. Do you think I am Nur Hamadeh? That's that! And
as for those stupid women, it will be a long time before they realize who I was and what I did."
    Zari sat by Miss Fotuhi's bed and said hello. Miss Fotuhi
looked away from the garden, noticed her, and returned her
greeting. Zari took four issues of the *Iran* newspaper out of her
handbag and gave them to Miss Fotuhi. Earlier issues were
stacked up next to her pillow. Miss Fotuhi opened up the new issues
one after another. She frowned when she saw the change in the
format and the newspaper's smaller size.

"Haven't you given the newspapers to the patients this time?" Zari asked.

Miss Fotuhi answered distractedly, "No, most of them were released from prison. Ali took two of the newspapers and ate them." Then she looked Zari over from head to foot. She seemed displeased with the long pleated sleeves of her blouse. She asked, "How many hundreds of meters of material have you wasted on the sleeves?" She crumpled up the new newspapers and threw them to the side of the bed. Then she turned to the old newspapers. She picked them up from beside her pillow, counted them, stacked them, rolled one, hit Zari on the head forcefully, and said, "They say Afsar Khanom, the daughter of Sardar, has died. And she didn't even have a shroud."

11

ZARI SENT Gholam away and set off on her way. She was thinking about the futility of her vow of charity and remembered Yusof's words: "What is the use of all this charitable work? The whole thing is rotten from the core." But no matter how hard she thought, she didn't know what she could do to fix things. The solutions that Yusof proposed seemed so dangerous to her that it made her shudder to even think about them.

At six o'clock, she arrived in front of the midwife's office. She felt her stomach wrenching. Two donkeys were standing in front of the office with their reins tied to the door knockers. In the small courtyard leading to the office, two women were crouched up on a bare wooden platform. Another woman was lying down behind them. It wasn't clear whether the women were young or old because they were so distraught. On another wooden platform, a male patient was writhing in pain. Right next to the waiting room, a woman was lying down straight on a bench, still and stiff. She was covered by a dark blue *chador* with blue dots. Up to her ankles her feet were bare. The soles of her feet and her toenails were dyed with henna. Her dark trousers were rolled up to just below her knees. Zari was taken aback. Surely the woman was dead. She was not so naive that she could not recognize death. But it appeared that the woman had nobody, because she was alone even in death.

There were no empty chairs in the waiting room. Among the patients there were only five pregnant women, their bellies swollen and faces blotchy. The other patients were either men or old women. A young girl in stained clothes with her head on the shoulder of a middle-aged woman entered, and shouted, "My heart! My heart!" A pregnant woman stood up, gave her seat to the girl and opened the window above her head. A wave of heat rushed into the room. The door to the office opened and a pregnant woman waddled through the waiting room. She was certainly in her last month. A nurse with disheveled hair came out and called, "Forty-eight." Zari caught up with the nurse, who was checking out the patients and calling out, "Forty-nine." Zari said to her, "I have an appointment for seven o'clock." The nurse responded, "My dear lady, it is useless to make an appointment these days. All sorts of patients are mobbing this place. The courtyard is packed. Didn't you see?"

"Yes, I did," Zari said. "One of them is dead, too."

"Yes," the nurse said calmly. "By the time they are brought here from the village on donkeys, they have already taken their last breath." The nurse almost shouted, "Isn't forty-nine here? Fifty." An old woman got up. She was covering her face tightly with her veil. She had a crab-like walk and was hunchbacked. The nurse let her into the office. Zari opened her handbag. The nurse hesitated. She followed the movement of Zari's hand, which searched but could not find her handkerchief. The nurse said impatiently, "If there's nothing the matter with you and you've come here for a baby, you'd better wait for a more opportune time." She opened the door to the office and went in.

She was right. Zari was in no hurry. She knew that this time, too, she would end up with Khanom Hakim. She decided to go home and wash herself clean and boil all her clothes. With those delicate children, she should not let anyone touch her. On her way home, she bought louse insecticide, rubbing alcohol, soap, and sulfur.

By the time she knocked at the garden gate, the sun had already set. A boy with a dark complexion and curly hair came to open the door. He stared at her with his round black eyes and laughed. She recognized him. She asked, "What are you doing here, Kolu?"

"I came with the master," Kolu said.

"Has he come back?"

And she ran. Yusof was sitting on a wicker chair next to the pool, smoking a hookah. He was still wearing his traveling clothes and was covered with dust from the road. His face lit up when he saw his wife. "Where have you been? I've been waiting for you. I came all this way to—why are you standing so far away?"

"You came back too soon," Zari said. "but I'm so happy that you did. But you shouldn't touch me. I should take a bath; I'm covered with germs. When you come, one forgets about one's worries." And she hurried to the house.

She returned to the garden, nice, clean, and perfumed. It had gotten dark. Yusof was holding his head in both hands. She walked to him, lifted his head, kissed his hair and asked, "You're not sick, God forbid?"

Yusof seated his wife on his lap. The wicker chair creaked. He kissed her neck, face, and bare arms. His lips were soft and hot. Zari got up and said, "Let me go turn on the lights."

Yusof held her hands and said, "Never mind."

Zari glanced up and said, "The sky is heavy. I wish it would rain so we could breathe easier." Yusof said, "Like my heart."

"It's midsummer, after all." She was preoccupied with the thought of Sahar. She thought, I hope he doesn't ask about Sahar.

"When I came home, it felt really empty. Where are the children?"

"Their aunt took them to Mehrangiz's house, to a sermon on Karbala, and Khosrow's gone out with Hormoz."

"You shouldn't send the children to such sermons."

"They wanted to themselves. Besides, they don't understand any of it. They just play with Mehri's children. Their aunt has sewn *chadors* for them and they imitate her when she prays." Suddenly it dawned on her and she asked, "Why did you come back so soon? And you've brought Kolu with you." Yusof said, "Send Kolu to the bathhouse tomorrow morning and get him some new clothes.

I have adopted him. I killed his father, so I couldn't stay in the village any longer."

Zari's heart sank. "But I don't understand. You killed Kolu's father? Our shepherd? You? Impossible."

Yusof held his head in both hands. "Don't talk about it, my head is about to burst."

"But tell me what happened," Zari asked.

"That is why I came back to town, to tell you. I dropped everything I was doing and came back to you to get it off my chest, but you weren't here."

Zari sat on a chair next to Yusof and let his head rest on her shoulder, stroking his neck, and kissing his earlobe. "You know dear, I'm not telepathic. How could I know you were coming? Now, tell me. I'll listen. Get it off your chest."

"He was supposed to take the last flock of sheep to the summer pastures. Before leaving, he killed two sheep, stewed them, and stuffed them in a sheepskin. I don't know why he did that. He had never done such a thing before."

"Well, dear, you said yourself that out of fear of famine people get greedy," Zari said.

Yusof got up and began to pace. Ignoring what his wife had said, he continued: "Nothing can be hidden from the village chief. He came and reported it to me in front of everybody. I wanted to ignore it, but do you think the chief would let it go? At dusk, when the shepherd brought the sheep back, he reminded me of it again. I had to question him. I asked the shepherd why he was two sheep short. He answered, 'I swear on your life the wolves got them.' The village chief interrupted, saying that if he was telling the truth he should swear by his holiness Abbas, take seven steps toward Mecca and swear by his holiness Abbas." Then he stopped. After a few moments, he continued, "I saw that his legs were trembling. Stupid me, I could see it, but I let him swear. That night, he got a stomach ache. I went to his house, which was a dump. He fixed his eyes on me like a sheep and asked for forgiveness. I shouted that I had forgiven him from the very beginning. You know me anyway. But it was no use. Tears began to pour out of the corner of his eyes onto his dirty pillow. I made him a wine and rock candy toddy. He didn't drink it. He said, 'How long can I go on sinning? Everybody knows that his holiness Abbas can't endure it.' I shouted, 'Man, I am the owner of the sheep and I have forgiven you.' He said, 'His holiness Abbas has stricken me down; you won't be able to do anything anymore. Have my brother take the sheep to the summer pastures.' "

Yusof sat in the chair next to his wife and continued: "He signaled to Ma'sumeh, Yarqoli's wife, who went and brought two sheepskins full of stewed meat, I don't know from where, and threw them at my feet. I wished then the ground would open up and swallow me."

Zari said calmly, "Look, dear, it wasn't your fault. It was the fault of that shameless village chief. So, the sheperd took a false oath, or maybe he ate too much. Or even more likely, he might have caught typhus. Or perhaps God wanted his son to have a decent life. We don't know anything about God's will, do we? Maybe God wanted his son to get an education."

Khadijeh came to the veranda and turned on the light. She then walked over to the beds in the garden. She spread the twins' beds on the wooden platforms on the other side of the pool and set up the mosquito nets. When she got to Khosrow's bed, she pulled the bed cover aside, spread out the mattress, and asked, "Ma'am, did you put Khosrow Khan's blanket somewhere?"

Zari, still sitting where she was, answered, "No. Did you use it for a pad under the iron?"

"No, ma'am."

"Then what's happened to it?"

"I'll be darned if I know. The same petty thief who stole the clothesline has probably snatched Khosrow Khan's blanket."

Zari suddenly became anxious. She thought it must be Khosrow's own doing. But why? Early that morning, when it was still dark, before the aunt came down from the roof for her prayers, Zari had awakened to the sound of footsteps. When she opened her eyes, she had seen Khosrow looking around stealthily. She saw him tiptoe over to the clothesline and untie it from the nail on the wall. He gathered it up in loops until he reached the elm tree at the end of the garden where the other end of the rope was tied. He put the

rope under his arms, crawled back into his own room, then quietly came back and went inside the mosquito tent. In fact, these
days, there was something wrong with Khosrow. His mind was
somewhere else and now and then his eyes stared fixedly ahead.
When he first heard about Sahar's death, he was grief-stricken, and
at any excuse tears would fill his eyes. When he reached for the sugar
bowl, his hand would tremble. Most of the time, he would hang
around the end of the garden, near the make-believe grave. He would
pull out the weeds and water the petunias and the potted flowers
with his own hands. But in recent days he had changed and
wouldn't even look at the make-believe grave. He avoided his
mother's eyes and gave short, incoherent answers to her questions.

She stood up. She had a feeling that Khosrow would have taken
his gun too, even though she was sure she herself had locked the
cupboard and taken away the key. Yusof's voice brought her
back to herself. "Why are you standing up? Sit down. Say something."

Like someone who has just been awakened, she asked, "What
did you say?"

"I know I've upset you," he said. "You are upset with me."

Zari answered absentmindedly, "No, you're wrong; it isn't
your fault at all. In the courtyard of Miss Masihadam's office I saw
the sick, who had been brought on donkeys from the villages, One
of them was dead. Typhus has spread to all the villages; it's all over
the city too."

With surprise Yusof asked, "What were you doing in
Masihadam's office? Are you . . . ?"

Zari was sick with worry. What a difference between what she
had on her mind and what he had on his! No one knows what's
going on inside anyone else's head.

"I went to get louse insecticide from the Sa'adat Pharmacy,"
she said. "The door was open, so I peeked in. Maybe that
patient wasn't really dead. She seemed to be . . ." Zari herself did-
n't know what she was saying. She didn't wait for more questions
and rushed into the bedroom. Without turning the light on, she
found her handbag, took out her keys, and went to the cupboard.
Fumbling in the dark, she opened the cupboard door. Her

hand was trembling and her stomach was turning. No, thank God, the guns were there. To reassure herself, she touched their barrels, breechblocks and handles. Cold and straight, they were leaning against the cupboard wall. She locked the cupboard, shut the parlor windows and doors, and walked over to the telephone. She cranked it once and asked the operator for Abolqasem Khan's house. She spoke so quietly that the operator didn't hear her. She repeated the name. As luck would have it, Abolqasem Khan himself answered. She asked if Khosrow was there and was told that he wasn't and neither was Hormoz. Through the receiver, she could hear Khan Kaka asking others in the house. Apparently, Hormoz had said that he was going to have dinner at his aunt's house. He said that she had invited him. Then Khan Kaka complained jokingly, "Why didn't you invite all of us? Do you think we would turn down a free meal?" Zari was on the verge of tears. She answered, "God willing, next time," and hung up the receiver. She was so frightened that she almost collapsed. Both boys had lied. They were up to something. They had taken the rope and the blanket. She would have to tell Yusof everything. As she walked out of the parlor the telephone rang. She picked up the receiver. It was Khan Kaka. When he thought it over, he, too, had started to worry. Zari pulled herself together and said, "Don't worry. I think they've gone to the movies or something. They'll come here for dinner. It's not late yet. As soon as they get back, I'll have them call you."

She opened the parlor windows and doors. She heard Mina. The children had come back. She went to the garden. Both girls were on Yusof's lap and he seemed to have regained his composure. Mina said, "Mother won't let us. She says, Lady Sun will get angry; she will heat up prods and stick them into our soft flesh." Khanom Fatemeh was sitting there, still wearing her *chador*. She said, "Sister, Mehri sends greetings and says she won't talk to you anymore. She said to remind you that you haven't once dropped by for the sermons this year!"

Mina, still seated, clapped her hands and said, "I won't talk to you till the Resurrection Day." She then turned her head and kissed her father under the chin and tried to get down.

Yusof held both children tightly in his arms and said, "All right, now, tell me all about it, my cutie dolls."

Zari was staring at the veranda lights and listening to the voices coming from the garden. She didn't know where to begin. Like the madmen she had seen in the afternoon, she was distraught, but had assumed an air of calm. Mosquitoes, tiny moths, and dragonflies circled around the veranda light, stuck to it, and fell down. In the garden, the crickets and frogs seemed to be having a heated exchange. Otherwise, there was neither sound nor movement. If the boys were coming toward the house, she would certainly hear their footsteps. She should tell them right now, send them all out to turn the city upside down, and find her son. Was she paying for the shepherd's death? Had God sent the shepherd's son to take Khosrow instead? Her stomach kept churning. Time stood still, as if it had gone to sleep under the heavy quilt of the sky. She wished the wind would blow, or that, like the wind, she herself could stir up the people and the trees. She wished the sky would clear up and become a garden with millions of eyes. She wished the trees would open up their chattering lips and begin to talk. Involuntarily she said, "Get up, let's go away from here." Yusof was holding Marjan's hair up and kissing the back of the child's neck. He laughed and said:

"Where should we go that's better than here?"

Zari said, "Go after Khosrow."

Khanom Fatemeh said, "Sister, Khosrow went with Hormoz to Khan Kaka's house."

Zari said, weeping, "No, he isn't there. He has taken a rope and a blanket along, but hasn't taken his gun."

Yusof put the children down and asked in amazement, "What for? Gone where?"

Zari said through her tears, "I don't know where he's gone. Get up; let's go find him. I know something has happened to my son. When I saw Kolu, I realized this was God's revenge. God has sent Kolu to replace my son." And she broke down into a sob.

Yusof got up and put his hands on his wife's shoulders. "You are upset," he said. "It's my fault for telling you whatever happens. Get these superstitions out of your head. Go call Khan Kaka's house. He might be there."

Zari said, "I already did."

Khanom Fatemeh said, "I'll put the girls to bed. Go over the hill; the Governor's house is on the other side of the hill. I have a feeling Khosrow and Hormoz are there."

Yusof looked at her and asked, "Are you clairvoyant, sister?"

The aunt emphasized, "The sooner you go, the better. I'll call Khan Kaka and tell him to get over there, too."

Yusof shook his head. "I don't understand," and then he had an idea. "They might have gone to Fotuhi's house, Hormoz's history teacher. But he's in Esfahan. I know he hasn't returned yet."

Khanom Fatemeh said, "Get up and go. Zari will tell you on the way."

They left from the small back door of the garden, which opened at the foot of the hill, and started toward the hill. Yusof asked, "Woman, what mess have you gotten yourself into? What have you made my son do? Maybe it is my own fault for not controlling my tongue . . . walk faster." He was taking such long strides that, in order to keep up with him, his wife had to run over the rocks. When they reached the top of the hill, she could walk no farther. On the other side of the hill, the Governor's mansion with its lights on seemed to be the only thing awake in the entire plain. Zari sat on the rocks, panting, and said, "Wait a minute." Her heart was racing wildly. Her stomach was turning. She vomited. She threw up with such force that it seemed as though her insides would come out as well. Yusof held her shoulders, then began to massage her shoulders and neck. He said, "You are driving me crazy. Well, tell me what's happened. What's happened that we have to come after the boys here?"

Zari said, "You go ahead; I'll sit here. If you don't bring my son back, I'll die right here. I'll put my head on this rock and die. Khan Kaka forced us to send Sahar to the Governor's daughter. I guess Khosrow has gone to steal Sahar from the Governor's garden. There are gendarmes guarding that place. They have killed my son." And she began to scream.

Yusof slapped his wife, the first time he had ever done so. Zari did not know that it would also be the last time. He said, "Shut up. In my absence, you are spineless." He let go of her and headed down the hill. He was wild with rage. Zari got up involuntarily. She wiped her lips with her skirt and began to run. She fell, but she got up again. She had to get to him and calm him down. She could see the huge figure of him reach the garden wall and stop. Thank God, he had stopped. It took all she had left in her to catch up with her husband. She was completely out of breath. She took Yusof by the hand.

Yusof was looking around listening to the sounds. He said, "We'll go to the guard's room. If we hear the boys' voices, we'll go in. They'd better not have touched a hair on those kids' heads."

Zari said, "Promise me if they're okay you won't make a fuss."

They knocked on the door and went in. Yes, the boys were there. In the guard's room, a young officer was sitting casually on a desk, and a cigarette in the corner of his mouth had curls of smoke rising from it—just like cops in the movies. When he saw them he asked, "May I help you? You've probably lost your way, too."

On the desk was a half-finished dinner tray. Khosrow and Hormoz were standing in front of the desk. Two gendarmes with rifles slung over their shoulders were searching their pockets. Zari recognized one of them, the man from Gholam's village who had taken Sahar. It was obvious that Khosrow had been crying. When he saw his father, he smiled, and brightened up Zari's heart.

The gendarme from Gholam's village took a few lumps of sugar out of Khosrow's pocket, put them on the desk, stood at attention and said, "Sugar, Lieutenant."

Yusof demanded, "For what offense have you brought my sons here?"

The young officer, ignoring his question, said, "Include it in their file."

Zari interrupted and said calmly, "Officer, these boys go on field trips in the afternoon." She saw the rope and the blanket on the desk and a bag that Hormoz was carrying with something wiggling inside it. She continued, "They collect rocks and . . ." She couldn't figure out what could be in the bag, so she added, "They collect insects, butterflies, and field mice and dry them. They also take a blanket with them to sit on and rest. Sometimes they also take a rope and play Tarzan or if they find two suitable trees, they tie it to the trees and swing on it." The young officer was clearly fascinated by Zari's voice and face. Zari continued, "Tonight, they were late, so we came after them."

Yusof involuntarily burst out laughing, and Hormoz corroborated what she had said. "Sir, we swore and told you that we were on a field trip. We lost our way. We saw the lights and came here toward them." The officer put out his cigarette in the ashtray and asked, "Why did you whistle?"

Hormoz said, "We whistled so some good-hearted person like yourself could hear it and show us the way."

Again Yusof shouted angrily, "What can two unarmed boys who only have a few lumps of sugar in their pockets do?" Zari held her husband's arm and pleaded, "My dear, don't get angry. You can see that the children are fine. There's been a misunderstanding. It will be resolved."

Yusof shouted more angrily than before, "They are treating my children like criminals. Do you know why they came here?" Zari knew that if Yusof were to tell the truth they wouldn't hear the end of it and none of them would be allowed to go. She interrupted her husband and, turning to the officer, said, "The gentleman has just come back from a long journey; he is tired."

The officer noticed the bag that Hormoz was holding in his hand. He asked, "What's in that bag?"

Hormoz answered calmly, "A snake, sir."

"A snake?" the officer said.

Zari suddenly understood. She was sure that Haji Mohammad Reza, the dyer, had given them the snake. She knew that he had pulled the snake's fangs. She said, "I told you they collect animals. This time they have found a snake. But I'm sure it's harmless."

"Would you like to see it, sir?" Hormoz asked.

He emptied the bag on the ground. A brightly colored snake came out of the sack. First it raised its head and cocked it at the lieutenant's shoes. Then it flicked its tongue out and slithered under the desk.

The officer hoisted his feet up. He shouted, "Kill it!" The man from Gholam's village tried to strike the snake with his rifle butt.

The snake escaped the blow. The officer shouted, "You threaten a government agent on duty with a snake."

He didn't finish his sentence. He jumped down from the desk and inadvertently stepped on the snake's head. The man from Gholam's village struck at the snake again. Suddenly, the officer stood at attention, saluted, and said, "Good evening, Your Excellency!" Zari turned around to see Khan Kaka, who was blinking. He smiled at Zari and said, "Sister, you bring your guests here?" The officer began to stammer. His foot was on the snake's head, the snake's back was broken, its tail still thrashing. He said, "Your Excellency, I had no idea it was Your Honor's brother, even though dignity and nobility are manifest in all his features. If I have been impudent, I apologize." And turning to Yusof, he bowed and said, "Why didn't you tell me?"

Then, facing the policemen, he added, "I'll have these bastards thrown in jail." And striking the officer who was closest to him, he said, "Idiot! You arrest the son of the most respectable man in the city and bring him to the guard station?" Abolqasem Khan calmly and majestically said, "Forgive him this time. Convey my regards to His Excellency. It's late, otherwise, I would enjoy the honor of calling on him."

The men were chatting away heartily. The boys told their fathers the whole story from the beginning. They were paying no attention to Zari. They were walking toward the hill, and she no longer had it in her to climb the hill and come down on the other side. She turned to a side street and then reached the main road. She was alone and walked rapidly. Several Indian soldiers were sitting by the stream along the road and another was standing under a tree urinating. As Zari walked by, he turned his whole body toward her, his trousers still open, and said, "Lady need!" Zari quickened her steps. A gendarme and a police patrolman passed her; they turned around and looked at her. She was hoping against hope that either her son or her husband was behind her. When she reached the side road where their garden was located and saw no one following her, on second thought, she was glad that she had gotten there on her own. When she arrived at the garden, she was surprised.

They hadn't arrived. The twins were sleeping under the mosquito netting. She sat by the pool and put her face in the water. Then
she sat at the edge of the pool and soaked her feet in the overflow
ditch. The water was lukewarm. She put her hand on the stone head
on the ledge. Whenever they had to irrigate the garden from the
well, the well water would pour into the pool through the mouth
of the stone head. Hoseyn Kazeruni would come and bring a little cushion, which he placed on the seat next to the pulley, and from
morning until sundown he would sit on the cushion and turn the
pulley with his feet. His hands were free, except for when the pail
of water would appear. He would take the pail and pour it into the
little pool that led to the reservoir. Alone, from morning until
sundown, this is all he did. And he went to other houses to do the
same. He didn't even sing. How does he keep from getting bored?
Zari thought. And to provide him with some distraction, she
would send the children to watch him and talk to him. But how
long could they stand watching him? And suddenly Zari thought,
My whole life has been just like this. Every day I have sat behind
a pulley, turning the wheels of life and watering the flowers . . .
     Khanom Fatemeh called her from the roof. She asked, "Did Khan
Kaka arrive in time?"
     Zari lifted her head and said, "Sister, please come down. I don't
feel like listening to their fussing."
     There was a loud knock at the garden gate. Gholam went to
open the gate in his short sleeves and felt hat, with a lantern in
his hand. They all came in. But Khosrow followed Gholam
toward the stable and went to Sahar's make-believe grave. In the
light of the lantern, Zari could only see his feet. Involuntarily, she
got up to see what he was doing. With his feet he kicked the flower
pots one by one. Then he sat on the ground and dug out the stones
arranged around the grave. He pulled them out one by one and
threw them into the garden. Sparrows could be heard moving in
the trees, and a bird flew in the dark. The others walked toward
her and sat on the wicker chairs. Khanom Fatemeh came down
from the roof. She was bareheaded and wore a long white nightgown.
     Khan Kaka said, "Sister-in-law, which way did you come
back? Halfway up the hill we realized that you weren't with us. We

came to the road looking for you." He took off his hat and wiped the sweat off his brow with his hand and asked, "I don't suppose there is any whiskey to be found in this house; won't you be charitable to us with a bottle of that wine Tavus Khanom makes for you? And of course there is no Dutch cheese around here; I'll be happy with the goat cheese wrapped in sheepskin and some thyme. After all, I'm content with whatever God provides."

Zari, still standing, was watching Khosrow, who was walking alone along the garden walkway. His footsteps could be heard on the gravel, but he was not visible in the dark. He came up to his mother and threw her the package he was carrying: the sack, the rope, and the blanket.

"Mother, why did you make up so many lies? Why?" Turning to his father, he added, "Father, ask them why they all conspired to deceive me. Would they have dared if you had been here?"

Yusof sighed and said, "I have come to the conclusion that I am incapable of changing anything. If a man can't even influence his wife—"

The aunt interrupted Yusof and said, "We were afraid you would do something foolish and endanger your life, just like you did—and don't shout so much—the children will wake up."

Khosrow raised his voice even louder than before and shouted, "Either the children are asleep or the ladies are afraid. What cowards and liars women are! All they can do is dig graves, bury, and then weep."

Khan Kaka blinked and said, "Sister-in-law, what happened to the wine?" Zari looked at him; she looked at all of them. How they all appeared like strangers!

Abolqasem Khan bit his lip and, turning to Khosrow, said, "But I told you that it was my fault, dear boy. Don't bicker with your mother so much." Then he turned to Zari. "Sister-in-law, get us the wine; I want to drink to the children's health."

Zari set out like a wind-up robot, went to the storeroom, and came back. Khadijeh followed her with a tray of drinks and snacks. She heard Khanom Fatemeh say to Hormoz, "You, who are older, should have come and told us. You frightened poor Zari half to death tonight."

"If we had told you, you would have tried to change our minds," Hormoz answered.

The aunt continued, "What if you had been spotted and shot at when you were climbing over other people's walls?"

"Well, we weren't spotted," Hormoz said. "and no one shot at us. Our plan was for me to climb over the wall, pull Khosrow up with the rope tied around his waist, throw the blanket over Sahar's head, take him out through the back door of the garden, and release the snake in the garden for revenge."

Abolqasem Khan poured wine in three glasses. He gave one of them to Hormoz and said, "To your health!" And addressing Hormoz, he said, "Drink from now on and try to enjoy this world. I hope you won't turn out to be like your uncle, who has ruined his own life and that of others around him by worrying about the people and the country. Brother, why don't you pick up your glass? I swear to God the world isn't worth crying alone in the desert for justice, your frustration gnawing away at you. A smart man of the world like myself has his smuggled whiskey provided for him. You can't refuse to take any advantage of these Europeans at all. Behind your back, they have the time of their lives and laugh at you. Let me give you all a piece of good news. As the saying goes, 'my donkey has crossed the bridge.' My position as a member of Parliament has been confirmed. The telegram of my approval arrived from Tehran this morning." He then stood up straight and snapped his fingers in the air.

Khosrow asked sadly, "Uncle, you're probably going to Tehran and taking Hormoz with you, aren't you? We had made such plans together."

Khan Kaka blinked and said, "Yes, boy, I'm going to take Hormoz. He's lucky that I'm going to take him. Here, you've really become two sheep-like disciples of that fellow Fotuhi. The fool has gone to Bushire to incite the seamen. He's gone to Esfahan to get a permit to start a Bolshevik Party here, damn it." He turned to Yusof and added, "I hear the fellows came to you first. Thank God you were wise enough in this one instance to turn them down. I don't believe in these party games at all. I was also invited to join the Baradaran Party. I didn't tell them I wouldn't. But so far, I have evaded them."

Then he laughed and continued, "Even so, it is not a bad thing. One brother flirts with Russia and the other with England. And when the time comes for them both to get caught, they will come to each other's rescue. But you're not the kind to come to your brother's aid, dear Yusof." He lifted his glass. "To your health!" he said, then rolled up some roasted chick pea and meat patties, pickled eggplant, and fresh herbs in a piece of flat bread. He handed it to Khosrow and continued: "I was there when the man who was reporting it to the Governor told us how beautifully you had spoken and stood up to them. I said, 'Well, after all, my brother is not chopped liver; he's got a Ph.D. in agricultural economy from the University of Manchester, or rather . . . Hardfart.' " He laughed and added, "To tell you the truth, I'm rattling off these names now. I didn't mention the name of your university there. In fact, I've forgotten its name. The man was saying that you told them you were not made for servitude, neither individual nor collective servitude. You told them you despised party discipline. I know that laziness prevented you . . . but in any case, for once in your life, you did us proud."

Yusof shook his head bitterly. "The man who was reporting it probably had his own ulterior motives and hadn't understood most of what I said or didn't repeat it because you were there."

Abolqasem Khan defended the man. "No, dear brother, from the report he gave the Governor, it was quite clear that he caught your drift."

"I told them basically that it is not as easy as they think," Yusof said. "I told them, 'Marxism or even socialism is a difficult ideology that requires careful education.' I told them, 'Adapting it to our way of life, psychology, and social attitudes requires maturity, broadmindedness, and unlimited self-sacrifice.' I said, 'I'm afraid it'll be like putting on a show with inexperienced actors. For a few days, the new actors and the novelty of their lines will draw a crowd to your show. But soon you will bring both to your audience and players despair, boredom, disappointment, and helplessness.' I told them, 'To do something for the people of this country you need an enlightened heart, clear thinking, and no outside interference."

Khan Kaka blinked and said, "And what actors . . . the Cat of

Shah Cheragh . . . Masha'allah the Hernia . . . Fotuhi . . . the Long-Faced Seyyed Aqa, the son of Qavam's wet nurse . . ."

Yusof answered sadly. "I didn't mean to insult anyone. Any day I would prefer one of those you mentioned to most of the players of this 'Golden Age.' "

Hormoz laughed. He had become light-headed. Abolqasem Khan threw a reproachful glance his way. Hormoz lifted his glass to his lips clumsily, his face contorted. He swallowed a sip and said, "My uncle is right."

His father raised his voice reproachfully, "Who asked you, little twerp, for your opinion?"

Khanom Fatemeh interceded. "Khan Kaka, let him speak his mind. Don't cut the child off like that in front of everybody."

Hormoz stammered, "That same Masha'allah the Hernia has so far sold two of the houses in the Tal-e Hasirbafha District he inherited from his father and used the money to have cooked lentils and rice distributed among the poor."

Abolqasem Khan blinked. "Son, don't keep making up stories. Get up, let's go. It's late. I was in such a hurry that I forgot my pass. We'll be lucky not to get stopped."

He got up and, addressing Yusof, said, "Do you think England will just stand by with her arms folded watching anybody do whatever the hell he wants in the south? You'll see that if the British aren't able to buy off all of them together, they will buy off a few of their big shots and leaders, and then woe be it to the fate of the gullible but sincere and blind believers!"

The uncle left and Yusof asked Khosrow, "How many times have you been to Fotuhi's house?"

"Four times."

"Did he encourage you to go steal the horse?"

"No. Just like you were saying tonight, he, too, said that we should try to find a solution ourselves. Hormoz said, 'Let's have a sit-in protest.' I said, 'No, we'd better go steal it.' "

"Shouldn't you have told your mother where you were going?"

Khosrow snickered. "Tell mother? I'm not a baby anymore. I'm a man in my own right now. Mother keeps covering things up. She only knows how to stop you from doing anything. This was the first thing that Mr. Fotuhi told us. He said, 'Bridges must be destroyed so there will be no way to turn back. All these things are like lessons; we must memorize them.' "

Zari said angrily, "That sure makes me feel proud! One has to have reasons to destroy the bridges. What's your reason? Have you ever gotten anything but love, kindness, and caring from your father and me? Have we for one moment neglected your lessons, school, food, or amusement? If Fotuhi wants to do anything, let him go take care of his poor sister in the insane asylum, who stares at the door waiting for him to come and take her to the 124,000-square-meter garden."

Khosrow said, "As Mr. Fotuhi says, when the society is set straight, then nobody will go crazy and every place will become a garden." Zari flew off the handle and said in a contemptuous voice, "Really? Could a man like Fotuhi set the society straight?"

Khosrow turned to his father and asked, "Can't he, father?"

The father answered, "Even if Fotuhi and the likes of him can't, at least they give the people the opportunity for a great experience."

Khosrow said helplessly, "I don't understand, father. Say things that aren't above the fifth grade." And suddenly getting back at his mother, he said, "No matter what he does, Mr. Fotuhi doesn't constantly tell lies, and he defends your rights behind your back."

Zari said in a calm and motherly tone, "I lied about Sahar on the instructions of your uncle. Moreover, I don't want you to grow up in a quarrelsome and violent environment. I want at least our home to be calm, so that—"

Khosrow finished his mother's statement. "So that, as Mr. Fotuhi says, we can be like a mule with blinders and never know where we are led. Just like—"

Yusof said imperiously, "That's enough."

"No, let him say it," Zari said. "He means a jackass like me. Now do you father and son want to hear the truth? Then listen. Do you remember the wedding day of the Governor's daughter? They came and borrowed my emerald earrings and they didn't give them back, no matter how long I waited. On the day of the foreigners' celebration, the Governor's daughter said that she was grateful for my gift. Then the business of the horse came up. I had decided to resist, despite Khan Kaka's insistence, and not to give into them this time. I knew that eventually we had to stand up to them. But I got scared. Yes, scared. I got scared of the gendarme who came for the horse."

Khosrow interrupted his mother and said, "That gendarme, the crazy fool, was from Gholam's village. You could have pulled the wool over his eyes. You know how to do that very well," and turning to Yusof, added, "The same gendarme followed me halfway up the hill and told me I could go ride my horse every morning. He said the little lady didn't mind, that she had said so herself. He said the animal's lost a lot of weight. He wouldn't let the little lady ride him in the beginning, but now she rides him a few rounds right there in the garden. But she hasn't the courage to ride the horse outside the garden. He said he himself taught Sahar to trot. He said Gholam beat him up." Khosrow began to cry like a little boy who has his toy taken away and given to another child. He was no longer the boy burning with desire to be a man.

Zari continued. "That same night, I wanted to tell you about the earrings, but you were already so angry, and I didn't want to make it worse. It's always like that . . . to keep peace in the family."

Khosrow finished his mother's sentence. "Whom I always deceive."

"When I said that's enough, I meant it," Yusof said in a stern tone, and in a calm, deep voice, added, "Your mother is not at fault. The situation here is such that the best school is the British school, the best hospital the missionary hospital. And when they want to learn embroidery, it is on a Singer sewing machine, the salesman for which is Zinger. Your mother has only known instructors and teachers who have tried to keep her away from reality and instead teach her politeness, etiquette, conformity, coquetry, embroidery, and how to smile. She always talks about peace . . ." And suddenly turning to Zari, he shouted, "Woman, what use is a peace based on deception? Why shouldn't you have the courage to stand up to them and say, 'These earrings were my husband's wedding gift to me, a memento from his late mother, who out of poverty became a housemaid in exile, but her thoughts were with the bride that her son would choose . . . and now, should I just give them up so easily? The earrings themselves and what they are worth are not so important. What is important is the memory and love behind them.' Woman, think a little. When you give in so easily, everybody pushes you around."

Khanom Fatemeh, who had been silent for a long time and was yawning, ran out of patience. "What's the matter with you—father and son ganging up on this poor soul? Giving up the horse wasn't her doing at all. I was a witness. I even told her to give up the horse. As for the earrings, I only heard about them from Ezzatoddowleh. At first, I was very upset, but when I thought about it, I realized she couldn't have done otherwise. What can one do against people who rule over everybody's life and property? Do you want to know the truth, brother? She is a pushover. She gives bribes so no one will bother you. Now, that's enough. Eat your dinner and go to bed. By tomorrow morning you will have forgotten the whole thing. I, for one, am going to bed." And she got up and left.

Khosrow got up too. "Now, you'll see what I'll do. I'm not my father's son if I don't get Sahar back out of their clutches. I'll write to the Governor personally. If he doesn't answer, I'll go see him in person. My father and my teacher, Mr. Fotuhi, are right. I must solve my own problems. If the Governor doesn't let me in, I won't cry. Nobody is ever going to see my tears again! Mother, it was only for your sake, because I knew you would be worried, that I cried when we were caught tonight. In front of Hormoz, in front of the gendarme, in front of that officer . . . If it weren't for these women, how quickly boys could become men . . . The women keep being afraid and scaring us men, too . . . Comrade Fotuhi . . ."

Zari said, "Yes, dear. In your opinion and that of your father and teacher, I am a coward, a weakling. I am always afraid that something might happen to one of you. I can't bear the thought. But I, too . . . when I was a girl, I, too, was brave in my own way." Turning to Yusof, she asked, "Wasn't it brave of me on that day of rioting to walk with you without having seen or known you before . . . what girl . . . ?" And she bit her tongue and said instead, "In that same British school, you are right, the headmistress kept humiliating us in order to civilize us, to teach us manners and how to live. Zinger kept making us feel indebted to him because he was teaching us sewing, so we would be able to make a living on our own. Khanom Hakim would say our recovery and cure was in her hands, but I knew in the bottom of my heart that they were only telling half the truth and that there was always something rotten somewhere. I knew that we were, all of us, constantly losing something, but we didn't know what it was."

"That's why I married you," Yusof said. "Why should you have changed so much?"

"But I told you; must I repeat it a hundred times? You are frighteningly frank and this frankness of yours—again, I know in the bottom of my heart—is dangerous. If I want to stand up to anyone, I must first stand up to you and then what a war of nerves will begin. Do you want to hear more truths? Then listen. It is you who have taken my courage away. I have put up with you for so long that it has become a habit with me."

Yusof shouted angrily. "Me? Stand up to me? I, who am like a tiger outside the house and in the house turn into your obedient lamb? Out of instinct, you put on a show of courage, a raw, unrefined instinct . . ."

Zari thought, If I shout a bit more, we'll have a really good argument. She thought about it and said, "Maybe I have always been a coward and not known it; I stood up to that headmistress several times without knowing what I was doing. That day, when they made Mehri break her fast, all the other kids ran away because they were scared, but I stayed. Maybe it just happened, I don't know. Maybe in those days, I had nothing to lose, but now . . ."

She didn't know what happened, but she lost all her self-restraint, patience, and tolerance. Suddenly, she stood up from the chair, hit her belly hard with her hand and said, "I hope this one in my belly is aborted this very night. For you, I have gone to the brink of death and come back. Khanom Hakim ripped open my belly and spread out my insides. On my belly she drew a map . . ."

She collapsed on the chair and burst into tears. She felt that no one in the world was as tired and depressed as she was. Yusof came up to her, held her head in his arms, and kissed her hair. Then he wiped her tears with his fingers. He put his hand under her chin, lifted her head, looked in her eyes, held back his own tears and said, "Don't cry, my darling. Why didn't you tell me before? I was absolutely caught by surprise."

Zari could not control her tears. She moaned, "Today, damn it, I went to have this one aborted. Wasn't I courageous to keep it? When you give birth to a child with so much hardship, you can't endure losing it so effortlessly. Every day I . . . every day I turn like a pulley on a well to water my flowers. I can't stand to see anyone trample them. Like Hoseyn Kazeruni, I don't do anything for myself with my hands. I have neither any experience nor knowledge of the world."

Yusof laughed. "Dear, instead of going to the insane asylum and tiring yourself and letting it upset you, you can go to the newly opened Iran-Britain Society and teach *Essential English II!* Would you believe Zinger has sent a message to me through MacMahon?"

Zari said through her tears, "You sure know how to make fun of me."

"You know I can't bear to see you in tears," Yusof said softly. "I wanted you to have a good laugh at this offer. But my darling, if you had told me the truth earlier this evening, we wouldn't have tortured you so. You said you had gone to Miss Masihadam's office but quickly brushed it aside. Why did you hide it from me and let me pounce on you like a hungry wolf and now be embarrassed to look at you?"

Khosrow had sat on the ground next to his mother. He hugged his mother's legs, but said nothing.

Zari wiped her tears and said, "You had just come back from your trip; you were depressed and upset. I didn't want to make you more depressed." She asked helplessly, "What should I do to satisfy you? What should I do to become courageous?"

Yusof said laughing, "I can teach you. Your first lesson in courage is this: First, when you are afraid to do something, if you are in the right, do it in spite of your fear, my cute kitten!"

"I am a human being," Zari said thoughtfully. "I'm not a cute kitten. Anyway, first lessons are given to people who are dead between the ears."

In bed under the mosquito netting, despite Yusof's cool hand that caressed her hot belly, and despite his kisses, Zari seemed to have forgotten all about coquettishness and playfulness. She kept wondering whether she had always been a coward or had become one, and whether Yusof was to blame. For one instant, she even concluded that marriage is wrong in principle. It is not right for a man to be tied down all his life to a woman and a bunch of children. Or, for that matter, for a woman to be so dependent on a man and a few children that she cannot breathe in peace. But she could see that all the joys of her own life depended on these attachments. The memory of those days of absolute detachment as a girl deprived her of sleep. The memory of the day when the headmistress had forced Mehri to break her fast was still vivid in her mind.

That year, Zari and Mehri were to get their elementary school diplomas. It was four months before the final examination when a letter came from the Office of Education stating that sixth-grade students must be taught the Koran and religious law at school. Zari knew that her mother's petitions had worked. But Zari's mother didn't have enough money for a private tutor to teach Zari the Koran and religious law. Letter after letter came, and announcement after announcement. And the headmistress was becoming more flustered every day with the persistence of the Office of Education. But Zari knew that all this pressure was the result of her mother's perseverance.

During those days, their course on etiquette with the headmistress had turned into a course on nagging about the Office of Education. The headmistress complained, "Our deal with the Office of Education from the beginning was that they should not interfere in our work." She would complain, "Where in the world am I supposed to find a Koran and religious law teacher? What extra hours do I have to fit such courses in? And, you are off on Sundays, so you can go to some old woman who teaches these things and study with her, or let your parents teach you." She used the old-fashioned Arabic word for parents, and very properly too. This one knew Persian well.

Mehri knew both the Koran and religious law. After all, Mehri was the niece of the spiritual guide of the dervishes. Keeping it a secret from the headmistress, she agreed to teach the Koran and religious law to her classmates when they came back to school after lunch. How hard Zari tried to pronounce "fasayakfikohomollah" correctly. But Mehri was very patient. She was a year or two older than the oldest student in the class . . . And then the month of Ramazan came. She had just taught them the prayer that is said during the solar and lunar eclipses or earthquakes. It seems like only yesterday.

The headmistress pushed Mehri down to the classroom floor, sat by her head, opened her mouth with her hands, put a finger in her mouth and tried to pour water down her throat. Mehri bit the headmistress' hand and the headmistress shouted angrily, "You miserable wretch!" Then Mehri sat up and said, "The filthy hand of you, an infidel, touched my mouth, so my fast is automatically broken. Give me the water; I'll drink it all. You'll be responsible for the sin."

The headmistress slapped Mehri and again Mehri fell to the floor. She then left Mehri and stood before the class to administer a scolding. The kids started to whisper and no one was listening. The Indian teacher, her eyes wide, only watched. The headmistress shouted, "There is no room for superstition in this school. Leave fasting and religious sermons to your aunts! Ask your mothers about menstruation and parturition! Fasting makes you physically weak. Why did I buy a horizontal bar, a balance beam, and a basketball net? For your bodies to become strong. Now you fast and ruin all my work? You certainly don't deserve any of this."

She kept shouting at the girls. "The bell has rung—why don't you leave the classroom? Mehri's punishment is to stay right here on the floor until sunset. Girls! Get out. No one is permitted to stay with Mehri."

The headmistress left and the Indian teacher tossed her hair over her shoulder and followed her. The other girls left too. But Zari felt that she could not leave. She bent over, took Mehri's hand, and helped her up. She shook the dust off her clothes, seated her in the teacher's chair, and looked for a handkerchief to wipe her tears. But she didn't have a handkerchief and she couldn't find Mehri's either. She wiped Mehri's tears with her fingers, kissed her, and

said, "I don't think your fast is broken. After all, you were forced
to drink the water."

Mehri kept crying. "There's only two or three hours before the
time to break the fast. I've observed the fast for twelve days. I even
started two days earlier as a sign of welcoming Ramazan. I had
decided to fast all thirty days of this holy month. I know that I'll
begin menstruating next year and I will never be fortunate
enough to get a chance like this again."

"Next year is a long way off," Zari said. "Besides, you taught
us yourself that women in menopause don't get periods. When you
go into menopause, you can fast the whole thirty days."

Mehri laughed and laughed and Zari was happy to have made
her laugh.

Mehri said, "I know who the tattletale was—Taji. That stupid
girl has become a Christian. I know that His Holiness Ali will strike
her down and she'll fail this year. Tonight there is a chanting ses-
sion for Ali and I hope my uncle curses her."

They arrived at the dervish friary together. The gate to the House
of Ali was open and a voice was heard chanting rhythmically, "Ya
Hu, ya Haq, ya Ali."

12

AFTER ALL the turmoil, fights, reconciliations, and sleepless nights, that very Friday morning Sahar headed back to their house on his own feet. They were all gathered on the veranda in the back of the house, which was not in direct sunlight and faced the hill Zari and Yusof had so anxiously and laboriously climbed the night before. Zari was ironing on the breakfast table. The hill, flooded in light, rested before her—as though no one had either climbed or descended it the night before. Khosrow was sitting across from her and had a pen, paper, and a few books in front of him on the table. He was leafing through a volume on *The Principles of Letter Writing* and reading, "Write a letter to the director of a department and request a position." "Write a letter to your uncle and ask him . . ." "Write a letter to your friends and invite them for the anniversary celebration of the birth of the Prophet." "May I be sacrificed to the dust of your bejeweled feet." "Wind has blown, bringing the scent of ambergris . . . I was blessed to receive your missive." He put the volume down on the table and said in a deprecating voice, "As Mr. Fotuhi says, it is all begging and flattery!" He picked up another book and leafed through it.

Although it was morning, the air was hot and there was no breeze. Zari felt perspiration roll down her neck to her spine. She wanted a cool drink flavored with things like betony or pussy willow extract, with a piece of ice that crunches under your teeth. When she was pregnant with Khosrow and later with the twins, the aunt went all out, and every day she prepared whatever she craved. She would order cane sugar, from Hasan Aqa, the herbalist, which was as white as snow and crunched under your teeth and made you feel like you were eating the very essence of health itself; and she said that it strengthened the baby's bone structure. She would buy sheep stomach, clean it herself, cook it with nutmeg, and feed it to her to tighten her belly. If she felt flushed, the aunt would make her drink gallons of tamarind juice, and if she was chilled, she would feed her rock candy melted in hot water. But ever since the aunt had decided to emigrate, she had lost all enthusiasm and didn't have patience for anyone, even the children. It was obvious, but Zari would not bring it to her attention.

Khosrow put down the book. "What writers! They haven't written a word about how to get back what is rightfully yours." He picked up another book, leafed through it, and read, "Two letters! I found it . . . What beautiful sentences!" He lifted his head and asked his father, who was sitting on an easy chair facing the hill and reading a book, "Father, what does it mean, 'His throaty voice was reminiscent of a cello?' " His eyes still on his book, Yusof answered, "It means like the bellowing of a cow. It won't do for Sahar. Son, write what comes to your own head."

The aunt's voice was heard telling Mina, "Give it to me. It's been through thousands of hands; it's dirty." The aunt was sitting on a small carpet facing the hill, leaning against the veranda railing, placing the golden *dinars* she had bought between the material and the lining of her jacket, and sewing them in long stitches. This was her only work in recent days, and she had just started on the second jacket.

Gholam came to the veranda and asked, "Are Kolu's clothes ready, ma'am?"

"Just a minute," Zari said.

Gholam said, "It's not my place to say, but why do they need to be ironed? Last night, all night long, he had dreams about cows and sheep. He kept waking up and looking for his kid goat. He was hey-heying so much in his sleep that he didn't let me sleep. This morning, he was sobbing. He says, 'I want my mama, my sister . . . my brother.' I doubt if he can stand it here."

Khosrow laughed, despite the fact that he was busy writing. Marjan was stacking up the aunt's gold *dinars* to make a tower, and Mina would knock them over and scatter them. As always, the plans and schemes were Mina's, who knew she was older because she had been born fifteen minutes before Marjan. Khanom Fatemeh shouted at them, "Get up; off with you. Money is not a toy. Go call Kolu to come here. Gholam, take them to the stable . . ."

The children pretended to cry and crawled under the table. Zari said, "Go put on the *chadors* that your aunt made for you and show them to your daddy."

Mina came out from under the table and said, "Auntie, will you give us prayer stones so we can say prayers and stick our little butts in the air?" When the aunt stood up to pray, they too put on their *chadors* and bowed up and down behind her. And when the aunt uttered the Arabic phrase, "walazzalin," they would suddenly prostrate themselves. Only God knew what these innocent worshipers wanted of Him. They would try very hard to pronounce "walazzalin," but couldn't and would tell their aunt, "Now you say it."

Zari finished ironing Khosrow's old shirt and trousers that she had widened, lengthened, and stretched at the seams for Kolu and gave them, along with the undershirt, underpants, and socks, to Gholam. "Sprinkle all of them with louse insecticide. Buy him a pair of *givehs,* too." She sat down. She felt as if her stomach were on fire, perhaps because of the heat of the iron.

"There is no more powder left," Gholam said. "I put it all in the ewer, mixed it with water, and sprinkled it all over the stable. The stable is infested with lice."

"Go and send Kolu here," Yusof said.

Zari said, "Let him take him to the bath first."

"He won't come, sir," Gholam said. "This morning he was like a wild animal. He wanted to run off into the hills. He said he would walk back to his mama."

After Gholam left, Khanom Fatemeh said, "Brother, you can't keep him here. It's like the baby deer that we finally killed. It really is none of my business. For a day or two, I will be your guest, and after that, my prayers will be with you."

Zari thought to herself that she was right. When she saw Kolu yesterday, his eyes looked like those of the fawn, large, as if blackened with *kohl,* bewildered, and scared. True, he smiled at his master's wife, but deep in his eyes was the fear of a cornered puppy.

"It's too soon for him to be taken out of his environment," Zari said. "No matter how good we are to him, it will be of no use. We'll only provoke his hostility and the curses of his kin."

Yusof said impatiently, "A few days of comfortable living and he will get used to it and won't mention the village any more. Next year, I'll send him to school."

Khosrow stopped writing, laughed and said, "Father, only if we send him to school in a gunnysack. He's quite wild. Besides he's too old; he won't be admitted."

Yusof, closing the newspaper, asked absentmindedly, "In a gunnysack?"

Khosrow said, "Yes, father. I saw it when they sent Davud Khan's son to school from the village. They brought him straight to school. I was in the second grade. At recess, we saw a nomad with a long moustache and a felt hat, slit gown, a shawl wrapped around his waist and *maleki* shoes come to school on a mule. On his saddle was a gunnysack, the opening tied securely, and something was wiggling in it. He got off the mule and with one hand tied its reins to the same tree that I tie Sahar's reins to whenever I take him to school. All this time he had his other hand on the gunnysack and was keeping it balanced. Then he picked up the gunnysack, put it on his shoulder, brought it into the school courtyard, and opened it. The khan's son jumped out of the gunnysack, wearing no shirt and a pair of long black trousers held up with a white string and took off, it wasn't clear for where or for what. He started to run aimlessly around the school courtyard. Do you think anyone could catch him?"

Zari gathered up the ironing things and took them to the pantry. She went to the cupboards. They didn't have a drop of aromatic extract left. She went to the kitchen. Khadijeh, wearing nothing but a pair of flowered panties, her sagging breasts and the prickly hair under her arms exposed, was frying eggplants on the stove. When she saw her mistress, she looked for her *chador.*

Zari went out the garden gate with her purse and two large pitchers to the neighbor's—the distillers. She went through the open gate onto the patio in the middle of the garden, where there were no flowers. The distillers were nowhere in sight. She almost shouted, "Anybody here?" She walked toward the house; she knew that the distilling vats were in the cellars. She had a strange desire to pour betony extract in a big decorated china bowl, mix it with sugar syrup and ice, stir the ice with her fingers in the bowl and with a deep wooden ladle with an engraved handle . . . She knew that even if the distillers were not there, she could go to the vats, fill both pitchers, and leave the money somewhere where it could be seen. When she reached the house she shouted once again, "Anybody here?" The old man's head appeared from behind the window of one of the cellars. With one eye, he looked at her through the stone lattice work of the window. He then came out. He was wearing pajama bottoms. He said, "Ma'am, you shouldn't have gone to so much trouble," and then, "Please come to the vats and take whatever you wish. We have been waiting for the last crop of sweetbriars, which hasn't arrived yet. The flowers will wilt. They say the city has been blocked off. A horse has run off with the Governor's daughter; they won't let any deliveries through."

Zari put the pitchers down. The distiller said, "I'll go to the garden; I've sent the kids after the load. Let me see if they've shown up. I know the flowers will wither. The city has turned into a land of infidels. Now, why does a girl need to go horseback riding so the horse runs off with her? Can one say to these infidels, 'Flowers don't have the endurance of human beings? And sweetbriars, for that matter, which have to be picked at dawn and put into the vats in the early morning. You can't keep the flowers in this hot sun.' "

Zari did not know whether to be happy or sad. After all, the Governor's daughter was also the child of a mother who had labored over her. Sahar is a noble horse; he wouldn't throw his rider. But how frightened the girl must be! And how worried her mother!

She took the pitchers to the cellar. What lovely perfume filled the air and how cool it was! They had removed the covers of the stone vats, made especially for boiling flowers, and leaned them against the wall. The tips of the bamboo cane pipes, which went from the vats to the reservoir, were dry, unlike previous times when she had brought the children to watch; no small streams of aro-

matic extracts were flowing from them. One of the reservoirs was
filled and the other was half filled with rose water. Full carboys
of rose water were lined up around the cellar. She opened a low
door, bent over, and went into the second cellar. She filled one of
the pitchers with betony extract from the first reservoir. How she
wanted to lie down on the damp dirt floor of the cellar next to
the vats of aromatic extracts and go to sleep.

When she returned home and went to the veranda, she heard
a commotion in the distance. But nobody else was paying attention, otherwise they would have looked up. The sound of a
crowd of people and automobiles mingled and came closer. She
looked at the hill. Not even a bird could be seen. Khosrow was
writing his letter and Yusof was leafing through the pages of a book
and laughing. She asked, "Where are the children?" No one
answered.

Again, her attention turned to the hill. Two automobiles, one
behind the other, were moving on an angle along the slope of the
hill. A voice said, "He's going toward the hill." A bunch of people appeared and started for the hill.

Khosrow said, "I finished my letter. Father, will you listen while
I read it to you?"

Yusof closed his book, rose from the easy chair, looked at the
hill, and asked, "What's going on?"

Khosrow got up and went to the ledge of the veranda and said,
"What a crowd has gathered by the hill! Four . . . five cars!"

A voice was heard, "Did you see him? There he is!" Then a commanding voice, "Don't shoot, idiot!" Someone screamed. The crowd
at the foot of the hill was getting larger by the minute. A policeman and two gendarmes . . . and two other cars, again at an angle,
passed the foot of the hill. The first car was honking its horn as
if it were going to the scene of a fire, and how much dust it raised!

Khosrow asked, "Is it a war, father?"

A voice was heard. "He went on the hill." And other voices were
lost in the din of the crowd and the rumble of the car engines.

"I think it's Sahar," Zari said. "Our neighbor, the distiller, said
a horse has run off with the Governor's daughter." Yusof put his
hand on his belly and, laughing heartily, said, "What a war! All this

mobilization for a colt! There he is: Sahar. He's standing on the top of the hill. Let's hope he doesn't throw the rider down from up there."

The aunt was still sitting with her back to the hill. She didn't even turn her head. Trying to thread the needle, she said, "It's just like threading a needle. If you hold the thread right in front of the eye of the needle and your eyes can see well, you will thread the needle right the first time. But if your eyes are half blind, like mine, you've got to keep wetting the thread in your mouth, thinning the thread with your teeth, and bringing it close to where you think the eye of the needle is. The thread goes back and forth so many times until finally it goes through by accident. Now, Khosrow, your horse has come your way accidentally. Go, let's see if you can thread the needle."

Yusof put his hand on his son's back and said, "Your aunt is right; go, son." Khosrow jumped down from the veranda and ran. Although she did not appreciate the aunt's oblique remarks, Zari knelt down by her, took the needle and thread, and threaded the needle for her. The aunt said, "But it is not always your fault, either. They don't let you go the right way from the beginning, and then you have to struggle and run into dead ends until finally you can make up for the mistaken path you've taken."

"Sister," Yusof said. "Since you have decided to emigrate, you've become quite a philosopher."

The aunt sighed and retorted, "Pillow-sobber."

Zari saw a car moving toward the hill with difficulty. On the peak, Sahar began neighing and swaying. His rider held his yellow mane tightly and screamed so loudly that her voice pierced through the hubbub of the crowd. The mare and the roan horse answered Sahar's neighs from the stable. Yusof said, "I knew that the first day they rode him outside the four walls of their garden he would gallop to his old stable."

"At least the animal has done something," the aunt said.

A new, long, black car arrived. A policeman saluted and the gendarmes presented arms. The driver jumped out. The man who was sitting in the middle of the back seat opened the door himself and got out. Zari recognized him. It was the Governor. Another car came and stopped right behind the Governor's. Zinger got out with two Indian soldiers. Zinger shook hands with the Governor.

The crowd kept getting scattered by the haphazard movement of the cars, and assembled again. The car that had driven
toward the hill backed up without honking its horn. The driver
was probably afraid that Sahar would be spooked and run off again.   ·
    The Governor and Zinger were both standing with their backs
to the garden. Then they turned toward the garden and the
Governor signaled with his hand. The driver stepped forward. The
Governor told him something and the driver started toward the
garden. But he didn't come through the gate that opened at the
foot of the hill, even though it was ajar. It was obvious that he was
going to go around the garden.
    Zari was looking for her son among the crowd, but could not
see him. Now was the time; where was he? The car of the commander of the army arrived, too. The commander and three
officers got out and slammed the doors noisily, and the car
moved on and, with difficulty and listing toward the Governor's
and Zinger's cars, passed them. The commander of the army looked
around. The officers placed their hands on their swords and
started up the hill. The Indian soldiers saluted the commander.
Zinger's hand was going up for a military salute when the commander took it and lowered it. The commander then saluted the
Governor himself. Now Yusof held a pair of binoculars, which he
sometimes used to watch the hill himself and sometimes gave to
his wife.
    Sahar neighed several times. The rider was holding tightly to
the horse and had her head down on the horse's mane. Sahar slipped
on some rocks and staggered.
    The commander of the southern army was holding a short, thick,
black crop. He left the Governor and Zinger and started for the
hill, shouting, "Gili, dear, take your foot out of the stirrup, sit side-
ways and jump down."
    The voice of Gilantaj was heard, "I'm afraid! I'm afraid!"
    Yusof said, "What an idiot!" Zari couldn't tell whether he
meant the commander or "Gili Dear."
    Sahar seemed to have noticed the officers. One unwound a rope
and tossed the noose toward the horse and rider. Sahar backed off,
the rider screamed, and both disappeared from view. The crowd

started up the hill. The drivers of the cars that had room to move jumped behind the steering wheels, revved the engines noisily, backed up their cars, and drove off. The commander shouted, "Come back, idiots! You've scared the animal. He was standing so calmly . . ." The officers all came back, the one with the rope and those without.

Yusof remarked, "If they had any brains, they would all stand aside and let Sahar bring the girl right here safe and sound."

Suddenly Zari caught sight of Khosrow hurrying up the hill. Her stomach began to churn. She went to the aunt, pleading, "Dear sister, pray, pray for him."

The aunt got up, directed her prayer toward the hill and said, "May God protect him, He is the most merciful of the merciful."

Khosrow had almost reached the top. He whistled with his two little fingers in the corner of his mouth, like he always did for Sahar, to make him come from anywhere in the garden and sniff his sleeves. The crowd suddenly fell silent. Zari looked at her husband. Yusof's whole face had lit up with a smile and his green eyes sparkled like stars. Khosrow whistled again. Sahar's head, turning to the left and right, appeared in sight.

Khosrow shouted, "Sahar, come on; I'm here." And he shouted to the girl, "Don't be afraid, child, he won't throw you." The crowd was so silent that one would have thought Sahar hadn't been frightened and run off and the rider hadn't been scared. Sahar neighed and went toward Khosrow. When he reached Khosrow, he stopped and, like a pet cat, bent his head before him. Zari knew that he was sniffing at Khosrow's sleeves and pockets and inhaling their scent. She knew that the animal's whole life depended on that familiar scent. Khosrow held the horse's head in his arms, kissed it, smoothed his mane, and held his hand in front of the animal's mouth. Zari knew that Khosrow had not forgotten the sugar lumps. Then Khosrow helped the rider dismount. In her riding boots and pants, she first sat on the rocks and then lay down. Khosrow was holding the horse's reins. He bent over and told her something. The girl sat up and screamed. Khosrow was standing in front of the girl and was obviously talking to her. He took her hand and helped her up. Then Khosrow held her under her arms and they and Sahar headed down the hill. Khosrow seemed to be talking to Sahar, because Sahar had stuck both ears forward. Near the foot of the hill, the girl left her companions and threw herself in the arms of her father, who had come toward the hill to meet her. As the boy and the horse reached the foot of the hill, people stood aside to make way for them. Khosrow mounted Sahar and galloped toward the garden.

13

THE MARE was ready to be harnessed. Yusof was about to mount when Kolu came running out of the stable, threw himself at the master's feet, and begged him to take him back to the village. How he had changed with a visit to the bath and barber and a set of second-hand clothes, even though he looked thinner, as if he had been trimmed down in these couple of days. His dark eyes were darting around in his tired face. First, the master tried to reason with him. "Dear child, you will stay in the city; you will go to school; you will become civilized; you will learn a thousand things from Khosrow." Kolu seemed not to have heard, because he did not understand what the master was saying and kept begging and pleading to be taken back to his mama and brother. Yusof boxed Kolu on the ear and said, "I'm not going to Kavar; for now, I'm going to Zarqan." He put his foot in the stirrup. Kolu burst into tears. He threw himself on the dirt in the garden, rolling in the mud. He howled like a trapped puppy. When Yusof bent down from the saddle to kiss his wife, Zari's eyes were wet. Yusof asked, "Do you want me to take him?"

Zari said, "No, he'll be tamed. He can't possibly know what's good for him. But, as you say, what is the use of your charity? Suppose you adopt this one as your son. What about his brothers and sisters? Who will adopt the thousands of other village children like him?"

When Yusof left, the aunt, who was holding a crystal bowl full of water and a few green orange leaves, poured the water on the ground for his safety, as was customary, and went to recite the An'am Sura, in the direction the traveler had gone. What is a human being? How soon a little hope or a happy incident can pique one's appetite for life! But when one faces nothing but dejection and despair, one feels that one has become like refuse, a corpse, or a carcass discarded in a rubbish heap. The aunt had again attached herself to their lives, although recently all she had been saying was, "Of what concern is it to me?"

Zari went to Kolu, who had not stopped rolling in the mud and was now in the middle of the garden. She squatted by him, caressed his hair and said reproachfully, "See, you've gotten your clothes all dirty." Kolu sat up, angrily took off his shirt, rolled it up into a ball and threw it at the master's wife. Zari said, "Look, if you can be a good boy, starting tomorrow I'll have Khosrow give you lessons. When you learn to read, I'll send you back to the village to visit your mother and show her that you can read her letters and write letters to her."

Kolu was silent. He seemed to be listening now, or perhaps he was worn out. "Nobody don't write no letters to my mama," he said. Zari stroked Kolu's sweat-covered back and said, "Get up, dear, wash your hands and face. Shake the mud off your clothes and put them back on." And since Kolu did not move, she asked, "What do you want me to buy you?"

Kolu burst into tears again and said through his tears, "Send me back to the village, mistress. I beg you, on the lives of your children, to send me back to my mama, my brother. Right now my brother is sitting by the stream playing his reed. Right now my mama is putting kerosene in the burner. I put out several traps to catch goldfinches; now the goldfinches are caught in the traps and there is no one to take them out. I put my sling shot on a ledge; Ma'sumeh will take it and lose it. Well, if I was there now, I could have stolen walnuts; I'd sit and crack them."

"The goldfinches are probably chirping and someone will go and let them out," Zari said. "I'll send someone to buy you walnuts and you can sit right here and crack them. And I'll give you a rubber band to make a sling shot."

Kolu smiled sorrowfully. "You make a sling shot with leather, not with rubber," he said.

"Well, I'll send them to bring you leather."

Kolu's mouth drooped. "Nobody will go to them. Their trap is far away from the village."

Zari began to tell tales. "Now look, the master is going from here to the village. He'll probably pass by where you had set the traps. He'll hear the chirping. He'll get off, take the goldfinches out of the traps and set them free."

"But the master ain't going to our village."

Khadijeh's voice was heard from the veranda, "Ma'am, telephone."

"Who is it?"

"Khanom Ezzatoddowleh."

What could she want from her? She probably expected to be fully thanked and would say, "I was the one who had the horse come to your son. Say, Good for you."

When she went into the parlor, she found Khosrow sitting by the window with his hand under his chin looking at the garden. She said, "Khosrow, for God's sake, go play with this poor fatherless boy a little." Khosrow did not move. He said, "Mother, get the idea that I'll give lessons to Kolu out of your head."

Zari went to the telephone. She learned that as soon as Ezzatoddowleh had left their house that day, her bad leg had acted up again and she had been confined to her house. She'd heard that her sister was thinking about going on a pilgrimage to Karbala; she missed Zari, her dear sister, and the twins very much; and they also owed her a visit. Tomorrow morning they were going to change the water of their bath house at home and she would like to invite everyone to honor her with their presence for a bath and lunch on Wednesday. No matter how many excuses Zari made, they were not accepted.

On Tuesday morning, Kolu came down with a fever. Zari darkened the pantry with bamboo curtains, put a bed in it, and put Kolu to bed there to have him close by. Kolu would open his eyes wide and look at his hands with his fingers spread apart. You could tell from his eyes that he wanted to see but could not. Khosrow, Gholam and the aunt all thought that Kolu should be sent to the hospital. There was no doubt that he had typhus, and they might all catch it. But which hospital? Even the first-rate doctors in the city had caught typhus, and it was said that Miss Masihadam and three nurses from the Namazi Hospital were in critical condition. Khadijeh had heard from Sakineh, the baker, that the city's best doctor, Dr. Abdollah Khan, would not leave Miss Masihadam's bedside. He would dip two large towels in ice water, wring them and constantly wrap them around the naked body of the patient. Sakineh, who had gone to visit Miss Masihadam, thought that she was already dead and they had put a shroud on her. She had begun to hit herself on the head and come out to the courtyard, and, in a gesture of mourning, put dirt from the garden on her head . . . And when they had calmed her down, they made her understand what the whole thing was about. So she went to the shrine of Seyyed Mir Mohammad and lit ten candles. It was even said that men and women were putting Korans on their heads during the sermons given at Mehri's, and they had performed the *Amman Yujib* prayers for Miss Masihadam. Also, Akbar Khordel had bought a sheep, gone around the patient's bed with it, then had slaughtered it, distributed the meat among the poor, and made a gift of its skin to Baba Kuhi, who in exchange had chanted prayers for the patient.

The aunt made Zari call Khanom Hakim who said, "Unfortunately, the beds of the missionary hospital exclusively for the foreign officers and soldiers have been, and all the beds filled have been, and even no room left has been in the corridors," and said so many "have beens" and "has beens" that Zari hung up without saying goodbye. Then, turning to the aunt, who was awaiting the results, she said, "Obviously, they built the hospital for the day they would need it themselves."

They put their heads together and began the treatment. They fed Kolu Persian and purgative manna. They soaked towels, wrung them, and wrapped them around his body. They made him drink gallons of watermelon juice. He was very thirsty and willing to gulp down any cool drink. They soaked fleawort, put it in a clean cloth, tied the end with twine, dipped it in a glass of cold water, and, whenever one of them had time, she would put the fleawort ball on the boy's blistered lips. The aunt unwrapped her bundle of white cord that she had put in the Shah Cheragh Shrine for a long time, cut two hand-lengths, tied them around Kolu's neck, and sat by his bed reciting the *Kasa* prayer. Despite all these efforts, it was clear that the aunt's spirits had dampened again. In truth, from the very morning that Zari noticed Kolu's high fever, the aunt had begun innuendoes such as: "Obviously, this orphan child has had a fever for several days, but we didn't notice it and thought that he was homesick. Yes, nothing can take the place of a mother's loving care."

Never mind the hospital; they could not even get a doctor to come to Kolu until late that afternoon. Kolu was now semi-conscious and delirious: "The goldfinches in the trap . . . chirp, chirp. Chirp, chirp. Beak on the dirt . . . legs in the air . . . then fly, fly . . . fly, fly . . . no water, no seeds. My daddy. My daddy's daddy. My daddy, I'm burning."

In the evening, Zari pleaded with Khosrow to go with Gholam to Miss Masihadam's house and ask Dr. Abdollah Khan to drop by for a minute to see their patient. But Khosrow wouldn't go. He said, "I want to take Sahar for a walk, and then go to Mr. Fotuhi's house with Hormoz. Father didn't say that I couldn't go."

Zari exploded. "What an obstinate child!" She shouted, "Fotuhi is crazy like his sister and is misguiding other people's children." She even wanted to add, "He is a pedophile," but she stopped herself in time and said to herself, "God save you, man. What a mess you've gotten me into. What in the world will I do if this poor child dies on my hands?" She swore that if Kolu recovered, she would immediately send him back to the village, whether Yusof liked it or not.

She did not want to ask Khan Kaka, but she had to. Gholam had gone after Dr. Abdollah Khan and returned disappointed. The doctor had said, "I have gotten old. The honorable inhabitants of the city should allow me to retire."

Had Khan Kaka not answered favorably, she would have gone to Miss Masihadam's house herself and begged and dragged the

doctor to the patient's bed. After all, a doctor cannot take sanctuary in the house of one patient and say to other patients that
he has stopped practicing—even if that patient is very young and
has worked hard for the people of the city.

Abolqasem Khan was home. He answered the phone and said,
"I'm surprised you remembered us, sister-in-law!" He was in a gabby
mood again. He would not let Zari get a word in edgewise. He
said, "I've heard that Sahar returned to Khosrow on his own. I was-
n't here that day. To escape from the concerns of my honorable
constituents, I had set out for the country. Can you believe they
think I am their real representative? Their petty requests have already
started. One says, 'Have my patient hospitalized.' Another says,
'Fight for my rights in the Justice Department.' One says, 'Register
my daughter in Mehra'in School free of charge.' But my dear man,
this appointment cost me seventy thousand *tomans*. In any case,
I've heard it was a sight to behold. Zinger said my nephew came
to the field like a ferocious lion. In his shirtsleeves and with cotton sandals on his feet, he pushed everyone aside. Now, sister-in-law,
why didn't Khosrow go in some respectable clothes? In short, he
said, 'As soon as the horse set eyes on him, like a lover who has
found his beloved, he sniffed and kissed him and hid his head in
his arms . . .' But the Governor's driver was complaining about
you, sister-in-law. He said, 'I kept knocking on the garden gate
but no one came to my rescue.' "

Zari explained, "We were on the veranda in the rear of the building and couldn't hear the door over the clamor of the crowd." Then
she forced herself to say, "Khan Kaka, I beg you for your help. Kolu
has caught typhus and is dying on my hands. I couldn't bring a
doctor or anybody to see him. They are all so busy."

"Which Kolu?" asked Khan Kaka. "Why does Yusof bring
the sick villager into the city? And into his house? Doesn't he take
pity on his own delicate children? Didn't he say the whole thing
is rotten from the core and our charity is of no use? That's what
he told you right in front of me, sister-in-law."

"You're right, but Kolu is our shepherd's son. His father just
recently died. He didn't have a fever when he came to the city. Now
he has come down with a fever." She knew if she told him that

Yusof had adopted him as a son, she would have to hear a long lecture about the disadvantages of adopting "another man's child" and what not.

Finally, Khan Kaka consented, saying, "For your sake, sister-in-law, and for the sake of your delicate children, I will arrange for him to be hospitalized in the missionary hospital."

"I called the missionary hospital; they have no room left."

In a proud tone, Khan Kaka said, "They will have room for me."

It was eight o'clock at night when Khanom Hakim called. First she complained, "Why you had not said the patient has been his honor Abolqasem Khan?" Then she said, "A bed prepared in the corridor has been, which separated by a screen has been from an Indian patient, and also the Indian patient stricken with typhus has been. Also, the pills that set aside for the family of his honor Abolqasem Khan's family have been I will give to those who in compact . . . contact have been with the patient."

Tents were erected in the courtyard of the hospital, and cots were put inside them. A sharp odor of phenic acid burned the nose. Most patients were fair-skinned and blonde. They did not have typhus; they were either sitting on the beds, heads bandaged and arms in slings, or were sleeping with bandaged eyes or legs in a cast. Four men sat around a table playing cards. Their yellow hair looked golden in the light of the mantle lamp which hung from the tent pole. There didn't appear to be anything wrong with them.

From the time they got in the *droshky* until they arrived at the prepared bed, Gholam was holding Kolu in his arms. When he set Kolu down on the bed, he put his hands on his waist. From behind the screen came the cries of the Indian patient, angry and saying things which Zari did not understand, "Seri rama, siri rama krishna." His crying got louder and again he uttered words that Zari guessed to be the names of relatives. "Sandra, Sandra, Kitu."

When she returned home, Khosrow had not come back yet. First she wanted to call Fotuhi, say whatever came to her mind, and vent her anger. But she soon gave up the idea. What fault was it of Fotuhi's? Other people's boys were looking for a way to become men and Fotuhi was a tool. She decided to wait for her son to come back, and then take him to task. First I will be calm with him, then angry, and finally I'll tear into him, she thought. He will never forget.

But Khosrow arrived home in a calm disposition and left no room for quarrels, questions, or anger. As soon as he arrived, he put his arms around his mother's neck, kissed her, and said out of the blue, "Mother, you are not of aristocratic descent, are you?" He was making his inquiries hastily. "Your father was a work-er . . . of a . . . class . . . oh, I've forgotten the name of the class . . . in any case, your father was a worker, isn't that right?"

"Why are you asking?"

"The comrades regret very much that Comrade Hormoz and I have a mark of aristocracy, and it will be a long time before we can erase this mark."

Zari burst out laughing and Khosrow confessed that the com-rades even opposed starched and pressed trousers. He said that he and Hormoz had decided to rub dirt on and wrinkle their trousers before going to the meetings, and as for ties, they had to be com-pletely forgotten. Then he admitted that he had made a little cut in the right knee of his new gray trousers and had pulled the thread around where he cut to make them look torn. Then he revealed that he had boasted to the comrades that his maternal grandfa-ther was very, very poor. He said, "Mother, I told them that my mother's mother ate dried bread with nothing else every day, and dried bread had broken her front tooth. I said, 'Now my moth-er takes bread for the prisoners and mental patients every week.' I said, 'In memory of the dried bread that broke her mother's tooth.' "

"You, too, have learned to lie," Zari said.

"The comrades were quite pleased," he continued. "Now, tell me. The day that you stood up to the British headmistress . . . many times you fought and struggled with her. You were saying it just the other night. These struggles are very important to me."

Zari was depressed and thought, What struggles?

That afternoon, a group of British who had just arrived from London were coming to visit the school. Classes were canceled that morning so that Ali Beyg, the Indian janitor, could sweep and clean the classrooms. The headmistress sent the girls home and said that she wanted all of them to return to school by that afternoon, neat, clean and dressed up, and to make sure to put on their clean, pressed white blouses. Zari's father had just recently died, so out of respect for her father's death she wore a black blouse under her black and white plaid school uniform. All the girls who were in mourning did the same. It was not forbidden anyway. Now, where the hell would Zari find a white blouse in the two or three hours she had, and with what money? Her mother was ill and bedridden. She said she had a shooting pain in her breast and small cysts the size of lentils under her arms. But she wouldn't let Zari touch her. She said, "What if the disease is contagious and you catch it?" Her mother couldn't be sent to take the silver ventilation ring off the top of the hookah or their small silver plate with scalloped edges to pawn at Dror, the Armenian silversmith, or rather, sell them, to buy white material for Zari. And besides, even if she could, how could the blouse be sewn in time? In the early months after her father's death, as her mother said, they were in quite a bind. There wasn't any regular pension or anything yet. Later on, the principal of the Sho'a'iyyeh School suggested they write a petition. He had summoned Zari's brother to the office, told him quietly that they could make such a request, and then had instructed him how to write the letter and to whom to address it. When Zari's brother came home and told them about it, the mother bent down and, prostrating herself to offer her thanks to God, said, "I knew it. I knew God Himself would find a way!"

But that day, Zari risked it. She washed the same black blouse, ironed it, and went to school, thinking, She can't kill me, anyway. As soon as the headmistress's eyes fell on her, she was so beside herself that she wanted to beat her. She shouted in anger, "You filthy brat, have you now become disobedient, too?" This one among all her compatriots had learned Persian well.

"I am in mourning," Zari said. "It hasn't been a month yet since my father died."

The headmistress shouted, "Now you even answer back? When did your father ever believe in such superstitions?"

Then she calmed down and said, "What a pity. Your English is better than that of all the other students. I want you to welcome

them in English and recite the poem "If" by Kipling. Otherwise,
I would expel you from school. Am I going to regret exempting
you from tuition?"

Now it was all out. Until then, Zari's classmates had not
known that she did not pay tuition. How can I look them in the
eyes again? she thought.

It was not clear how in a matter of fifteen minutes the headmistress found a white blouse Zari's size and gave it to her, saying, "Put it on."

But Zari was stubborn. "I am in mourning. My father has died,"
she insisted.

The headmistress took the matter into her own hands. In
front of all the students, she carefully removed Zari's plaid uniform, but when she got to the black blouse, she pulled it so hard
that she tore off a sleeve. Then, careful again, she put the white
blouse on her.

Zinger had arrived before everyone else and gathered the girls
in the school garden. Most of the girls had bought sewing
machines from him. He checked the girls over and said: "Like this.
They enter the hall, you pretty ones bow. These give out of own
pocket expenses. They give large school for Christ's path." Then
he called Zari and said, "Zahra, you said welcome; lady stretch hand
to you. You kiss lady hand!"

The assistant headmistress rang the bell and all the girls lined
up and marched to the auditorium to wait. Zinger came into the
hall, followed by a group of old women and men, hunched up and
straight, medium height and short. Zari counted sixteen of them.
Zinger was being more respectful to one of the old women. It
seemed as if sparrows had been buried on her hat. One of the sparrows had opened its wings as if about to fly, but had not yet taken
off. The head of a baby sparrow was also visible.

Zari stepped forward and said her welcome. The headmistress
had a smile on her thin lips, and all the while Zinger had his eyes
fixed on the face of the old woman wearing the hat with the sparrows. The old woman extended her hand, Zari shook hands
with her, and Zinger frowned.

Then Zari joined the other girls, together they sang "Christ in

Heaven," and finished it in voices louder than ever, "Say hallelujah!
Say hallelujah!" Their Indian teacher opened the Bible, tossed back
her long braids that were draped over her breasts, and read the letter of Paul the Apostle to the Corinthians: "If I speak in the language of angels . . ." But when it was Zari's turn to recite the poem,
instead of "If," involuntarily Milton's poem about Samson's blindness sprang from her mouth, "O dark, dark, dark, amid the
blaze of the noon."

At the time of their departure, the headmistress squeezed
Zari's arm and said, "Impudent wretch!" This one knew Persian
well, words that even Zari and her classmates did not know.

14

KOLU'S ILLNESS and the ensuing problems made Zari completely forget the invitation to Ezzatoddowleh's house. But Ezzatoddowleh had not forgotten it. That distinguished lady had probably gone to a great deal of trouble preparing everything, because early Wednesday morning she called to remind them of the invitation.

Now it was the aunt's turn to be difficult.

"You can go," she said. "I, for one, am not going. I went to the bath house the day before yesterday. Sister, you didn't stop me from going. Besides, I don't have the patience for Ezzatoddowleh's pomp and ceremony. She spreads a supper cloth from one end of the room to the other, but her crossed eyes watch every bite you take. She doesn't take her eyes off the sugar bowl to see how many lumps you take. And she probably sees double."

Zari had never in her life been as tired as she had been in recent days. She said, "Sister, the party is for you. Besides, Ezzatoddowleh is your friend." She almost said, "She is your avowed sister and your peer," but she did not say it and continued, "In fact, sister dear, of late you have cut yourself off from us. I thought to myself, because you have your trip in mind, you want to get us out of your heart altogether."

The aunt said, "You're absolutely right. I don't want to miss you when I get there. Besides, I don't want these poor children to keep asking for me as soon as I turn my back."

Finally, the aunt consented. They traveled the avenues in a *droshky,* and the smaller streets and alleys on foot. Khadijeh first would carry Mina and then put her down and carry Marjan. The child who had to walk would take Zari's hand and be led by her cautiously over the rocks in the alleys. They passed through the narrow Qahr-o Ashti alleyway and stopped on the right, just before Sardozzak, in front of the large gateway to Ezzatoddowleh's house, for Khadijeh to catch her breath. The aunt read the Arabic verse inscribed in tile over the house gate, "Lo! We have given thee a signal victory." She threw a glance at their old house across from Ezzatoddowleh's and said, "Look how run-down it is!"

The door was open. As they were passing through the large cool entrance hall, the gate keeper was sitting on a bench with his hands under his chin. As if jumping up from sleep, he suddenly moved and stood up. He took off his felt hat and said, "Please come in." At the door of the outer courtyard, an old black woman was standing with a crystal bowl. She took the lid off, greeted them, and said, "Please have some." The adults each took a piece of jasmine-scented almond confection and put it in their mouths, and the black woman bent down and held the bowl in front of the twins. She then stood up and held it in front of Khadijeh. At the door of the inner courtyard, which was an orange grove, Ferdows was standing in a blue silk *chador* holding a platter of cool, fragrant *dastanbu* melon, which she offered them, just as the black woman with the almond candy had done. Zari put a cool slice of *dastanbu* against her face and smelled its mild aroma, feeling as if she had smelled all the soothing fragrances in the world.

In the large *howzkhaneh,* the fountains of the small marble pools were on. Ezzatoddowleh was sitting on a double-folded blanket in the most prominent place. She apologized for not being able to rise to welcome them, because her sciatica wouldn't leave her alone even in the middle of the summer. She said, "You have honored me; you are so terribly kind to have come. I am so honored that you have consented to come and uplift my spirits."

Ferdows, the wife of Kal Abbas, the gatekeeper, came in with a cashmere bundle, placed it in front of the aunt, and helped her

take off her black *chador.* While Ferdows was carefully folding the
black *chador,* the aunt opened the cashmere bundle, looked at the
stack of *chadors,* chose a plain blue one, and took it out. Ferdows
unfolded the *chador* and put it on the aunt. She then folded the
black *chador,* placed it on top of the stack of *chadors,* wrapped the
bundle, and took it away.

This time, she brought limeade in a decorative china bowl, in
it a china ladle matching the designs of the bowl. She carefully put
the bowl in front of Ezzatoddowleh. The old black maid brought
cut crystal glasses arranged on a silver tray and placed them next
to the bowl of limeade. Ezzatoddowleh delicately poured the
limeade in the glasses, and turning to the aunt, said, "How fortunate Qodsossaltaneh is. I would also have wished to become a
resident pilgrim to such an imam, if it weren't for my sciatica." Zari
had long forgotten that Khanom Fatemeh's aristocratic title was
Qodsossaltaneh.

The aunt said, "First of all, have them shut off those fountains.
Moisture is not good for your legs."

Ezzatoddowleh gave no such order and Zari thought, The leg
ache is a sham . . . and I wish she would get to the point, the reason for all this hospitality and entertainment. And just to say something, she again complimented Ezzatoddowleh on her hair.

Ezzatoddowleh smiled and touched her hair, which was as
beautiful as the black color of bezoar, and said, "Acquaintances,
even the Governor's wife, kill themselves trying to find out the formula that I use . . . but I haven't told anyone. Everyone who sees
it says, "What beautiful hair!" And I respond, "It's your eyes that
see beauty! But Zari dear, I'll tell you. You are like my own
daughter. Your mother, God rest her soul, and I were like one soul
in two bodies. I really wanted you to become my daughter-in-law.
That poor child Hamid only liked you from among all those girls.
Well, it was not to be. I mean, you played hard to get. But your
hair, the color of acorns, is also very pretty and has not yet
turned white. It would be a shame to dye it. As soon as you dye
hair, it suddenly all turns white."

"May God grant you a long life," Zari replied. She thought to
herself, Thank God I didn't become your lecherous son's wife.

Ezzatoddowleh looked at both of them. That is, Zari couldn't tell whether she was looking at her or at the aunt. She said, "I'll tell you, but, for the love of God, don't tell it to anyone else. This is a family secret . . . henna, coffee, cocoa. I add the cocoa to it myself; it softens the hair. Soak one soup spoon each of henna, coffee, and cocoa in chamomile tea and rub it all over your hair. Then cover your hair with fresh walnut leaves and wrap your head overnight or from morning to late afternoon."

Zari couldn't care less about a hair coloring recipe. Had her mother been alive, well, maybe. Her mother had pledged that if God would restore her health, she would take a set of silverware to the shrine of Abolfazl Abbas and then come back and dye her hair like Ezzatoddowleh's. She said she would get the formula out of her by hook or by crook. And where is mother now? Zari prayed to God Ezzatoddowleh would not expect too much in return for all this show of generosity.

When they went to the dressing room of the bath, the black maid was sitting next to His Master's Voice gramophone. She started it when she saw them. "You've gone and broken your promise . . ." The walls of the changing room were white marble halfway up from the floor, and the other half and the ceiling were covered with painted figures. Zari had seen the same bath house and the exercise room behind it on that day, the day that their teacher had dragged all the girls of marriageable age in the ninth grade to Ezzatoddowleh's house under the pretext of an excursion to the historical sites. The house actually was one of the attractions of the city and no important foreign dignitary would visit the city without seeing it.

That day Hamid Khan obviously had taken over the role of the visitors' guide. The large room with sash windows did not yet have electric lights, and Hamid Khan, with the help of a kerosene lamp, was trying to show the girls the artwork on the ceiling. The ceiling was covered, from one end to the other, with pictures of men's and women's heads next to each other. The women had tiny little mouths, eyes like gazelles, and long wavy hair, and the men looked like the women, only with a tuft of hair and no earrings.

That day Zari did not really notice Hamid Khan look her over. But the following week, when Ezzatoddowleh intruded on their private cubicle in the public bath and began to watch her naked body with her crossed eyes, she immediately understood. Her look sent chills down Zari's spine. That woman's eyes seemed to want to strip something away from her. And she had her nerve: She put her hand under Zari's chin, held her face up to the little light coming from the bath window and said, "May God protect her . . . God protect you . . . I have never seen a body this white and smooth, like Chinese porcelain. Your eyes are the color of dates. I've never seen eyes this color. God has created you for the love of His own heart. 'God's blessing on the most beautiful of creatures!' I swear to God, if you weren't in the bath, I would have thought you had put on rouge or something." Zari wanted to hit her hand and free her chin. But how could she? In the British school, every week, they had two hours of a course on etiquette, and every day of the week they studied good behavior. Of course, that meant they studied the Bible. But at least the course on etiquette was about manners. And would Ezzatoddowleh let go? "Teeth straight and white; the neck so beautiful, like it was carved out of marble; and those eyelids . . ."

The twins were so fascinated by the paintings that they would not let Khadijeh undress them. They had especially liked the painting of a man on a horse with a finger to his mouth and a naked woman combing her long hair. On the day they had come sightseeing, Hamid Khan kept the girls waiting in the changing room of the bath for a long time to thoroughly explain to them a painting, which was a scene from the story of the legendary lovers, Khosrow and Shirin. A naked woman with large breasts was sitting next to a spring combing her long black hair. A screen of sorts separated the woman from the rider, a man with thick hair and a moustache wearing a royal hat. Even though he was supposed to be behind the screen, all the details of him and his horse were visible. And the woman had nothing covering her genitals, either.

Zari promised the twins that if they let Khadijeh undress them, she would send them in the afternoon to see the *zurkhaneh*, the exercise room next to the bath, in which there were representations of Rostam and his double-pointed beard, the tiger skin he was wearing, the skin of Akvan the Demon that he had killed and skinned.

In the bath, the aunt performed ritual ablutions and left. She did not want to get a splitting headache from the scratchy records. But Zari tried to stay as long as she could. First, she sat on the step inside the warm water pool, letting her body be engulfed in the water. Her limbs relaxed. Leaning her head on the side of the pool, she closed her eyes. When she came out, she sat on a sparkling white tray and pulled the white embroidered loincloth up to her breasts. The black maid, naked as the day she was born, brought in a platter of watermelon and put it on an empty copper bowl. She had cut the watermelon in zigzag shapes. The eyes of Mina and Marjan grew wide with surprise at the sight of the black maid. Marjan was about to burst into tears when Mina's question changed her mind. "Mother, but this one has a skin. You said that they pulled his skin off and the man with the beard is wearing it!" Zari laughed and the black maid said, "God protect you, you beautiful little things! Let me go and put some wild rue on the fire to ward off the evil eye."

Naneh Seyyed, the most skillful bath attendant in the city, came in with a shiny pitcher, its rim all engraved with prayers, and was taken aback at seeing Zari. But she said hello. She had covered her genitals with a red string that she had tied around her waist, and a red loincloth, folded like a handkerchief, which passed through the two sides of the string and knotted between her legs. On that day, too, this same Naneh Seyyed had been in their cubicle in the Shapuri bath. She had come to wash Ezzatoddowleh, who had instructed her to wash Zari first. With the usual small talk and pleasantries she had first washed her right arm, and when she got to the second arm she had scrubbed so hard that it hurt. When Zari merely said, "More gently," she took the washing mitt off, threw it at Zari and said, "If you know how, do it yourself." And how happy Zari had been. She didn't have the money anyway to hire a bath attendant or give her a tip.

Now Naneh Seyyed took the pitcher to the warm water pool, filled it, and walked over to Zari, poured it over her shoulders and sat on the floor in front of her. Zari noticed drops of sweat on her nose. She pulled the bath paraphernalia, arranged on a tray with legs, toward her. She took some salt out of a small copper bowl, rubbed it on Zari's feet and, using a fine pumice stone with a silver cap, gently rubbed her heels and the soles of her feet. It tickled, but Zari wouldn't make a sound. The black maid came in again, circling her fistful of wild rue over the heads of each and every one of them, even Khadijeh and Naneh Seyyed, and left. Then the smell of burning wild rue seeds came from the dressing room.

Zari was sitting on the outer step of the warm water pool and Naneh Seyyed was gently rubbing her hair with fuller's earth mixed with rose petals. What a pity to smear this shiny white marble with mud, she thought. But she submitted to the gentle hands of the bath attendant and thought of all the fragrances that she still could smell—*dastanbu*, jasmine, lime, wild rue, roses—and she wished this happy mood would last for a long time.

15

EZZATODDOWLEH DID not get to the main point until that afternoon, and then, with what detailed explanation, prefatory remarks and marginal annotations! The guests were sitting on a twelve-piece platform over the pool. The platform was covered with carpets; over the carpets were placed cool striped mats, and cushions with floral prints were scattered against the platform's tall lattice railing. Ezzatoddowleh was sitting at the prominent end of the platform and fanning herself. Khanom Fatemeh and Zari were seated on the two sides of the platform. But they were not fanning themselves. The air had cooled, and the jasmines, in large flower pots around the pool, like half-sleeping stars, were looking at the sun, which couldn't bring itself to leave the orange grove. Ezzatoddowleh had gotten rid of Mina and Marjan by sending them with Khadijeh, Ferdows, and her children to the police chief's garden to watch the Pahlavan Kachalak puppet show.

Zari couldn't figure out how the subject turned to her charity and then to the women's prison. Zari explained, "The women's prison is relatively calm. There are no restrictions either, since the women's offenses are usually no more serious than stealing a ewer." And, yes, she can easily sit with the women prisoners on their little carpets—carpets brought by their relatives—and listen to their complaints. But the food that she takes to the men's prison, the Karimkhani Citadel, she just delivers to the prison office, and

what the prison guards do with it only they and God know. But
the guards believe that anyone who steals from another's rations
will be stricken with leprosy. She said, "One day, I insisted on taking my ration in person into the men's prison. That day, they were
cleaning the sewer well, which is in the hallway, and what a
stench! Enough to turn you off life altogether."

Then the subject turned to the madam director of a charity house
who had been jailed recently. Zari said, "I wanted to see this woman
jailed, but I didn't report her. The district officer who was with
us could have reported her if he wanted, as he seems to have done.
Khanom Mahin and I had been delegated by the Women's
Association to inspect the houses in the Mordestan red light district. No matter how long we knocked at this woman's door, no
one opened it. The district officer kept kicking the door. Finally,
the madam director herself opened it. It was already dark. We
inspected all the rooms. Mahin checked some of the beds and she
ordered that the pillow covers be changed and sheets be provided for the mattresses. In the end, we went to the madam's room
to give her lice powder and disinfectant chemicals. I saw something wiggling under a short-legged sewing machine in the corner of the room. First I thought it was a cat. You could only see
its black head. I switched on the light and signaled to the district
officer. He went and pulled out a seven-or eight-year-old girl from
under the sewing machine. The girl was wearing a crinkled,
gold-embroidered dress. Her breasts had not yet fully developed.
She was trembling like a sparrow caught in snow. Despite my mild
temper, I got angry. I said, 'Woman, aren't you ashamed to put
a girl this young to work?' She swore by everything holy: 'This girl
is my niece and she is my guest for one night.' Then she confessed,
'What can I do, dear lady? There are lots of customers. An
Indian sergeant major has been waiting for some time for a little
girl. You can't disappoint the customers. We are constantly being
ordered from above to keep the customers happy, and now you're
criticizing us. What's behind your coming here, anyway? Isn't it
to clean this place up so the foreign guests won't have a bad time?
I've been in this business for years and years and no one has ever
inspected it before.' "

Zari paused. But when she realized that her audience was eager to hear more, she continued. "Then it became clear that the madam had put ten or twelve of these children to work, and that day she had sent them over the roof to escape, all but this one, who couldn't escape in time. And what bracelets! The woman was wearing at least ten sets of gold bracelets."

"What a shameless woman!" Ezzatoddowleh said. "I hope, by my holy ancestor, she pays for what she has done to all those innocent children," and added, "They have arrested our Naneh Ferdows, too. When you go to the prison tomorrow, you'll see her."

Zari was waiting for the aunt to ask, "Since when have you become a *seyyed* to swear by your holy ancestor?" But the aunt did not ask that question. She merely inquired, "On what charge?"

Zari now understood what it was all about. She realized what Ezzatoddowleh wanted had to do with the women's prison and Naneh Ferdows. So she waited. But was Ezzatoddowleh likely to get to the point quickly? Instead, she sighed and said, "All I suffer is the fault of my child. That ingrate husband of mine—may God not rest his soul—didn't know how to raise a child. He didn't even let him be taken for compulsory military service. He put sand in his urine and bribed the military doctor into signing a letter saying that the child had a bladder stone. Had he gone through military service, he may have straightened out. May God not forgive you, man! He took a fifteen-year-old boy whoring, and when my poor child was sixteen years old, he got gonorrhea. And his wife doesn't know how to straighten him out either. How I wished to have Khanom Zahra become his wife. It wasn't destined to be. Like father, like son. May you not rest in your grave, man! May God not forgive you!"

Khanom Fatemeh said, "But I heard that he has lost his zip and has settled down."

"Settled down? With all those expenses and his shrew of a wife? I kept saying, 'Son, come fix up this house, with such a big courtyard, and live here.' He didn't listen. That is, his wife wouldn't hear of it. She said, 'I get depressed in the small streets and back alleys of the city. No matter what, my house has to be on the corner of two streets.'" Ezzatoddowleh paused, fanned herself a little, and began again, "From the olden days, they have always said that an only child either becomes half-witted or crazy. When he was five years old, he flew kites with colorful lanterns, at seven or eight he became a pigeon fancier. When one's fate is woven in black . . . now, he's a grown man and still playing with pigeons. He has built nests for three hundred pigeons on the roof of his house. Every afternoon, he flies pigeons. He claims that when the pigeons fly off the roof, his heart begins to pound and will calm down only when they come back to roost."

The aunt sighed and said, "He was my young son's playmate. When my boy died, I couldn't stand to look at your Hamid anymore. But now age has reduced my anguish . . . I miss Hamid."

"He will come to pay his respects. I told him his dear aunt was going to be here. He promised to come early this evening to greet you. He also misses you a great deal."

The black maid brought in the afternoon snack and set it on the platform—all sorts of seasonal fruits, several kinds of imported cookies; then she carried in a brazier full of burning charcoal on a copper tray with scalloped edges and placed it in front of the aunt. The maid made tea in a red teapot with floral designs. The opium bowl was made out of china and had floral designs that matched the teapot. The flowers on the opium bowl and the teapot were white poppies. The brass tongs and the poker gleamed like gold.

Ezzatoddowleh continued. "All I suffer is because of my child . . . you know he sends the foreign officers and soldiers here under the pretext of seeing antiques and they sell us whatever extra stuff they have, which I then sell through Naneh Ferdows, for example, cookies, soap, shoes, socks, silk cloth . . ."

The aunt asked harshly, "Do you think no one has found out? Everybody knows that a distinguished woman like you has become a smuggler. I wasn't going to bring it up during this meal. The other day in our own house I hinted around but you denied it, and I didn't press the point. In the Domil teahouse, in front of everybody, your son's driver told the story of your smuggling from Jahrom. He said you and Naneh Ferdows left thin and came back fat. He said you spent two whole hours wrapping your body in silk brocade, and in the trunk of the car you put two gunnysacks stuffed full of goods and made them look like two lovers embracing. If you had been caught, the fine would have been twenty thousand tomans. Why are you being so greedy, anyway? Reputation and dignity are nothing to trifle with."

Ezzatoddowleh bit the corner of her lip. "He's probably the one who exposed us. I kept saying, 'Boy, don't fire this driver in the middle of this famine and disease-ridden summer.' But he didn't listen. How I suffer at the hands of my child. I'm sitting here early in the evening. He comes in with a pot full of *tah chin,* a plateful of cool apricots, and a platter of large tangerines. He says, 'Mother, I was worried about you.' Then he kisses my hand, kisses my feet, and puts his head on my chest. After all this endearment, I know that the next day I'll do anything he wants me to."

The aunt opened the lid of a bejeweled box, took out a piece of opium, and smelled it. "What good opium!" she said, warming it up and packing it into the opium bowl.

Zari said, "I beg your pardon for being so impudent, but you have a great deal of land and property."

"May God not forgive you, man, on this dear evening!" Ezzatoddowleh said. "What land and property? He would steal the title deeds to my land, put a *chador* on his sister, and take her, pretending to be me, to the office of Aqa Sheykh Gheyb Ali. He would sell my land, and his sister would hold her veil tight over her face and put her fingerprint as signature at the bottom of the documents. Then he would spend the money on women. How much he spent on that room—his private room where he brought prostitutes, with that double bed he had imported from India . . . made of ebony!—I'll never know. He bought any piece of used playing cards, queens and aces, he could find in this town, and stuck them on the walls of that room. He hired a painter, brought him here, and had him paint men and women copulating in various poses. And what was left of the money in the end, when he was confined to the house, he smoked away and wasted on opium."

The aunt puffed on the opium pipe and said, "He left enough for you and seven generations after you to live respectably. But if your sarcastic remarks are also directed at me, I am not wasting anybody else's money on opium; it's my own. Besides, I've pledged that as soon as I set foot in the shrine of Imam Hoseyn, I will give up opium. I will break the opium bowl right there, may God Himself help me."

"Sister, how sensitive you've become!" said Ezzatoddowleh. "Why are you so touchy? I swear on the life of my only son that I wasn't insinuating anything about you. But about giving up opium, I have no doubt that you can do it. You're the kind of person who can do whatever she wants."

Khanom Fatemeh took a long puff. "What good opium!" she said again. "Where do you find it? When you inhale the smoke, it reminds you of the poppy fields. How often I went horseback riding in those fields! Field after field full of poppies, and every field a different color. At sunset the fragrance makes both you and the horse intoxicated. And when it begins to form its fruit and the yellow moss-green bulbs seem to talk to you and shake their heads, you're almost sure that they're alive. They have something that no other flower in the world has. They start to score them at dawn. Dew is still glittering on the bulbs and the pretty-colored sap oozes out drop by drop."

"Since you like it so much," Ezzatoddowleh said. "I'll make some pills from this opium to take with you, enjoy, and remember your sister by. I have a recipe for opium pills."

"Satan be cursed," the aunt said. "Even if it kills me, I'll give it up. What does the beauty of the fields have to do with its poison?"

Zari was anxious. She had planned to visit Kolu in the afternoon, but now it was too late. She was worried about Khosrow, who was with Hormoz. She knew that tonight they were going to Fotuhi's house together, even though last night Khosrow let it slip that because he was under age, he had not been accepted in any group. But Mr. Fotuhi had been kind enough to let Khosrow sit in on the meetings of the group to which Hormoz belonged. This group was the same one whose comrade members felt sorry for those who had a mark of aristocracy.

Zari turned to Ezzatoddowleh and said, "I think I understand now. Naneh Ferdows was carrying smuggled goods and was caught."

"I wish it were that simple," Ezzatoddowleh said. "This time it was arms."

The aunt put her opium pipe down by the side of the brazier. "Good God!" she said.

"Yes, two Brno rifles, ten revolvers, and a box of ammunition. God knows, we were very cautious. Four times before, Naneh Ferdows had taken similar loads safely to their destination, but this time she was caught. I'm sure the driver gave us away and got a reward for it, too. I hope he pays for his disloyalty, the ingrate. She was supposed to take the merchandise at dawn, before it got light and the women's bath opened, and deliver it to Mirza Aqa Hanasab near the Khani public bath."

"Which Mirza Aqa? Your Nanny's son?" Zari asked.

"No dear. My Nanny's son disappeared, you know. They say he's become a Bolshevik."

Ezzatoddowleh continued. "To deliver the merchandise to Mirza Aqa Hanasab and say out loud, 'Mirza Aqa, this is the mistress's bath bundle. I'll leave it here. During the women's bath hours, give it to the bath keeper's wife.' And Mirza Aqa was supposed to say casually, 'Boy, come take this bundle and put it in the back room of the shop.' I wrapped the bath bundle myself. Naneh Ferdows didn't even know what was in it. I put the guns with the top of one facing the bottom of the other in a little rug and rolled the rug lengthwise. And even though it made my hands bleed, I closed the ends with safety pins so the guns wouldn't slip out and the fringes of the carpet on both ends would cover them up. I put the rolled up carpet on the bath tray with the basin next to it and placed the box of bullets inside the basin. I put the revolvers in a bath towel, wrapped them up in a cashmere bundle, and tied it up. I set the bundle in the basin so that a part of it would show, and then sat down praying for the protection of the merchandise."

The aunt said, "God help us. You sure pray for strange things!"

Ezzatoddowleh ignored her. "At dawn that morning, we helped Kal Abbas put the tray and the basin on Naneh Ferdows's head.

It was very heavy, but she didn't have far to go. Again, I recited
prayers for the safety of Naneh Ferdows and her load and sent her
out through the inner courtyard door. Kal Abbas had already
checked the alley from one end to the other."

The aunt asked, "Who told you she'd been caught?"

"I was saying the morning prayers when they knocked at the
door. My heart sank. It seems that before she reached the bath
house, she was stopped by a policeman and a gendarme. They probably threatened her, searched her load, and asked her whose it was
and where she got it. Kal Abbas said you could tell from her face
that she had been beaten and had cried too. In any case, she had
told them enough. She brought them to the house. Now, see what
a loyal and clever man Kal Abbas is. He opened the door, and the
policeman asked him if he knew the woman. He says, 'No, sir, I
don't.' Naneh Ferdows bursts out crying and says, 'Shame on you;
you're my son-in-law. You don't know me?' She says, 'What is this,
has the world come to an end? Have you gone blind that you can't
recognize me?' Kal Abbas says, 'You slut, why do you lie this early
in the morning? How would I know you?' "

The aunt puffed once more on the opium pipe. "What a
mess you've gotten yourself into! Well, you were saying?"

"By now I had gone to the outer courtyard and was listening
and trembling. May no Moslem ever hear and no infidel see such
a thing! Naneh Ferdows was screaming, 'I will swear on the
Koran that I brought the stuff from this house. I didn't even know
there were guns and bullets in it. And this man is Kal Abbas, my
cuckold of an ingrate son-in-law, who takes the side of strangers
and not the side of his wife's mother. They disgraced my daughter, I didn't say anything; now they want to disgrace me. I spit on
you, on your face, Kal Abbas! You, too, have put on a cuckold's
horns. You help them. That other time, too, you helped them.'
And so she wailed, shouting such curses that sent chills down my
spine. She said, 'Oh God, where are You? Are You blind?' "

Ezzatoddowleh stopped and began to fan herself. The aunt and
Zari did not say a word. Zari was biting her thumbnail. And now
what can I do? she thought. Obviously she would not get to the
point until she had told them all the details.

"I don't know if it was the policeman or the gendarme who shouted, 'Woman, stop this blasphemy.' He shouted at Kal Abbas too, 'Go wake up your master; I'll ask him.' Kal Abbas said, 'May your life be long, the master passed away a long time ago.' The same voice said, 'Well, let's ask the mistress of the house.' I had all but fainted and was sitting on the ground. Kal Abbas said, 'The mistress is away on a trip; she's gone on pilgrimage to the shrine of Imam Reza.' The same voice shouted at Naneh Ferdows. 'Didn't you say that this was the mistress's bath bundle and you were taking it to the Khani bath house?' Kal Abbas didn't give Naneh Ferdows a chance. He laughed and said, 'Sir, we have a bath in the house. The mistress never goes to the public bath. If you want to, come and I'll show you.' And then he said, 'Go settle your quarrel somewhere else. I've got a thousand things to do.' Again, I don't know if it was the policeman or the gendarme who said, 'Get going, woman.' And Naneh Ferdows asked pleadingly, 'Where are you taking me?' The policeman or the gendarme said, 'First to the lieutenant, who will send you to jail.' The foolish woman shouted, 'Let me see my child, then I'll go anywhere you want. But they took her away. Thank God Ferdows and her children were sleeping on the roof of the room with the sash windows and didn't notice the commotion. But now hear about me. May no Moslem ever hear and no infidel see such a thing. I was shivering as if I had a fever and couldn't breathe. I sent Kal Abbas quickly after Mirza Aqa Hanasab."

Finally she turned to Zari and said, "But, dear Zari, you can solve this problem. We have made some inquiries from a distance. We know that Naneh Ferdows is in the women's prison. Now, darling that you are, when you go to the prison tomorrow, visit with Naneh Ferdows. Talk to her. Plead with her on my behalf never to mention our name. At the last moment, Kal Abbas had nudged her foot with his to make her understand that she should keep her mouth shut, and apparently she has caught on, or else she's tired and has temporarily stopped talking. Zari dear, please tell Naneh Ferdows to say on the day of the trial that the mistress had gone on a pilgrimage; Kal Abbas had bought the merchandise from some Indians, wrapped it in the mistress's bath stuff, gave it to her, who is his mother-in-law, to take and sell in the bazaar. Mirza Aqa Hanasab was the buyer of the merchandise. If she doesn't tell it like this, our family will be ruined, our reputation of many years destroyed."

The aunt said bitterly, "Is it all right for Kal Abbas's family to be destroyed? What has that poor henna grinder done? I don't want to scold you. In fact, what business is it of mine?"

"Qodsossaltaneh, please don't make Zari change her mind," Ezzatoddowleh pleaded. "After all, what are sisters for? I promise I'll repent. Besides, neither the Hanasab family nor Kal Abbas's will be destroyed. I informed Hanasab in time, and he fled and is now with his tribe. And I have made Kal Abbas agree. Tell her I have made her son-in-law agree. We have asked around. If a commoner smuggles arms for money, the punishment won't be more than a year or two in jail. They confiscate all the merchandise and fine you double its price. That's not even worth one hair on the heads of Zari's children. I'll pay the fine. And I'll give five thousand *tomans* to Kal Abbas when he gets out of jail. I promise I won't let anything happen to his wife and kids. Tell her to get Mr. Harfabadi as her attorney. I'll also have contact with the judge and the prosecutor. I'll send her to Karbala on pilgrimage, as I have so often promised her. This time, I'll keep my promise."

She put her hand under the sheet and took out two envelopes and a box, gave them to Zari and said, "Bazmara! Turn on the lights." The lamps on the tall posts in the courtyard, which looked like carriage lanterns, came on.

"Give these envelopes to her, sister," she continued. "In the first one I requested an attorney on her behalf and the second repeats what I have said. She can read. She can read the Koran. But she doesn't know how to write. Make her dip her finger in the ink in this box and put her fingerprint at the bottom of the first letter, and then give the letter to the prison office and get a receipt. Tell them that as a good deed and an act of charity, you yourself wrote the letter for the prisoner. Everyone knows that you are a charitable lady who does good deeds; nobody will suspect you. But make sure to get both letters back from her. Never, never leave these letters with her. Do this in the name of God, will you? I could send her daughter Ferdows under the pretext of visiting her, but I don't trust the girl. Her eyes have a strange glitter in them these days. I'm afraid mother and daughter will gang up and make a real mess for us. If they wanted to take revenge, what better chance than this?"

What would be courageous, if I did this or not? Zari wondered. Taking two envelopes to the prisoner, repeating all that chit-chat, probably pleading with Naneh Ferdows, taking the fingerprint, waiting until with her little knowledge of reading she goes through both letters, and doing all this in front of the madam who considers her responsible for her own arrest, is a daunting task. Could she take the risk and carry it through? In this deal, who would get what she deserved? She would be mediating for a guilty person to appear innocent, and for an innocent person to take the blame. Yet, she wasn't afraid of Ezzatoddowleh. Would it be equally courageous if she turned her down? If they couldn't succeed through her, they would find some other way and would buy their respectability by any means. And as for Kal Abbas, it wouldn't make much of a difference whether he were in a real prison or imprisoned in this house. But despite all of this, why should she be a dealer in injustice? The right thing to do was to advise Naneh Ferdows to tell the truth and to not fear how Ezzatoddowleh and others would react. But couldn't they use all the money and influence they had at their disposal to fool the woman and destroy her family? Naneh Ferdows was, in any case, a partner in the crime and had submitted to the kind of disgraceful life they had prepared for her.

Ezzatoddowleh's voice interrupted her thoughts. "Zari dear, why are you weighing it so much? This is nothing really important!"

Zari put the envelopes and the ink box in front of Ezzatoddowleh and said, "No, I won't do it. I'm sorry."

Ezzatoddowleh asked with astonishment. "You won't? Why?"

Zari didn't answer. Ezzatoddowleh said in a tone that is used to coax children, "What if I get your emerald earrings back from the Governor's daughter? You will still not do it? Before I could do anything about your son's horse, this problem came up."

"The earrings are no longer important," Zari said. "You'd better let the truth come out. You said yourself it was a pity Hamid Khan didn't go into the military service. Now this is itself a sort of military service."

The aunt laughed so hard that she began to cough.
Ezzatoddowleh laughed too, but nervously. "You don't seem to
understand the difference between Kal Abbas and Hamid," she said.
"If Kal Abbas is convicted, he will get a jail sentence of a year or
two, but if we are involved, we stand to lose everything. Then the
issue will be arms smuggling against the national security.
Harfabadi says that in accordance with Article 171, punishment
for such smuggling is execution, or if the sentence is reduced, life
imprisonment. And the most he can do is to settle the matter with
ten to fifteen years imprisonment. Nobody will believe that we have
a lot of expenses and we did this for money."

Tears came to her eyes and she said, "When a person's fate is
woven in black . . . so this is what friends and avowed sisters are
. . . they abandon you in your hour of need." Then she shouted,
"Bazmara! Get my heart drops!" and continued, "I know why you
won't do it. You didn't like us from the very beginning. What have
we ever done to you? Or perhaps now you regret that we did not
insist and you did not become our bride. Beggars can't be choosers.
I know. Now you want to have your revenge. With that hot-tem-
pered, crazy husband of yours, you deserve to . . . he's made an
enemy of everybody!"

Hamid Khan entered with greetings, fat and jovial. He took off
his shoes at the foot of the platform and walked to it in his socks.
He put his arms around his dear aunt's neck, kissing her over and
over again. Zari noticed that Ezzatoddowleh hastily wiped her tears
and when the son's eyes fell on her, she laughed. The son actually began kissing her from her feet up. He sat cross-legged next to
his mother and asked, "How's it going? How are you? What's up?"
He pulled himself toward the aunt, put his head on her shoulder
and caressed her braided hair. He narrowed his eyes, fixed them on
Zari and said, "Khanom Zahra, may God protect you, you are really
ly like a Kerman carpet. The more you are used, the better you look!"

He held Khanom Fatemeh's hand, kissed it and said, "Auntie
dear, how many years has it been since we've seen each other?"

Khanom Fatemeh did not answer. She poured a cup of tea and
put it in front of him. She scraped the opium pipe with a pocket knife, carefully cleaned the hole in its bowl with a needle, and
asked, "Should I put some opium on for you?"

Hamid Khan said coquettishly, "Oh, how I have suffered in your absence, dear aunt."

He turned to Zari and said, "I had no brothers and sisters; instead God granted me two mothers."

He puffed many times. His became talkative and began to relive his memories. "Do you remember?" he asked the aunt. "I used to sit on your lap and, even though I was three or four years old, I'd say, 'Mommy, up up, give me boobies to suck up, ummmmm,' and then begged you to lie down and put your breast in my mouth? I loved you like my mother. She took care of me so much. I remember the kids had thrown stones and broken the leg of my peacock-feather pigeon. You had come to visit your sister. I was hugging my pigeon and, as Mama says, I was shedding tears all over my face, and saying, "For God's sake somebody do something for my poor pigeon." My pigeon was in such pain that his cooing was worse than any cry of agony in the world. You came and soaked chick-peas in water, pounded them, mixed in egg yolks and myrtle, and applied it like a plaster to my pigeon's leg. By the time you had finished wrapping its leg, the pigeon had started to coo."

Zari felt she had nothing else to do here. She shifted her weight to show she was ready to leave, but Hamid kept on talking. Again he asked the aunt, "Remember the night in the garden? We had all stayed overnight in the country. The musicians couldn't hire a *droshky* and had to spend the night, too. But there weren't enough beds for everyone. My mother, who would never miss the opportunity of sleeping in my father's arms, didn't have room for me. Nobody else let me share their bed either. I had Oriental boils. I had seven of them on my face and the one on my nose had pus in it, and everybody knew it was contagious. The patio was full of mosquitoes and flies, and everybody knew that flies were carriers of Oriental boils. I was left standing there not knowing where to sleep, and I was really sleepy. It was very cold, too. Even though you had a child sleeping in your arms, you called me and said, 'Come here and sleep on this side by me.' I had cried and you wiped my tears and especially kissed my infected nose. When your son died, I wouldn't show my face around you, so you

wouldn't get sad. One day in the Vakil Bazaar, I saw a woman who
looked just like you, the same figure and shape. I followed her and
said softly, 'Auntie.' The woman turned around, slapped me and
said, 'Auntie, my foot, Auntie my . . .' "

He watched Bazmara put a small medicine bottle and a glass
of water on a tray before his mother. He asked, "Dear mother, are
you taking medicine again?" Ezzatoddowleh said, "It's nothing. My
heart is just beating fast." He looked searchingly at Zari and asked,
"Khanom Zahra, I hear you are going to the prison tomorrow. Will
you visit our prisoner?"

Ezzatoddowleh was counting the drops. When she reached fifteen, she said, "But not as we wanted," and continued the counting from sixteen. Hamid frowned and was flustered. He picked
up the opium pipe from the side of the brazier, packed in some
opium, and began to puff. He asked, "Why? You're probably afraid.
Well, you should be afraid." Unskillfully, he put the opium pipe
down beside the brazier, threw his arms around the aunt's neck,
and said, "But my dear aunt is not easily frightened. She will kiss
my boil this time, too, isn't that right, Auntie? Certainly you don't
want to see me on the gallows. Now, if anybody else but you goes
there, they'll get suspicious."

Zari saw Kal Abbas, who had passed through the orange grove,
come toward the platform and say, "Ya Allah." The aunt put on
her *chador*. He stood by the platform, called Hamid, and whispered
something in his ear. Hamid put on his shoes and rushed off. Zari
got worried. Had something happened to her children? This
woman is capable of anything. Had she taken the children hostage
somewhere and now the mother and son were creating a scene to
force her to agree to their deal? Why hadn't she thought of it before?
Why did she let them go to the police chief's garden at all? And
bitterly she thought that the "Pahlavan Kachals" of the puppet show
were right here, but the children wouldn't understand anything by
watching them. In a trembling voice, she asked the aunt, "It's late;
where are the children?" Now she was ready to agree to anything
. . . if she had to choose between courage and her children, obviously she would opt for the children. Yes, Hamid was going to come
right now and start the game. The aunt looked at her sharply and

said, "Don't worry, they'll show up." I'll wait, she thought. There is no reason to worry. Good thing I sent Khadijeh with them. She remembered the poem that Yusof so often recited: "With a thought, their fear and their fright——." No. She had given the poem her own twist. The poem Yusof recited was: "With a thought, their peace and their fight/With a thought, their reputation and disgrace."

Hamid came up the platform accompanied by a broad-shouldered woman in a *chador* who was covering her face tightly. He laughed and said, "Mother, do you want a guest?" Zari immediately recognized the "woman." She had entertained that same person in that same *chador* in her own house. Involuntarily she said, "Malek Sohrab Khan!" And then she put her hand over her mouth. Sohrab sat down and took off the *chador*. He was thin, his head and face covered with dust, and he had several-days' growth of beard. Ezzatoddowleh laughed so hard that tears came out of the corner of her eyes. Sohrab gave a tired smile and said to Zari, "I first went to your house. No one was there." He held his head in his hands. "I wish Yusof were in town. I should have listened to him."

Bazmara brought a ewer and basin set so shiny that it looked like gold. She was holding a thick towel with a flowered pattern and a piece of soap shaped like a pear. The soap they had put in the bath for Zari was in the shape of an apple. Was it for these knickknacks that they put themselves in danger? Nevertheless, the presence of Sohrab at that time of night put the problems in a different light. Ezzatoddowleh said, "Sohrab, we have just changed the water in the warm water pool. Why not treat yourself to a bath?"

"They might call," he answered. "Perhaps I am wrong and they haven't deceived us. I came straight from the battlefield. First, I went to the colonel. Really that cross-eyed one has much in common with Yazid. He thinks this is Arabia. Let him die thinking he is Lawrence of Arabia. He didn't let me in. He sent a message that he had caught a cold. How do you catch a cold in the middle of summer? Then I went to Zinger. That fox said, 'I am having a busy mind. I cannot you admit.' The idiot hasn't learned Persian after so many years of living here. If they have deceived us, we have needlessly shed the blood of our own brothers, though he did say he would call."

Ezzatoddowleh signaled to him with her head, which everybody noticed. So she was obliged to ask, "Did you go to them in this *chador?*"

"No. I had put on the cavalry uniform of Captain Mohammad Keshmiri-Kermani. His identity card was in the pocket of his uniform. Ten of us had pounced on him. First we undressed him. Then we shot him in the neck. Afterwards I went to Mirza Aqa Hanasab's house and changed clothes."

Zari heard the children in the outer courtyard and sighed with relief. Hastily she asked permission to leave. Ezzatoddowleh, only too happy to grant her wish, called out, "Ferdows, come bring my sister's *chador* . . . and bring my prayer bundle. Make sure your hands are clean."

"Have you heard anything about the war here in the city?" Sohrab asked.

"No," Zari answered. "The newspapers haven't mentioned a thing."

"You mean they write something in the newspapers once in a while? There it was rumored that the corpses of the colonel and the officers were brought to the city and given an official funeral procession." He paused. "But we did nothing wrong, except to set our hopes too high. After my meeting with these cunning foxes, I felt that if I kept that unfortunate man's uniform on for another minute, I'd go mad."

The young maid brought the cashmere bundle containing the aunt's black *chador* and also Ezzatoddowleh's prayer things. Zari noticed Hamid's face. When Ferdows bent over and put the prayer bundle in front of Ezzatoddowleh, his eyes sparkled and he looked her over from head to toe. Following his gaze, Zari noticed Ferdows' pretty legs and figure. Her legs in transparent stockings really looked like upside-down sugar cones. Her blue silk *chador* would slip aside on the crepe de Chine dress printed with red flowers and green leaves. The soft curves of her body were so properly in place that no one would have believed this woman had aborted three babies and given birth to three others.

But the aunt did not touch the bundle. She said, "Khanom Ferdows, take the children something to eat and keep them in the outer courtyard until we come. Tell Bazmara to come and gather up the opium set."

Totally unaware of what had happened, Ferdows filled some plates with fruit and cookies. It was obvious that she had no idea why the mistress was looking askance at her. The mistress pushed the corner of the sheet aside, performed a ritual ablution with the dust on the carpet, adjusted her facial veil several times until it completely covered her bezoar-colored hair and fit snugly around her face. But what a face! She looked like she had just taken quinine. She was even at war with God. She spread out her prayer rug with an angry gesture and started her prayers sitting down.

Deep down, Zari was happy that she had stood her ground anyway. If only Yusof would come back sooner. Never before had she had so much to tell him. Her experiences in the prison and the insane asylum were interesting, but not to Yusof. Often he would say, "Zari, I feel down. Say something." And how she would search her mind for a happy and soothing memory or experience. For a long time, she had had nothing, no pleasant memory or event left to tell Yusof. She knew that lately her stories were repetitive and her husband was only enjoying her voice. And now Zari had once again put up resistance.

She was sure that Ezzatoddowleh would be traversing the heavens for a while, and, to spite them, she would stretch out her prayers as long as she could. And they, out of respect, would keep silent. But they would eventually run out of patience and Sohrab would soon begin to talk. Her curiosity was so piqued that she knew if Ezzatoddowleh herself would not make them leave, she would stay until the whole story was told. The black maid came and took away the opium set. Zari said, "Sohrab Khan, you were talking about the battlefield."

"In fact, I meant to tell my friends all the details so that if one day I happen to set out for the mountains and become an outlaw, or leave and disappear, or my nomad blood boils and makes me take vengeance and say to myself, 'Let them drown and me with them,' they should know why I did any of these things. I wish, like my brother, I had listened to Yusof. He knew. He is a friend of MacMahon. They sit together and translate poet-

ry, the poems of a courageous poet who is said to have been bold
enough to challenge the rules of prosody." He shook his head
and recited: " 'On what part of this dark night should I hang my
tattered garb?'

"But Zinger gave us his word. He said, 'The first stop, Semirom;
the second stop, Shiraz; and then Esfahan and Tehran.' And
what atrocities we committed. Let me say it myself: And what mistakes our brothers made. What an ugly war it was!"

"Brother, I may be stupid," Hamid said. "but I didn't understand a word you said."

"This MacMahon is a war correspondent. You have no idea."

Hamid said, "Come on, man. Don't take it so hard. Be grateful you are safe and sound. Now, that's all water under the bridge.
In my opinion, you should smoke some opium. You'll forget all
about it. Do you want me to have them fix it for you?"

"I'm not the kind of person who numbs his senses with opium.
If I can't atone for my sins, I'll do away with myself. Right now,
I'm ready for anything."

"What if they call?" Hamid asked sarcastically. "Then you
will forget even your cardinal sins, won't you?"

Zari thought this was the only sensible thing he has said in his
whole life.

Sohrab agreed with Hamid. "If they were going to call, they
would have done so by now. They trust you and your mother."
He continued. "The Russians wanted thirty to forty Iranian soldiers, maybe more . . . it was rumored they wanted about five divi-
sions for behind-the-line services—that is, for the provisions—soldiers armed only with guns to guard the ammunition warehouses and the roads, help with transportation and unloading, or to
take care of the wounded and the field hospitals. Obviously their
rivals, even though they are allies for now, do not want, as Yusof
Khan says, to have a communist cell established in Iran. They say
the Iranian army has not had proper training, that it can't even take
on a bunch of local outlaws, and with this war, that was proven
to them in practice."

"If you knew that was the case," the aunt said, "why did you
fight your own compatriots?"

Hamid laughed. "Dear aunt, these people are dying to fight. To them, fighting is as enjoyable as hunting. But I don't even want to hurt a fly. Do you remember that fox hunt, Sohrab? How happy I was that the fox outwitted you and you couldn't shoot! Even though I covered my ears, I'd get sick to my stomach when the gun knocked you in the shoulder."

Ignoring Hamid, Sohrab told the aunt, "These were all rumors. I understand the truth now. I just heard on the way here that a Russian observer is at the Khungah Pass. But they were telling us the whole time to have our crowns ready, that we were the successors to the Achaemenid dynasty. They would get the weapons to us any way they could. Twice, according to a prior arrangement with them, we looted them. They had loaded guns and ammunition in a private car, disguised as a shipment of coins they were taking from Khuzestan through the Bakhtiari Mountains to the Shahi Bank in Esfahan. They had done exactly the same thing in World War I, only on mules. According to their own instructions, we ambushed the car and left the driver on the road with his arms tied. The driver was expecting us; he flashed his lights for us. But we confiscated the car, too."

"But I heard you actually killed a bank director and robbed the bank," Zari said. "Was this the same time?"

"No, that was another time. Well, in any case, one needs money for such work. Friends helped too. Hamid and others got weapons to us . . ." And turning to Hamid, he added, "My dear Hamid, these last bullets really came in handy, even though you charge too much . . . and the revolvers, how heavy they get in the sun."

Ezzatoddowleh had apparently finished her prayers. She said, "Why should you say these things in front of strangers?" She paused and continued, "If you really want to know the truth, we, too, were caught. Our Naneh Ferdows has been arrested. These days, never mind the friendship between sisters, you cannot even trust your own eyes."

"Who is Naneh Ferdows, the mother of this pretty servant girl here?" Sohrab asked.

"Did she steal your heart, too, so soon?" Hamid asked. "When I told my mama, this woman emits sparks that set your heart on flame, she wouldn't believe me."

"Good God," Ezzatoddowleh said, lifting both hands to her ears to continue her prayers. She had probably not yet said her night prayers or was paying God back for her previous sins.

Sohrab suddenly remembered. "Mirza Aqa Hanasab's wife mentioned that your go-between had been caught. But I didn't know her name was Naneh Ferdows. She said her own husband has fled. Before any other decisions are made, we must send Mirza Aqa's wife and children to him. Hamid, first thing in the morning or even tonight, go to Zinger and tell him that it was in carrying out their plans that we were trapped. Tell him from me that they have twenty-four hours to respond. If they don't show up, I know where their jugular vein is. As God is my witness, I'll take a few fighters who, like myself, are ready to give their lives and . . . We have done all these things to make sure that their pipelines don't even get a scratch."

Zari had figured the whole thing out now. If you commit a sin but succeed, that sin is by general consensus not a sin, but if you don't succeed, then it is a sin and must be atoned for. She wanted to speak her mind, but who would listen to her? Hamid, who did not think of anything in this world but women, whiskey, and pigeons? Or Sohrab, who had been blinded by ambition? Or Ezzatoddowleh, who quarreled with God? Or the aunt, whose only concerns were emigrating to Karbala and giving up opium? She advised in a motherly fashion, "Sohrab Khan, it's still not too late. From now on, cooperate with Yusof, like Malek Rostam Khan."

"Everyone's nature is different," Sohrab answered. "He is of the land and I am of the wind. I'm not the kind to wait and set my hopes on the distant future. I want to grab my future right now. I want to die, like the colonel, by the bullet or by the axe, not in bed. I want to be the last one to leave the fortress, and not on my own two feet. I want them to drag me out, shoot me dead, and chop me to pieces with an axe. I want to stare at my killers until they envy me and are amazed at my indifference to life and death."

"His nomad blood is boiling again," said Hamid.

"You were fearless from the time you were a child," Zari said.

"You were a poet, too. I recall, for your first wife—"

Sohrab interrupted. "Now, too, fearless poets are needed." And turning to Hamid, he asked, "I don't know, have you ever gone from Shahreza, from the southwest, to Semirom?"

"No," Hamid answered. "But if you remember, once we went together from the northwest foothills of Dena to Semirom for the wedding of the son of Esfandiyar Khan Kashkuli. I remember. We stopped at the Semirom spring and a really beautiful girl, as beautiful as the full moon, gave water to the driver from her jug and poured water in the car radiator from the same jug. And oh how she walked, the damn thing—tall as a cypress; she roamed gracefully like a partridge, as if the ground were indebted to her, as if saying, 'It is I who honor you with these delicate feet.' "

"Is this the time for such recollections?" Sohrab asked.

"It is always time for such recollections." Hamid sighed and, turning to the aunt, said, "Auntie dear, you did a bad thing sending Ferdows on a wild goose chase. Call her. You call her. I'm dying for a glass of gin with lime." Then turning to Sohrab he said, "You know, brother, these hopes of yours and your tribe end up in nothing but headaches and killings. As for me, everything I do is for money, to have the beautiful and delectable things of this world—women, wine, worsted wool fabric from Manchester."

Sohrab put his hand on Hamid's knee and said, "Wait a minute; I think the telephone is ringing," and got up. The telephone was actually ringing. Ferdows came into the courtyard, everyone's eyes fixed on her. Sohrab was standing. Ferdows said, "Zahra Khanom, Khosrow wants to know if you are coming for dinner or should they go ahead and eat without you?"

"We're leaving right away," Zari responded and, turning to the aunt, she said "Shall we go?"

Sohrab sat at the edge of the platform. "This time, I won't let the real foxes pull the wool over my eyes." Hamid said, "A man who is so sure of himself won't be pushed around so easily . . ."

Ezzatoddowleh shouted, "Ferdows! Bring my sister's *chador!* Are you deaf?" Could she have gotten rid of them more obviously? The aunt's *chador* was in the bundle in front of her.

"The night is still young," Hamid said. "Where are you going so early? I know that you got depressed because he talked so much about killing and slaughter. Let me tell you the story of his fox hunting—it will cheer you up."

Zari was too embarrassed to say that she had heard the same story several times from Malek Sohrab himself. She put up with Hamid's telling the story in embellished detail.

They had wanted to trap a fox that had been sneaking into Hamid's chicken coop every night. But the fox was more cunning than they were. One snowy night they set up a dead hen on a snow mound so that when the fox comes to get the hen, Malek Sohrab can shoot it. But the fox doesn't go straight to the hen. It digs a tunnel under the snow mound, takes the chicken from underneath, and escapes. Of course, later when they see that there is neither a hen nor a fox, they realize they've been had.

On their way home, Zari kept wondering why Hamid had insisted on telling this story. Was he trying to remind Sohrab that he couldn't take on the foxes? And she thought, He pretends to be simple-minded, but he is very sly!

While waiting for dinner to be brought in, Zari turned on the radio, but no matter how she tried, she couldn't find the Radio Berlin Persian program on the dial. They had only recently bought the radio. But they didn't use it much, because it was too hot in the parlor where they had put it. Besides, it was too heavy to move around. When Yusof was in town, he'd play around with it, bringing out loud scratchy noises from here and there that gave you a splitting headache, until finally he would find Radio Berlin and listen to the man who rattled off heartfelt insults. Then one man called all prominent people Jews, and, as Yusof would say, cursed them as if they had personally killed his father. In the morning he would turn on the Shir-e Khoda exercise program and praise it for its recitation from the *Book of Kings*. On Fridays, when Yusof was away in the village, Zari tried to keep the twins amused with Sobhi's stories, even though they were too fidgety to sit quietly and pay attention for half an hour.

After dinner, she turned on the Iran and the World program.

There was no reference at all in the news to the incident in the south. She flipped through the local newspapers. The most important domestic news was in the obituaries. She picked up the newspapers that were mailed to them from Tehran and which she collected and took to the insane asylum for Miss Fotuhi once every two weeks.

She opened the first newspaper: "The Ministry of Provisions To Be Dissolved." "Sugar Lump and Granulated Sugar Coupons. Lump sugar and granulated sugar rations are set as follows from this date on. Three hundred grams of lump sugar, four hundred grams of granulated sugar."

In the second issue, the only item that could be related to what she was interested in was this: "Fars Society Made Up of Fars Residents in Tehran To Be Established." Then there were items like "Shutdown of *Mard-e Emruz*," which looked normal to Zari. But she didn't give up and several days later in a newly published news-paper, on the third page, she came across the headline, "Strengthening the Abadeh and Semirom Garrison."

She read on. "According to reports received, the Boyer Ahmadi and Qashqa'i outlaws have robbed trucks carrying provisions, ammunition, and clothing, which had been dispatched by the army to strengthen the Semirom garrison. They attacked the Semirom garrison on June 29 and martyred a group of officers and soldiers. This matter is now under investigation in Tehran and it has been decided that the garrisons in Abadeh and Semirom will be strengthened."

16

WHEN KOLU came out of the hospital he was too weak for Zari to fulfill her promise and send him back to the village. His head was shaved and a copper cross hung around his neck. His eyes were darting around and when he stood up, his head wobbled and his legs shook. He had obviously been dismissed too soon. Zari ordered him to go to bed.

Kolu told of a bearded man in a long black gown who always carried a book and had a charm, like the one he had given Kolu, around his neck. But the chain on his charm was very long. He had appeared on the morning of the day that Kolu's Indian neighbor was dying. He had passed by Kolu's bed. Then Kolu had heard his chant. He had chanted loudly. Kolu neither understood the language of the bearded man when he was chanting nor the language of the Indian. In fact, there, nobody understood anybody else's language. No, only that old woman with buckteeth and the bearded man, when he wasn't chanting, understood our language.

The Indian had one night walked on his own two feet to Kolu and kissed him. He had cried so hard, as if Kolu were his own son, and kept saying, "Sandra! Kitu! Kitu!" In fact, that Indian constantly called out, "Kitu! Sandra!" Or maybe he thought Kolu's name was Kitu or Sandra. Kolu was by his bed on the last night as he lay snoring. Suddenly his jaw dropped and his eyes opened wide, just like Kolu's father.

The man in black seemed to live at the hospital, because he showed up every day. At first Kolu thought he was His Holiness Abolfazl, who had come to cure him. But when he found out that his Indian neighbor had died, he was sure that the man in black was not His Holiness Abolfazl. In any case, that same man had put the charm around Kolu's neck and told him that he should kiss the charm every morning, and that he should go to the village and bring his uncle, so he can give his uncle a charm too.

On three occasions, the man read stories out of his black book. Kolu only liked one, the story of the shepherd boy. That boy too played the pipe. He was a friend of the king's son and had killed a giant with his slingshot and rocks. The man in black kept saying, "Jesus is everywhere and has paid for everybody's sins with his own blood." Then he had taken Kolu by the hand into Jesus' house, a very big, dark room that frightened Kolu. But no matter how much Kolu had looked for Jesus, he hadn't found him. That man in black had shown him the picture of the owner of the house. He had also shown him the picture of the mama of the owner of the house. It was a woman with a baby in her arms. She looked like Goldusti, the wife of Kolu's uncle.

Kolu wanted very much to find Jesus, but when he gathered from what the man in black said that Jesus is a shepherd and is looking for his lost lambs, he was sure that Jesus had gone into the fields, and it would be a long time before he could find those poor animals.

Early Wednesday morning, Yusof returned from the village. When could he have left to have arrived that early in the morning? When he knocked on the door, Zari could not imagine it would be her husband. He had gotten a night pass just recently, after much hassle. How quickly he had used it. Zari had just turned up the flaps of the mosquito tent to come out. She went to welcome her husband, who dismounted from the mare. But he was not alone. Another man, with his eyes closed, was on the roan. She rubbed her eyes and looked at the man. He was wearing Yusof's jacket over his bare body. He looked like he was dead, because he was tied on the horse with a rope. Gholam and Yusof untied the rope and put the man gently on the ground. The man opened his eyes to look, but it was obvious that he couldn't see. Blood was clotted on his right temple. His unshaven beard was full of dust and his long underwear were spotted with dull red stains. The man put his hand on his bare belly. Yusof asked, "Is the bath heated?" Zari answered, "No, but we'll heat it up."

Before Gholam took him to the bath, in the dressing room Yusof examined his wounds, washed them with soap and water, and put some iodine on them. The wounds were superficial. All this time the man's eyes were closed.

When they sat down to breakfast on the back veranda, Yusof explained. "When we started off at dawn, we found him by the stream near Zarqan Gate. He was lying there naked, in those long underwear and tattered socks. First we thought it was an animal or something. We flashed a light and saw that it was a man. I thought somebody must have robbed him. I got off the horse. He begged us to get him to the city. He said he was coming to our garden, but his legs wouldn't carry him any farther. So he fell right there. I said, 'You can go with Seyyed Mohammad. He'll put you on his saddle and take you to the garden. When you feel better, he'll take you to the city.' But he kept begging me to bring him to the city. He said, 'You'll find out how important it is to take me to the city. If I'm not going to get to the city, just leave me here; someone else will take me to the city.' Since I had invited a few guests for this morning, I said, 'All right, I'll take you to the city.' First, he kept up with me on the horse, but by the time we reached Bajgah, he was worn out. He couldn't even hold the horse's reins. So I tied him to the horse with a rope. I guess he's either very tired or very frightened. These days we are going to see lots of scenes like this. He kept talking about a truck on fire. Maybe he's a truck driver."

Kolu came and kissed the master's hand. His legs didn't seem strong enough yet, and Zari was afraid he might fall. Yusof hastily patted him on the head, as if he had not recognized him. Zari explained, "This is Kolu. He has just escaped the angel of death."

When Kolu left, Yusof said, "I really didn't recognize him at first. He's lost a lot of weight! I thought this child might come down with typhus. A messenger from Kavar told me his whole family has caught it. You were right, our shepherd had typhus. It has spread throughout the villages in that area. In this hot weather, the messenger said, it looks like the villages have all been abandoned. But they haven't. In every house you visit, you see beds spread out and villagers lying down. On top of all the work I have, I must get medicine and doctors for them."

"I doubt if you can find a doctor," the aunt said.

"I'll send one of Dr. Abdullah Khan's apprentices," Yusof said. And, turning to Zari, said "Get up dear. Wake the children. I want to see them. And bring me the newspapers from the past two weeks."

As Zari got up to go, he added, "Zari, we have a few guests coming today. When they arrive, don't let anyone bother them. Keep the garden gate open. They're coming by car."

As she passed through the pantry, Zari saw Gholam with a plate of fresh pistachios and hazelnuts. It was as if the green skin of the pistachios had been rubbed with rouge, and the fresh hazelnuts looked like artificial flowers cut from tiny leaves. Gholam said, "They were in the mare's saddle-bag."

Zari had realized from the beginning that Yusof was preoccupied, otherwise he would never have come back from the village without bringing his wife the first pick of the fruit. When he handed her the first pick of the fruit, it felt like he was giving her the whole village, with all its fragrances, crops, lovers' springs, and orchards.

She hoped he would ask her to say something, so she could tell him everything she had stored up. She noticed Yusof cutting out parts of the newspaper and setting them aside. She knew he would see the news of "Strengthening the Garrisons of Abadeh and Semirom" and, God willing, he would ask her for some explanation.

Yusof saw that report and clipped it out, but he set it aside without comment or question.

Yusof instructed Gholam to put Mina and Marjan on the mare and get behind them on the saddle himself. With Khosrow riding Sahar, they went for a ride in the direction of Masjed Vardi Orchards. Yusof insisted that they take Kolu along, but Khosrow didn't want to double up on Sahar and Kolu wasn't strong enough to walk. It was decided that he should rest on Gholam's bed in the stable and not come out until he was called. Khadijeh was so busy that she was only too happy not to set foot outside the kitchen and have the mistress herself serve the guests. The aunt was in the *howzkhaneh,* sewing the rest of the gold *dinars* into the jacket. And the stranger was sleeping like a log in the pantry. Yusof occasionally went in to listen to his breathing and sometimes sent his wife to check on him. He had told Zari that if he woke up and asked for food, she should feed him, dress him up, and send him on his way. The man's breathing was normal and sounded healthy. But he was frowning in his sleep and had put a hand on his lips.

Yusof was anxiously pacing in the garden. At every sound, he turned his gaze toward the garden gate. Finally a green car with its headlights on drove in. The driver had obviously forgotten to turn the lights off, for the sun had arrived long before the guests and was already caressing the branches.

The car stopped in front of the house by the pool. The driver got out, noticed the headlights, and went back and turned them off. Zari recognized the driver. It was Majid Khan, one of those who had made a pledge together with her husband to take charge of the city's bread supplies. The other passengers were a man accompanied by two women in black *chadors.* She recognized the man by his resemblance to his sister. It was Fotuhi. She also recognized the women when they got out and said hello. They were Malek Rostam and Malek Sohrab, who were putting on darker veils every day.

All signs indicated there was something important afoot. As she was carrying in their tea, she heard them shouting. When she entered the parlor, she realized that they would not reach an agreement very soon. First, all five of them fell silent for a moment and took their tea pensively, without even thanking her. Sohrab and Rostam had wadded up their black *chadors* and thrown them on the floor. She picked them up, folded them slowly and listened. As she put the *chadors* on an empty bench, Sohrab said, "Khanom Zahra was a witness. She knows how I felt that night. That butchery has become a nightmare for me. Now, I am ready to do anything. I will pay for it with my own blood. Isn't that enough? I am prepared to swallow dynamite and set myself on fire with gasoline beside one of their oil docks. I am not afraid of death. But I am afraid of our plan failing. Yusof Khan, make a proper plan that has at least a 30 percent chance of success . . ."

Yusof looked at Zari and said, "Zari, check on our guest, the stranger, will you?"

She knew that she had been politely asked to leave, even though she very much wanted to stay. She stood behind the door eavesdropping. Sohrab's voice was now pleading, "My uncle is still hopeful. I am even prepared to deceive my uncle and get at least two hundred guns from him. But Fotuhi, you insulted me. You, too, are someone else's lackey. If not, what business is it of yours to think about Stalingrad and worry about whether or not they receive weapons?"

Why in heaven was she standing there eavesdropping? With three demanding children and one more on the way, what could she do? It hadn't even been an hour and she was already worried about the children—they might have been thrown off the mare, they might get heat stroke on a hot day like this, even though she knew that the alleys of Masjed Vardi were quite shady.

She prepared the hookah for Yusof. Coward or courageous, with her kind of life and upbringing, it would be impossible for her to engage in anything that would disrupt the normal flow of life. A person must be physically and psychologically prepared for things that smell of danger, and she had been prepared for peace and tranquillity, not danger. She had neither the courage nor the endurance. If she weren't so attached to her children and husband, things might be different. The first pick of the fruit, caresses, conversations, affectionate gazes, on the one hand, and witnessing the wonders, on the other . . . such a person could not take risks. It is true that like a pulley over the well, day after day she had monotonously moved in a circle; it is true that morning to night each day she had turned the wheel of life with her feet, like Hoseyn Kazeruni, and had never had a free hand to do anything for herself. Where had she read, "The hand is the tool of all tools?" But the smiles, glances, words, caresses, and the familiar smell of those she loved were her reward. Every tooth that her children cut; every new curl that she saw in their hair; their first chirps and twitters that would then become words; the words that they rattled on, correctly or incorrectly; the first sentences that they made; their sleeping, which made them look like angels; and their soft skin that felt like a fresh leaf. No. She wouldn't really be able to do anything. The only brave thing that she could do was to not keep the others from being brave and let them—with their free hands and thoughts, with their tool of tools—do something.

If only the world were in the hands of women, Zari thought. Women give birth. They are creators, and they know the value of their creation, the value of endurance, patience, monotony, and being unable to do anything for oneself. Perhaps because men have never been creators, they'll take any risk to create something. If the world were in the hands of women, how could there be wars? If they take the blessings that you have away from you, what then?

She remembered the day that Khan Kaka had just bought a car. There was still no war, and no quarrel had started between the brothers, and if Khan Kaka nagged occasionally, it concerned Yusof's conduct as a landlord and his treatment of the villagers. They went hunting in Khan Kaka's car. Khosrow was there too. The driver accidently hit a fawn and the fawn crumpled into a lifeless bundle of flesh and bones. They stopped and moved the crumpled corpse to the side of the road. Its mother got there with another fawn following her. She circled her baby again and again and then rammed herself against the car. The poor thing didn't know it was metal. She was butting against Khan Kaka, Yusof, and Zari. She was confused. Her hind legs were slipping, and she looked at each one of them, gazing with her big eyes, eyes that looked as if they had been blackened with *kohl*. She seemed to be asking, Why? Why? Khan Kaka began to cry. The game had come to them on her own feet. But they turned back.

She put the hot charcoal on the hookah, took a puff, and before taking it to the parlor, she checked on the stranger, who was sobbing in his sleep. She wanted to wake him up, but she changed her mind. The stranger looked athletic.

It was obvious that the quarrel was still going on. She hadn't gone in yet, but she could hear Sohrab. "Now that I've figured it out and know exactly what to do, why do you prevent others from helping? You say I'm an ambitious and dangerous person and woe be the day that I get anywhere . . ."

She entered the room and put the hookah in front of her husband. With the doors closed, the air in the parlor was warm, and sweat was beading on everyone's foreheads and noses. Majid had taken off his jacket and opened his shirt collar. Zari went to the cupboard, brought out straw fans, and put them on the table. Then she took small plates, knives, and forks out of the cupboard and set the table so quietly that she made no noise at all.

Sohrab was saying, "This action is not just dangerous for me. I know that I am no more than a step away from death. If I don't do this, the nightmare of that incident will drive me crazy. You say this action is a kind of show. Man! I am welcoming death with open arms." He put a hand over his eyes and suddenly wept. Zari looked in amazement and put a fan on his lap. Sohrab immediately stopped weeping, laughed, and said to Zari, "Then, every Thursday I will wait for you to bring me bread, dates, and cigarettes." Addressing everyone, he continued, "Khanom Zahra is like my own sister. I told her and her sister-in-law my plans before telling you. Unfortunately, some unscrupulous people also heard. But it doesn't matter anymore. Even if you don't help me, I'll do it. But, my brother must give me armed men and Yusof must give us provisions. I myself have thirty trustworthy men ready to give their lives."

It was strange. Zari had cut open two watermelons and both turned out yellow and unripe. She took this as a bad omen. The third watermelon was not bad. She wanted to cut the edges in zigzags, but she thought, Who is going to look at the zigzag shapes of the melon now?

She put the large platter of watermelon next to a map of Iran that they had spread on the table. They were all bending over and looking at it, and Malek Sohrab had his finger on a point. "If we reach Yasuj, it won't be too far from Basht," he explained. "Then we'll go to Gachsaran."

"It will take a long time before we can get the people over there to support us," Yusof said. "But there is no other way and this is just the first step. As for the saboteurs, Mr. Fotuhi must—"

Turning to Zari, he said, "Khanom, don't make so much noise."

"All right," she replied realizing that she was being asked to leave. As she did, she heard Majid say, "I don't think the Laborers Party headquarters would approve such an action. If you agree with it yourself, that's one thing."

On Yusof's instructions, she set the lunch on the parlor table. They had all taken off their jackets and ties and had picked up fans.

At lunch, Yusof asked for wine, and Zari brought out two bottles of red wine from the cupboard. They had probably reached an agreement; why else would he ask for wine on a hot afternoon like this? When she was pulling the cork out of the bottle, it broke off and half of it fell into the bottle. It was obvious that Yusof had been watching because he said, "Don't worry, dear. The cork was dry."

She poured wine for everybody. The guests lifted their glasses and said, "To the health of Khanom Zahra." She dropped her head and thought, What good is health alone?

They were talking and joking, oblivious to Zari's presence. She was there to put the salt shaker in front of them, fill their glasses, or put the chicken gizzards on Majid's plate, because he liked them. Majid answered Yusof with his mouth full, "You're right."

Yusof was saying, "It was easier for our fathers. And if we don't move, it will be harder for our sons. Our fathers confronted one challenger and unfortunately submitted to him. Now, we are facing two challengers. Tomorrow a new challenger will also arrive and the day after tomorrow others, all guests at this table—"

Malek Rostam said, "Even if we can accomplish nothing, we will show our children the way—"

"Even if I am alone myself and the enemy numbers in the thousands," Malek Sohrab said. "I won't turn my back to the field—"

"And for thousands of years everyone's blood shall boil to avenge us, brother," Malek Rostam said. He downed his glass and continued with, "The blood of Siyavash!"

Yusof extended his glass to Zari, but the conversation had filled her with such fear that she dropped the crystal carafe and broke it. She thought, Oh God, what kind of people are these men? They know it is useless, but to prove their existence, their manhood, and courage, and for their children not to later spit on their graves, with their own free hands, they dig . . . bite my tongue . . . God forbid. She was choking on the tears that had welled up, but she would not let them out. She bent over, gathering the pieces of crystal. What odd things come to women's minds, and at what times! For no reason, she remembered one night when Yusof had sighed in his sleep and she had awakened, turned on the light on the table and had watched her husband's earlobes in the light of the lamp for a long time—just like red velvet that a hand has brushed against the grain.

The stranger slept until sunset and then came to the garden in Yusof's pajamas. He sat by the pool, washed his face, and watched Yusof and Majid playing backgammon. The other guests had left in the afternoon, when the heat was at its peak. From the man's comfortable movements, his face, and the instructions that he was giving Yusof and Majid—"Block his stone . . . you have no choice . . . spread out"—it was obvious that he wasn't a truck driver.

Khadijeh brought him food. The man had quite an appetite. By the time Zari came back with the aromatic beverage he had asked for, he had devoured the food.

The stranger got up, looked around the garden and said, "You've got a good life. But what a pity, it seems you have no children. Wouldn't it be nice to have ten or twelve children running around in this garden? Zari asked, "Do you have children?" The stranger sighed and said, "I have two boys."

It was some time before the stranger opened up and confessed that he was a military captain, and excitedly told them all that had happened. He was in the middle of his story when the twins came back. The man fell silent and looked at them with envy. Yusof kissed the children. He ordered Khadijeh to take them to the aunt on the roof and to keep an eye on them so they did not fall or touch the hot brazier. The man continued his story, more excited than his audience. Later, when Khosrow and Hormoz arrived, he routinely answered their greetings.

17

I WAS THE commander of a convoy of yellow provision trucks that left Shiraz and reached Abadeh. All together there were fourteen trucks, forty-five soldiers, and five noncommissioned officers who were assigned to protect the trucks. A third lieutenant, just graduated from the military academy, a young man of nineteen or twenty, was my immediate subordinate. Three of the trucks carried provisions, a fourth military uniforms, a fifth fuel, and a sixth weapons. We also had an ambulance. I was ordered to take the convoy to Abadeh and wait. No one had given me any written orders. In Abadeh we received a telegram saying that we should deliver the supplies needed by the Esfahan division and then go on to Tehran. I had been on several other assignments with Rezvaninezhad and knew him well. The unfortunate man had fourteen dependents and his parents were blind. His brother was also with us. Both brothers were warrant officers.

"We stayed overnight in Abadeh. Late at night we were coming back from a night out on the town, when I saw a light in one of the trucks. I went in. I saw Rezvaninezhad and his brother sitting there. They were having bread and tea. I felt sorry for them. 'Come on, let's go out together,' I said. 'Be my guest. We'll go to the Municipal Kabob Shop and have rice and kabob and *arak*. The *arak* there is so powerful that if you pour it on the ground and strike a match it'll start burning.' He said, 'Captain, do you think we couldn't have thought of going out drinking? Do you think we don't want to have a good time like you? We accepted this assignment to get two hundred *tomans* each in extra pay to take home to our children.'

"We started out the next morning, and at noon we stopped the convoy by a river. We were supposed to wait there for a car. When I got out, I saw a few nomads wearing double-flap felt hats and sleeveless shepherd's cloaks. They were on the other side of the river watering their unsaddled horses. As soon as one of them saw us, he jumped on his horse and took off for the mountains on the left. We went to the orchard next to the river to have lunch. A few of the men in felt hats were in the garden, but they were wearing thin *abas,* as thin as my mother's *chador.* We didn't realize they were spies. When the tank commander came, he made us understand. He said that we must get into battle formation, because the road we were going on was under siege. Until then, we all thought that we had a simple assignment. We only had to go to the Semirom garrison and deliver provisions, weapons, and fuel and return safe and sound.

"I told the tank commander, 'My friend, we don't have troops. How can we pass through a road under siege?' He said, 'They won't attack in the daytime. We'll go through during the day. If we start right now, we'll get there in the afternoon. If we can, we'll return; otherwise we'll spend the night in the garrison and start on the road early in the morning.'

"We started out but when we turned left, it became clear that the road had been tampered with. Every twenty meters, our trucks either fell into potholes and stalled or got stuck in mud and spun their wheels. You couldn't even make five kilometers an hour. We didn't turn on the truck lights, and the we stayed close together. Had we made it to the Khorus Galu Pass, we would have reached those unfortunate people. The obstructions on the road were planned by a native army deserter. Later on, we found out that he had planned their battle formation. That officer had been condemned to death, escaped, and taken refuge with them. They called him Colonel, but he wasn't a colonel.

"The tank engine overheated. It went another ten feet and stalled. By then it was dark and bonfires dotted the higher elevations. It

was clear that they were the strongholds of the Qashqa'is and Boyer
Ahmadis. We were just at the mouth of the Khorus Galu Pass. They
were above us on both sides, but they weren't bothering us. They
only made frightening noises: 'Lilili, huhuhu, lilili, huhuhu.'

"When we opened the hood of the tank to let it cool, we saw
that the water pump had a hole. We decided to repair it in the light
of a hurricane lantern. While the repairs were being done, we gathered up the men to dig trenches around the truck as a precaution
and had the soldiers stand watch while we patrolled. I told everybody that we neither had the right nor the ability to turn back.
All the truck drivers were sergeants. The head sergeant said,
'Captain, the soldiers have just received their ranks. They don't know
how to fire guns.' I told the head sergeant, 'Then distribute
their weapons among the officers and the sergeants.' Their share
turned out to be a gun and fifteen bullets apiece. We also had five
machine guns to protect the armored tank—two on each side and
one in the back.

"We sat in the trenches with our guns cocked and ready for the
attack. I wore a revolver under my uniform. We had no food or
water. And the weather was very cold. We could neither turn back
nor go forward. The tank commander and his aides were trying
to repair the pump, but they never did succeed. The enemy kept
making those 'lilili, huhuhu' sounds until ten o'clock and still did-
n't bother us. The car commander, a captain like me, lost all hope
of repairing the pump and, out of fear, got diarrhea. He said there
were two thousand of them—a thousand Qashqa'is this side of
Khorus Galu and a thousand Boyer Ahmadis on the other side.
He said, 'They'll tear us to pieces. I wish the tank—' I didn't let
him finish. I said, 'You're ruining everyone's morale. For now, go
inside the tank, close the hatch, and sit down.'

"It was certainly past ten, and it was quite dark. No light, no
moonlight, no lamps. We didn't dare strike a match. We could only
see their bonfires dotting both sides of the mountain. 'Don't
waste bullets,' I told the sergeants. 'If the target is not in sight, don't
shoot until they come to our rescue from Semirom or Shahreza.
When the tank commander joined us, he said that a convoy
had started out from Shahr-e Kord and should be in Shahreza by
now.

"It was certainly past eleven when I heard the sound of hooves coming from behind us. There must have been ten or twelve riders. The head sergeant said, 'Sir, they're coming.' From the sound of the hooves, I gauged that they were about thirty meters away from us. The sergeant at the end of the convoy, who had a machine gun, said, 'They're coming.' There was utter silence and absolute darkness. They had come to check and see if we were asleep or awake. Three or four of them shouted, 'huhu, huhu,' and the sound of bullets hitting metal was heard, 'whizzz, pop, whizzz, pop.' They were shooting at the trucks. The shower of our machine guns drove them away.

"In the early morning light, I could make out horses and riders appearing on top of the mountain and then disappearing. Suddenly the horses and their riders started down the mountain. The ground in the trenches was cold. Again there was the sound of 'whizzz, pop, whizz, pop.' The bullets hit the trucks. I said, 'Do not fire. Shoot only when they come down.'

"The sergeant who was the driver of the last truck was an old man. He said 'ouch' and fell. I went to him. The sergeant from Esfahan said, 'Sir, get down. Get down on the ground. Bullets are flying everywhere.' I dragged the old man toward the ambulance and we laid him down on a stretcher inside the ambulance and waited for God's will to be done. Three minutes later, a bullet pierced the shoulder of one of the soldiers. Then the belly and thigh of another. The soldiers took those two and laid them down on the other stretchers in the ambulance. The ambulance only had these three stretchers. It was a brown Ford with the Lion and Sun emblem.

"Their people were crawling down the mountain. A hundred and fifty meters from our trenches, we could see a brick building in an orchard. They would reach the back of the orchard and take positions. When they came into our firing range, a Turkoman sergeant, the driver of the first truck, said, 'I can take a side road, get to the top of the mountain and check their position, if really . . .' I didn't let him. By then it was too light. It was seven, seven-thirty in the morning. On the top of the mountain, about sixty or seventy were 'huhuing' and shouting all together, 'Soldiers, weapons down, surrender. Soldiers, weapons down, surrender.' I said, 'They can eat shit; we will not surrender.' By nine or nine-thir-ty, twelve people had been shot when I heard, 'Attack! Huhu, attack!' And they headed down the mountain. We jumped into the trucks and the Turkoman driver and another sergeant tried to turn the trucks around any way they could. There was no other choice. We had to abandon the tank and at least save the weapons and fuel trucks. I am ashamed to say that we left behind the wound-ed. They were crying. Not all of them . . .

"They rushed out. There were about a thousand men, maybe more. The Turkoman driver slipped out from behind the wheel in time, but the other driver got hit and the road was blocked. We had to get out. They were crawling forward on their chests and firing. I had one bullet left. They had gotten within ten steps of us. Rezvaninezhad lifted his head to shoot; he fell. He said, 'Khandan,' and fell. I guess Khandan was his child's name. The poor fellow had fourteen dependents. The bullet had blown his brains out. I saw the grey mush of his brains with my own eyes. His brother went to help him. They shot him, too. They had nailed both brothers at the same time. I sat on the ground and with the bullet I had left shot the guy who had killed the two brothers in the chest. His friend ran to him and shouted, 'Papa, Zargham, did he kill you? Papa?'

"I crawled under the weapons truck and slowly dragged myself into one of the trenches. The sergeant in the trench was dead. I laid down on the dead man like a bloody corpse. The Boyer Ahmadis were galloping and jumping over my head and kicking dust over me. The looting started. First they took the weapons, and then I could hear the voices of their women, who were ulu-lating, 'Lili, huhu.' I heard the sound of a bugle and drums. I heard their song so many times that I memorized it:

> Over the hill, down the hill, is an army camp, not far.
> Sohrab Khan, look into the glass, see how many there are.
> I'm drunk, I'm drunk, I'm so drunk.
> The government's ankle's in my hand
> I'm drunk, I'm drunk, I'm so drunk.
> A short Brno is in my hand.'

"A Qashqa'i came up to me, put the heel of his shoe on my shoulder and said, 'You bastard, you are alive; get up. I saw you lying down. Give me the pistol. Get up. Get up.' A dark, dwarfish Boyer Ahmadi also arrived. I gave the pistol to the Qashqa'i and the two began to fight. I saw the Boyer Ahmadi kill the Qashqa'i and take the pistol. Again I laid down on the corpse in the trench and almost passed out. I was tired and thirsty and I was so angry I almost had a stroke. The Qashqa'i and Boyer Ahmadi women had arrived and were throwing the gunnysacks of provisions out of the trucks. They untied the sacks or tore them open and poured tea, sugar, rice, chick peas, and beans into their own sacks. I saw a Boyer Ahmadi take the newly graduated third lieutenant's gun from him and make him undress, stark naked. The third lieutenant managed to hold a gunnysack in front of himself. One of the women snatched the gunnysack away, put onions in it, and tied the top. In the end, the women and children of the upper village came with donkeys and put what was left into their saddle bags.

"We had put three sergeants who had been shot or had their bellies ripped open on the ambulance beds. The ambulance had a Lion and Sun emblem on it, but they didn't realize it and set the ambulance on fire. You could smell charred flesh and bones for a long time. Then they set the trucks on fire, too.

"Again, another Qashqa'i came and put the heel of his shoe on my shoulder. 'Get up,' he said. 'Take off your coat.' I got up, mustered all my strength, and pushed him against the burning fuel truck. Then a thin, dark rider came toward me. He had a club in his hand with a knife stuck on its tip and he was holding his gun at his waist. He said, 'Take off your coat. I won't kill you, so your clothes won't get bloody.' He got my uniform, my insignias, and my army boots. My insignias were gold. My mother had bought them for me at New Year, when I received my promotion. He ripped off my watch with his knife and with the same knife took the revolver from my side. They took two undamaged trucks with them, trucks with army uniforms and ammunition. I heard later that they put on the uniforms and attacked the Semirom garrison.

"I slipped away into the mountains. I heard someone moaning. I thought I'd take his clothes and wear them. It was a sergeant, the driver of one of our own trucks. He was covered in blood. I asked, 'Are you shot?' He said, 'No, I gave them my gun and escaped in time.' I said, 'Get up and come with me.' He said, 'Captain, sir, I beg you, my suitcase, the souvenirs I bought from Shiraz.' I said, 'From now on, no more Captain, sir.' And we started up the slope of the mountain. We passed their trenches. They were made of stone, white stone, each with room for four people, and were full of empty cartridge shells. Now we were going toward Abadeh off the main road. When we passed the mountain ridge, a Qashqa'i horseman appeared. We laid down on the ground next to a bush. He came and stood by our heads and said, 'Hey, soldiers, bastards, I saw you. Get up. Get up.' He said to the sergeant, 'Is that you, bastard? Mirza Hasan? Where is your gun?' The sergeant got up and automatically began to undress. He took off his army boots and was left with a shirt and long underwear. He bundled the rest, tied it, and handed it to the Qashqa'i horseman. The horseman said, 'You bastard, how fat you've gotten! You're looking nice and healthy, Mirza Hasan!' I said, 'You'll have to waste two bullets to kill us both. Don't kill us. On the other side of the mountain they're looting the trucks. Everybody is taking away rice, chick peas, beans, sugar, tea, onions, army uniforms, bullets, and guns.' I said, 'If you hurry, you can get there in time.' He looked at the sergeant and said, 'Is he telling the truth, Mirza Hasan?' The sergeant said, 'Yes, brother.' The horseman took a pair of slippers out of his saddlebag and said, 'This melon skin is for you, Mirza Hasan.' It was a pair of soft ladies' slippers. He had probably stolen them. Yes. I forgot to tell you, a husband and wife and twelve government officials from Abadeh caught a ride with us, and when we turned left, they got off. They had probably been robbed on the road to Izadkhast. The sergeant gave the slippers back to the horseman and said, 'Keep them. I can't use them. Take them to Sister Golabtun. And say hello to her for me.' The horseman said, 'I'm taking Golabtun a dress with marigold prints; I'm taking her a gold necklace; I'm taking her a mirror.' I said to the horseman, 'Then go now, so you can take food too.' When he left, I asked the sergeant, 'Are you related?' He said, 'Yes. He's my cousin. But my name is not Mirza Hasan. Mirza Hasan is what they call thieves.'

"I think it was two in the afternoon. An airplane came by and made some noise and circled above the military convoy. The Qashqa'is and Boyer Ahmadis popped a few shots and it left. So much for military aerial assistance!

"Now we two were left thirsty, hungry, and barefoot, in shirts and long underwear, and we had a pair of ladies slippers that fit neither of us. We headed down from the ridge of the mountain to a little puddle of water in the valley. We rubbed our faces with the muddy water. The sergeant said, 'I can't walk anymore' and laid down right there. I said, 'As you wish. I'll leave you here and be on my way. But I walked slowly. When I had gone about a hundred meters away from him, he called me, caught up with me, and said, 'Hey, Captain, sir, I was considering going to the black tent of Sister Golabtun. It's not too far.' To tell you the truth, I felt embarrassed. I didn't answer him. We came out of the valley together. We saw a few villages teeming with people.

"We caught up with a little boy on a donkey and an old man following behind. He was a peddler. He had a loaf of bread. He gave half of it to us and said he had no water. I told him, 'We are drivers. They set our trucks on fire and took our clothes, as you can see.' He said, 'The river is a *parasang* away. But be careful. They have no mercy. Look at the top of the mountain. They say the Qashqa'is and Boyer Ahmadis have become outlaws. They have fought the government on the other side of the mountain.'

"It was early in the evening when we reached the river and drank water. I told the sergeant, 'Don't drink too much—you'll get bloated.' We rested for ten minutes and waded across the river. We saw two Boyer Ahmadis sitting by a fire and having tea, their horses tied to a tree. They asked us who we were and where we were going. I told them the Qashqa'is had robbed us and that we were truck drivers. The sergeant told the one smoking a clay pipe, 'Let us have a puff of your pipe. We are hungry.' He handed us the pipe. When we gave it back to him, it was spent. He dumped it on the ground and said, 'What's left?' Then he gave us his water gourd and said, 'Off you go.' Nothing else.

"A few peasants with shovels on their shoulders were walking toward the village. We caught up with them and joined them. They

asked, 'Who are you?' I said, 'We are drivers; our trucks were set
on fire and . . .' We kept going until we reached Abadeh. When
we entered the city, it was eight at night. We found the sergeant
in the gendarme station. He said the lieutenant was in the teahouse,
but the station chief, a captain, had gone to Shiraz. He took us
to the teahouse. I told the lieutenant how we had been trapped.
I told him how they had attacked, looted, burned, and slaughtered.
They gave us hot tea with sugar and then we went to the guard
station. The lieutenant called his assistant and said, 'This is the
captain. You should hear what he's been saying. It wasn't as simple as we heard. It was even worse than crossing the Serat Bridge
on Judgment Day. The soldiers didn't even know how to shoot.
They were greenhorns. They were crying and saying, 'Captain, sir,
we don't know how to shoot.' And turning to me, he said, 'When
the convoy left Abadeh, I breathed a sigh of relief. I thought the
poor colonel would not have to beg so much for reinforcements
anymore. God help them.' Then he ordered his deputy to close
the gate to the tower, gave instructions for guarding it, and went
to the wireless himself to report to the gendarmerie and ask for
help. He said, 'They are sure to come for us tonight.' They did
their best for the two of us. They gave us clothes and scraped together a little money for us. Even those old gendarme clothes and shoes
were a great blessing to us. The lieutenant said, 'Wash your
hands and face and go spend the night at the house of the village
chief. But don't let him know that you're officers or he'll kill you
before tomorrow morning.' We left with the gendarme who was
to accompany us and passed through a sheep pen. The village chief
came out of his room. He had a red beard. He took us to a room
with a dirt floor and no carpeting. He took two old quilts, which
were on top of a wooden box in the corner of the room, spread
them on the ground, and asked, 'Have you had supper?' We told
him no. Then the daughter of the village chief brought in some
dirty milk in a black dish and put it in front of us. She opened
the wooden box with a key and gave us two loaves of black
bread, which we ate. And she locked up the box. We slept like logs
until the next morning. They didn't find out that we were officers.
In the morning, they gave us hot tea and black bread. Again we

went to see the lieutenant. He was even kinder than the night before. We waited until noon so he could get permission for me to return to Tehran. By noon, five other people, wounded and naked or half naked, got to Abadeh with the help of the peasants and came to the guard station. They were the patrol guards of the Semirom garrison and reported that the main battle had started the previous afternoon.

"Finally the lieutenant reached the gendarmerie. He was ordered to help us, but they said explicitly that we should all return to Shiraz immediately. It was decided that we would start off for Deh Bid on two or three donkeys and hitch a ride when we found a car with room for us. We cleaned and bandaged the wounds of the injured as best we could, and the lieutenant got together some civilian clothes and gave them to us. He also handed me eighty *tomans*. In the meantime, our Turkoman driver appeared riding a Qashqa'i mare. He was the only one who had escaped unscathed. He told us, 'A Qashqa'i took my gun, got off his horse and went looting. He told me to hold his horse for him until he came back. As soon as he wasn't looking, I jumped on the mare and came straight here. Last night, I slept somewhere safe and had rice, *khoresht,* and *dugh,* And this morning, I went to a bath house and had a massage and a nice drink of cold water. At noon . . .'

"We put the wounded on the donkeys and started out on foot behind them. Whenever one of us got tired, we took turns riding the Qashqa'i mare our Tukoman driver had brought as his spoils. We also had bread and cheese and a jug of water. We arrived in Deh Bid at ten o'clock that night. At the Deh Bid gate an officer was standing with a riding crop and boots. I looked at the officer and said, 'I am an officer, too.' The officer had a new riding crop, shiny boots, and a new uniform. I told him briefly what had happened to us and asked him for a car to take us to Shiraz. He said, 'This whole area is crawling with bandits. No vehicles are allowed through.' He took us to the gendarmerie guard station. The gendarme chief welcomed us and said that he had been expecting us. He had gotten word from Abadeh. They brought us roasted chicken, *arak,* and yogurt with cucumbers. We had sat down to eat and the gendarme chief had gone to the wireless when they

came. But they were neither Qashqa'is nor Boyer Ahmadis. They
were Doshman Ziyaris. The gendarme chief was shot right there
at the wireless. If looting can be profitable for two tribes, it can
be profitable for a third. I haven't seen my other companions yet.
I escaped from the back of the guard station tower and headed down
the mountain into a large pasture until I reached a walnut tree.
I wanted to lie down and go to sleep under the tree, but it was very
cold and dark and there was the constant sound of shots being fired.
I walked and sometimes ran until dawn. There was no moonlight,
no stars, no lights. And I didn't have any matches, either. I had
the eighty *tomans* in cash the lieutenant in the Abadeh gendarmerie had given me. If I had had any matches, I could have
made a fire to sleep by. In the morning, two shepherds came with
their flock. I said hello to them. I said, 'I am a truck driver. I was
robbed last night, and I'm hungry now.' The shepherd made a fire.
One of them milked a sheep and gave me the milk in a black bowl.
The son of the shepherd, a boy of seven or eight, showed up with
a bundle, which he gave to the shepherd and said, 'I ran all the
way, papa; it's real hot.' He was right—the black bread was still
hot. I heard a shot and a bullet hit the bowl of milk right in the
middle. They were the same people from the night before. One
group went to the sheep and herded them away and, as they headed down the mountain, they shot the two sheep dogs. A few of
them came and tied the arms of all three of us. They didn't
bother with the boy. They made us walk ahead of them until we
reached the khan, who was sitting on a chair in front of his
tent. On the way there, I told the little boy, 'When we get to the
khan, fall on the ground at his feet and plead with him not to kill
your father and your uncle for the love of his own children.' I said,
'If you do this, when they let us go, I'll give you something
nice.' The boy did as I had said. But they kept us for six days, and
when they were about to leave, they took our clothes and let us
go. As for the eighty *tomans,* they took that on the first day. And,
again, I kept going along on foot until I got myself to Zarqan, where
I saw you.

    "Now, listen to what had happened to those unfortunate peo-
ple. The real slaughter was in the Semirom plain and the Semirom

garrison. Those patrol soldiers said they had one day's rations to eat for four days. I know they weren't at all prepared to resist. They had guns but no bullets. And we couldn't get to them. The same officer that I saw at the Deh Bid gate with the boots and the riding crop said, 'The Boyer Ahmadis and Qashqa'is sent a letter to the Colonel that he was condemned to death and he'd better surrender. The Colonel wrote in response, *Our tents will be our graves!* He said the poor colonel had lost hope in the Esfahan division and had resorted to asking for help from the Abadeh garrison. He said, 'Now the wireless of the Semirom garrison is silent.'

"One of the patrols of the Semirom garrison, whose arm wound I bandaged myself, told me on the road, 'We saw through the field glasses that they had mounted three machine guns on three mules and were coming.' I asked him, 'How about the tank?' He said, 'They set the tank on fire. It was still burning as we were running away.' He said, 'We reported it to the poor Colonel. The Colonel first had us set up tents on the four sides of the spring so we wouldn't be short of water, and we dug trenches around the tents. He had planned a circular line of defense. The poor man kept encouraging us to resist. The Colonel said, *The fire power of the light and heavy machine guns will mow them down.* He said he was sure help would come. The Abadeh radio had reported that the motorized convoy was on its way. He instructed us patrol soldiers to let him know as soon as we saw the head of the convoy and we would receive a reward. He said the outlaws didn't have heavy artillery and the range of their guns was no more than four hundred meters. When we reported to him that the outlaws were coming with three machine guns loaded on mules, he went pale. He said they had ambushed the reinforcements. Alas, the poor man spoke to us like a father. He lost all hope of your coming and was forced to change his defense strategy. He said they would all come from the back road, which follows Khorus Galu. He hastily made a battle formation and the soldiers took position on the ridges of two fairly high mountains that overlooked the road. The poor soldiers had one bullet apiece. On those ridges where the soldiers sat in ambush, there is a half-dead forest of mountain pistachio, almond bushes, and lotus trees. On the slope of the hills we hastily erected the hospital and kitchen tents. But what kitchen? What hospital? We had one day's rations for four days.

"That patrol warrant officer of the Semirom garrison said, 'They attacked from three directions. The sound of their bugles and drums echoed in the mountains and valleys. The Boyer Ahmadis came from the northeast of Semirom village, the Qashqa'is from the northwest, and another group came down from the Dena heights, passed through the groves and vineyards, and tightened the circle around us. The cavalry captain, a first artillery lieutenant, a few noncommissioned officers, and I went to the tower to convince the Colonel to stop the fighting and raise a white flag. I saw the Colonel sitting behind the desk, his hands under his chin, staring straight ahead. He listened to what the cavalry captain had to say and shook his head. Then he asked if any one had a cigarette. This time, the cavalry captain pleaded and said this was not a war anymore, that this way we were waiting for a massacre. In a sad tone, the Colonel said we might get help at the last moment. The cavalry captain got angry and told the Colonel, *Sir, for ten days you've been trying everywhere. What reinforcements? When? Why are you putting up resistance? To get us all killed?* In the same sad tone, the Colonel said, *I can't force you to stay, but I myself will stay. And forget about the white flag.* As we came out of the tower, I got shot. I tied a handkerchief on my wounded arm and got myself to Semirom village. The people in the village said that the Qashqa'is and Boyer Ahmadis would keep coming, taking Iranian military uniforms, putting them on, and leaving in a hurry. Since they mixed in with our poor soldiers, they probably thought the reinforcements they had so anxiously awaited had arrived and they may have even cheered.' "

When the captain's story ended, Majid got up, yawned and said, "What a small world!" Zari said, "As they say, 'mountains don't meet, but people eventually do.' " Yusof looked at her, laughed and said, "Dear, you have slowly started to figure things out, too."

Next morning, the stranger who was no longer a stranger left for the headquarters wearing Yusof's clothes. They were too wide and too short for him. They didn't hear from him until the following week, when his letter arrived from Tehran. He expressed his gratitude and mentioned the court-martial that he had ahead of him and the case made against him. He said it all reminded him of the story told about the famous coppersmith in Shushtar who was blamed for a crime committed by an infamous blacksmith in Balkh, but had to pay for the other's crime. He also wrote that he had decided to resign from the army and, no matter what, to take his wife and two sons and go to Switzerland. But he made no mention of the two hundred *tomans* he had borrowed from Yusof.

18

ON THURSDAY afternoon, Zari went to the insane asylum with Gholam. The director was not there so she was accompanied by the head nurse, a woman who resembled the maid Khadijeh. She knew that Miss Fotuhi would be upset about the newspapers, which had been cut out here and there. In the women's ward, of the former patients, only the paralyzed woman who hugged the *givehs* in her sleep and Miss Fotuhi were left. But there were quite a few new patients. Four were sitting on the beds, and there was a screen around one of the beds. In the middle of the room three patients were sitting on straw mats and playing the little children's game of "crow, fly." When Zari entered, one of them said, "Bread and date, fly!" Zari smiled. Fortunately, she had brought bread and fruit, which Gholam set down. The same woman said, "The princess, fly." They began jostling about and playing "punch the dough."

The head nurse did not allow her to approach the bed that had the screen around it. "They have sent plenty of fruit and flowers for this patient," she said quietly. "The only thing is that she doesn't eat anything. For now, they have given her an IV. They are preparing a private room for her. Her relatives say she has worked so hard in this heat that she has strained her brain. But the doctor says it is due to both typhus and being overworked. May God cure her, for the sake of Imam Ali." She added, "A woman comes late at night when everybody has gone to sleep, performs her ablutions and begins praying to Her Holiness Fatemeh. Ezzat was on duty last night. She said the woman was prostrate in prayer for a very long time, and Ezzat was worried. She got closer. Thank God, she heard the woman saying, 'Oh Fatemeh, help me. Help! Help!' She pleaded with God, saying, 'Help! Help!' fifty, a hundred, I don't know how many times. The woman spent the night here. It was long past the curfew. Now Dr. Abdollah Khan has prescribed donkey meat, if they can find it. They have to make patties out of donkey meat; maybe she'll feel like eating them."

When she finished her distribution, Zari went to Miss Fotuhi, who was sitting by the window with her back to the other patients. Zari said hello and put the newspapers at the side of the bed and stood a little farther back. She knew that as soon as they were opened, they would meet with the same fate as the ones she had brought two weeks ago. Miss Fotuhi suddenly got up from the bed and said, "My brother! I had a hunch that my brother would come and take me to the 124,000-square-meter garden." Zari looked out the window but could not see anyone. Without paying attention to her, Miss Fotuhi set out on her way. She was mumbling to herself, "How rude! Stupid jerks . . . I'll show them right now."

In fact, it was not long before she returned with her brother and sat on the bed. She was crying and saying, "Why did you come alone, dear brother? Why didn't mother come? You never come, but when you do you're empty-handed!"

Mr. Fotuhi greeted Zari, who was getting up to leave the brother and sister alone. "Khanom Zahra," he said, "I have some business with you." Miss Fotuhi got angry. "Let her get the hell out of here. Every week she comes here, putting on airs, and shows off to me!" She asked again, "Why hasn't my mother come? Take me to the 124,000-square-meter garden. I feel depressed in this cage. What kind of brother are you? You should have at least gotten a private room for your sister."

She was holding the brother's hand tightly, kissing it, pressing her tearful eyes on his dark, veined hand, and asking again why her mother had not come. She was worried that the enemies might have confiscated their garden . . . those enemies who constantly attach electrodes to her body. They attach them to her legs, her arms, and her heart and make her heart beat irregularly. She placed the brother's hand on her heart and said, "See!"

The head nurse, Gholam, and all the patients were looking on, even the patients who had been playing "crow, fly" a few minutes ago. Fotuhi kissed his sister's salt and pepper hair and said, "Dear sister, you know that mother is dead. I've told you a hundred times."

Miss Fotuhi said, "Now you see here, brother. I know that my mother is not dead. They have deceived you. When you put her into the coffin, she quietly got out and hid. Ever since then, she's been hiding somewhere in the 124,000-square-meter garden and you haven't gone to look for her." She swallowed and said, "I swear to God, last night, in the middle of the night, they came to me with a knife and cut out my liver, took it, and stuffed straw in its place. Since this morning my mouth tastes like straw."

Fotuhi said impatiently, "My dear, where did we ever have a 124,000-square-meter garden?"

Miss Fotuhi said, "Take me. I'll work as your maid. We'll live together and won't bother with anybody else. We'll plant wheat in that large garden of ours. We'll plant black mulberries. We'll plant cucumbers. We'll install beehives. I myself will make a kiln and bake bread. We'll bring roosters and hens and hatch chicks. And we won't let anybody in, either . . . We'll buy narcissus bulbs and plant them in our own flowerpots, wrapped in cotton . . ."

A nurse came in and whispered something to the head nurse who said, "Very well. Put the flowers around the room and set the fruit on the table. Then come back; help me move the patient. Wait a minute. Take her suitcases for now." The nurse went behind the screen and came out with two new suitcases. Gholam took one of the suitcases from her and they left the room together.

Zari and Mr. Fotuhi stopped under a dusty pine tree in the flowerless garden of the insane asylum. "I came to see you here," he said. "Yusof Khan has probably told you that I would come today and tell everybody of my decision through you." No, Yusof had not said anything to her. He probably wanted their meeting to look natural.

"Since yesterday, I have considered all aspects of the issue. And this morning, I brought up the subject in the meeting of the party leaders—of course, without mentioning any names. Only as a pro-posal from myself. Everybody opposed it." He was shifting from foot to foot, swallowing, and stumbling on his words. "Nevertheless," he continued, "you know we have not officially announced the existence of our party. We are waiting for the right moment. But to separate from my comrades and go to Khuzestan with a group of people who are of the same mind as me . . . You know, I am in charge of students. With my group, a bunch of chil-dren, what can I do there?"

"Then they were right," Zari said. "They shouldn't have invit-ed you. You are not concerned about friends and allies. You're not even concerned about your own sister."

She was amazed at her own harshness, although she felt it was justified. She was irritated with Fotuhi anyway. Without any sign of being offended, he said, "We must build the society in such a way that nobody's sister goes mad. My sister's madness is a symp-tom of the malady of our society. When we organize the masses and come to power, we will administer justice." He then paused and added, "In my opinion, it is still too early for this action and it will result in nothing but chaos and confusion. And it is not as easy as Malek Sohrab thinks. I don't believe they should give their reins to a hot-headed youth like Malek Sohrab. And I am sure they won't. Yusof Khan is more experienced than all of us. He said him-self that until there is a forty percent chance of success, taking such a risk will be suicidal."

He was still speaking when Miss Fotuhi came toward them. She was tripping on the white sheet she had wrapped around herself. She shouted, "Kill me and relieve me! Take your penknife out of your coat pocket and kill me. I have put on my shroud and I'm ready!" When she reached them, she let go of the sheet. She was stark naked. The nurses ran out and surrounded her. She hit one of them with her elbow and threw her down. And shaking her fist at her brother, she said, "Oh you thief of people's wives! Meeting under the pine tree! Is that it?" She was stronger than all of them. They would catch her and she would escape their grip and shout, "You took my land and property! You sold my 124,000-square-meter garden to spend on this slut!" She ran around the empty pool in the courtyard and screamed, "Oh people, know that I am the greatest woman in this country. I am a poet. I have composed fifty thousand couplets. This slut has my poems." She stopped to catch her breath and continued, "This slut has my poems published in *Shafaq-e Sorkh* newspaper in her own name. I am the daughter of the Prophet himself. Then Her Holiness Fatemeh . . . like Her Holiness Fatemeh, I am chaste, pure, and immaculate. My brother has swindled me out of my property. He has cut off the heads of my father and mother. All these narcissuses you see have sprung from their spilled blood. Make a bouquet of these flowers and put them on my grave." And then she cried hard enough to break one's heart, saying, "Me, the bastard, the unfortunate bastard, me . . ."

She talked such a blue streak she wore herself out. The nurses covered her with a *chador* and a hefty man picked her up and took her to the office.

Zari was leaving. The head nurse came to her and said, "Thank God, Miss Masihadam is feeling very well. We transferred her to a private room. She can have visitors now. Go see her. I'll bring you a pain killer or something."

So the patient they were all so keen to serve was Miss Masihadam. Even though Zari was tired and had a headache, she decided to visit the woman she had heard so much about. She knocked on the door and went in. Miss Masihadam was sitting on the bed and was swinging her head back and forth. As she moved her head, her curly black hair would fly through the air, cover her face, brush away from her face, and again . . . They had actually put flowers all around the room. It was evident from some of the bouquets that a woman gardener had picked and arranged them, or someone had searched through a field or farm and put together that bunch of wild flowers or armful of wheat stalks. One bouquet in particular caught Zari's attention. In the middle of it, there were a few stalks of purple wildflowers that grew by streams or in wheat fields. They were surrounded by a row of fragrant Mohammadi rosebuds firmly tied together. Around the buds were blossomed red roses, and the same arrangement was repeated up to the last row, which consisted of tuberoses. The entire bou-

quet was tied together with a string. Miss Masihadam kept swinging her head and did not even glance at the flowers or pay attention to the pastries arranged in large crystal bowls in the middle
of the room. Zari guessed that the covered bowls contained various homemade pastries, which someone must have baked for the
patient in this heat. Miss Masihadam tired, stopped moving her
head, and noticed Zari, who said hello. Miss Masihadam gazed
at Zari, but her eyes seemed vacant, even though they belonged
to someone quite young. Her eyes were hollow and despairing. Miss
Masihadam was so thin that she seemed shriveled. Her chest bones
showed through a thin, white nightgown. Her breasts seemed to
have sunk. Her complexion was yellower than the sunlight that
fell on the top row of bricks on the wall across from her.

"I hear you are feeling much better," Zari said. Miss Masihadam
was chewing on her nails and staring at her. She said, "I've heard
this voice somewhere before." She squinted and suddenly laughed,
a sparkle of recognition appearing in her eyes. "I recognize you!
I recognize you! You are Tal'at Khanom." She put her hand to her
heart and said, "I was so afraid! You didn't die then. I knew God
would answer my prayers. I asked God to take six months off my
life and instead not have you die by my hands. Come closer and
let me see you with my own eyes."

Zari knew that she had the wrong person, but she didn't say anything. If the thought of a friend or a sister or a patient staying alive
would bring a spark to her eyes and a smile to her lips, why should
she take this happiness away? As she sat on the bed next to her,
Miss Masihadam took Zari's hand, squeezed it, and in an amaz-
ingly sane manner explained, "When a child is born, if its color
is pink like silk, if it screams so the mother hears its voice, if it
pees—shshshsh . . ." She put her other hand over her mouth, gave
an innocent laugh, and continued, "then you feel rested and
you are so happy with yourself, as if you have created the child yourself! But when your child came, this first pregnancy, oh, it didn't
seem to have any color. There was no blood in the cord. I hit it,
and hit again; it didn't scream. I felt so exhausted. It was the first
baby I had delivered dead. Suddenly, I saw that no blood was coming from you either. I knew that you were bleeding somewhere

inside your belly and blood was collecting right there until your belly swelled up like a drum. I flicked my finger on your belly. Oh, your eyes moved, your pulse moved, your heart moved. I heard the outside door. Your mother had taken off into the alley and your husband came in and said, 'Did you kill them both?' And he told me, 'You are a murderer!' " She then pressed Zari's hand harder and complained, "Why did you play dead even though you weren't dead? Huh?"

Zari did not answer and Miss Masihadam continued. "You know, we doctors must get accustomed to death. We must not be afraid of its signs. But I was afraid; I felt as if a storm had come, scrambled all the conductors in my nerves and brain, thrown them in a pile, and jumbled them up. I felt like something had shattered in the pit of my stomach and dropped. They think I've gone crazy. But I'm not crazy. I'm just very, very depressed."

Zari tried to get up from her side, but Miss Masihadam wouldn't let go. She said, "I saw with my own two eyes that the ceiling cracked open and a winged person in black came and held you under his wings. But they don't believe it. I pleaded with the winged person in black. I said I was ready to give my whole life so that he would not take Tal'at. He said, 'I'll take her to heaven under the Tuba Tree.' 'Take me instead,' I said. Now, tell me, please, how come he brought you back? Was there no room left in heaven?"

She was pressing Zari's hand very hard and talking non-stop. She said, "Will you now do something for me? You know I've promised to go in your place."

"Of course!" Zari agreed.

Miss Masihadam put her mouth to Zari's ear and whispered, "Buy two *mesqals* of good opium, pulverize it, and before nightfall, before the old man comes, get it to me. But don't tell anybody. If the old man is here, drop it quietly into my shirt and leave. Okay?"

Zari bit her lip and Miss Masihadam burst into tears and said, "When the sun sets, I get so depressed that . . . it's as if they bring a load of steel and pile it on my heart."

She began to swing her head again. Her long hair was hitting Zari's face. Zari was pulling her head back and trying to get her hand out of the woman's grip at the same time, but in vain. And Zari had such a headache.

Finally, an old man with white hair and a cane came in and Zari, pleased, guessed that it must be Dr. Abdollah Khan. The old man came to the patient and put his hand on her shoulder. "Dear, you've started again!" His voice was not commanding. Instead it was very soothing. The patient's head stopped moving and she laughed at the old man. "I kept her so you could come and see her with your own eyes. You see? There was no room, so they returned her."

The old man turned to Zari and asked quietly, "Did she say a lot of nonsense?"

"On the contrary, she made a lot of sense."

Miss Masihadam shouted, "Do you see how the old man has become senile? Ask Tal'at what was going on at the end of the line, what was going on past the line. Because she's gone to the end of the line and come back. I thought she'd become part of that jug of water. I was afraid to drink water. I thought she'd become part of the flowers. I wouldn't look at the flowers for fear. You've talked so much nonsense, the old man's become senile. You scratched up my brain." And she winked at the old man. "Only death is true. All else is lies. Tal'at, please tell him death had wings and took you away. He tells me I have worn myself out and am imagining things!"

"I really must go," Zari said.

The old man accompanied Zari and murmured, "I have brought scissors with me to cut her hair. She can't stand the sight of her mother and relatives and won't let them near her. Do you know how to cut hair? It is really in the way."

"I know how, but it is late," Zari said. "I have guests tonight."

"Suppose it takes five minutes?"

Perhaps the patient heard the old man's whispers or guessed what he had said. In any case, she shouted, "Old man, have you gone mad?" She held her hair tightly with both hands.

"It won't take a month for your hair to grow back even fuller, dear," the old man said. "By then you'll be all better. I want to be the one to toss wedding candy over your head. Hurry up darling. I'm getting too old." What a soothing voice! He could tame a person with that voice, even someone who was in a hurry, even someone who was imagining things. Miss Masihadam signaled Zari over

and said, "Come closer, I want to say something in your ear." And
turning to the old man, she said, "You go to the other end of the
room and cover your ears." Zari was obliged to go back and put
her head near her mouth. She whispered, "When you are cutting
my hair, stick the tip of the scissors in my artery. Okay?"

She sat calmly while Zari wet her hair, combed it, and cut it
in little boy's style. Then Zari handed the scissors to the old man
and gazed into his eyes, which glittered in spite of his age. He nodded knowingly and Zari realized that he understood the secret that
had been whispered to her. The old man put the scissors in his pocket, and Zari said goodbye. She did not know whether the glitter
in the old man's eyes was a reflection of his white hair and eyebrows or a sparkle of awareness. Miss Masihadam was staring at
them. Suddenly she shouted, "Go get lost. Go wherever the hell
you want. Go to the end of the line." And she started swinging
her head again.

Zari had not yet stepped outside the room when the head nurse
came in and gave her a pill wrapped in a piece of paper. "I had
to go out and buy this for you," she said, adding, "The director
went to the Health Department this morning to get our ration of
medicine, but he isn't back yet. We don't even have a single pill
left. If we don't get them by tonight, with all these crazies . . ."

She did not finish what she was saying and went to the water
jug in the corner of the room. She picked up the glass that was
put over the jug. Zari unwrapped the pill. The old man said, "Wait,
Khanom Zahra. A pain killer is not such a good idea for a pregnant woman."

Zari looked at him in surprise and asked, "Do you know
me?" She thought and added, "I recognized you, too. You're Dr.
Abdollah Khan." She looked at him again. His face looked as if
he knew all the secrets of the world. She thought, If his fingers touch
my forehead . . . this is a man who has treated people's ailments
all his life; he has consoled them, has kept their secrets, when in
their best interest, he has reminded them of their secrets . . .

Zari was in a hurry. She had to get home as soon as possible.
Now her head hurt so much it felt as if it would burst, and her
heart was as heavy as Miss Masihadam's. MacMahon was coming

to dinner. She was hoping that he hadn't arrived yet so she could at least lie down in the dark for an hour.

Gholam was sitting by the *droshky* driver and smoking a clay pipe. When he saw her, he got up, emptied the pipe on the ground and helped Zari to get in. How slowly the *droshky* was moving, clicking along, and when it passed a car, the horses were spooked and the *droshky* driver had to pull to the side. It seemed like she would never get home. But she did.

Yusof and MacMahon were in the wicker chairs on the patio in front of the house. Mina and Marjan, sitting on MacMahon's lap, were leaning toward the table. With one hand he was guarding the children and with the other he was turning the pages of the book they were looking at. When Zari reached them, they clapped their hands and laughed. The men and the children were happy. But she knew that if she sat by them, the sorrows that had piled up inside her would depress them too. And with her headache she couldn't stand smiles and pretenses. Upon seeing her, MacMahon carefully put the children down and stood up. They shook hands. "I apologize for being late," Zari said. "I'll drop by the kitchen and join you shortly."

She went straight to the bedroom and dropped on the bed, dress, shoes, stockings and all, and sank her head in a pillow. The pain had spread around her eyes, ears, and the left side of her jaw. If it doesn't get better, she thought, I will ruin their evening. For a moment, she decided to take two aspirins, but remembered what Dr. Abdollah Khan said and changed her mind. The old man's hair had not turned white treating the people of the city for nothing. He was a knower of secrets. How he had discovered the secret of her pregnancy with one glance of those bright eyes!

Someone came in and switched on the light. "Turn that off!" Zari commanded.

She heard Yusof ask, "Are you sleeping?"

"Please turn off the light."

He turned off the light and came and sat on the floor by the foot of the bed. "What's wrong?"

"I have a headache," Zari said.

Yusof took off her shoes and quietly put them on the ground. He then massaged the back of her neck and her temples. "Would you like me to bring you some smelling salts?"

"You go to your guest," she said. "When I feel better, I'll come too."

"I can ask him to leave," Yusof said.

"No. But if you go, I'll be more comfortable."

Yusof left and after a while came back, turned on the light on the table and said, "Turn your head so I can start my treatment. I bet you'll get well." Zari turned around and saw him place a tray on the vanity stool. Steam was rising from the bowl of water on the tray. He soaked a small towel in the hot water, wrung it, and put it on her face. Twice, three times; then he held her head in his arms and said, "Try to drink all of it." It was a honey and lime drink. He then kissed her—her forehead, her eyes, the back of her ears—and said, "Now, close your eyes and go to sleep." He put two pieces of cotton soaked in rose water on Zari's eyelids. "Why do you tire yourself so?" he asked.

Zari began to cry. "Why should there be so much misery?" she sobbed.

Yusof picked up the cotton balls that had fallen on the pillow, soaked them in the rose water again, squeezed them, and put them back on Zari's eyes. "You are not responsible for all the miseries!" he assured her.

Zari sat up. The cotton balls fell on her lap. "You aren't either," she said. "So why do you put yourself in danger?" She paused. "I saw Fotuhi. He's excused himself from cooperating with you."

"Now I understand," he said. "You got frightened and got a headache."

Zari said, "That's not all. His sister attacked me. And Miss Masihadam took me for one of her patients who died in childbirth. God, so much misery! So much loneliness!"

"Someone must do something," Yusof said.

"If I beg you not to be that someone, will you agree?"

"Look dear, when you are flustered like this, I get distracted."

Zari threw herself in her husband's arms and said, "We have three children and one on the way. I'm so afraid."

"Do you want me to consult with the *Divan* of Hafez to see what the future has in store for us?"

"No!" Zari answered, trembling.

"Would you like me to bring the radio and turn on some music?"

"No," she said. "Just promise me that you won't be that some-one. I know that you people want to go to Khuzestan and do something dangerous."

"I have an idea. MacMahon's story has been published. I'll ask him to read it to you. I know his story will make you feel better."

"All right. Put the pillow behind me. I'll sit up. I feel better already." But she was only pretending.

First Khadijeh came to take the tray. "My poor mistress," she said. "May God give me all your pains. The master was so afraid. He thought you had caught the fever that is spreading in the city." She left and soon returned with the round table from the corner of the parlor, left again and returned to arrange the dishes, bottles, and glasses. Zari had given her all her instructions in the morning. She had even prepared the chicken and gravy before Zari had left for the insane asylum in the afternoon. She had told Khadijeh to keep it cool by putting it in a basket over the well of the water reservoir. Now she asked Khadijeh, "Has the children's aunt come yet?"

"No, she hasn't," Khadijeh said. Sighing, she continued, "May God Himself bless us with such an opportunity. I wish she would get me a contraband passport from that fellow too. I wouldn't go now. I'd hide it till the Imam wishes this sinful slave to go on a pilgrimage to him." She paused once more. "Bless him, I cracked an egg, as an augury, to see who had cast an evil eye on you. It turned out to be the master himself."

Khadijeh left and Khosrow and Hormoz came in. Khosrow put his arms around his mother's neck. "You are my own good looking mother," he said. "Do you want me to fan you? What can I do to get you out of bed?" Hormoz smiled and, still standing, asked how she was. Khosrow put his face to his mother's and said, "Mother, let me and Hormoz eat dinner in my room."

"Why, dear?" Zari asked.

"We've decided not to say one word to the British officers. We won't even bother with their Indian soldiers anymore."

"But MacMahon is not British," she said. "He's Irish."

"What's the difference?" asked Hormoz.

"He's not even an officer," she persisted. "He's a correspondent."

"He is probably a spy," said Hormoz. "Otherwise, why should a young man like him not wear an officer's uniform in wartime? He's younger than Zinger. I'm sure Zinger sends him here to get my uncle to talk."

Zari was sympathetic in a motherly way. "One shouldn't judge people one doesn't know this way."

She wanted to continue and say that he even dreams about the independence of his country and writes poems about the Tree of Independence. But she decided not to and consented to their request. She didn't have the energy to explain all this and defend MacMahon.

As the boys were leaving, Zari asked Khosrow to tell Khadijeh to feed the children and put them to bed.

When Yusof returned, he switched on the overhead light even though the table lamp was still on. The extra light bothered Zari's eyes, but she didn't say anything. And when MacMahon came in, he turned on the lamp on the vanity table, too, and sat on the stool near it. Zari hadn't noticed until then that MacMahon was missing the middle finger on his left hand. She saw that he was heavier than before, and his forehead was quite wrinkled. She said, "I heard your story has been published. I'm very happy."

MacMahon smiled. "I'll read it to you, even though I'm afraid it will make your headache worse." And turning to Yusof he continued, "Is your liquor rationed?" He spoke in clear, crisp English. Perhaps his Irish accent had been modified or he was trying to sound more neutral.

He took a sip of a fresh drink and began to read. His voice was like a lullaby and Zari closed her eyes. Yusof was sitting on the edge of the bed.

19

THE OLD Chariot Keeper gathered up his white flowing beard, a memento of millions and millions of years, and dusted the Golden Chariot of the Sun with it. Then he reached for the Golden Key that hung on his belt and headed eastward. Yes, it was time now. The Sun, tired and weary, was returning from its journey. He opened the Gate to the East with his key. The Sun was late, and when it arrived, it was covered with dust and it yawned. The Chariot Keeper brushed off the dust of the journey, which had settled on the head and face of the Sun, with his massive white beard and polished its rays. The Sun mounted the Chariot to begin its journey in the sky. But it did not leave immediately, and the Chariot Keeper waited. The Sun said, "The Master has sent you a message, that is why I was delayed."

"He is the Commander," the Old Chariot Keeper said.

The Sun continued, "He sends his greetings and says, 'I want you to clean out the Celestial Storeroom, collect the odds and ends and either burn or throw them away.' But most important is this command: to take the stars of his subjects out of the cupboard and send them to those on Earth. He wants everyone to become the owner of his own star."

The Old Chariot Keeper began to grumble, "Do you think cleaning out the Celestial Storeroom is an easy task? For five hundred thousand years, or maybe even more, things have constantly been piled up in that storeroom. It is so full you can hardly get in."

"You know the Master yourself," the Sun said. "When he gives an order, I know he keeps track of everything."

The Sun set out and the Old Chariot Keeper grumbled as he walked toward the Celestial Storeroom. He mumbled, "Wipe their whole species from the face of the earth and get it over with for everybody's sake. They will never straighten out. What a waste it was for you to have entrusted to their bosoms the sparks from the fire of your own heart! No matter what you do for them, they are the offspring of that disobedient baboon. You've seen yourself what horrors they have wrought upon each other. Now you want to hand over the reins to them? How long do you intend to spoil them? How lenient do you intend to be with these earthling brats? From the time they first stood on their own two feet, you've been excited, you've been talking about the noble human race. I know the noble human race. As I have heard, they have no other talent but killing, slaughtering, and oppressing the weak."

He kept walking and grumbling quietly. He walked on until he reached the Celestial Storeroom. There he first went to the Tablets of Destiny, clay and stone tablets on which the fate of the subjects was prescribed in odd scripts. He broke all the Tablets of Destiny and threw them into space. He threw away great numbers of odds and ends, such as old wings of archangels and favorite cherubs, burned-out stars and meteors that had not reached their destinations, and then went to the files on ancient gods. How many cases were piled one on top of the other! He collected all the files in the corner of the storeroom and went to the adjacent hall, to the replicas of the gods that were made from the files. This hall was exclusively for replicas of ancient gods—replicas of tree, animal-bird, and animal-human gods; snake gods; star, fish, and sun gods; and finally purely human gods, with and without wings. In the corner of the hall his eyes caught sight of a battle-axe, which he used to strike down Ashur and Siva. He was so livid with these types of gods. He saw Gilgamesh and, surprised, he said, "What the hell is this? Finagling yourself a place among the gods?" In the blink of an eye he turned him to dust and blew the dust away.

When he got to the attractive goddesses with nice figures he stood there looking and recalling his youth. In those days Ishtar, Isis, and Anahita would tease and taunt him, or throw a wink his way. Anahita would give him her jug of water; he would take a sip and feel happy.

As he was breaking the replicas of the goddesses, he even had tears in his eyes. He did not break Anahita's water jug. To tell the truth, it was with regret that he even smashed Marduk, Mithra, Qetzalcoatl, and Apollo. After all, these gods, in their heyday, were not hard on their subjects and were even sympathetic to them. But as soon as the god of Benue saw that the Chariot Keeper was breaking the Tablets of Destiny, which he had mostly written, he disappeared.

Gradually the Old Chariot Keeper began to get hot. He came out of the hall and looked at the sky. The Sun, in its Golden Chariot, had reached the center of the sky. He returned to the storeroom and pulled out the documents on the holy cities and mountains, documents on Ur, Nineveh, which later became Karbala, Benares, Chichen Itza, Jerusalem, and other holy cities, and then the documents concerning the Himalaya, the Zagros Mountains, Mount Olympus, the Andes, Mount Sinai, Golgatha, Mount Hera', and any other sacred mountain that was a residence of ancient gods, or other mountains which were the meeting place of the Master and his favorite subjects. He piled the documents about the cities and mountains on top of the files of the ancient gods.

There was nothing else left in the Celestial Storeroom except one file containing a few pages about the sacred trees, such as the Tree of Knowledge, the Palm Tree, the Lotus, and others. On its other pages was recorded the information concerning the charms, prayers, and diversions that the Master had created over these 500,000 years for his noble human race. The Old Chariot Keeper put all the documents, papers, and files from the Celestial Storeroom under his arm and piled them up in the corner of the sky. He clapped his hands and created a spark, which he threw on the pile of files and documents, and set them all ablaze.

But he did not wait to watch them burn. He went to the cupboard, as he did every day just before dawn, to store up the stars that he swept up with his Celestial Broom, and locked its door. Well, if he didn't put the stars in a safe place, the stars would be scattered all around and anybody who came by would want to play jacks with them—the Sun, for example, the angels who had nothing else to do, or the cherubs. He took the Golden Key from around his neck to the cupboard, opened the cupboard, and called out, "Hey kids, come and help." His voice resounded in the sky and from various corners, millions of cherubs rushed to him. All sorts of gunnysacks, in their size proportional to the population of the villages, towns, and cities of every country, were prepared in the blink of an eye, along with all sorts of ladders, whose steps were made of the rays of the Sun. The cherubs had their work cut out for them, but they really liked it. One cherub read the list of names, another held the gunnysack open, and a third put the stars into the gunnysack in the order in which the names were read. When the gunnysacks were filled with stars, the Old Chariot Keeper tied the tops, sealed them, and handed them to the cherubs. Each received a gunnysack with a list of names and in return gave a receipt for it. He also assigned a general supervisor and five assistant supervisors to them and ordered the ladders to be secured toward Earth.

It was a sight to behold. Imagine millions of sunbeam ladders with millions of cherubs carrying gunnysacks full of stars on their shoulders and descending the ladders like whirligigs. In his life, he had seen many interesting sights . . . the day when the Angel of Fire stood before the Master, bad-mouthing Him, and then left angrily . . . the day that Gabriel's wings burned . . . the day the Master ordered all the waterlilies to bloom on the lakes of the Earth and sent the Light of Knowledge to the man who was sitting cross-legged under the tree . . . the day when he sent that pigeon to earth . . . the day that he supped with one of his favorites . . . but no day ever before like this.

The task of the cherubs on Earth was to knock on the doors of houses, and put everybody's star in his own hand and say, "From now on, you are on your own!" They were free to change the wording of the message as they saw fit.

The Old Chariot Keeper went to the West to see the Sun off. The Sun dismounted its Golden Chariot, entrusting the Chariot to the Chariot Keeper and said, "I hope you are not too tired."

The Old Chariot Keeper said, "I've got to think of something for the Master's robe. Tonight and all the other nights his robe will be without stars until he gets a chance to create new stars." The Sun said, "But, is that your fault?" and coldly said goodbye and left.

The Old Chariot Keeper was happy that his work was done. He stroked his massive beard, which was just like cotton, and said to himself, "Now that I have a little time, I should attend to my own appearance." Pity. He shaved off that handsome beard, which reached all the way to his toes. He kept beating it like cotton until the whole sky was covered with fluff. He brought Anahita's water jug, broke it, and poured it on his head, washing his body clean. He became quite youthful and the Celestial River of the galaxy filled with this water.

Obviously, on Earth the sky looked cloudy. There was thunder, lightning, and it rained, but the cherubs were not afraid. They knew that the Old Chariot Keeper had broken Anahita's water jug.

The Sun came and went three times and there was no sign of the cherubs, the supervisor, and the assistant supervisors. Every day, the Chariot Keeper sat in the corner of the sky watching the planet twirl around the Sun like a whirligig. In time, he began to worry. I hope they haven't lost their way, he thought. I hope their sunbeam ladders didn't get wet from the water in Anahita's jug and burn up. He was so depressed that he was about to tear off his clothes. The sky was empty, empty of stars, empty of cherubs, and the Master had not sent any message in all this time.

On the morning of the fourth day, he heard noises from far off, like the flapping of wings or the singing of the breeze. Then the noises became more distinct—like celestial songs, the melody rising from the orbiting planets and galaxies. The ladders rose toward the sky and the cherubs appeared. The Chariot Keeper smiled. How the cherubs had grown, how tall they had become in such a short time!

He went to welcome them and he searched for the supervisor and his assistants but did not see any of them. Most of the cherubs did not recognize him at first, but those who did said together, "Why did you change your looks? We missed playing with your beard, that's why we came back."

All at once they talked about their experiences on Earth and made such a ruckus that you couldn't hear to think. The Chariot Keeper made a roaring sound that was louder than all the others. "You're driving me crazy!" he shouted. Then when everybody was quiet, he asked, "Where is the supervisor I sent with you?"

A cherub taller than the rest stepped forward. "He didn't come back. He decided to stay there. He appointed me supervisor in his place."

"What happened to the assistants?" the Chariot Keeper asked.

"They decided to stay, too," the new supervisor said.

"You know, 180,325 cherubs decided to stay on Earth. With the supervisor and the assistants, that makes 180,331."

"Why? What was going on on Earth?" the Old Chariot Keeper asked.

All the cherubs said together, "Earth is very interesting. Everything is alive there."

The Chariot Keeper covered his ears. "You are deafening me," he said. "Only one of you speak. Supervisor, you talk. Tell me about it."

The new supervisor said, "You know, the Earth is genuine. It is real. It is not imaginary or illusionary. It is not made of clouds and winds and ethereal things. It is solid. One's feet stand on a firm place, not everything and everybody with their feet in the air."

"What did the humans look like?" the Chariot Keeper asked.

"They are all shapes," the supervisor said. "There are no two alike among them, and they are all real. They have flesh and blood. You know, everything grows there. Everything is in a state of flux. Everything is bound by the laws of creation, evolution, and extinction. There, nothing and nobody is immortal."

"When I saw you, I realized that myself," the Chariot Keeper said. "Now, tell me about your mission."

"We had a very good time," the new supervisor continued. "We enjoyed their celebrations. They had wars, too. There was poverty and disease. We wept for them."

"What did you do with their stars?" the Chariot Keeper asked.

"We took their stars and gave them to each and every one, the children, the young, and the old. The assistants gave a report of their work on every continent and I have summarized all their reports for you."

He took out a folded piece of paper from under his right wing and read it as follows: "As you had ordered, the task of the cherubs was to give everyone his own star and say, 'I gave you your star so that you know that from now on you are free. You are your own relief, support, and refuge.' The reaction of the people of the Earth was as follows: The children's eyes sparkled at seeing their stars. They took the stars and played with them. When we were leaving, they were still playing. The old said, 'It's too late now.' But now hear about the young and the middle-aged who are in charge of most of Earth's affairs. All of them received their stars but most did not comprehend the Celestial Master's purpose, no matter how it was explained to them. Some lost their stars very quickly. Some hid their stars in their shirt fronts and smiled for having a star in there. But a small group of the young and middle-aged understood it all very well. Of this group, some said, 'We've been like this from the beginning. We've never expected anything from any star, neither in Heaven nor on Earth. We have never believed in fate, nor have we ever blamed anyone for having a good or bad star . . . ' This group spoke very pompously and the cherubs did not quite understand what they said. Even the Earth people who spoke the same language didn't understand them . . . Some from the same group said, 'How wonderful that everyone's heart is lit up with his own star.' This group was made up of odd people, and in almost every country there were a few of them. Some of them had beards, but none as long as the one you used to have. This group immediately got to work and checked their dictionaries and omitted a lot of words from them. Words such as fate, fortune, luck, destiny, and predetermination, and rules and regulations, and all their synonyms, equivalents, or cognates. They were making new words out of the roots of 'freedom' and 'liberation,' as we were leaving."

The Chariot Keeper smiled. "One of these days, I'll make a trip to Earth," he said. "Your description makes it worth seeing."

MacMahon fell silent. Zari opened her eyes, as if she had awakened from a pleasant dream. She said, "What a story!"

"Did you understand all of it?" Yusof asked.

"Any part I didn't understand, I made up for in my own imagination," Zari answered and, turning to MacMahon, said, "To tell you the truth, at first I was expecting it to be the story that you wrote for the children."

"Your daughters sowed the seed of this story in my mind," MacMahon explained. "First, the ideas of the sweeping of the sky and the gunnysacks full of stars in a dark cupboard were planted in my head. But to tell you the truth, no matter how I tried to write a story for them, a story for children, and pay my debt to them, I couldn't. It turned out as you heard."

Yusof laughed and poured a glass of wine for MacMahon. "This is very good wine," MacMahon said, taking a sip. "Where can one buy some?"

"You know, now that I've heard your story again," Yusof said, "it occurs to me that the subject that interests you is what you repeat in your poems, too. You're trying to atone for the sins of others."

Zari could not figure out what her husband meant. She opened her mouth to ask, when Khan Kaka called from the parlor. "Hey, folks. Where are you hiding?" Then he appeared there, blinking as he said, "I heard there was a spread in this house tonight so I came on the run."

20

WHEN KOLU had recovered, he made a slingshot and the sparrows in the garden could no longer rest on any branch because of him. It was a wonder that of all the windows in the house, only one in the pantry was shattered. That day, Zari had slapped Kolu on the hand and said, "You're driving me up the wall." Kolu ran under the sour-orange trees, began wailing, and once again asked for his mama and brother.

Every Sunday morning, before the sun rose, Kolu would get up, undress, and jump into the pool with the copper cross around his neck, always waking Zari up. Then he would get out of the pool and, as Gholam reported, put on his new clothes. With or without breakfast, he would go to the man in black at the missionary hospital. Just before noon, he would come back home and, as soon as he arrived, instead of saying hello, he would declare, "I am a Christian." But it would not be noon yet before he would forget and swear by Abolfazl al-Abbas. That last Sunday, however, Kolu came home later than usual. Zari was in the kitchen preparing food for Yusof's trip, so they could have dinner as soon as they arrived in Zarqan that night. Kolu came to the kitchen and lectured Zari and Khadijeh for some time about Christ. He also spoke of Judas and asked if he could find that ungrateful wretch in the Jewish district. Then he sighed and said, "I am Christ's lost lamb." He put his hands together, held them before his lips and continued,

"Oh Christ, Who are in heaven, come, and if you are telling the truth, find me and take me to my mama."

Khadijeh shouted at him. "Stupid boy! Say, God forgive me. Go wash your mouth."

But Zari said firmly, "Leave him alone."

"From tonight, every night I'll appeal to my Lord Jesus Christ until he gives in and comes to my rescue," Kolu said. "What kind of shepherd is he anyway to let his lamb get lost and go sit in the sky? If he is telling the truth, let him come down and take me. If he takes me, I'll give him my daddy's pipe that I hid under the bed rolls. But if he doesn't, may Abolfazl al-Abbas strike me dead, if I get hold of him I'll land a rock right between his eyes with my slingshot."

He took three copper crucifixes from a pocket and, showed them to Zari. "The old bucktoothed woman gave me these crosses. I'll take one for my mama, one for my uncle, and one for my uncle's wife as souvenirs." He held one of the crucifixes in front of Khadijeh and said, "Kiss it!" Khadijeh pushed Kolu's hand away and said, "Stupid boy. Go back to your mama." None of us has ever accepted him as a child of the family, Zari thought. Not even me. Not even the children's aunt.

"The old bucktoothed woman said, 'Christ is everywhere,' " Kolu continued. "He is in our village, too. She said, 'To any child who calls out, *My Lord Jesus Christ,* the Lord Christ will right away answer, *Yes, my child.*' But I am now grown up and can't hear his voice."

On the afternoon of the same day when Kolu and Yusof left for the village, Zari thought, Now what will he think? Will he think Christ has found him?

The boy was so happy he couldn't contain himself; even though he knew he wasn't going to his folks immediately, he forgot his slingshot. First he was going to Zarqan with Yusof, until someone could be found to take him to the summer pastures. The poor boy thought if he only got out of the garden, no matter where he went, he would be closer to his village.

They left and Zari stayed behind, with nights full of nightmares and disturbing dreams, nights that seemed as if no morning followed them. As time passed, her thoughts became more uneasy, her dreams more disturbing.

The aunt was a master at interpreting dreams. Everyone, even strangers, knew this. Often people they had not met or did not know would phone and tell the aunt their dreams. She would always answer with, "I hope it is a good omen," and then interpret their dreams with the hope of a heavenly reward. She also had a handwritten script to consult whenever she was at a loss. But even the aunt could not interpret two of Zari's dreams. Nor could she find the key to those dreams in her book of dream interpretation, no matter how much she pored over it. That is why Zari had these two dreams repeatedly, the aunt reasoned.

In Zari's dream she was standing stark naked in the middle of an unknown square with thousands of men and women watching her. It was examination time and she was standing in front of a frowning, dark examiner, but tried in vain to find the answers to his questions. No matter how she racked her brain, sweated in anxiety, and felt her heart race, she could provide no answer to any question, and the next morning she could not remember what the questions were.

The aunt instructed her to beg a piece of bread from a beggar and eat it so the questions would stay in her mind.

One night, Zari dreamed that a two-headed dragon had swallowed her husband as he was galloping along on the mare. When she looked carefully she saw that the two-headed dragon resembled Sergeant Zinger. He was wearing a Scottish kilt, which was embroidered all around. The aunt interpreted this dream easily. She said, "Zinger will be a public laughing stock. But Yusof, like Jonah, will learn patience and tolerance in the belly of the whale and the darkness inside the whale will endow him with light so that he will understand all the secrets of the world."

A few nights later, she dreamed that with his own hands the Governor had thrown Yusof in a baker's oven and Yusof, charred, had staggered like a blind man out of the oven. Interpreting this dream, the aunt said that fire signifies the same fire that became a flower garden for Abraham, the Friend of God. That Yusof came out of the fire means that he has passed his ordeal. Even though the aunt's words reminded Zari of the story of Siyavash, she did not say anything. After all, that night in the tribal chief's tent—the night that Malek Sohrab had bet a new Brno gun with Zari, which Zari never paid up—all that night, they had talked about Siyavash and teased Zari for knowing John the Baptist and not knowing Siyavash, and they explained to her that Siyavash had passed through fire and come out vindicated.

The aunt continued the interpretation of the dream. "Obviously, the oven is the same oven in which the wife of Khuli hid the children of Moslem. As for being charred, it is a sign of being vindicated, because obviously a woman's dream is the opposite of what it seems."

On another night, just before dawn, Zari dreamed that Kolu had struck Yusof right between the eyes with a stone from his slingshot. The aunt did not interpret this dream at all, stating that early morning dreams need no interpretation.

Ten days after Yusof's departure, it was rumored in town that Malek Sohrab had become an outlaw. Everyone who walked into Zari's house had something to say. Gholam would say, "He set off for the mountains with a thousand armed men and is hiding where no man can get his hands on him." Khosrow would say, "He's reached the outskirts of Yasuj with two thousand fighting men. But he hasn't come down the mountain yet. That's my man!" Hormoz would show up with "Aunt Zari, you know that I like bravery. But a brave man should also know when the time is right." Yusof's brother, Khan Kaka, would come to fetch Hormoz and was hurrying to take him to His Excellency the Governor, but Zari would insist that he sit down and would donate, as Khan Kaka himself would say, the oldest wines made by Tavus Khanom and be hospitable and sympathetic to him until she would draw it out of him that "I have heard that Bibi Hamdam went to the headquarters . . . and without permission opened the door to the army chief's room, and dropped herself in those big baggy pants at the general's feet . . . to ask for mercy for Malek Sohrab. She said she'll go and bring her son in. The general said, 'The sooner you do this the better.' Bibi Hamdam took a Koran out of her dress and said, 'Swear on this Koran that when my son comes you will leave him alone,' but the general kicked the old woman's hand with his boots." Sakineh, the bread baker, would come to Zari and say, "Bibi Hamdam has hired forty Koran reciters to chant together aloud and recite the Surah An'am. Every day. It makes the hair stand on end. 'Oh God, I plead with you on the chastity of Sadiqeh Tahereh to return this son to his mother. And along with that, free the son of this sinful humble slave from the evils of military conscription.' "

In despair, Zari began reading newspapers again, but she couldn't find even the slightest reference in any newspaper to Malek Sohrab's name. Her habit, nevertheless, brought her across a report that was published in the most reliable local newspaper. She was alone in the garden that afternoon when she took the newspaper from the delivery man. It had been two weeks since she had seen Yusof.

"Commendation," read the headline. Then "Her Excellency Khanom Ezzatoddowleh, a charitable and benevolent lady, was assigned by the Women's Association to inspect the houses in the Mordestan District as well as the women's prison. Under her supervision, all the houses in the above-mentioned district have been cleaned and disinfected. Also, this gracious lady magnanimously paid out of her own pocket the fines for a woman prisoner who, out of ignorance, had engaged in illegal means of making a living. Her ladyship was instrumental in obtaining freedom for this infirm and shelterless woman. The Office of the Governor General of Fars commends this humanitarian and benevolent lady."

Even though she was not surprised by the report, Zari became depressed. She crumpled the newspaper, threw it in a corner, and took refuge in the orange grove. She paced under the sour-orange trees, feeling like she had no energy left for anything that required thinking. She decided to go to the stable, call Gholam, and ask whether he had heard anything new about Malek Sohrab. But she changed her mind. The poor man is in his shirtsleeves, she thought. He's probably taken off his hat, too. In this heat, he may not be dressed. Maybe he is smoking his clay pipe. For a moment, she thought she'd call on Bibi Hamdam, but once again changed her mind. She couldn't stand the clamorous mingling of the voices of the Koran reciters. She also knew that as soon as Bibi

Hamdam set eyes on her she'd begin to wail, asking her for a solution and say, "Now tell me, what should I do?" But if Zari knew what could be done, she herself would not be so distraught. Everyone knew that Bibi Hamdam's life depended on Malek Sohrab's, and it was obvious that despite all his pomp, before his mother Malek Sohrab was no more than a child.

She considered going to Mehri's house to fetch the aunt and the children, but she realized that in that heat, she could not stand wearing a long-sleeve dress and putting on a scarf to please Mehri's second husband, Mohsen Khan. He was a strict man.

She knew that her depression and anxiety was to a great extent due to being tired. Every summer she would go to the village for two or three weeks, for a change of air. By walking and horseback riding, she prepared herself for the coming fall and winter. But in this summer of disease, famine, war, and her own pregnancy that had caught her by surprise, she was a prisoner in her house, plus the prison and the insane asylum. She thought about arranging a weekly get-together with her former classmates, perhaps in the afternoon. She thought she would host it first, and then Mehri. Mehri would agree as long as Mohsen Khan allowed it. Their husbands didn't get along, but she and Mehri remained the same old friends whether or not they saw each other.

She went to the bedroom and looked in the shelf drawers for knitting needles and yarn to knit her anxiety and depression into knots of yarn, but could find neither the yarn nor the knitting needles. Instead she took a box full of glass beads along with a sewing box to the veranda and sat down to string some beads. She looked at the garden. It seemed to have lost its freshness; dust had settled on all the trees, their leaves had burned and turned yellow. For a moment, she thought the trees were stunned and staring at her. Then she saw that the trees were trembling, shaking their heads, and soon after settled down. They are preparing to go to sleep, she thought. But the sparrows on the top branches are awake and are bickering at each other like old women in a public bath.

The sun had left the garden when she heard the neighing of a horse, the mare, not Sahar. Thank God, Yusof is back from the village. It is true what they say, that hearts can communicate. As soon as Zari felt that she could no longer stand his absence, he returned. She decided not to let him know that she felt his trip had taken too long, how she had worried, and how he had left her alone with disturbing thoughts and dreams, frightening rumors, and unjust commendations.

Gholam came out of the stable as Yusof's foreman, Seyyed Mohammad, arrived riding the mare and leading the roan. Zari, feeling her heart sink, got up, scattering the glass beads all over the carpet. Maybe Yusof has gone somewhere for something, she thought. Seyyed Mohammad dismounted, gave the reins to Gholam, and whispered something to him. Gholam threw his hat on the ground. Seyyed said something else, and Gholam took the horses to the stable as Zari ran up and asked breathlessly, "Where is the master?" "The master is coming in Malek Rostam's car," Seyyed Mohammad said. "Don't worry. Nothing has happened."

Even so Gholam and Seyyed were acting mysteriously. Gholam ran out of the garden without his hat. Seyyed came to the pool and washed his hands and face and combed his thick moustache. He then took a stone from the garden walkway, washed it, put it on the ground and stood to prayer. But Seyyed isn't the praying kind, Zari thought. And anyway, what kind of prayer was this? No proper ablutions, and even though the day was done, there had been no call for evening prayers from the *muezzin*.

First the aunt arrived. It was odd. She did not speak a word to anyone and in her street *chador,* without a prayer mat, stood on the veranda and prayed. She had not brought the children back, either. Some time later a car came carrying Khan Kaka. Zari was certain that something had happened, but she didn't want to ask. She had neither the courage nor the heart. They, the sister and brother, started it themselves.

Then Malek Rostam's light green car stopped by the pool. She knew now what had happened, but she would not believe it until she saw it with her own eyes. Malek Rostam and Yusof's friend, Majid Khan, got out, and she knew that her husband would not get out. She knew that he would never again get in or out of a car. Where had she read that so-and-so sat on the wooden horse? Yusof was sitting up straight in the back seat, his *aba* over his shoulders and a hat lowered over his eyes. She heard the aunt's voice saying, "Hello. I hope you're not tired, brother. You've come home—" And she wailed. Khan Kaka was screaming so loud that his voice surely reached the neighbors seven houses away. Zari put her hand on Yusof's hand. It was cold, fingers stretched out, separated, and stiff. She looked at his face, which was yellow; lifting the hat she saw that his eyes were closed. His chin was tied with a handkerchief covered with congealed and dried blood. She saw but could not believe. She asked, bewildered, "Without a goodbye?" Gholam screamed and Zari asked again, "Alone?" And now everyone wailed and she thought, How could they make these noises and why couldn't she? The aunt sitting on the pavement by the pool was tearing at her clothes. Zari kept asking, "Why?" And then the car, the trees, the people, the pool, whirled around and disappeared.

When she opened her eyes, she found herself lying on the veranda carpet. All the lights in the garden were on. Were there guests? She could smell a mixture of clay and straw. The aunt was rubbing her shoulders. Her face, neck, and body were wet. Noises came from everywhere. They had sat Yusof on a wooden platform next to the pool, and Gholam was sitting behind him, supporting him, while rocking and constantly saying, "My master!" He didn't have a hat on. Haji Mohammad Reza, the dyer, his arms purple up to his elbows, was trying to take Yusof's boots off, but couldn't. Khan Kaka was standing over them. He said, "Haji, cut the boots," and shouted, "A knife!" There was no *aba* over Yusof's shoulders. There was no hat on his head, either, and Zari thought she was dreaming. Of late, she had been having disturbing dreams. So this was another of those dreams. She was dreaming that a man had been forced to sit on a wooden platform and was having his boots cut with a knife, but Zari couldn't make out the man's face . . . she was dreaming Malek Rostam was holding the cut boot and shouting, "Oh my!" What do they call this shouting from the pit of your stomach? she wondered. Crying? Yelling? Wailing? No, it's a nice word that I have forgotten. Then she thought she was seeing in a dream that Majid had put his head on Yusof's *aba*, which was on the wooden platform, and was sobbing. Or maybe she wasn't dreaming, because, after all, her eyes were wide open.

Khan Kaka came to the veranda and blew his nose into a white handkerchief. He seemed to have a cold. His eyes and long nose were quite red. He blinked and said, "Sister-in-law, how soon you became a widow! You are not thirty years old yet. Oh, oh."

The aunt said, "Control yourself, man. Don't frighten a pregnant woman more than this!"

"Pregnant?" Zari asked.

Zari realized she was pregnant, but her brain absolutely refused to believe what had happened. She asked the aunt, "How did you find out?"

"From your eyes."

Zari felt again that she was dreaming. She was dreaming a person was crumpled up and asleep on the wooden platform and in this heat they had put Yusof's *aba* over him. But she didn't know the man. She was dreaming three men were sitting on the children's bed talking about the crumpled up man. She could distinguish the voices.

Khan Kaka's voice: "My sister is right. The times were not right for him. Brother, if your soul is present, forgive me. I wished to have your intelligence, common sense, and education. Because I didn't, I made fun of you. Brother, like a free-spirited cypress, you—"

Majid's voice: "Yes. Don't upset yourself now. He knew that his time and the time for people like him had not yet come. But he said, he told me so often, that our duty is to make that time come sooner."

Malek Rostam's voice: "I know that today or tomorrow, they will catch my unfortunate brother Sohrab. They'll set up the gallows on the drill field and everyone will go and watch."

The voices mixed with screams and cries: "You think one doesn't want to say and act properly? But when one starts downhill, there is no way to go but down . . ." Whose voice was that?

There was the sound of footsteps on the gravel in the garden walkway. When the sound reached the veranda, it would stop and continue again. Zari had closed her eyes. She felt like a withered pomegranate, all the vital saps drained out of her body. She felt as though a snake had crept down her throat and coiled around her heart, waiting there with its head erect, ready to strike her. And she knew that for the rest of her life this snake would remain coiled around her heart and that whenever she remembered her husband, it would strike her chest.

Giving in to the aunt's insistence, she got up. The aunt held her under the arms and took her to the parlor. All around the room, there were women sitting on the chairs or on the carpet. Most of them were fanning themselves and speaking in whispers. The men were in the other rooms. She could hear their voices. It seemed as if they were all standing watch behind the garden gate and waiting for her husband's corpse to arrive, and for the blood to streak down from his yellow hair and coagulate on his blond moustache. Only then would they come in. When the women saw her, they stood up. But she could not quite distinguish anyone, except Ezzatoddowleh, who looked like a mesmerizing serpent. For a moment, Zari stared at her face and bezoar-tinted hair, and then the yellow, red, blue, and black glass beads mingled before her eyes, shining and forming strange patterns. Most of the women looked at her carefully, shaking their heads and crying. From the other rooms, she could hear the voices of men and the wails of Khan Kaka, "If someone knows it, tell me . . . I am at a loss . . ." But Zari's eyes and tongue were dry— no tears, no words. Nothing.

She returned to the veranda and sat on the carpet. Khosrow came in through the garden gate riding Sahar and galloped toward her. He dismounted, came to his mother, and asked, "Is it true?" Zari bent her head and began to pick up the glass beads. She asked, "Did you pass?" All the lights were on. How could he have not seen the crumpled up corpse of his father under the *aba?* But he kept asking, "Is it true, mother?" Zari said, "How late you are!" Khosrow explained, "Those of us who passed bought *paludeh* for the kids. Our janitor came and said, 'Your uncle called and said your father has been shot, but he is only wounded. He's gotten on his horse and gone straight home.' Is it true? Where is he now? The hospital?"

She took her son in her arms, kissed him, and then her tears gushed out.

Later, many came and put their arms around her and shed tears of pity for her, for her having been widowed so young, for her having four children to raise without a father. How soon everyone found out that there would be a fourth child. Ezzatoddowleh came too, but she neither put her arms around Zari's neck nor did she weep. She only said, "I hope this will be your last sorrow. Well, at least he's left you enough to raise your children respectably." She left without saying goodbye, placing her hands on her waist and climbing down the steps with difficulty. She went to Malek Rostam, who was sitting on a wicker chair by the pool. Malek Rostam stood up and she sat down. It was obvious that Ezzatoddowleh was talking to Malek Rostam, and he was listening. It seemed that he shed tears too, because he kept dabbing his eyes with a handkerchief. A voice said, "The *droshky* is ready." Ezzatoddowleh got up, Malek Rostam took her arm, and together they walked to the end of the garden.

A few hours later, Zari was lying on a wooden platform in the *howzkhaneh* and Khanom Hakim was standing by her. The fountain in the little pool was on and a wet, cold handkerchief was on Zari's forehead. She felt the sting of the doctor's syringe. One, two, three . . . she saw Khanom Hakim put the cold metal stethoscope on her belly and listen. "The baby has been healthy," she said. "Tonight has been time for burial." And she heard Khanom Fatemeh's answer, "You keep to your medical work. As if my brother has committed a crime to bury him at night."

And again came the voice of Khanom Hakim. "Why have you been bitter? All three children have been from my hands. The fourth child also has been from my hands." And Zari knew that she was being addressed. "Why not sooner to have been coming to me?"

Zari did not answer, and the aunt said harshly, "It's all this 'have been, have been' that has pushed people to the edge . . . I wish—"

"I wish you'd get the hell out of here." Zari imagined someone saying this, and yet the aunt did not finish her sentence. Nevertheless, Khanom Hakim, as if having heard what the person had said in Zari's imagination, complained in a trembling voice, "This the payment has been for service and self-sacrifice? We have been in a strange city, dry climate, away from brother, sister, and friend. Medicine has been free. Treatment has been free."

And this time, that someone imagined by Zari shouted, "Get lost! All of you, get lost!"

Khanom Hakim had gone and Zari saw Khosrow with a fan in his hand and felt a soft, cool breeze on her face. She mumbled, "Khosrow." Khosrow brought his head close to her. Zari continued, "Do something for your mother . . . Go to Dr. Abdollah Khan early tomorrow morning . . . tell him what calamity . . . ask him to come and see me for a minute." Khosrow got up and said, "I'll go right now." Zari said, "No, dear. Go early tomorrow morning."

The aunt came in and Zari heard, "Boy, get up, go eat your dinner, and then go to bed. On the soul of your father, get up." She thought, How soon they swear on a father's soul . . . sometime later, Khadijeh's voice: "A man is here, he says that he's come to offer his help as a pious deed. He says last night he dreamed that one of Ali's fighters entered the city of God . . ."

She knew that they had set up a tent around the pool and that they wanted to perform the ritual ablution on her husband's corpse in the garden pool. She knew that they would drain the pool tonight and channel the water into the garden, and the water that had washed her husband's corpse and cleansed away the dried up blood would irrigate the trees. And Hoseyn Kazeruni would start the pulley over the well and fill the pool from the well.

Her eyes stirred as she heard Seyyed Mohammad ask, "What should I say? Much better to say nothing." Was he answering someone's question? Zari opened her eyes and saw Seyyed kneeling down by the door of the *howzkhaneh* and rolling a cigarette. The aunt was sitting on the wooden platform by Zari's feet. Khan Kaka and Khosrow were there, too. Seyyed put the thin cigarette to his lips, wet it, struck a match and said, "What can I say, by God? Nobody could figure it out. The villagers would give their life for the master. I don't know. Maybe the gendarmes, maybe others. To claim that Kolu's uncle hurried in from Kavar, shot the master, and rushed back is nonsense. It debases the whole matter; it is even an insult. Whoever was involved spread this rumor. I got on the horse to go to the lower pasture. Kolu came and stopped me and said, 'I shot the master.' I said, 'Shot with what?' He said, 'With my slingshot.' Later I heard he had said with a gun. Then he'd said, 'My uncle shot him.' I know he had been coached. They think they've fooled everyone. No matter how we searched, there was no sign of Kolu's uncle in the village. How could he have come without anyone seeing him? Yes, Kolu's uncle had a hunting gun. The master himself had bought it for him after his brother's death.

". . . It was early morning when we went to the warehouses on horseback. The master broke the seals with his own hands and distributed beans, dates, and flour among the villagers. He was teasing them and joking around with them. He was telling the women, 'If you sell them and buy gold bracelets or think about going on pilgrimage, we won't get along anymore.' He told the men, 'If you dare exchange the merchandise for cash and use the money for new beds and new wives . . . don't let us get cross with each other.' Everybody was happy. The master was the happiest of all.

"Before noon, we went to the upstairs room in the fortress. The master sat on a little mattress. We had pulled up the mosquito netting. Elyas brought the hookah and put it by the master. I asked, 'Would you like me to take off your boots?'

"The master said, 'No, I'll smoke the hookah and we'll go to the lower pasture.' "Then he asked, 'Has the camel driver come?' and I said yes.

"Elyas said, 'Master, Zinger's agent has come again.'" Khan Kaka's voice interrupted Seyyed's tale and Zari thought, How can a man who shouted so loud before talk like this now? Khan Kaka said, "Everybody who came tonight whispered in my ear, 'Hush hush, mum's the word, this is a dangerous matter. From higher up—'"

But the angry aunt would not let Khan Kaka finish. "Is that so! Now they want to hush up that young man's murder. Khan Kaka, listen to me. Get an attorney. If you don't have the guts to, I will." And Khan Kaka said sarcastically, "But, sister, I thought you wanted to go live as a resident pilgrim in Karbala."

"My Karbala is right here now," the aunt cried. "See what happens only a night after somebody's blood is spilled? And it hasn't been one night yet."

"Sister, you women don't understand what's at the bottom of

all this," Khan Kaka said softly. "Suppose I do get an attorney. Who
are the people they'll arrest for this murder? Kolu and his uncle,
or a few other unfortunate villagers, or maybe even Seyyed right
here. They'll make it so we either forgive the so-called murderer,
or Kolu, who is still a minor, will be identified as the murderer.
Am I wrong, Seyyed?"

Seyyed said, "If a judge is going to rule so unjustly, I am
ready to go and incite the peasants in all the master's villages to
rebel."

"What's the use?" Khan Kaka said. "What little money is left
for these orphans will be wasted. Moreover, what if they arrest you
first? Do you think they can't?"

"Uncle, in that case, Hormoz and I would go and start a riot
in the villages," Khosrow said. "Mr. Fotuhi will help too. And if
the property of us orphans is wasted, it doesn't matter. I'll make
a living by my own hands; I know, I can't now. Now, my mother will work as a seamstress to make a living for us until I grow
up." And suddenly he began crying.

Zari wanted to get off the wooden platform, put her arms around
her son, and cry with him, but she could not. She couldn't even
open her mouth to say to her son, "Don't cry, darling." What had
Khanom Hakim's injections done to her?

The aunt cursed and said, "God, why did you make me a
woman? If I were a man, I'd show everyone what manhood
means."

Zari expected Khan Kaka's temper to flare, but instead he
only complained softly, "Make fun of me and say that I am not
a man. But what can one do but submit and consent?" A moment
later he added, "All right, these are all problems for later. Give me
a little time to see what I can do."

Khosrow asked Seyyed Mohammad, "Isn't Zinger's agent the
same fat one with the pock-marked face?"

"Yes, that's him," Seyyed said. "He came up. He said, 'Sergeant
Zinger sends his greetings and wishes you well.' The master said
he was kind. The agent said, 'Tell the master to get off his high
horse. What is the use of distributing the wheat among the peasants? A peasant doesn't think about what will happen to him tomor-

row. He'll go and sell it on the black market at several times the price.'

"The master laughed—this was the last time that he laughed—and said, 'Go tell Zinger instead of him and the likes of him getting fatter every day, let the peasants get some money.' The agent reported that Sergeant Zinger said, 'It is in your own best interest not to touch the rest.' The master said, 'When did I ask Zinger to tell me what is in my interest?' I can still hear everything they said . . . The agent told him that Sergeant Zinger said he could break the locks on the warehouses and take the wheat—not only the wheat, they need barley, beans and dates, too. And he said he had a written decree from the Governor. He said, 'Dear sir, we'll give you cash, is that bad?' Quoting Zinger, he said, 'If worst comes to worst, we will buy it second-hand from the peasants. And still we won't be paying more. The government has doubled the rate of exchange of the pound sterling.' Then he bent over and whispered something in the master's ear that we couldn't hear. The master got angry and shouted, 'To hell with them all! Don't try to threaten me with the gendarmes, because I am not afraid of them, either. If you really dare, go with the gendarmes and break the locks of the warehouses. You have a decree.' Then the master calmed down. He said, 'Now the food supply has nothing to do with their war. It is now in the hands of the company, and the company has gotten into the grain trade.' The agent wiped the sweat on his forehead with a handkerchief and said, 'Dear sir, please don't oppose them, don't fight these people; it will turn out bad for you.' Then he said, 'Aren't we compatriots?' The master said, 'Yes, unfortunately, we are.' The agent said, 'These people don't need your wheat and food supplies, but they are afraid you might get something started.' The master said, 'In fact, that is exactly my intention. In Hamadan, they closed up the stores and didn't let a grain of wheat leave the city gate. Here they have destroyed the Qor'an Gate.' Again the agent whispered in the master's ear, mumbling to him for two or three minutes. When he finished, the master became pensive. He was upset, but he did not waver. He only said, 'Go tell Zinger I give Sohrab only food supplies, not arms.'

"I was about to leave the room; I hadn't reached the door yet when I heard the shot. I turned back. I saw the hookah tip over, the master fall over, and blood start gushing out. Mohammad Mehdi and Elyas rushed in to help, but the agent didn't move. I shouted at him, 'Get the hell out of here! Get out of my sight!' "

"Maybe Zinger's agent shot him," said Khosrow.

Seyyed responded, "The agent that I know is such a coward that if you say boo to him he'll run all the way to Timbuktu." He continued, "We moved the master off the little mattress. I picked up the mattress. A hole had been dug under the mattress the size of the palm of a hand. The master still had a little life left in him. He opened his mouth to talk, but couldn't. I brought my head close to him. He said, 'Kolu . . . Kolu . . . Take him and return him to . . . his kinfolk. Zari . . . Zari. My children.'

"I dispatched a messenger to Kavar, to Malek Rostam, and sent Kolu with the messenger before the ignorant people could tear him to pieces. I took the camel driver and Mirza Aqa Hanasab with me to the lower pasture and waited until the provisions were loaded on the camels. I got a receipt from Mirza Aqa and came here. And here is the receipt. I don't know if I did the right thing or not. But if the master were alive, he would have done the same."

"What was Mirza Aqa Hanasab doing there?" the aunt asked.

"He had come with the camel driver from Malek Sohrab's camp," Seyyed replied.

Zari tried to sit up but could not. "I wanted to raise my children with love in a peaceful environment," she said. "But now I will raise them in hatred. I will put a gun in Khosrow's hands."

"Who could blame you?" Khan Kaka said. "They really did it to us. But blood cannot be washed with blood; it must be washed with water. We must wait and see what happens."

Zari lay down and slept, dreaming that a strange tree had grown in their garden, and Gholam was watering it with blood from a small watering can.

21

ZARI WAS awake. It was as if she could hear someone talking inside her head, continuously saying nonsensical things, things that Zari knew she herself had heard or read somewhere. Sentences rattled off one after another, but she had not anticipated them. To what part of her memory had they been clinging that they were showing up now?

"Oh well, all those who knew loyalty have left this land!"

"O dark, dark, dark, amid the blaze of noon . . . I am Ilanoddowleh, I am Veylanoddowleh, fire, fire, I am on fire. There is fire in my own head . . . that you are younger and cannot endure it. Mischief flows from this vaulted ceiling . . ."

She squeezed her eyes shut to block the invasion of the bothersome phrases. It got worse. Now the painting that a madman in the insane asylum had painted appeared. It depicted a butcher shop. She even saw the portrait of His Holiness Ali and the young butcher with his severed hand on the wall of the shop, and the shop was full of butcher hooks, as far as the eye could see. But instead of sheep carcasses, people were hanging by their feet on the hooks, blood dripping from their throats.

She opened her eyes. It was certainly past midnight. They had no electricity, so candles were lit. She saw Khan Kaka sitting on the carpet holding his crossed legs in front of him. The aunt was sitting across from him. Khosrow was there. Malek

Rostam was there, too. Seyyed Mohammad was standing by the door of the *howzkhaneh.* The smell of opium, cigarette smoke, alcohol, and charcoal were mingled together. Floating between sleep and wakefulness, she heard the voice of her husband's foreman. He was talking about the memorial service. His voice was scratchy and his chest wheezing—as if he has just climbed down the Mortaz Ali Mountain with a carboy of wine on his back and was now going to the tomb of Haft Tanan. He opens the top of the carboy and drinks; from his thick moustache red drops trickle down onto the nameless graves. He puts the carboy under the cypress tree and goes to sleep on the cold stone. When will the wine in the carboy turn into Rare Wine? At dawn? When the sun rises? She thought, Those days when people could find Rare Wine to drink and become Hafez are over. Now they must swallow gunpowder wine. Those times when people sat by the stream and watched the passage of life, sang, and of all the bounties of the world contented themselves with one rose-cheeked beloved, are gone. Now they must stand by life's flood embankment and be so forcefully struck by it on the face that they forget their names . . . By the way, what was the word for the shouting that comes from the pit of your stomach? It was a word that fits this kind of shouting. It must be a word that means piercing. That is, if one is unable to shout that way when faced with a flood, a thunderbolt, or one of fate's blows, one's heart will be pierced. Then people whose hearts have been pierced get into a brawl, beat each other, and end up in jail. Or they crack up and go mad. And a spoiled, silly, pampered woman takes bread and dates to the prisoners and the insane every Thursday. She has made a vow. And now that woman herself may be struggling on the verge of madness. That is probably why her mind works like this, like a clock, such that she can't stop her mind's activity.

Suddenly she was overcome by fear: "Am I going mad?" She wanted to sit up, but it felt as if she were glued to the mattress.

When she lapsed into deep sleep, she would have dreams. When she was awake, she could hear someone talking incoherently in her mind, or events would emerge out of the recesses of her memory and become vivid before her closed eyes, as if they were happening right then. Or scenes appeared in her mind that she could not remember having witnessed or heard about. She tried to keep her eyes open and ears alert, to see that the aunt, Khosrow, and others existed and that she knew them and could hear what they said. But she could only control her eyes, ears, and mind for a while, and sooner or later drift away from reality.

She heard the aunt say, "In spite of her bad legs, how did Ezzatoddowleh get herself here? She probably came to check things out. When she looked at Zari, her eyes glittered. I thought to myself, Zari, how you made your enemies happy!" and she wailed.

Then she heard Malek Rostam: "She asked me about Malek Sohrab. First she said she'd heard that he was under siege. I asked, 'Where did you hear that?' She was taken aback. She said, 'Well, they'll catch him somehow and then God help Bibi Hamdam; all one's suffering is the fault of one's children,' and she cried. Because of her contacts with the Governor's family, I thought she knew something or other and tried to find out where she had heard that Sohrab was under siege. She denied it altogether and said, 'When did I say such a thing? I said people around him gave him away.' She changed her story a hundred times . . . she said Malek Sohrab had gotten tired, he hadn't received provisions, and had turned himself in. When I was helping her into the *droshky*, she said, 'I have heard Bibi Hamdam has pleaded for mercy to His Excellency and has gone to deliver her son to his execution,' I almost pulled the wig off her head and gave her the beating that she deserved. I said, 'Khanom Ezzatoddowleh, if you have any news, tell me.' I pleaded with her on the life of her pampered Hamid. She said, 'All I told you were rumors.' I got into the *droshky* with her and hurried to Bibi's house. I knocked on the door for a long time, but she didn't open it. Have they given her a verbal pardon, only to break their promise later? Have . . ."

Abolqasem Khan's voice: "Pardon me for saying so, but with the hell Malek Sohrab raised in the Semirom war, I doubt if they'd give him a pardon. That's like the story of the husband who told his wife, I told you to dance, but not that well."

But Zari could clearly see in sleep or wakefulness: It is dawn and people are coming to Bagh-e Takht with carpets on their shoulders. Women have on *chadors* and facial veils. They are wearing bell-shaped *chadors* and braided facial covers; and men are walking on all fours. My God, it's as if the people of the city have lost their minds! Wasn't this the same city whose ground was said to be kissed by angels? It had a nice name. I've got to remember who it was that had described Shiraz. The same name as . . . Mohammad ebn Yusof Saqafi. I used to know the phrase by heart. This is a land from whose bosom several thousand grand mystics shall spring. The place where Sufis tread, the source of guardianship, the mystic substance of the Immaculate Family. Hey! Hey! Then where are they? Where are these people who are not coming? I've heard a hundred times that all those who recognize the guardians left this land. They asked the swallow, "Why don't you come in winter?" He answered, "What did you do for me in summer?"

And here is Naneh Ferdows. She has a carpet in a bath basin on her head. And here is Ezzatoddowleh, with Ferdows holding her arm to help her as she limps along. Oh my, look. Ezzatoddowleh is sitting on the carpet in front of all the people. She has no veil and her hair is the color of bezoar. No. It's as if she has a wig on which looks like a turban. And here is her son Hamid Khan. The jerk reaches out and grabs and pulls Ferdows' breasts. And he keeps pulling and pulling. Ferdows gets up to go. Her legs in the transparent stockings are just like upside-down sugar cones. All the people, amazed, with their fingers to their mouths, look at Ezzatoddowleh and her son and giggle.

Oh where has Ezzatoddowleh's husband been? How could he be here? Probably escaped from the grave. But he's been dead for a long time. Look, in this hot weather, he is wearing a cashmere gown and a rimless hat. And his hat is very tight and is pressing his forehead. There is a hole punched in the corner of the hat . . . Now I know. He's come back to kill Mas'ud Khan the Gold Teeth again. He puts his hand inside his cashmere gown and brings out a long pistol and points it at Mas'ud Khan the Gold Teeth and bang . . . bang . . . bang. He drags the corpse on the ground and leaves it on the grass by Seyyed Abolvafa. But it seems Mas'ud Khan has not died. He rolls on the grass between the cucumbers, zucchinis, and eggplants and opens his eyes and looks at the people who have rushed to watch him and sighs, "Water."

Now there is a riot in the city. Mas'ud Khan is dead. He died in Haj Aqa's arms in a *droshky.* There is no one to calm the people down. They are looting the Jewish district. They pour into the houses. The people hurry to the roofs and put a British flag above the doors of their houses to indicate that they are under the protection of His Majesty's British government. What chaos! The men who were on the roofs come down, clomp, clomp, clomp, and each with a basin on his head. They put down the basins. In every basin, there is a severed head with blood dripping from it. What a ruckus they make.

They have tied Malek Sohrab's hands behind his back and he keeps laughing uncontrollably. He sways from side to side. Children follow him clapping and sing, "They've brought him, they've brought him, look at the wedding suit they bought him."

Now they are erecting gallows in the middle of Bagh-e Takht. What a racket they are making! Why didn't they do this before, so Malek Sohrab wouldn't have to wait so long? The men's eyebrows are so bushy that they cover their eyes. The men brush their eyebrows aside to see better, and women sit on the carpets and raise their heads to peek. There is room for everybody. But all of them have something wrong with their eyes. How they wiggle! Maybe their eyes have moved to the tops of their heads. No. The men had their eyes under their eyebrows. But the women have wrapped themselves so well in their *chadors* that one does not know where their eyes are.

They bring Malek Sohrab to the gallows, but instead of putting the noose around his neck, a soldier with a gun strapped over his shoulder comes and ties him with a rope to the post of the gallows. Malek Sohrab looks at the soldier with astonishment and says, "Not so tight; don't tie it so tight. It hurts my leg." And then he says, "It's fine now," and laughs. He laughs so hard that his laughter resounds throughout Bagh-e Takht. The same soldier wants to blindfold Malek Sohrab with a black handkerchief. Malek

Sohrab says, "That's not necessary at all. Pull the trigger quickly. In the temple. Right between the eyes. In the heart. Aim
wherever you wish. And it doesn't matter whether you do it
sooner or later. I am standing right here. I have been waiting here
for you for a long time. You can chop me up into pieces with an
axe." Oh my, the ropes turned into such snakes! Thank God, Haji
Mohammad the dyer came. He has wrapped felt around his
hand; he catches the snakes by the head one by one and smash-
es them on the ground.

And here is Bibi Hamdam, with her baggy pants. She should-
n't have come. Why should the mother come to see her son's hanging? Maybe she is being dragged here to pay for her treatment
of Malek Sohrab's first wife . . . Weren't Sohrab and his first wife
like lovers? Yes, they were. Then Bibi Hamdam alluded to the
lack of fire in some furnace, meaning her daughter-in-law's
inability to bear children. The Koran reciters came too. No need
to count them. They harmonize their voices and sing the
al-Rahman Sura in unison.

Malek Sohrab's unfortunate wife used to say, "Bibi Hamdam,
if you wouldn't keep humiliating me, we wouldn't even think about
it and ruin our happy life." And she also told the story of a woman
who couldn't have children. What a night that night was! They were
in the village and Zari was pregnant with the twins. Her pregnancy
was a reminder to Bibi Hamdam that her daughter-in-law could
not get pregnant. None of them could sleep, because it was too
hot. The palms of Zari's hands and the soles of her feet burned
from the heat.

She'd stick her feet out of the mosquito netting and the gnats
would attack them. She was dying of thirst. A little farther away,
Malek Sohrab and his first wife were sleeping in another mosquito
tent and Bibi Hamdam was sleeping in the room. And there was
so much noise. First the sound of mourners beating their chests
and shouting: 'Ya Hoseyn, Ya Hoseyn!' Then the sound of dogs
barking. Then the sound of sheep's bells. The poor things were
dreaming and stirring in their sleep. The sound of crows disput-
ing whether the sun was coming up or not. And Zari kept thinking about the story that Malek Sohrab's wife had told . . .

"Once, a woman who wanted to have children went to a dervish. The dervish said, 'You must fast for forty days, and on the fortieth day go to the top of the mountain and bathe by the waterfall. But there is one condition: When you get to the waterfall, you must not think about monkeys. You can think about anything else, but remember, don't think about monkeys.' The woman followed the instructions five times, and every time, after forty days of hardship, she got herself to the top of the mountain and stood under the waterfall but could not get the thought of monkeys out of her head. Every time, the only thing she could think about was a huge, hairy monkey. Finally, the woman went back to the dervish and said, 'Your prescription did not work. Had you not mentioned monkeys, I would not have thought of monkeys in a hundred years. But now . . .' "

And here is Sergeant Zinger in a short kilt that he himself has embroidered all around! He sits at the Singer sewing machine and keeps on sewing. Is this a time for sewing? How fast he pedals. His eyes run from one end of the fabric to the other. He is doing a zigzag. No, it is eyelet work. The material is perforated like the heart of Zoleykha. Now he's up and making a speech. "Ladies! Gentlemen! Give to charity. We have brought you civilization as a gift." His eyes fall on Zari. He laughs and says, "Lady, hand you stretch, you be kissing lady hand."

People applaud, but not for Zinger. They applaud the cherubs who are heading down the sunbeam ladders with gunnysacks full of stars. The cherubs come among the people and hand everyone his own star. Zari takes her star. The cherub says, "Now you know best. The Celestial Master is tired. Real tired." But Zari loses her star. Now she looks everywhere. She looks on all the shelves. She takes all the odds and ends out of the storeroom. She looks into all the chests in the closet, but she does not find her star. She wanders off into the garden. She looks on all the ledges; she looks under all the trees. She asks the maid Khadijeh, "Have you seen my star?"

A weeping voice said, "Since you can't find any saffron, go make quicklime *halva!*" It is the aunt's voice.

And a sad voice sighs, "Quicklime *halva* can be made, but can't be eaten." It is Malek Rostam's voice . . .

And again the voice of the aunt, who's rambling on: "Khadijeh, go cook a yellow rose *halva* . . . for my red rose who yellowed, who has withered; oh how I have no more tears, and yet my sorrows remain."

The door slammed, someone came in, and Zari opened her eyes. Seyyed Mohammad said, "They answered the telephone. His reverence the Sufi master said you may have the memorial service in the House of Ali. The House of Ali is open to all."

And the voice of Khan Kaka: "For one to be a parliamentary representative of the city and not be able to have his brother's memorial service in the Vakil Mosque . . . Well, Khosrow, write . . . What date is the day after tomorrow?"

And Khosrow's voice: "Thirty-first of Mordad."

And Khan Kaka's voice: "Write, On the occasion of the death of the young—"

And the aunt's voice: "Death? Write martyrdom."

And again the voice of Khan Kaka: "Sister, it would be nice if you would let us do our work. He has agreed to publish the obituary only after making sure that I felt indebted to him, but he made a thousand conditions . . . one condition . . ."

And the voice of Malek Rostam: "I also believe you should write martyrdom."

What a smell was in the air. If only some passerby would come in and throw out the brazier of fire. If only a passerby would ask, "What is the problem with this patient who is lying down on the bench like a corpse, like carrion? Let me take her to the garden and put her under a seven-graft fruit tree. Outside, the sky is full of stars." Zari's heart was beating fast and would flare up with pain, then beat fast again and flare up again. When she closed her eyes, she'd see a truck on fire, burning. The officer comes and lies down in a trench over a dead soldier.

And once again the aunt's voice: "It's cat shit. They left the charcoal storeroom open again; it has gone there to shit. Khadijeh, come take the brazier, I give up."

And the aunt's voice once more: "Did you sweep all the rooms? Did you drain the pool? Did Gholam sweep the garden?"

. . . And now Zari sees a little girl, whose hair has been braided and tied with a bow, standing outside the herbalist's store at Kal

Moshir. On the instructions of the physics teacher, she asks for seven ingredients to make black shoe polish. That shoe polish will never be real shoe polish. She makes something messy like a black frog spawn and no one knows if it is the fault of the girl, the physics teacher, or the herbalist. The herbalist has gone to look in his storeroom and brings the seven ingredients. It is afternoon and she is in a hurry to go to school for the fourth period and make shoe polish. Suddenly, a horseman arrives. Sitting straight on the horse, the horseman looks exactly like the King of the Fairies. And green eyes . . . the horseman's eyes are emerald green in the sun, and now that he is standing in the shade they are moss green. He asks, "Dear girl, do you know the way to Sang-e Siyah District?"

The girl is frightened, because there is nobody else around that afternoon. Nevertheless, she asks, "Do you want to go to the tomb of Siboveyh?"

"No, dear," the horseman answers. "I want to go to the dervish friary."

"Are you a dervish?" the girls asks. "Do you want to go to the House of Ali?"

The horseman laughs; his white teeth sparkle. "No, dear. I am not a dervish. My foreman is a dervish. He has taken ill and is resting in the dervish friary. I want to go and see how he is."

"Well, go straight. Then turn right, then left, then left again . . . but you can't go on horseback. The streets and back alleys are full of rocks."

She has already given the directions; why doesn't the horseman leave? Why is he checking her over? Yes, I understand. He is puzzled at why, of all those women and girls, this one has no veil. I must explain, otherwise, he'll think I'm Armenian, she decides. She says, "My father was Mirza Ali Akbar Khan the Infidel. He has left a will saying that I should never wear a *chador.*"

The horseman removes his hat. He has a hat with a strange rim, but it is not a Pahlavi hat. He bows to the girl and says, "I didn't ask you why you have no veil," and then he leaves.

But what will? As if there was a will! That very afternoon, with the black messy shoe polish left on the girls' hands, there is news of a riot in the city. The British headmistress lines up all the girls.

"Put your braided facial coverings in your school bags," she says. "They'll bring you veils from your homes." But, contrary to her habit, she does not complain, "This nation does not deserve civilization." Then she sees the girl with the braided hair and bow. She asks, "Zari, do you know how to wear a *chador?*" It is not knowing how to wear a *chador* that is important. Zari knows that there is nobody to bring her a *chador* and veil. Khanom Hakim has cut off her mother's breast and she is in the missionary hospital. It will be a long time before she gets well. Her brother has gone into the military service, and it will be a long time before he returns. And how would their old senile maid know there is a riot in the city and think of bringing her a *chador?* Well, when everybody left, Nazar Ali Beyg, the school's Indian janitor, would go and bring her a *chador* and facial veil. And it will be a long time before all the girls leave.

The servants come for the girls and bring veils, and the girls put them on their faces and leave. She is still there. She is there and so is Nazar Ali Beyg, and now it is already dark. And she is afraid. Nazar Ali Beyg has a long moustache, one end of which is high and the other end low. And his face is slightly crooked. Nazar Ali Beyg explains that the thugs and riffraff have poured into the streets and bazaars and are tearing up people's braided facial coverings and rimmed hats, and in the end they will come here and break all the doors and windows. She is afraid of Nazar Ali Beyg because he keeps saying, "Missy, good missy!" But at the same time, she does not want him to go and leave her alone in this big school. The girl suddenly has an idea: I'll call the dervish master's house, so Mehri can send me a *chador.* She is happy to have come up with the idea. She hopes to God that the horseman she saw in the afternoon is still at the dervish master's house. She telephones and then sits by the pool and fantasizes. She fantasizes that she is sitting with the King of Fairies on his saddle and they are galloping toward Baba Kuhi and she is singing for the King of Fairies: "The lips and teeth of the Turks of Cathay/ Should not have been created so beautiful."

Someone knocks at the school gate. Yes, it is he, and the girl smiles upon seeing him. But this time he is on foot, without a hat, and is carrying a package wrapped in newspaper. He hands the pack-

age to the girl and says, "Take it and put it on. I'll take you home."
Nazar Ali Beyg says, "Sahib, good Sahib."

The girl does not know how to keep the *chador* on her head;
it slides off. The man asks Nazar Ali Beyg, "Do you have a safety pin?" Nazar Ali Beyg puts his hand on the back of his coat collar and takes out a straight pin.

She leaves with the man. The girl cannot see well and is almost
tripping. She asks, "Why did they trouble you?"

The man answers, "There wasn't anyone else. The dervishes had
each crawled into some hole. Khanom Mehrangiz, the niece of the
Sufi master, asked me to bring you this *chador* on my way. She said
your name is Khanom Zahra. My name is Yusof." The headmistress
of the British school had taught them that when being introduced
they should extend their hand, smile and say, "Pleased to meet you!"
But how could she extend her hand? Both her hands were
occupied, one holding the *chador,* the other the books. The man
continues, "I knew your father. I studied English with him, until
I went to Europe. In his own right, he was a great man. He could
motivate his students with grand hopes." The girl remains silent
and the man says, "Khanom Mehri says that your mother likes oper-
ations. She enjoys having parts of her body cut and thrown away.
Every day she makes up an excuse to go to the missionary hospital.
One day, she says her toe has become stiff. Another day, she says
she has a cyst in her breast."

The girl asks, "You mean Mehri says my mother doesn't have
cancer and goes under the surgeon's knife for nothing? I wish to
God that were so."

The girl is looking at the man's shoes. Suddenly she stops
and says, "Your right shoe lace has come untied." The man bends
over and ties his shoe.

How quickly she had become intimate with this stranger! It is
as if she has known him for years. And now what is the man thinking? He accompanies her with such ease and opens his heart up
to her, too. Thank God she has a *chador* and veil and nobody will
recognize her. Thank God there is not a soul about in the Jewish
district. Hopefully he won't think she set this whole thing up to
see him, even though she really had. And Mehri had realized it and

helped her. She says, "Mehri's face is as beautiful as a flower petal, isn't it?" The man smiles and says, "I didn't see her face. She was wearing a *chador.*"

The girl explains, "Up to the sixth grade we were classmates. Every day after lunch we gathered around the heater and she taught us the Koran and religious law. Then she told us stories that she had read in the *Thousand and One Nights.* She has a good voice, too. She sang poems from the *Masnavi* for us. She sang: 'I know the king in any dress . . .' I have forgotten the first line."

The man recites: "I seek to have eyes that know the king . . . know the king in any dress."

The girl tries hard to control herself. She really wanted to say, "I recognize you!" In fact, that is why she recited this poem.

The man asks her, "Has anyone ever told you that your voice is as soft as velvet?"

The girl doesn't say a word.

The man says, "Well, you were talking about Khanom Mehrangiz."

The girl says, "Oh, it's nothing. She left school to get married. I don't know why her husband divorced her a year later. He died young. They say the Sufi master cursed him."

The man asks, "Do they stuff your heads with this kind of superstition in the British school?" The girl is offended and keeps silent. The man asks, "What grade are you in now?"

And the girl, still hurt, answers, "Eighth Persian and ninth English."

There is no one else in the streets and back alleys. No one has turned on the street lights. The girl wants to take off her facial veil but she doesn't have the courage to do so. It's good that she knows her way home by heart. She knows where all the potholes are and can even walk home with her eyes closed.

The man says, "Khanom Mehrangiz talked about you constantly. She said, once you recited the poem about Samson's blindness for the Oriental Missionary Council and really showed the headmistress."

The girl says, "That poem just came out of my mouth by itself. I didn't mean to be ornery or anything like that."

The man laughs and says, "You are noble!"

Now they have reached the head of the bazaar and both remain silent. A few oil lamps have been lit in the bazaar and placed on the platforms by the shops. But all the shops are closed. Seven or eight policemen are hanging around in the bazaar. A commotion is heard, from the sword cuttlers bazaar. In the bazaar there are few people going about their way. The man says quietly, "They've lined them up again!" And the girl does not understand what the man means. Perhaps she didn't hear it right.

They pass under the arch, which is darker than anywhere else. The man takes the girl's arm and the girl feels herself flush all over. Her whole body gets hot, hotter than she has ever been in her life . . . Now they reach the door of the girl's house. The girl asks the man to come in and have something to drink, but in her heart she hopes to God that he will not, and he does not.

The man says, "I remember, you had a calcicanthus tree in your house."

The girl says, "We still have it."

The man says, "It's hard to grow, but once it takes root, it blooms every year . . . and what fragrant, lasting blossoms!"

She was torn between wanting him to leave and stay. She asks for no reason, "Have you done your military service?"

"I am supposed to go this fall."

"It takes two years, doesn't it?"

"Try to grow up more quickly," he says.

Once again Zari does not understand what he means. Later, when she tells her mother about what had happened that day, her mother agrees that God has sent that horseman to rescue her daughter. Then, three years later, when the same man comes to ask for her hand . . .

What a commotion! It was nice daydreaming. She seemed to feel better, so the nightmares and hallucinations had left her. Someone is yelling in the garden, "Ya Hu, ya Haq, ya Ali." It is Seyyed Mohammad's voice. Gholam's voice can be heard: "Khadijeh, what happened to the lime juice?" Zari thought, He has gone into a trance. She said out loud, "Take him to Haft Tan." The aunt comes toward her. She asks, "Did he wake you up?" Zari opened

her eyes. Only the aunt was still in the *howzkhaneh*. Zari said,
"They'll wake the children up. The children will be afraid."

The aunt said, "Don't worry. Mehri will keep the children
tonight; she'll keep them tomorrow, too. And I took Khosrow and
put him to bed on the roof after a lot of pleading with him."

The noises in the garden have not subsided for one moment.
She can hear Koran recitation, like a murmur, from somewhere.
Someone is vomiting. Someone is cursing loudly and saying,
"You're sitting up there watching? If you dare come down here for
a second and have a taste of what you've been giving to these folks—
Oh, to hell with the—" Someone is beginning to sing: "One house
full of drunks, new drunks have arrived!"

The aunt put her hand on Zari's forehead and said, "They sat
together and drank so much *arak* that they all got drunk," and continued in a motherly tone, "You try to sleep."

Zari said, "Won't Khosrow wake up and fall off the roof? I wish
you had sent him to Mehri's house, too."

The aunt said, "Hormoz is sleeping on one side of him and
Majid on the other."

"Ya Hu, ya Haq, ya Ali." It was Seyyed Mohammad's voice from
a distance. Closer, the monotonous weeping of a man disrupted
her thoughts and dreams, and Zari felt this weeping would never
cease. She opened her eyes. She saw Malek Rostam sitting, holding his head in his hands, and wailing. Khan Kaka was sitting there,
too, so pale that Zari thought it was Khan Kaka who had died.

The aunt said, "Malek Rostam Khan, for the sake of this
unfortunate woman, don't cry. She'll wake up."

Khan Kaka said, "I told Khanom Hakim to give her a shot to
make her sleep. I said if she stays awake, she won't last till morning. This sorrow will destroy her by tomorrow morning. I wish
she had given me a shot, too."

The weeping has not stopped, but Zari's mind has escaped the
thought of misery and sorrow . . . She sees herself hand in hand
with Yusof, passing through a wheat field. The wheat is golden and
ripe. With the evening breeze, the wheat stalks have dropped their
heads. Zari and Yusof reach a stream and sit by it until it gets dark
. . . They are sitting in the dark, holding hands, and Zari feels that

there is no one else in this world but she and Yusof. She puts her head on Yusof's shoulder and listens to his heart. How long they sat in darkness without talking. That night, they sat by the window in the dark and looked at the garden . . . That night in Baba Kuhi, Baba told their fortune with the *Divan* of Hafez, reading: "All this is not the fruit of the workshop of existence!" He read to the end of the ghazal. He said, "It is like the blink of an eye. Its distance is like the distance between the lip and the mouth." Then Baba went to his own room and Zari and Yusof sat in the dark and looked at the city. They came down the mountain in the dark, holding hands . . . That night, in the children's room, Yusof picked up the keys off Marjan's pillow, turned off the light, took Zari's hand, and both stood in the dark listening to the children breathing . . . That night in the mosquito tent they slept stark naked and they woke Khosrow up and Khosrow called to his father. Yusof hastily put on his pajamas, went to his son and said, "Go to sleep, son. It's nothing." And he came back and both sat in the dark in the mosquito tent and their hearts beat so fast that they could hear each other's hearts, and they waited until Khosrow's breathing became regular. And all those days and nights that came and went . . .

And again the aunt's voice. She did not want to hear it. Her daydreams were pleasant, but the voice imposed itself on her dreams: "I myself have a black scarf and black dress, but Zari doesn't. That poor young man hated black. When Zari's mother passed away, he did not let Zari wear black for more than forty days. I had to give her dress and scarf to Haji Mohammad Reza to dye them black tonight. I had him dye all the sheets, too. He said he would work all night to dye the sheets and the dresses. It is warm, so they will be dry by morning."

And the voice of Khan Kaka: "The sheets?"

And the voice of the aunt: "I want to cover the rooms with black. I will cover the cushions that I set around the room with black sheets."

But Zari is in the village, not in the basement of their house. She is in the village and knows that today they are harvesting the last field, and she knows that Yusof is sitting by the mill waiting for her. She is supposed to meet him before the sun leaves the field, and she knows that she has a long way to go. She comes out of the landlord's house. The village women are sitting in their *chadors* by the stream that flows from the landlord's house and are washing tea glasses and saucers. When they see Zari, they greet her. Zari inquires about their health and makes small talk. She points to the belly of Kolu's mother and says, "You've got another bun in the oven." She looks at Goldusti, the wife of Kolu's uncle, who has just become a bride and who is heavily made up with rouge and powder and has her eyes lined with *kohl,* and says, "You seem to be having a good time." Kolu is there, too. He is hanging around nearby. Zari touches his thick hair and says, "Run to Seyyed Mohammad and tell him to saddle the horse and bring it here." Kolu laughs and runs.

Zari mounts the horse and passes by the harvested fields. The wheat is piled up like a flood of gold. The men press the straw, tie it with black rope, and load it on donkeys. In every field she passes, the men say hello. She answers with, "Not tired, I hope," and passes by. She reaches the upper village. She is surprised. They have blocked the doors of the winter pasture houses with mud. It seems there is no one in the village. Yes, there is. She sees a few nomad women who are going their way. But the tribe had gone to the summer pastures. She had seen them leave herself. They stopped a few days in the upper village and then left . . .

She passes more men and women in the fields. The sun hasn't actually set when she reaches the last field. The men are still harvesting, and the women gleaners are sitting in a row at one side facing the field. They all have black scarves on their heads. They know that Yusof always tells the men, "Don't reap too thoroughly, so the gleaners get something too." And for this reason, the women gleaners bring two gunnysacks with them.

She sees Yusof wearing a thin *aba* and sitting on a carpet in front of the mill and smoking a hookah. Yusof sees her, too, and, still in his *aba,* comes to meet her. He lifts her down from the horse and says, "Come under my *aba.* You've been sweating, I'm afraid you'll catch a cold." Then he says, "The sun was shining on your hair and made your hair the color of pussy willows from a distance."

Zari sits under Yusof's *aba* on a rug. It is now sunset and the miller is watering three four-o'clock bushes in the little garden in front of the mill. He is white with flour from head to toe. Flour has even settled on his hair, eyebrows, and eyelashes.

The miller puts a tin tray on the rug. On it are two loaves of round flat bread that he has baked, a bowl of yogurt that he has made, and a bunch of fresh green onions. He has put salt and pepper for them on two pieces of paper. Zari takes a big bite of the bread and hands it to Yusof. Yusof laughs and says, "I know you're hungry, you've come all this way. Eat it yourself." How hungry she is . . .

Behind the mill there is the landlord's or Yusof's summer garden that is irrigated by the water that turns the mill. Yusof takes his *aba* and goes to the summer garden, and when he returns, the skirt of his *aba* is full. The miller has brought in a tin brazier full of burning charcoal. A mended, blackened teapot sits in the corner of the brazier. He places the brazier at the edge of the carpet. Yusof has brought several ears of corn. He removes the teapot, puts the corn over the charcoal, and fans the coals.

. . . Zari and Yusof come to the gleaners. Their gunnysacks are full. They have tied every two sacks together with rope. The men help them and put the gunnysacks on the women's shoulders. Zari walks with a middle-aged woman who has started on her way after everyone else and asks, "Mother, why are you wearing a black scarf?"

The woman does not seem to hear. Instead of answering, she prays for her: "May you live a long and prosperous life, dear. May God increase your fortune."

Zari asks again, "Why are you all wearing black scarves?"

This time, the woman hears. "Bless you, dear," she says. "Tonight is the Eve of Savushun. Tomorrow is a day of mourning. If the khan's guide has come and we set out now, we will arrive when the cock crows . . . When we arrive, they play the kettledrums . . . they play the drums . . ."

"Where is Savushun?" Zari asks.

The woman has obviously not heard. "No, dear," she says. "We will go on mules. Your servant Mohammad Taqi has brought the

mules. He is waiting for us under the Hair Tree. He charges a sack-
ful for the fare."

The woman stops. She has now become talkative. "When we
arrive, we sit around the square. They serve hot tea. They bring
long loaves of bread, gingerbread, rose water drink, *rish-e baba*
grapes. They'll serve lunch and dinner on the day and eve of
Savushun. They have firewood in the middle of the square. They
make a fire. Suddenly you look and see the night go pale. But the
sun hasn't come up yet when that dear one appears on the mountain riding his horse. He looks as if he is saying his prayers while
he is riding. He puts a Koran on his head and prays for all
Moslems. 'Almighty God.' He is wearing black himself. His horse
is black. He comes and jumps over the fire on horseback. We
women ululate. We make a clamor. The men wail. Boys whistle.
They play the kettledrums; as they beat the drums suddenly you
see the rays of the sun appear and the square lights up."

Zari likes the woman's chatter. "Well, what happens next?" she
asks.

The woman has fallen behind the other gleaners, her eyes following them. Zari notices and says, "Go catch up with them. You'll
be late."

"By the time they pack up and get the children on the mules,
I'll catch up with them," she says. "My dear, you are our benefactor
. . . and you've asked me to tell you about this."

"All right," Zari says. "Let's go together—you can tell me on
the way." And again they walk together. The middle-aged woman
says, "I'd give my life for him—he comes to the square all alone.
He circles the square slowly. He is deep in thought. How can he
fight so many cursed enemies by himself? From one side of the
square, the Princes of Earth come so he may give them permission to help him."

"Princes of what?" Zari asks.

The woman says, "A group of people carry earth in their
hands and have brown hats with paisley designs. These are the
Princes of Earth. Another group carries fans and fan themselves.
These are the Princes of Air. A group in black clothes has torch-
es in hand. These are Princes of Fire. They come to help from three

corners of the square. Finally, from the fourth corner, a wandering dervish comes chanting the name of Ali . . ." The woman sighs, "Oh Ali, dear, do not abandon your people . . . for the love of . . . The dervish's drinking bowl is full of rose water drink. The dervish takes the reins of the rider's horse and says, 'Take a sip in the memory of the thirsty lips of Hoseyn.' But he pours the drink on the ground and sends away all the princes. All alone, on horseback, he remains still, waiting for the cursed ones. He neither carries a sword nor bow and arrow. And the sun has covered the square from end to end . . . Those cursed ones gallop on horses from the four corners of the square. Thirty or forty people pounce on his blessed head. They fight . . . they play the kettledrums and keep pounding them. They play so fast that it rends your heart.

"Finally they chase him and pull him off the horse. They put the horse's reins around his blessed neck. They put the horse's saddle on his back. They tie his arms, but he doesn't even say 'ouch.' His bare black horse stands there and neighs so loud that the sound echoes through the whole square. One of these cursed ones has put on an executioner's cloak. He comes and takes the horse's reins, which they have put around His Holiness' neck. He is on horseback himself and that lonely captive is on foot. He runs him around and around the square, and he keeps falling and getting up. His head and body get bloody. His black clothes get torn and dirty . . . but he doesn't cry out or complain." The middle-aged woman weeps and wipes her tears with the corner of her black scarf. She wipes her nose, too, and continues in tears, "Then that cursed one gets off the horse, and with his sword strikes his blessed throat. He covers his face like a sheep and puts his head on the edge of the basin. He sharpens his knife right in front of us. Oh, he sharpens it so . . . But, by the will of God, the knife does not cut. Then he lays him down on his face and puts the knife on his neck. The trumpet keeps playing a sad tune. Suddenly, you see his horse get covered with blood. Its whole mane is soaked with blood. Our elders say that once during the time of Sowlat, the black horse of His Holiness could not endure it and collapsed and died of grief. Several times I myself have seen tears in the poor animal's eyes.

"We women put straw on our heads. Our men each hold two mud bricks in their hands and rub them together and dirt and straw falls on their feet. They hold their mud bricks up and rub them together and dust and straw falls on their heads . . ."

Zari feels tears welling up in her eyes. She is about to put her arms around the middle-aged woman's neck and cry along with her, but they have already reached the Hair Tree. The woman prays for her and says goodbye; and this is probably Mohammad Taqi who comes forward. He helps pick the gunnysacks off the woman's shoulder and helps her get on the mule . . .

Zari and Yusof get on the horses and gallop together. Zari asks Yusof, "Do you know what Savushun is?"

"A kind of mourning," Yusof says. "All the people of the upper village will go to it tonight."

"Is that why they have blocked the doors to their houses with mud?" Zari asks.

"Yes. Their trip will take several days."

Zari says despondently, "A village with houses that have no doors and whose people meet under the Hair Tree to go together to Savushun!"

"That means mourning for Siyavash," Yusof says. "The people of the upper village leave every year after harvest and return at threshing time."

Both remain silent. It has gotten dark in the winter pastures. They ride, staring straight ahead. Zari's eyes are filled with tears. Quietly, tears roll down her cheeks, so quietly that Yusof would not know . . . but she is already sobbing. She weeps out loud.

A hand wiped her tears. It was the aunt's hand. She said, "I beg you on the soul of Yusof not to cry."

Zari sat up and said, "I was crying for Siyavash . . . At first, I didn't know him; I hated him. But now I know him well, and I feel very sorry for him . . . I was standing under the Hair Tree and weeping for Siyavash. It's a pity I don't have long hair, otherwise I'd cut it and hang it on the tree like the others."

What could she have said that everyone became quiet and stared at her, a kind of stare and silence that could not be endured? Zari felt as if something actually broke and crumbled inside her. Who was it that said to her, "A storm came to the field of my body?"

Khan Kaka put his hand on his waist, stood up, came to her and said, "How many times did I say to that poor young man not to let this weak and vulnerable woman go to the insane asylum so much? But he would not listen."

The aunt said, "Bite your tongue, man. To say such a thing is like wishing it to happen."

"Everyone told me about Savushun," Zari said. "He was alone and there were a thousand of his enemies; of course, he did not want to stop them single-handedly."

Malek Rostam, still sitting, said, "Mr. Abolqasem Khan, please sit down." Then he whispered quietly. But Zari could hear, "Don't be afraid; she has not gone mad. What's wrong with crying for Siyavash?"

Khan Kaka hit his head and said, "Who is Siyavash? What is the Hair Tree? The world has turned upside down and crumbled on my head. Under the rubble . . . Oh my, oh my."

"I have gone to Savushun many times myself," Malek Rostam said. "When religious passion plays were banned, that was banned too. And the Hair Tree is known in all the winter pasture lands."

Zari explained, "The first time I saw the Hair Tree, from a distance I thought it was a wishing tree, and they had tied black, yellow, and brown pieces of cloth to it. When I went closer, I saw that, no, they had hung braided hair on the tree—hair of young women whose husbands, sons, or brothers had died young."

Why was Khan Kaka afraid? He heard all they said but, in the end, did not believe it. Why did the aunt become doubtful and say nothing else, while Malek Rostam agreed that one could weep for Siyavash? Zari rested her head on the pillow again and thought, If they would let me, I'd be happy with my own thoughts. In my imagination, I'd ride a horse. I'd go through the harvested fields. I'd sit by Yusof hand in hand by the stacks of wheat. I'd put my head on Yusof's lap and Yusof would massage my temples and say, "I bet you'll get all better."

22

FINALLY, THE night, thick with fear and nightmares, released Zari. At sunrise she got up. Her knees were weak and her mouth tasted as bitter as gall. She came to the garden and listened to the whooshing sound of water pouring into the pool from the stone head. She rinsed her hands and face. The cool air, the neat garden, the scent of soil in the flowerbeds, the chirping of early-rising sparrows, and the clean water that had now half filled the pool made her feel better.

Wooden platforms had been placed beside the pool in the shade of the house. They were covered with carpets. Khadijeh came and put a tray on one of the platforms. She greeted Zari and said, "I knew you'd be well by morning. Thank God! I performed an augury for you. I broke an egg and put some wild rue in the fire. I made so many vows and pleas to God." She spread a breakfast cloth on the platform and set out plates and knives and went to get the samovar. She returned with the boiling samovar and made tea. Zari sat by the breakfast cloth. Her stomach was aching with hunger. Khadijeh said, "Last night, no matter where we looked, we couldn't find the keys. There's probably lump sugar, granulated sugar, tea, and saffron in the storeroom. I know we have a carboy of sugar syrup—by the way, ma'am, we need more fans."

Zari asked, "Where is the Koran reader reciting? Is his voice coming from the direction of the well by the reservoir?"

Khadijeh stopped, stared at her, and said, "They've put the body by the reservoir well, between gunnysacks full of ice. It's cooler there than anywhere else." She was standing watching Zari. She said, "During the night, you were taken away and another person . . ." and finished her sentence this way: "My poor mistress, you've exhausted yourself. Your face is two fingers-width . . . Do you remember my cousin who had swallowed opium? I found her in the nick of time. In the morning she looked just as you do now."

Gholam came in through the garden gate followed by Haji Mohammad Reza the dyer. Gholam was carrying an iron in one hand and had draped Zari's black dress and scarf on his other arm. Haji Mohammad Reza wore a long-sleeve black shirt and, with hands matching the color of the shirt, he was balancing the bundle that he was carrying on his head. Zari took the dress and scarf from Gholam and went into the bedroom. She put the dress on with difficulty; it had gotten tight. She put her hands into the dress pockets. There was a crumpled up, blackened two-*toman* note in her right pocket. She looked into the mirror involuntarily. She could hardly recognize herself. She switched on the light and looked carefully. A few strands of her hair had turned white. Her lips were dry and cracked, and were lined all around; her eyes were sunken, and the circles under them had turned purple. She thought, When they say that somebody's whole head of hair turned white overnight, it is a lie.

She went into the parlor, which was empty of all its furnishings, even the radio. Gholam and Haji Mohammad Reza were spreading black sheets on the cushions arranged round the parlor. Haji Mohammad rose when he saw her, and in a distraught manner, offered condolences. The poor man stayed up all night to dye these sheets, Zari thought. Haji Mohammad Reza seemed to read her mind, because his satisfied glance ran across all the black-covered seats.

When she came to the garden, Khan Kaka and Khosrow were eating breakfast. Khosrow wore a black shirt, which hung over his gray trousers. Zari sat at the head of the breakfast cloth next to the samovar. She poured tea for herself, and when the aunt came in, she poured her some as well. Her hands were trembling and she felt dizzy. The aunt cracked two eggs. She carefully emptied the whites in the bowl placed under the samovar faucet, dropped the yolks into a cup, added sugar and began to beat them. Zari was watching Khosrow, who was now going out through the garden gate. Her thoughts involuntarily came to her lips, "The poor man has stayed up all night to dye us all!" Still beating the eggs, the aunt lifted her head and, to divert her attention, said, "Sister, did you find your keys?" Zari asked absentmindedly, "Keys?"

Zari smiled and said, "A few minutes ago, Khadijeh was shocked when she saw me. She said I look like someone who has swallowed opium and has just been saved from death. She said I have aged a thousand years overnight. No, she didn't say this; I don't remember what she said . . . I couldn't recognize myself in the mirror."

"How dare Khadijeh!" the aunt said. "Such matters are none of her business."

Khan Kaka looked at Zari. He stared at her and shook his head. He said, "Didn't I tell you, sister? Last night you said I had my eyes on this family's wealth and I was making things up."

Zari spoke her thoughts again. "I guess Khosrow went after Dr. Abdollah Khan."

The aunt bit her lip. "With time everything will be fine," she said, hastily pouring milk over the egg yolks, stirring them and handing the cup to Zari. Zari suddenly realized what Khan Kaka meant. Blood rushed to her face. Her heart began to beat rapidly and again she felt as if something had shattered and crumbled inside her.

She explained, "In the insane asylum, the first thing that every mad person says is that she is not crazy and that they have brought her there for no reason. But Khan Kaka, you can be sure, I have not gone mad. After all . . . after all, Yusof, too suddenly . . ." She did not finish her sentence. She wasn't even sure of what she was saying. Had she actually gone mad without realizing it herself? A fear greater than the one in the nightmare of the night before, a fear greater than all fears she had experienced in her life, took over her whole being. She broke into a cold sweat and felt the palms of her hands become moist. She had to show Khan Kaka, and more importantly, prove to herself that she had not gone mad. She ate her breakfast elegantly, even though she was no longer hungry. She thanked the aunt for the milk and egg mixture, although she could barely swallow it. Then she got up. She called Khadijeh and Gholam. She sent Khadijeh to borrow straw fans from the neighbors and stop by Mehri's house to get the keys from the children. She sent Gholam to find sugar and tea anywhere he could.

Khadijeh returned with an armful of fans and said, "Khanom Mehri and Mohsen Khan were fighting; I didn't dare go in." Gholam returned and said, "I went halfway down the street—no one has opened their shops yet."

And all this time, Zari watched the garden gate waiting for Dr. Abdollah Khan. First, Hoseyn Aqa, the herbalist, and his brother, Hasan Aqa, the dry grocer on the corner, came in dressed fully in black. Then two of the neighboring distillers arrived, sweating under their loads. They had each tied a piece of black cloth on their bare arms, otherwise they wore their usual pajama bottoms and sleeveless undershirts. They put their loads next to the pool, opened the tops of the gunnysacks and rolled them outward. Then, taking turns, they held their hands under the water pouring out of the mouth of the stone head, filled their hands with water, and sprinkled it on the roses and sweetbriars inside the gunnysacks. The sweet fragrance of roses and sweetbriars filled the patio. Zari was watching the flowers and thinking, What a distance they must have gone; they must have picked flowers all night. How many thorns must have pricked their hands. Why didn't the youngest son go with them? I hope he hasn't caught typhus.

Gholam, wearing no hat, walked over to Hoseyn Aqa and said, "Brother, I came by but your shop was closed. Could you please get us sugar, tea, and saffron?" Hasan Aqa, Hoseyn Aqa, and the distillers set out to leave. On the garden walkway, they came across the old man, the distiller, who had put on Gholam's old suit and wrapped a black shawl around his neck. They stopped and talked to the old man, and the old man went back with them the same way he had come.

A *droshky* stopped at the garden gate. Zari wanted to run and welcome Dr. Abdollah Khan and make him say to everyone,

"Khanom Zahra has not gone mad; she is absentminded because she is distraught. Don't keep watching everything she does and says. You will make her worse and drive her crazy!" But it was Ferdows who got out of the *droshky* and took Ezzatoddowleh's hand. Ezzatoddowleh dismounted with difficulty, gave her arm to Ferdows, and limped along on the garden path until she reached Zari, who was standing, astonished, on the patio. The sun was just coming up. Before Zari had a chance to overcome her surprise at seeing Ezzatoddowleh that early in the morning, she had put her arms around Zari's neck, kissing her and saying, "Last night, the news was so sudden that I didn't have my wits about me. I left without saying goodbye. I had no idea at all what I was doing or saying. All God's creatures slept last night, but I could not. You are like my own daughter. Your late mother and I were like one soul in two bodies. Bless her soul, bless her soul, she always said to me, 'Ezzatoddowleh, I am going to leave you. I trust my child to you.' Alas, alas!"

She sat on the wooden platform, the same one on which Yusof's crumpled corpse had rested the night before, but was now covered with carpets. She rubbed her leg and said, "Where is my sister?" She was dressed in black from head to toe—gloves, scarf, stockings. When had she found the time to dye her hair black? In fact, why was it even necessary for her to dye her hair black? Ezzatoddowleh continued. "I told Ferdows, 'Get up dear girl, let's go early in the morning. We might be of some help. After all, what is a sister for?' " Zari was wise enough not to say what came to her mind. If this one would accuse her of being mad, she was done for. She will store up enough things to tell the Governor's family for a week, she thought bitterly.

"My dear, my darling," Ezzatoddowleh said, "what sort of dress is this you've put on? A dyed dress which has even gotten shiny. It will be embarrassing in front of all the people. And it has gotten tight, too."

Zari was watching the door and not responding to her. Ezzatoddowleh continued, "Dear daughter, why are you so absent-minded? Go take off your dress like a beautiful lady and have Ferdows widen it for you. It probably has enough room. She'll take out the seam . . ."

She can see everything with those crossed eyes of hers, Zari thought. But she did not move. Ezzatoddowleh said, "By the way, I forgot, I brought you something that I know will cheer you up. A memento of your late husband. No, you're not paying attention to me at all. Look, here!"

Zari was obliged to turn her gaze away from the garden gate and look at her. Ezzatoddowleh took a small box wrapped in white paper out of her handbag and handed it to Zari. Zari held the box, but did not know what to do with it. Again, she stared at the garden gate. "Open it,"Ezzatoddowleh said coaxingly.

Zari inattentively ripped the paper, revealing a black velvet box. She opened the box. Her emerald earrings sparkled in the small velvet box. She became depressed. The earrings that Yusof, with his own hands, had put on her ears on their wedding night. In the shade Yusof's eyes were the same color as those emeralds.

Ezzatoddowleh smiled and said, "I knew that would make you happy. Last night, I went straight from here to the Governor's house. I said to myself, I am the one who handed over my daughter's earrings to them, and I must get them back myself."

Zari said, "Who do you think you're fooling?" And shut her eyes. She was dizzy.

Ezzatoddowleh displayed neither anger nor irritation. She said, "Ferdows, my child is distraught with sorrow. My innocent child! Take her into the room. A tight dress is not good for a pregnant woman." She put her hand to her eyes and wept; then she calmed down and advised her in a motherly tone, "Zari, put the earrings in a safe place; it is going to be crowded here today."

Zari set out, walking like a rusty wind-up robot whose springs, nuts, and bolts have come loose. Ferdows was holding her arm so she wouldn't fall. They went together to the bedroom She took off her dress, put the velvet box on the vanity table, and lay down on the bed.

"Where is the sewing box?" Ferdows asked.

"I don't know," Zari said. Her head was spinning and her stomach turning. This is probably how madness begins, she thought.

She wished Ferdows would stay quiet. But Ferdows talked. She said, "Khanom Zahra, good thing you and I are alone. These people are capable of anything."

I wish you'd shut up, Zari thought.

"Are you paying attention to me?" Ferdows asked.

"No," Zari said.

"I want to warn you," Ferdows persisted. "Mother and son did not sleep last night and schemed against you. I sat awake on the roof and listened. God Almighty. In the middle of the night she colored her hair with black dye and henna . . . I swear, it's amazing they don't claim to be gods."

Zari did not say anything, but she had become interested. Ferdows had found the sewing box and was taking out the stitching in the seams of Zari's dress. Zari thought, What a clever woman she is.

Still busy with her sewing, Ferdows continued. "When the mistress came back, Hamid Khan kissed her hands and feet. He begged, pleaded with her, and in short said, 'Mother, no matter what, I must have this woman.' God forbid, he said that every night that he slept with his wife, he was thinking of you. He said he has made all of his three children with you in mind. May God protect . . . a grown-up man talking about his heart aching for you. You wouldn't believe the things he said."

Zari did not want to know, but Ferdows continued. "Well, I'll spare you the details. The mistress wouldn't consent. She said that you bring bad luck. She said, Would your brother-in-law let Hamid lay his hands on your wealth? She said you are pregnant and no one can marry a pregnant woman. Hamid Khan said, I'll wait. The mistress . . ."

Had Gholam not knocked on the bedroom door and announced that Dr. Abdollah Khan had arrived, Zari would have vomited. "Wait a minute," she told Gholam. "Let me put my dress on." She said to Ferdows, "Khanom Ferdows, hurry up."

"In a minute," Ferdows said. She would not stop, and Zari let her talk. It didn't matter now. Dr. Abdollah Khan had come and would set Zari's mind at ease one way or the other.

Ferdows said, "He begged so much that the mistress consented. He said, 'Then, mother, start on it tomorrow.' What lies! What lies she made up right before my eyes! My mistress was born a liar. How she put on that act of sympathizing with you. Don't be fooled by her, she is thirsty for your blood. It's done." And she handed the dress to Zari, who put it on and breathed more comfortably. Perhaps she had gotten dizzy because her dress was too tight.

Ferdows looked Zari over from head to toe and continued, "She never went straight to the Governor's house. Hamid Khan made her call the Governor's daughter. They gave a piece of jewelry in exchange and got your earrings back. My cuckold of a husband, Kal Abbas, went and took the jewelry there and brought back your earrings."

"Thank you very much," Zari said. "Now go tell the doctor I am ready."

Dr. Abdollah Khan came in with his cane. He looked more broken than when Zari had seen him in Miss Masihadam's room. Or Zari had not looked at him carefully that day. The doctor sat on the edge of the bed, took her hand in his own, and said, "Oh sister, what use is it for a human being to reach my age? When a young man like your dear husband dies, I hate myself. I tell myself, 'Old man, you are desperately clinging to life and the young are gone.' "

"But my husband didn't die," Zari said sadly. "He was killed."

"I know," the old man said. "Your son told me everything on the way. I congratulate you. An intelligent son like this can fill his father's shoes. May God grant both of you success." He paused and added, "An old man like me shouldn't come to a house that has lost such a young man. I am too old and decrepit. Those kindred who mourn him have a right to look at me, shake their heads, and think to themselves, 'Old man, you are alive while our young man was martyred.' "

"No one would look at you like that. You are the blessing of the age," Zari said.

Dr. Abdollah Khan took Zari's hand and kissed it. Zari pulled her hand back, embarrassed. The old man sighed and said in a calm, deep voice, "I don't know where I read that the world is like a dark room into which we have been sent with closed eyes. One of us might have his eyes open. Some might want to or try to open their eyes. Or someone might be lucky—a light might suddenly shine through a hole, and that person will be able to see and understand. Your husband was one of those rare people who had forgotten to close his eyes from the start. He had his eyes open and his ears cocked. Alas, he did not have enough time."

The doctor talked like someone who knew and understood everything. In his long life, if there was a God, He had revealed Himself to him, even if only once . . .

The old man continued. "Often, I told Khanom Qotsossaltaneh, 'This brother of yours is a rare man. He has insight; he has achieved insight.'"

Zari said, "You have insight too. You, too—"

Dr. Abdollah Khan interrupted, "Now, tell me what's the matter. Your son was pleading with me to come and see you. I said, 'Dear son, for the wife of a man like that, I am ready to go to the ends of the earth. Besides, I love your mother, too. She is quite a woman.'"

Zari was not afraid, abashed, nor embarrassed to tell to Dr. Abdollah Khan the truth. She said, "Since last night I have been distraught. I don't have my wits about me. I am afraid I am going mad . . . I am tempted to mimic the insane people I have seen." And she wept and said, "All last night, I was burdened with nightmares. Khanom Hakim gave me three shots. But they did nothing. I couldn't sleep. Horrible scenes came to my mind. I was talking nonsense. Since this morning, I have been dizzy."

The old man got up, stood by the window, looked at the garden, and with his back to Zari said, "I don't want to hear you talk like that. If you were worried, even if you were talking nonsense, you had a reason. And Khanom Hakim couldn't have given you a sedative. She has given you a camphor shot to strengthen your heart and the other two injections were distilled water."

He came back and sat by Zari. Zari asked innocently, "Are you saying that I have not gone mad?"

"By no means," Dr. Abdollah Khan said.

"And I won't go mad?" she asked again.

"I promise you won't," he said.

He looked Zari straight in the eyes and continued in a soothing voice, "But you have a malignant disease that I cannot cure.

It is an infectious disease. You must uproot it before it becomes chronic. And sometimes it is hereditary."

"Cancer?" Zari asked.

"No, my dear. Why don't you understand? It's fear. Many have it. I said it is infectious."

He again held Zari's hand and added prophetically, "I already have one foot in the grave. But listen to this old man, my dear. In this world, everything is in one's own hands, even love, even madness, even fear. A person can, if he wants, move mountains. He can part the waters. He can turn the world upside-down. A human life is like a story. It can be any sort of story—a sweet story, a bitter story, a sordid story . . . a heroic story. The human body is fragile, but no power in this world can rival man's spiritual powers, provided he or she has the will and awareness."

He paused to give Zari a green bottle with a white lid. "This bottle contains a sort of salt," he said. "Keep it in your pocket and whenever you feel you are getting ill, remove the top and take a whiff. And drink a glass of pussy willow extract with rock candy." Getting up, he said, "I know you are a lady, a real lady. I know you are brave and strong enough not to try to escape reality, however bitter it may seem. I want you to prove that you deserved such a man."

He took his cane from the edge of the bed and said, "If this bit of news will make you happy, then let me tell you. The day before yesterday, Miss Masihadam was released from the insane asylum. She feels much better, and by the time you have your baby, she will be quite well."

Zari was like a bird released from its cage. A knower of secrets had brought her glad tidings. Not one star, but whole constellations lit up in her mind. She knew now that she would be afraid of no one and nothing in the world.

They walked to the garden together. Khan Kaka was sitting on the children's bed with Malek Rostam and Majid Khan. When he saw them, he got up and came toward them. He blinked and said, "Well, doctor, what do you think? What did you figure out?"

The doctor said, "If you ask me, your sister-in-law has done more than well to be able to stand on her feet. Her anxiety and distress are quite natural. This is no laughing matter. Those of you around her, just leave her alone."

Zari accompanied the doctor to the garden gate. In her mind, she was searching for something appropriate to express her gratitude to the old man, but she could not find it. Perhaps the old man realized her inability, or perhaps he wanted to tell her to hold on, or perhaps just for himself, but in any case, he murmured the poem:

> *Try patience, oh heart, for God will not abandon*
> *Such a dear gem in the hands of a demon.*

Zari knew the doctor was a member of the Hafeziyun group that held vigils and read poetry by the tomb of Hafez every Thursday night. Yes, they drink wine, too, and even sprinkle libations over his tomb. And they play music, too.

"Recite more poetry," she said calmly. "Poems that will strengthen me." The old man smiled and recited:

> *Let us do something, otherwise we shall be ashamed*
> *On the day that our souls depart for the other world.*

He stopped under the elm tree to catch his breath and explained, "I didn't recite this poem for you, I recited it for myself."

"You have done your work in this world," Zari said. "Your story is a heroic one, but my unfortunate husband's was a sad, unfinished story." And without intending to do so, she leaned against the tree, put her hand on her forehead, and wept quietly. The hot tears rolled down her face and clung to the tip of her chin.

23

THEY HAD come for the funeral procession. First the relatives and close acquaintances arrived. The women were seated in the *howzkhaneh* and the men in the parlor. Ezzatoddowleh was in the most prominent position. Ferdows, wearing a tight black dress and looking despondent, was serving. The way Ezzatoddowleh issued orders, anyone who didn't know might think she was the next of kin. Upon seeing any new arrival, she would start talking about Yusof being young and unfulfilled, about his beauty and wisdom, his speaking English so fluently, his having left his innocent wife and children behind; she went on and on, weeping loudly. And sometimes she beat her chest, though gently. To keep herself from being affected by Ezzatoddowleh's words and crying, Zari constantly sniffed the smelling salts that Dr. Abdollah Khan had given her. The aunt was nowhere to be seen. When Ezzatoddowleh began with, 'My son, my son, my woes, my woes,' and spoke of a cypress whose roots were severed and had toppled to the ground, Zari left the room.

It was past eight-thirty in the morning when Khan Kaka's friends came. But there was no more room left in the parlor, so they sat on the children's beds in the courtyard. Zari sat across from them, next to the gunnysacks full of roses and sweetbriars that had been placed on the edge of the pool. The pool was now full of clear water.

Hoseyn Aqa and Hasan Aqa each carried a full gunnysack on their shoulders and were passing by Khan Kaka's friends to find the pantry. Their neighbors, the distillers, followed them, each with a carboy on his shoulder. Again, the younger son was not there. Then three other men arrived with large empty copper bowls on their shoulders. Zari's eyes filled with tears upon seeing them.

Khan Kaka came out of the parlor to join his friends. A fat, dark man spoke quietly, others listened to him anxiously; the manager of the city newspaper was shaking his head and a former member of parliament was nervously fingering his prayer beads.

Ferdows came to her with a tray of iced drinks and said, "You take one first. This one is pussy willow extract with crushed rock candy. Did you see what a show of mourning she put on? Now she's pretending to have fainted."

Zari took the glass and asked, "Who told you I was supposed to drink pussy willow extract with rock candy?"

Ferdows said, "The mistress had me eavesdrop. Let her take her wish for you to miscarry to her grave. You are not like me, with nobody. She asked me, 'What were Khanom Zahra and the doctor saying all that time?' I told her, 'Mistress, I couldn't figure out what they were saying, they were whispering. I only know that the doctor said the world is like a dark room in which the pictures are all upside-down, and all of us are in a daze wandering around in this world.' The mistress said, 'You dimwit. What a waste it was for a distinguished lady like me to spend so much time on educating you.' Khanom Zahra, even if there is only one day left of my life, I'll take my revenge on them. When my mother was in prison, it was a good opportunity—"

Zari interrupted Ferdows. "Take the drinks to the gentlemen—the ice in them will melt."

Ferdows walked to Khan Kaka's friends. The notary public, who looked Chinese, said something to Ferdows, and she laughed.

Gholam went to welcome a man dressed in black whom Zari did not know. They cleared a path for two porters holding candelabra on their heads. Soaked with sweat, they came over by the pool and the men helped put the wooden trays on one of the platforms. A half-naked man, carrying a huge banner used in passion plays, decorated with flowers, tulip-shaped lamps, cashmere shawls, and a large feather that waved in front of it, cautiously bent down and brought the banner in through the garden gate. The men in the parlor looked through the windows; the women had come out of their room to watch. But Ezzatoddowleh was not with them.

By nine or nine thirty, the garden was filled with men dressed in black, and they were still coming in, group by group. The last group carried chains, and they eventually brought a Qasem wedding chamber, which made Zari want to scream upon seeing it. But she controlled herself, taking the bottle of smelling salts out of her pocket and busying herself with the lid.

Khan Kaka's friends came toward her. The former parliamentary representative of the city had cut his hair in close-cropped German style; his hair was white and he no longer had the prayer beads in his hand. The notary public really looked Chinese. The manager of the newspaper took Zari's hand and said that they all had to attend a meeting in the Governor General's Office to discuss the city's bread supplies. He apologized for their not being able to take part in the funeral procession. But they all commiserated with Zari, "Abol," and her honor Khanom Qotsossaltaneh. They expressed hope that, God willing, the loss would be compensated by long life for the surviving family and that they would never suffer the loss of children. The others listened, and, when he finished talking, they left. But the newspaper manager would not let go of Zari's hand and said quietly, "You'll pardon me if I don't publish the news of the incident. I published the memorial service announcement just for your sake and out of friendship for Abol."

Zari pulled her hand away and said, "But memorial service announcements have always been allowed."

A few moments later, Khan Kaka sat next to her, very pale and nostrils trembling. He blinked hard and said, "Sister-in-law, you are still wiser than all of them. For God's sake, say something to these crazy people. My stupid sister doesn't understand. She'll make them even more angry. She says, 'I want you to make a Karbala out of this city that has gone to the dogs.' And the city thugs keep saying 'Bravo!' to her and cheering her on." And since Zari did not stir from her place, he begged, "Sister-in-law, get up, on the soul of that unfortunate young man."

Together they went to Khosrow's room where, as Khan Kaka called them, the city thugs were gathered. Malek Rostam and Majid, wearing black ties, stood by the door. Zari's gaze went from Haji Mohammad Reza, the dyer, who was squatting by the door, to the others. Seyyed Mohammad, Hoseyn Aqa, and Hasan Aqa had their backs to the window. She recognized Masha'allah the Hernia, who was tall and broad shouldered. Fotuhi was without a tie. Mr. Morteza'i was in his clerical garb. Those three were sitting on Khosrow's bed. The men who had taken the oath with Yusof and a few other men dressed in black, whom Zari did not know, were sitting on chairs brought in from the parlor. The aunt was standing behind Khosrow's desk—tall, with a black scarf that she had tied like a facial veil. None of the men had shaved.

Khan Kaka said, "Here is the wife of the deceased. Do whatever she says. You have shut down the bazaar; you have done that already. As for taking this corpse for a circumambulation around the Shah Cheragh Shrine, and for the people to lash themselves front and back with chains, and for Mr. Morteza'i to perform the prayer for the dead, and to stand on the portico of the shrine and preach, God forbid, don't even talk about it. With the foreign army in the city . . . there'll be a riot . . . You dragged all these people here for nothing . . ."

Majid looked at Zari and said, "Khanom Zahra, you know yourself that we had taken an oath with Yusof. Now that they have killed him, they want us just to sit with our hands folded and not even have a funeral procession for him. And for a simple protest like this, you—"

Zari did not let him finish. "They killed my husband unjustly. The least that can be done is to mourn him. Mourning is not forbidden, you know. During his life, we were always afraid and tried to make him afraid. Now that he is dead, what are we afraid of anymore? I, for one, have gone beyond all that . . ." Her voice was trembling. She took the bottle of smelling salts to her nose and inhaled its cooling scent.

Khan Kaka said, "Really, sister-in-law . . . you have done us

proud! Why don't you understand, woman? When so many people get moving, if someone incites them to riot, who can stop
them?"

"For now, it is you and our brother's corpse," the aunt said.
"Don't sit by and let his murder go unnoticed." Zari looked at her
and was reminded of Her Holiness Zeynab.

"I know for a fact that they'll stop you," Khan Kaka said. "Then
there'll be a slaughter. I won't allow it. That poor young man never
even allowed an ant to be harmed. He treated his peasants as if
he were their elder brother. Don't torment his soul."

"I lived with him for fourteen years," Zari sighed and said, "and
I know that always bravery . . . truth . . ." The snake that had
remained coiled up around her heart raised its head and struck.
She was so choked up that she could not finish her sentence. But
the lights had lit in her mind, she had seen the light and she knew
that no one in this world could ever extinguish it. She swallowed
and said, "Do all you want today. If you don't do it now, there will
never be another chance."

Turning to Khan Kaka, she added, "Today, I have come to the
conclusion that one must be brave while alive and for the living.
Unfortunately, I realized this too late. To make up for this ignorance, let us weep properly for the death of the brave."

"Bless your mother's pure milk!" Seyyed Mohammad whispered.

The men in black whom she did not know said, "Bravo!"

Morteza'i recited the Koranic verse: "And there is life for you
in retaliation, O men of understanding."

Fotuhi said, "This way, we will prove that we are not dead yet
and that we know the value of the blood that has been spilled."

"Tomorrow or the day after will be my brother's turn," Malek
Rostam said. "They'll catch him in these hot merciless mountains
and bring him to the city to the music of horns and bugles and
hang him for being a rebel, and everyone will go to watch."

Khan Kaka openly vented all his anger on Malek Rostam. "You
talk as if your brother is the son of the Holy Prophet. Of course
they'll hang him. No one has forgotten the fratricide in Semirom.
How much government property was looted! How many innocent

people were killed! If sins must be atoned in this world, he must pay for all that slaughter." He blinked hard and continued, "Is it possible for anyone to be that ambitious! Turning a different color every day like a chameleon—one day, a servant of Germany, the next day a servant of the British, and another day, anti-British! As merciless as Shemr Zeljowshan, the murderer of Imam Hoseyn,—"

Malek Rostam interrupted. "When a living person finds that he has made a mistake, he makes up for it . . . but now is not the time to put Malek Sohrab on trial, and you are not the judge."

"But as for you," Khan Kaka said sarcastically. "You have shown up in public without weighing the consequences. If I were you, I'd put on a *chador* and head for the mountains through the back door of the garden."

Malek Rostam's nomad blood boiled. "Some put on black *chadors* to go to the Consulate to see the Consul. My brother and I put on *chadors* to hide ourselves from the eyes of the friends and supporters of the Consul."

Fotuhi interrupted. "Gentlemen! Now is not the time for arguments. We were supposed to decide about the funeral procession. Khanom Zahra agrees—"

"But I oppose it," Khan Kaka said. "Naturally, I am the rightful guardian of my brother's children. Sister-in-law, be wise. Listen to me."

Zari could no longer stand up. She sat on the bed next to Fotuhi and said, "He has not even been buried yet. I don't want to argue with you. But while he was alive, you and others tried to keep him quiet and he was forced to shout louder and louder until he got himself killed. Now . . . let the people show in his death that he was right . . . Moreover, with his death, justice and truth have not died. There are others—"

Khan Kaka blinked and said angrily, "Women like you who follow their husbands like sheep are the cause of premature death."

"Khan Kaka," Zari answered calmly. "Don't make me say it, but his blood is on many hands, including yours. Even I may be guilty."

Angrier than before, Khan Kaka shouted, "Now you've found your tongue, too? That's really something to be proud of. I'll say it before everybody. You've gotten your hands on somebody else's money and have forgotten that there is such a thing as a man and such a thing as a woman. The woman is the lining, the man the outer garment. It is the lining that gives the garment its shape. For every wrong step that that young man took, you said well done . . .”

Zari felt that the snake, remaining awake inside her, was talking and thought, Snake tongue! and said, “You are worried about your position as a member of parliament . . . worried about your plans during your term of office—having an eye operation, ordering a set of false teeth by Dr. Schtomp. Didn’t you say it yourself? And maybe even taking a wife.”

Khan Kaka looked at her stunned. “Damn!” he swore. And just as suddenly he calmed down. “You don’t know me yet. I am the kind of man that when my wife died . . . for sixteen long years, without a wife and spouse, alone in bed . . .” Zari wanted to say, “What about the temporary wives, one after the other? What about the daughter of the shoemaker who rubs the gall-bladder stones of an ox on her body in the bath to get fat?”

She was ready to go to extremes and was in such a state that if she had a gun and knew how to use it, she might have fired it. She stood up and said, “Just a few minutes ago, before your notary public . . .”

Majid Khan mediated. “Please, I beg of you. Mr. Abolqasem Khan, Khanom Zahra, is this the time for such talk?”

Fotuhi gestured for everyone to be silent. “Let’s not waste our time arguing about the particulars of each other’s lives,” he said. “Let us discuss the matter differently. The murder of Yusof Khan is a private matter from your perspective and a social matter from ours.”

Abolqasem Khan interrupted Fotuhi. “I know the rest by heart. You want to take the utmost advantage of this murder. You want to start a riot and get innocent people killed. There are several truckloads of soldiers standing on the main road, with the foreign troops that are in the city . . . You know best.”

The coffin was covered with roses and sweetbriars, and it was decided that it would be carried through the garden walkway on the shoulders of Hoseyn Aqa, Hasan Aqa, Majid Khan and Mr.

Fotuhi. Malek Rostam insisted on being a pallbearer, but Zari made
him change his mind and said, "Of all Khan Kaka said this one
thing was true: You have shown up in public without weighing
the consequences." And she made him promise, "When we leave,
put on Khadijeh's *chador* and get yourself to a safe place through
the back door of the garden."

"It doesn't matter anymore," Malek Rostam said. "Let whatever
is going to happen, happen." Abolqasem Khan asked the ladies
to stay for lunch; he said he was sure a bite of bread and cheese
could be found in this humble house, but that it would not be advis-
able to take part in the funeral procession. He said that her honorable eminence Ezzatoddowleh would also stay behind.

The banner and the candelabra proceeded, and the Qasem wedding chamber followed the coffin. Khan Kaka gave his arm to one
of Yusof's allies and took a black handkerchief out of his pocket,
which he sometimes lifted to his eyes. Zari and the aunt accompanied him.

The stable door was open. The roan horse had its head in the
stall, but the mare and Sahar were standing calmly on the side road,
Khosrow and Hormoz holding their reins. Zari's heart broke
when she saw the horses and the boys.

The saddle on the mare was covered with a black cloth, and
Yusof's hat was on the horn of the saddle with his gun slung around
the mare's neck. A white sheet spotted with mauve ink to make
it look like a blood-stained shroud was on Sahar. When the
mare saw the corpse, she pricked up her ears and thumped her
hooves on the ground so hard it sounded like drums. Zari felt that
she was pounding on her heart. And she neighed twice. It seemed
as if tears flowed out of the mare's eyes onto her nose; her nostrils
flared. Zari remembered what the middle-aged woman had said
years ago about the story of Savushun.

Khosrow and Hormoz led the horses behind the Qasem wedding chamber. Khan Kaka hurried toward Sahar, took the shroud
off, crumpled it up, and threw it under an elm tree. He then boxed
Hormoz's ears so hard that his glasses were knocked to the
ground. He shouted, "What ridiculous game is this you are playing? The whole affair has fallen into the hands of women and chil-

dren! Take the horses to the stable, you idiots . . . Bastar—. . . God forgive me, they make you blaspheme."

The banner had now reached the garden gate. The half-naked man bent down, his shoulders and back glistening with sweat. They all stopped. Hormoz picked up his glasses. He took out the broken right lens and put the glasses back on. A car honked and stopped by the garden gate. An Indian soldier got out. He brought a bouquet of white flowers in the shape of a cross and decorated with a black ribbon out of the car. He came into the garden and advanced toward Yusof's corpse, wanting to put the flowers on the coffin. The pallbearers stood on tiptoe and held the coffin up over their heads out of his reach. Khosrow let go of Sahar's reins, walked to the Indian soldier, and took the flowers from him. He pulled the flowers one by one from the cross and threw them in front of the horses. The horses smelled the flowers, but did not eat them. The Indian soldier, with wide eyes, looked at the crowd dressed in black—the crowd grew so silent, it seemed not to be there. Abolqasem Khan put his hand on the soldier's back, led him toward the car and whispered something to him. Obviously, the Indian soldier did not understand what he said, because he said something in a language that everyone heard but could not understand.

The car honked and left. Then the youngest son of the distiller arrived, sweating and running, with an armful of wildflowers. Khosrow took the flowers and smelled them. The pallbearers bent down and Khosrow put the flowers on the coffin.

Now the sun had invaded every nook and cranny. When they came out of the garden, Zari saw that all the shopkeepers had cleared the road leading to the main street. On both sides of the road, under the hot sun, Haji Mohammad Reza had hung swaths of dyed black cloth along rows of poles. He usually hung colorful fabric—red, blue, green, orange, and sometimes dyed silk and wool—out in the sun.

They had not gone halfway down the road when she saw Gholam, without a hat, bringing the twins. When they reached her, he spat on the ground and said, "Mohsen Khan called; I went and brought them." Zari and the aunt stood aside for the crowd to pass, but the crowd stopped and waited until Zari bent over and

kissed the children. Mina gave the keys to her mother, and said,
"Take us along. We want to watch, too. Oh God, what lights! How
many stars!"

Khan Kaka, who had walked forward a few steps, returned and
said, "They will be trampled underfoot. Sister, go leave them with
Khanom Ezzatoddowleh."

"No, sister," Zari said, "leave them with Ferdows."

The children began to cry and the aunt's pleading and coaxing
did no good. Gholam picked up Mina and the aunt picked up
Marjan, and the crowd let them pass.

On the main street, policemen were standing around alone or
walking in pairs. On the side road, across the main street, a
truck full of soldiers was waiting. When the policemen saw the
funeral procession, first they stopped and watched. But when the
procession went to turn onto the main street, the head policeman
blew his whistle and all the other policemen ran and lined up on
the main street, blocking their way. But the banner had already
turned onto the main street, and the feather in front of it was greeting the crowd of people gathered on the roofs of shops and on the
sidewalks. What loudspeaker had called so many townspeople into
the street?

The head policeman came toward the crowd and shouted,
"Gentlemen, all but the relatives of the deceased must leave," and
waited. Khan Kaka continued standing with his back to the
crowd. Zari looked behind her. The men dressed in black were still
coming out in groups through the garden gate. A voice said, "There
is no God but God." And the crowd repeated the sacred words in
unison.

The head policeman spoke for Abolqasem Khan, "Do you hear
or not? His excellency Abolqasem Khan is grief-stricken and
cannot speak to you . . . to thank you. It is warm. He bids
farewell to you, gentlemen, and God be with you."

A calm voice rose from the crowd, "We are all relatives of the
deceased."

Hoseyn Aqa, who had a shoulder under the coffin, signaled for
Seyyed Mohammad to take his place and walked over to the head
policeman. "Sir," he said, "a young man has been shot unjustly.
We are mourning his death. That is all."

The head policeman said out loud, "I am telling you gentlemen to kindly disperse. Go. Open up your shops. If you do not, they will revoke your business permits. This is an order. Do you understand? If you do not carry it out, I will have to resort to force . . ."

This time Masha'allah the Hernia came forward. "Captain," he said, "you know what kind of man I am. When I say something, I stand by it. We don't want a riot, you know. We are mourning our fellow townsman. Suppose this is Karbala and today is Ashura. You wouldn't want to be a Shemr, would you?"

Someone invoked, "Ya Hoseyn." And the crowd replied in a drawn-out chant, "Ya Hoseyn!"

Or suppose it is Savushun and we are mourning Siyavash, Zari thought bitterly.

The head policeman shouted sternly, "I said disperse. I'll break your candelabra," and turned to the candelabrum on a man's head. The man was standing face to face with the line of policeman on the main road. The companion of the man with the cande-labrum nudged the other man's arm with his elbow and whispered something in his ear. The man moved to the right and stood by the dry stream, and the pendants of the candelabrum jingled. The head policeman turned around and signaled to the truck full of soldiers. The truck began moving. It turned around and stopped noisily on the main street beyond the banner. The crowd watched the truck. An officer got out. He was fat, his face soaking with sweat, and he had three stars on his epaulets. He came and stood by the head policeman and said, "As God is my witness, I don't even want to see one of you get a bloody nose. We also have wives and chil-dren. Go back to your businesses."

The crowd came alive with the captain's soft tone. Masha'allah the Hernia came forward. "Captain, you know who I am," he said. "As long as I am with them, I will not let a hair be harmed on the heads of my sisters and brothers. We'll take the corpse to Shah Cheragh, circumambulate the shrine, perform the called-for acts of contrition and self-flagellation—"

The captain lost his composure. "Shah Cheragh? The heart of the city? Who has given you such permission? You don't seem to understand kind words. Get back to your businesses."

He walked a few steps toward the main street and signaled to those in the truck. The soldiers, guns in their hands, got off one by one and lined up behind the policemen. The captain turned back to the crowd, tilted his head to wipe the sweat off his forehead with his hand, and said, "This one is a troublemaker whether he's dead or alive!"

Zari thought she was the only one who heard the captain insult her husband, but Hoseyn Aqa turned to Abolqasem Khan and said, "The corpse of that unfortunate young man is not yet buried and you let them insult him like that?" The captain slapped Hoseyn Aqa's face so hard that his nose began to bleed. He then shouted at him, "Put a lid on it!"

Abolqasem Khan took a silver cigarette box out of his pocket, opened it, and held it in front of the captain. He blinked and said, "Captain, please. You look familiar. Aren't you the son of Aqa Mirza Mehdi, the porter at the Rowghaniha Caravanserai? Your father had respect for the dead."

"Is this the time to drag out my mother and father's family tree?" the captain shouted angrily. "Why do you whip the crowd into a frenzy?" And then, turning to the crowd, he shouted, "I told all of you to get lost!"

Hoseyn Aqa, his hand cupped under his nose, asked, "Which way? You've blocked our way." The captain struck Hoseyn Aqa several times on the back of the neck and said, "Here you go shooting your mouth off again! Didn't I tell you to shut up?" And they scuffled. Masha'allah the Hernia held the captain's arm from behind. The head policeman blew a whistle and the policemen and soldiers attacked the crowd. They hit them with billy clubs and gun butts left and right. The path opened to the main street. Fotuhi, Hasan Aqa, Majid, and Seyyed Mohammad put the coffin on the ground along the side of the road and followed the crowd to the main street.

The main street was blocked. Cars stopped one after another on both sides. The horses of several *droshkies* were spooked. The sound of the *droshky* drivers cursing, their whips striking the horses, the honking of the cars, their futile efforts to back up, and the commotion of the crowd mingled with the sounds of the chains with which the men were lashing themselves.

The man holding the candelabrum on his head wanted to cross the dry stream bed over to the sidewalk but he was jostled by the crowd. The candelabrum fell from his head and broke on the ground. With the empty wooden tray still on his head, the man bent down and started collecting the broken pieces of crystal. But the banner was saved, brought to the sidewalk, and leaned against the wall. Some also helped to open a pathway to take the Qasem wedding chamber into the garden.

Now the whole crowd poured onto the main street. The coffin covered with flowers was left at the side of the road next to a wall. Only Zari and Khan Kaka were left standing by the coffin. Without saying a word to each other, they helped pick the coffin up off the ground. It was heavy. The sweetbriars and roses had withered. But the wildflowers had stayed fresh. Zari looked toward the main road searching for help. A shot was fired. The men and women who had been watching from the protection of the shop roofs retreated.

Zari's eyes caught sight of Khosrow, who was shouting, "Let me go!" A policeman had grabbed both of her son's hands, and Hormoz, with his one-lensed glasses, was beating the policeman on the chest. Bloody and unconscious people were being carried on the shoulders of others. The clothes of many had been torn and parts of their bodies showed through. And so much dust had been raised. There was no one to help them pick the coffin off the ground, and Zari would not agree with Khan Kaka to drag the coffin on the ground all the way to the garden. Her stomach was turning and, after a time, she remembered the smelling salts.

Four buses with their horns blaring opened a path, scattering the crowd. They continued past the empty soldier's truck, and with difficulty drove onto the sidewalk, forcing aside the few people left there. The buses stopped, far beyond the banner, one after the other, and Indian soldiers peeked from the windows. The crowd that had paused and retreated drew together, and the commotion started once again.

The captain walked over to Zari and Khan Kaka and told Khan Kaka, "You can take the corpse and bury it. I'll find you a car. When you incite the public—" He took a handkerchief out of his pocket and wiped his face, which was soaked with sweat.

"I have my own car," Khan Kaka said.

An Indian officer from the bus made his way to the captain. He saluted him and said, "On leave, okay. Soldiers make pilgrimage Shah Cheragh, okay. Only two days, leave, okay." The captain said loudly, "You can see that the road is closed." And the Indian officer said, "Good! Good!" But Zari was certain that the captain also knew that no pilgrim would ever reach Shah Cheragh from the direction they had come.

She saw Majid and Haji Mohammad Reza the dyer holding Hormoz and Khosrow by the hand and making their way to the side road. They helped Khan Kaka lift the coffin, and together put it on their shoulders without letting go of the boys. They went into the garden, with Zari following them, and put Yusof's coffin by the reservoir well. Khan Kaka sent Haji Mohammad Reza once again after ice and prayed to God that he would not come back empty-handed. The garden was full of wounded people. On the wooden platforms were several men with bared chests, faint and bloody. Two men were washing their faces and drinking at the pool, even though the water was no longer clear.

Zari walked into the *howzkhaneh* hoping to find the twins. She found Ezzatoddowleh lying on the wooden platform with Ferdows seated on the floor at her feet fanning her. The fountain of the goldfish pool was on. No one else was there.

Zari found the aunt and the children in a bedroom. The curtains were drawn and made the bedroom almost dark; nevertheless, Mina saw Zari, stood up on the bed next to the aunt, opened her arms, and threw herself into her mother's arms. Zari kissed her on the eyes. The child's eyelashes were still damp. Marjan was in the aunt's arms. She did not get up. She looked at her mother with wide eyes.

Mina said, "Mother, the old man didn't say Narcissus and Tangerine; he kept saying, 'Ouch! Ouch!' His head had an ouchie. It was bleeding."

"You were supposed to stay at Aunt Mehri's house," Zari said.

Mina was looking at the curtain of the window that opened to the veranda. "Why did you let all those people into the house?" she asked. "Now they'll take my brother's horse and my daddy's horse and go. That boy had an ouchie here," and she put her hand on her arm.

"I said," Zari asked again, "why didn't you stay at Aunt Mehri's house?"

Mina pointed to Marjan, sitting in the aunt's arms, and said, "This scaredy-cat cried. She said, 'I want my mommy.' My aunt didn't let us look . . . she kept her head like this under the tree and blood came out."

She paused and then put her arms around her mother's neck. "Aunt Mehri and Daddy Mohsen were fighting. Aunt Mehri cried. Daddy Mohsen said, 'I'm afraid.' He grabbed Aunt Mehri and hit her. And this scaredy-cat cried."

"I didn't want it to turn out like this," the aunt said. "I had no idea that it would turn out like this."

"But I don't regret it," Zari said. "As Yusof would say, 'A city must not be completely without men.' "

The aunt sighed. "I wanted them to mourn for that martyr, but I didn't want it to come to fighting and bloodshed. As my late father used to say, 'In every war both sides lose.' "

Mina, her arms still around Zari's neck, said, "Daddy will come and get angry. My brother will say, 'Where is my horse?' I'll say, 'Brother, Sahar got an ouchie and died.' Okay?"

Now that she had the keys, Zari could take the first-aid kit from the cupboard to bandage the wounded. The commotion had not subsided, and the sound of shots would not stop. Now, in the middle of all this mess, the telephone rang. Khan Kaka went to the telephone. It must have been for him, because he took so long, and afterward, as he left through the garden gate, he looked hurried. A little later, Hormoz also left. But Majid was still holding Khosrow's hand and sitting next to Zari on the bed. Zari was rubbing oil on Khosrow's swollen hand, which had been bruised by the policeman. She asked, "Does it hurt a lot? I think it is out of joint." Khosrow said, "No mother, I am not more precious than my father. When he was shot—" He did not finish what he was saying and, laughing, said to his mother, "Besides, even if hurts, it will get better."

Zari smiled and said, "Now, you've become a real man."

They took Yusof's corpse at night from among the gunnysacks of ice and put it in the trunk of Khan Kaka's car. The aunt, Zari, Khosrow, and Hormoz sat in the car and passed by the shrine of Seyyed Haji Gharib, telling themselves that they had performed the ritual circumambulation in spirit, if not in deed. Khanom Fatemeh was crying and saying, "I could die of grief thinking about your loneliness." But Zari had no tears. She did not know whether the aunt meant the loneliness of the holy man of the shrine or the loneliness of Yusof. She thought, I wish I had tears too and could find a safe place to weep for all the exiles and the lonely people of the world, and for those who have died unjustly and must be buried in stealth at night.

The grave in Javanabad Cemetery was ready. By the light of the lantern Gholam was holding they put the corpse into the grave. Seyyed Mohammad wanted to perform the burial prayer, but he could not remember it. On a sign from Khosrow, Gholam removed the shroud from Yusof's face; he buried his face in his hands and wept. Gholam and Seyyed threw handfuls of soil on Yusof and the aunt wailed, saying, "My martyr is right here. My brother is right here. Why should I go to Karbala?"

But Zari was sick of everything, even death, a death that had no circumambulation of the shrine, no prayers for the dead, and no funeral procession. She thought, I won't have anything inscribed on his gravestone, either.

When they arrived back home, a few messages of condolence had come. Among them, MacMahon's condolences particularly touched her, which she translated for Khosrow and the aunt:

"Do not weep, sister. In your home, a tree shall grow, and others in your city, and many more throughout your country. And the wind shall carry the message from tree to tree and the trees shall ask the wind, 'Did you see the dawn on your way?' "

GLOSSARY AND NOTES

aba: a coarse fabric of wool or hair fiber with felted finish usually worn by men over other clothing, nowadays worn predominantly by clerics.

Abbas or Abolfazl al-Abbas: brother of Imam Hoseyn. He was martyred in Karbala.

Agha Mohammad Khan Qajar: the founder of the Qajar Dynasty who reigned from 1779–1797.

Akvan: or Akvan-e Div, the famous demon fought and killed by Rostam, the Iranian champion hero of Ferdowsi's epic *Book of Kings.*

And there is life for you in retaliation, O men of understanding: Koran, Sura II, 179.

aqa: an honorific used for males, roughly equivalent to "Mr." or "Sir;" can be used before a first name or surname, after a first name, or alone as a form of address.

arak: Persian for vodka.

Ashkabus: a warrior in Ferdowsi's *Book of Kings* who was killed by Rostam.

Ashura: the tenth day of the Islamic lunar month of Moharram, on which the martyrdom of Imam Hoseyn is commemorated.

Ayesheh: the daughter of Abu Bakr, the second caliph, and wife of Mohammad; not liked by Shi'ites.

Baba Kuhi: shrine of Sheykh Abu Abdollah Mohammad ebn Abdollah, known as Bakuyeh, in the mountains near Shiraz; a popular place of excursion.

Babi: a follower of Seyyed Ali Mohammad of Shiraz (1819–1850), the founder of Babism, considered a heretical sect by the Shi'ite populace in Iran.

Bagh-e Behesht: literally, "Garden of Paradise," a garden in Shiraz.

Bagh-e Takht: a garrison center in the northern part of the city of Shiraz.

bezoar: any of various concretions found in the alimentary canal of certain ruminants; formerly believed to possess magic powers and used in the orient as a medicine or a pigment.

Bibi: in this text, "mother," although rarely used in contemporary Persian.

Book of Kings: in Persian, *Shahnameh,* Iranian national epic by Ferdowsi, consisting of 60,000 couplets of verse, completed in the early 11th century. The poem is a history of Iranian kings from mythical times to the reign of Khosrow II (A.D. 590–628), as well as the story of the overthrow of the Sasanian Dynasty by the Arabs in the mid-seventh century.

Boyer Ahmadi: Iranian nomadic tribes of what is now Kohkiluyeh and Boyer Ahmad Province in southwestern Iran.

Brno: reference in this text is to the Brno gun, originally manufactured in Brno, Czechoslovakia, later known as the ZB or Bren gun, manufactured in Enfield, Middlesex, England.

chador: a long veil used to cover the head and worn by women over their clothes.

Commander of the Faithful: title of Ali, the first Shi'ite imam, son-in-law of the Prophet Mohammad.

crow, fly: or *kalagh-par,* a game for small children, who sit in a circle with an older child or adult who names different birds, animals or objects, after which the children are supposed to raise their hands and say *"par"* or "fly," if what has been named can fly.

danstanbu: a small, fragrant melon generally held in the hand because of its refreshing scent.

Dena: a mountain in northwestern Fars Province; its peak is the second highest in Iran.

dinars: 100 *dinars* equals one *rial;* ten *rials* equals one *toman;* a *toman* is about 13 cents.

Doshman Ziyari: a nomadic tribe in Fars Province.

Draw not near unto prayer when ye are drunken: Koran, Sura IV, 43.

Dror: probably a variant pronunciation of the Armenian name Dro.

droshky: a low, four-wheeled open carriage.

dugh: a beverage made of yogurt and water or carbonated water seasoned with aromatic herbs, generally served in summer.

Esfandiyar: known as *ru'intan,* or invincible, but killed by Rostam in Ferdowsi's *Book of Kings.*

Ezhdahakosh: a clan of the Qashqa'i tribe.

Farsimadan: a clan of the Qashqa'i tribe.

fasayakfikohomollah: Arabic phrase meaning, "Then God shall be sufficient for you."

Fatemeh: daughter of the Prophet Mohammad and wife of Ali.

giveh: handwoven cotton shoes worn in most Iranian rural areas.

Hafeziyun: literally, devoted admirers of Hafez, the reknowned Iranian lyric poet, who lived in the 14th century in Shiraz.

Haftan: a shrine of seven nameless dervishes in Shiraz.

Haj or Haji: honorific title given to a Moslem male who has made a pilgrimage to Mecca.

halva: a cooked paste made of flour, oil, sugar, and saffron; usually served at funeral services, along with coffee.

Hend the Liver Eater: the mother of the Omayyad caliph Mo'aviyyeh, who in the Ohod War carved out and, with her teeth, tore into the liver of Hamzeh, the Prophet's uncle.

howzkhaneh: a room with a pool and fountain or fountains, usually on ground level, found in traditional Iranian houses, where families find relief from the hot temperatures in summertime.

I have breathed into him of my spirit: Koran, Sura XV, 29.

Ilanoddowleh and Veylanoddowleh: the suffix *-oddowleh* usually indicates an aristocratic title; used in jest in this context to mean roofless or wandering aristocrat.

Imam of the Age: title of the 12th Shi'ite imam, Mahdi, who is believed to have vanished in A.D. 873 and is expected to return to establish justice in the world. During World War II, German propaganda presented Hitler to Iranians as the Imam of the Age.

Imam Hoseyn: third Shi'ite imam, grandson of the Prophet Mohammad, mourned in Iran more than any other martyr. He was killed while leading an unsuccessful revolt against Yazid I, the Omayyad caliph, at Karbala in A.D. 680.

Imam Reza: Ali ebn Musa (A.D. 770–813), the eighth imam of the Twelver Shi'ite sect, believed by Shi'ites to have been martyred by Ma'mun, the Abbasid caliph. His shrine in Mashhad is considered the most sacred site in Iran.

Jalaloddin Menkoberni: or Jalaloddin Kharazmshah, the last king of the Kharazmshahiyan Dynasty, who fought bravely and tried unsuccessfully to prevent the Mongol invasion of Iran in the early 13th century.

Kaka: term for "brother" in Fars Province.

Karbala: city, now in Iraq, where Hoseyn, the third Shi'ite imam, battled against the Ommayad army and was killed along with his followers; location of the shrine of Imam Hoseyn.

Kavar: a village south of Shiraz.

khan: a tribal chief; also used as an honorific title, generally used after the first name.

khanom: honorific used for females; can be used either before a given name or surname, after a given name, or alone as a form of address.

khoresh: also *khoresht,* any of a variety of stew-like dishes usually served atop steamed rice.

Khosrow and Shirin: famous lovers immortalized by Nezami in a story in verse by the same name. Khosrow II or Khosrow Parviz (A.D. 591–628) was the Sasanian king who fell in love with Shirin, an Armenian girl, who was also loved by Farhad, a stone carver.

Khuli: a man cursed by Shi'ites for having hidden the severed head of Imam Hoseyn in the bread kiln of his house. His wife saw light emanating from the kiln and discovered her husband's secret. She is also supposed to have hidden the two children of Moslem ebn Aqil to protect them when their father was killed by the supporters of Yazid I in Kufeh.

kohl: a preparation of antimony or soot mixed with other ingredients, used to darken the edges of the eyelids.

Leyli and Majnun: legendary lovers. Majnun's story of love for Leyli is put into verse by Nezami, the 12th–13th century romantic poet.

Lion and Sun emblem: Iranian government emblem; in this case, emblem of the Iranian relief organization of the time, equivalent to the Red Cross.

Lo! We have given thee a signal victory: Koran, Sura XLVIII, 1.

malek: literally "king" or "prince;" used here as an honorific.

maleki: a superior quality *giveh,* usually with pointed toes.

Mard-e Emruz: a newspaper. The title literally means "Today's Man."

Masnavi: or *Masnavi-ye Ma'navi,* spiritual verses by Jalaloddin Rumi, known as Mowlavi, one of the greatest Persian mystic poets who lived in Qunieh in Turkey in the 13th century. His verses are used for chanting by Sufi dervishes.

Ma'sumeh: the sister of Imam Reza, the eighth Shi'ite imam, whose tomb in Qom is considered one of the holiest shrines in Iran.

Mazandarantaj: a play on the name of the Governor's daughter, Gilantaj. Mazandaran and Gilan are both provinces in northern Iran, by the Caspian Sea.

mesqal: measure of weight equal to approximately 5 grams.

miyur: a soft, light cotten.

Mohammad ebn Yusof Saqafi: brother of the infamous Arab commander, Hajjaj ebn Yusof; supposed to have rebuilt the city of Shiraz in the first century after the Arab invasion of Iran.

Mordestan District: literally, the Dead District, the red-light district in Shiraz. Mordestan is probably a corruption of the word Murdestan, literally "myrtle garden."

Moslem: Moslem ebn Aqil, a cousin of Imam Hoseyn, who was sent by him to Kufeh as his deputy but was killed by the supporters of Yazid I.

mosquito netting or mosquito tent: translation of *pashehband,* a tent of sorts made of thin cotton material in which bedrolls are spread, used for sleeping outdoors in the summertime.

muezzin: a Moslem crier who calls the hour of daily prayers from the minaret of a mosque.

Najaf: city, now in Iraq, where the shrine of the 1st Shi'ite imam, Ali, is located; a center for religious learning.

Nakir and Monkar: two angels believed to come to the grave for questioning on the first night of one's death and who are supposed to punish sinners.

naneh: "mother;" usually used in rural areas.

Nay Prison: prison where Mas'ud Sa'd Salman (d. A.D. 1121), a famous poet who spent much of his life in prison, spent three years. Nay was built for the political prisoners of the Ghaznavids.

Nur Hamadeh: an early Lebanese feminist.

Pahlavan Kachalak: literally, "little bald champion," puppet-show characters particularly popular in Fars Province. The term also denotes the puppet show in general.

Pahlavi hat: a form of brimmed hat popular in Iran during the reign of Reza Shah Pahlavi (1926–1941).

paludeh: a starch-based dessert eaten with lime juice; a summer-time specialty of Shiraz.

parasang: six kilometers.

passion play procession: rendering of *ta'ziyeh,* a form of religious drama reenacting the death of martyrs, particularly those who were killed in Karbala along with Imam Hoseyn.

qaran: one-tenth of a *toman;* a *rial* is also one-tenth of a *toman.*

Qasem wedding chamber: Qasem, son of Hasan, the 2nd imam, who was betrothed but was martyred in Karbala before his marriage. In Iranian mourning rituals, a decorated box-like structure is carried to remind mourners of his untimely death.

Qashqa'i: nomadic tribe in southwestern Iran.

qeran: monetary unit equal to one rial.

Ramazan: Persian pronunciation of the Islamic month of fasting, Ramadan, the 9th Islamic lunar month.

ranginak: a local confection of Shiraz made of dates, walnuts, browned flour, and ghee.

rish-e baba: literally, "daddy's beard;" large, elongated grapes.

ritual ablution with dust: or tayammom, a substitute for ablution with water before daily prayers, resorted to when water is not available or would be harmful to the worshipper.

Rostam: the most famous legendary hero of Ferdowsi's *Book of Kings.*

Sadiqeh Tahereh: title of Fatemeh, the daughter of the Prophet Mohammad.

sangak bread: a variety of flat Iranian bread baked on hot pebbles.

sang-e siyah: literally "black stone," a district in the city of Shiraz.

Sardozzak: district in the city of Shiraz.

Serat Bridge: a bridge over Hell leading to Paradise, believed to be thinner than a hair and sharper than a sword, over which everyone must cross on Resurrection Day. Sinners will not be able to cross and will fall into Hell.

seyyed: honorific title that precedes a male name, used to indicate that one is a descendent of the prophet Mohammad.

Shah Cheragh: shrine believed to be that of Ahmad ebn Musa ebn Ja'far, a brother to Imam Reza in the city of Shiraz.

Shahreza: small city south of Esfahan and north of Shiraz.

Shemr: Shemr ebn zel-Jowshan, hated by Shi'ites for having severed the head of Imam Hoseyn in Karbala.

Sheykh San'an: a well-known character from *Manteq al-Teyr,* or "The Conference of Birds," by one of the greatest Persian mystical poets and thinkers of the 12th–13th centuries, Attar. Sheykh San'an was a prominent, pious man with hundreds of followers. After traveling to Rome, he fell in love with a Christian girl and consented to pray in a Christian temple and became a swineherd to prove his love for her.

Siboveyh: Iranian scholar of Arabic grammar (d. A.D. 796), buried in the Sang-e Siyah District of Shiraz.

Siyavash: legendary Iranian prince, son of King Kavus, who was betrayed by his stepmother and forced to undergo a trial by fire.

Sobhi: Fazlollah Sobhi (d. 1962); a popular radio personality who told children's stories over the radio for some twenty years, from the early 1940s to the early 1960s.

Sohrab: champion in Ferdowsi's *Book of Kings,* son of Rostam. He was unwittingly killed by his father. A version of this tragic story is found in Matthew Arnold's *Sohrab and Rustum.*

tah chin: literally, "arranged on the bottom," Iranian dish made of rice, eggs, and yogurt, mixed with butter, saffron, and spices, which forms a thick cake-like crust at the bottom of a pot of steamed rice.

tar: a musical instrument made of a double sound-box (of unequal size) covered by a thin skin, with a neck of six strings which are plucked with a plectrum to create a velvety and brilliant sound.

"To what part of this dark night . . .": line from a poem entitled "Vay bar Man," or "Woe Is Me," by Nima Yushij (1895–1960), considered the father of modern Persian poetry, who revolutionized Persian poetry by breaking away from the conventions of classical meter and imagery.

toman: one *toman* is ten *rials,* or about 13 cents at the official rate of exchange.

Tuba Tree: or Tree of Happiness in Paradise, said to be laden with various kinds of delicious and fragrant fruits, of which all inhabitants can partake.

walazalin: literally, "and those who go astray;" the last phrase of the opening sura of the Koran, which is used in daily prayers.

wooden platform: translation of *takht,* large wooden structures which in traditional Iranian homes were placed in the courtyard for outdoor family activities in late afternoons and evenings in summertime, and on which bedrolls and mosquito netting would be placed for sleeping outdoors.

Ya Allah: a multi-purpose phrase; here used by a man entering a room as a warning to allow women to veil themselves; equivalent to knocking on a door.

Ya Hu, Ya Haq: incantation calling on the name of God in Sufi chants.

Yazid: Yazid ebn Mo'aviyyeh, the Omayyad caliph (A.D. 680–683), abhorred by Shi'ites for being responsible for the killing of Imam Hoseyn.

Zeynab: Sister of Imam Hoseyn, who became a prisoner of war after the Battle of Karbala, regarded as a model of virtue and bravery by Shi'ites.

Zeynab Ziyadi: not to be mistaken for Zeynab, the sister of Imam Hoseyn. Not an actual character in traditional religious drama, the character of Zeynab Ziyadi, or "the unwanted Zeynab," is based on a woman who, during a *ta'ziyeh* performance being held for Naseroddin Shah Qajar, attempted to enter the performance center to view the play, claiming to be a fictitious character called Zeynab Ziyadi.

zither: a musical instrument with a shallow sound box and 30 or 40 strings.

Zoleykha: wife of Phutiphar, who was in love with Joseph, son of Jacob.

SIMIN DANESHVAR was born in 1921 and continues to live in Iran. She received her Doctorate in Persian literature, worked as a Fulbright scholar with Wallace Sttegner at Stanford University, and was a professor at Tehran University. Her collection of Persian short stories, published in 1948, was the first by an Iranian woman writer and *Savushun* was the first novel ever published by an Iranian woman.

M.R. GHANOONPARVAR is the author of *Prophets of Doom: Literature as a Socio-Political Phenomenon in Modern Iran* and has translated numerous works from Persian literature, including Jalal Al-e Ahmand's *By the Pen* and Sadeq Chubak's *The Patient Stone*.

BRIAN SPOONER has spent much of his life in Iran. He became involved in Persian literary studies as a student at Oxford University in the late 1950s. In the 1960s, as Assistant Director of the British Institute of Persian Studies in Tehran, he travelled extensively in the east and south of the country and carried out ethnographic studies of the rural and tribal communities. He is currently professor of anthropology and director of the Middle East Center at the University of Pennsylvania.

Printed in the United States
15671LVS00002B/158